PEG LEG ANNIE

The Story of Anna Morrow

A Novel

Howard Frisk

Western Echo Publishing

Western Echo Publishing
P.O. Box 593
Sumner, WA 98390
WesternEchoPublishing@gmail.com
www.WesternEchoPublishing.com

Cover and book design by Howard Frisk
Printed in the United States of America

Paperback ISBN 979-8-9937500-0-2
eBook ISBN 979-8-9937500-1-9

To Sandra Lowen, the inspiration behind this book

Chapter 1

The August sun bore down on Rocky Bar, Idaho, turning the bustling mining camp into a wavering mirage of heat and dust. The main road was scarred with hoofprints and wagon-wheel grooves, baked hard as stone. From her perch on the mercantile porch, a girl lifted her hand to her brow and squinted through the distant veils of dust stirred by a passing freight wagon, searching for anything out of the ordinary. The air was thick with the scent of sun-warmed pine and horse manure, mingled with the faint sweetness of bread baking somewhere down the road. Flies droned lazily around her head, occasionally tapping against the windowpane behind her. Off in the distance, the stamp mills pounded tons of quartz ore with a steady rhythm—a powerful march that echoed off the surrounding mountains. The whole town seemed to breathe with it: worn-out miners shuffling through the dust, women moving like ghosts between false-front stores, horses flicking their tails, a dog across the road panting in the shadow of an empty rain barrel—all of them caught in the slow, relentless heat of an Idaho summer afternoon.

"Why does it always have to be so hot around here?" Annie said to herself. The Rocky Bar Road, the only road through town, was covered in fine dust this time of year, a stark reminder of the relentless heat that baked the remote mining town every summer. Even the occasional gust of wind felt dry and gritty in her mouth, stirring up clouds of powdery earth that danced around like restless spirits. Yet, Annie preferred this dusty discomfort to trudging through the slick mud that turned the Rocky Bar Road into a treacherous mire after every rainstorm, or worse yet, waist-deep winter snows. She gazed down the road and noticed how the thin wisps of smoke rising from the chimneys of the false-front stores drifted away in the same direction.

Every once in a while, she could feel the warm breeze on her face. Annie was small in stature for her age, yet she had a muted sturdiness about her, as if she had been formed from the same raw beauty of the North Idaho mountains that surrounded Rocky Bar. Her complexion was pale because she avoided the harsh sunlight as much as possible. She wore her dark brown hair parted neatly in the middle and twisted into a tight knot at the back of her head, with wisps escaping whenever the wind picked up along the trail.

Her eyes—clear, watchful, a soft brown that could turn steely without warning—missed nothing. There was a pinched set to her mouth, not from meanness but from years of holding back words better left unsaid. A narrow jaw and slightly hollow cheeks gave her an air of quiet resolve, the sort of determination that didn't announce itself but showed plainly in the way she carried crates of apples or steadied a frightened horse.

Annie's clothing was typical of what was popular among the teenagers of Idaho's mining camps: a faded calico light blue dress worn smoothly at the elbows, her apron stained from endless chores at the mercantile. There was a certain care in the way she kept herself—clean hems when possible, straight seams, a tidiness that stood in gentle defiance of the dusty roads. Despite her slight frame, Annie gave the impression of someone who could endure far more than she ever claimed—an unassuming girl whose strength lay not in spectacle but in her unyielding ability to accomplish whatever task was assigned to her.

Across the road, Annie spotted a few old-timers slouched on the porches of the buildings that had shade. Wandering down the middle of the street were a few young boys on horseback who didn't seem to know where they wanted to go. She had something worthwhile to do—helping at the mercantile, working the apple peeler.

Annie's favorite place in the world, if she had to choose, was the rickety bench on the porch of the Rocky Bar Mercantile. *It wobbles every time I sit down. I should fix it. Whoever built it didn't use enough nails.*

She sat alone under the store's awning; her dress already clinging to her perspiration-covered back. Annie set the apple peeler on the three-legged stool between her legs. She turned the crank, tossed a peeled apple into the tin bucket, and jammed another one on the peeler. The curved blade scraped across the apple, curling the skin away in perfect ribbons until the white flesh beneath gleamed, allowing her to savor its sweet scent. *Jonathans and Winesaps are my favorites, but today I got a crate of Gravensteins. I like how the Gravensteins are green with red streaks. What a pretty design. I could do this for hours, and sometimes I do, especially when I want to forget things, like my dreadful home life.*

Every so often, a cool breeze swept down off the mountains into town and blew away the dust in the road, only to have it build up again with a warm breeze coming up the valley. It was like a reverse tug-of-war between the cool mountain air and warm breeze from the valley, each blowing the dust toward the other. That afternoon, the first real breath of a strong wind in days sent a snarl of her dark brown hair across her face. She brushed it aside, but it only tangled worse because of the sticky apple juice on her fingers. She wrinkled her nose, flicked her hair over one shoulder, and set her jaw with quiet resolve. *These are more apples than I've ever seen, and Mrs. MacGregor expects every last one peeled by two o'clock. Seems like everyone has to have their applesauce. But I guess I shouldn't complain.*

Annie liked the part-time work at the mercantile. *In the mines, nobody cares what sort of slob you look like, but at the Rocky Bar Mercantile, it matters.* She liked to wear a blue ribbon tied around her long hair, and she scrubbed her hands clean before working. *It's important to look respectable, even in a place like this where respectability is a foreign idea. I'm glad that I'm not like some girls, like those scrappy Bannister twins.*

They're always tumbling around behind the blacksmith's shop, with dirt on their faces and shaggy haircuts. Mrs. Bannister could use a lesson in cleanliness and cutting hair.

Annie considered sitting on the porch bench, peeling apples, to be the perfect spot for daydreaming. She could absent-mindedly turn the crank while being miles away in her own world. She remembered last week, when her friend Hazel had snuck up behind her as she sat peeling apples. Hazel was quick-witted and found the right words to either tease or soothe. *"You know,"* Hazel had said, nudging Annie's side with her knee, *"you could walk into the parlor of that fancy Alturas Hotel and put every so-called lady in the territory to shame. Even if you showed up covered in apple peels and smelled like cider."* Hazel was like a bundle of sunshine, fun to be around, bright and cheerful, unless she was poking fun at me.

She was a year ahead of Annie in school, and they would often walk home together. Some children at school called Hazel "Blondie" when she wore her hair in long braids, but she took it as a compliment.

Annie laughed at the mental image. *"You're just sweet-talkin' me 'cause y'all want some applesauce,"* Annie had replied, sticking out her tongue. *"Y'all ain't gettin' some just 'cause you're my best friend."* Hazel had blushed, then darted off down the dusty road towards her home, her blonde braids bouncing behind her.

With that mental image fading, Annie let her mind wander as she returned to cranking the squeaky apple peeler, settling into its meditative repetition. *Don't they ever oil this thing?* She took satisfaction in the clean spiral of each peel, the pile of peeled fruit growing in the tin bucket, and the faint ache it left in her wrist, a sign of honest work.

The townspeople, meanwhile, moved around in their usual fashion: a parade of bedraggled miners who had finished their morning shift, busy merchants, wannabe cowboys, and ragamuffin children. She watched them, observing their faces, their habits, their arguments, and alliances. Annie did not need to be social. She liked to observe people instead. She didn't have many friends, but she cherished the few she had, especially Hazel.

4

Around one o'clock that afternoon, Annie caught a movement at the edge of her vision and looked up. A stranger was walking up the center of the road, boots hammering the packed dirt with deliberate, weighty steps. He was a tall man, broad-shouldered and straight-backed, with a presence you noticed even if you'd never seen him before. Dust covered his boots, and his red plaid shirt sleeves were rolled high, revealing hairy forearms. He looked like he knew where he was going.

Annie kept peeling the apples, but her eyes stayed fixed on the stranger as he got closer. *He could be a miner looking for work, a prospector, a scoundrel looking for trouble, or maybe just a drifter. We get plenty of those around here.* She paused her peeling to wonder which one he was.

Mrs. MacGregor emerged from inside carrying a twenty-pound sack of flour, her short arms straining, and a scowl stitched on her face. Mrs. MacGregor was a portly woman who was forever busy with something. Annie rarely saw her sit down, even though there was a stool behind the mercantile counter. Her hair was thick and reddish-brown except for a few strands of gray that fell in loose waves when she let it down. It was pinned up for practicality, though a few rebellious strands usually slipped free.

I heard that Mrs. MacGregor's parents came from Scotland many years ago. Mr. MacGregor never worked in the mines; instead, he sold goods to the miners. Good choice. Running a mercantile won't get you killed. Can't say the same for the miners.

A scattering of fine lines at the corners of Mrs. MacGregor's eyes made her appear older than her years, but they added to her softness rather than diminishing it. She wore plain dresses, simple but well-fitted, despite her less-than-attractive figure. There was a confidence in the way she moved, as though she enjoyed the physical labor of running her mercantile. She also carried an air of resilience—a woman who had seen the rough edges of Rocky Bar, endured them all, and learned to hold herself with hard-won dignity. Despite her rough exterior, Mrs. MacGregor usually managed to say something nice to Annie every once in a while.

Mrs. MacGregor noticed Annie was not moving. "Don't just gawk at him, Annie, keep working," she snapped, setting the sack of flour down with a thud. "Them apples ain't gonna peel themselves." Mrs. McGregor remained on the porch with her hands on her hips.

Annie ducked her head, embarrassed, but she couldn't help glancing up again at the man. He stopped on the road and studied the mercantile, arms crossed. He cut a commanding figure. Tall and broad-shouldered, he carried himself with the confidence of a man accustomed to being in control. His dark hair, worn a touch long, was slicked back from a strong brow. A neatly groomed mustache framed his mouth—thick, well-kept, and unmistakably the mark of a man who took pride in his appearance despite the dust and chaos of frontier life. His eyes were piercing slate-blue, cool and appraising, the sort that could size up a stranger in an instant. Annie felt the weight of his stare. They held a steady, unblinking intensity—more watchful than threatening, but with an edge that warned he wasn't a man to be ignored.

Hazel appeared out of nowhere, jumped onto the porch and landed on the bench next to her with a thump.

"Don't sneak up on me like that, Hazel. Y'all scared the bejesus outta me."

"Ha. I caught you daydreaming again. What's it about this time?"

Annie gave her a sideways glance and shook her head.

Hazel's maturity aged her beyond her fifteen years. Her long blonde hair was usually up in a bun except on those days when she wore it in braids. Her skin, with its clear, freckled look from spending time outdoors in the sun, complemented her blue eyes. She wasn't the sort of girl who sought notice, yet people around town looked twice all the same. There was a quiet composure about Hazel that appealed to Annie, a kind of self-possession uncommon in a rugged mining camp like Rocky Bar. When she smiled, which wasn't often enough, it emerged like sunlight slipping through a cloud. Her yellow dress was plain, sewn from calico, and the hem worn from the rocky paths of the camp.

She leaned over and whispered into Annie's ear, "Who's that?"

"Don't know. Never seen the likes of him before."

"He's looking at you," Hazel teased, smiling as she poked Annie in the side.

Annie rolled her eyes, but her stomach fluttered all the same. She pretended to focus on her work, but now the apple peeler's rhythm felt different.

"Hazel."

"What?"

"Your dimples are showing."

"You're jealous because you don't have any."

"Maybe so," Annie replied as she tugged on one of Hazel's braids.

Mrs. MacGregor glanced down at them. "You two are something else."

The stranger waited a moment longer, then sauntered across the street to the porch in long strides, his boots thumping on the lower steps in front of the porch. As he got closer, Annie could see that his features were rugged but not harsh, the face of a man both seasoned and self-disciplined.

"Afternoon, ma'am." His voice was low and even, giving the impression of a man who rarely needed to raise it to be heard. There was a steadiness to him, a sense of controlled power.

"Afternoon," Mrs. MacGregor replied. "What can I do ya for?"

"Just some grub for the boys at the mine," he said, and handed over a folded piece of paper.

Who was he? Annie risked a glance up, but he didn't look her way. Instead, he kept his eyes on Hazel, then the peeled apples, and then down the road. Annie found it both unsettling and, in some odd way, intriguing.

Mrs. MacGregor took the paper, disappeared inside, and the porch fell silent except for the sound of a bay horse trotting by, led by a small boy. The man glanced over at Annie, and for a heartbeat, their eyes met. She felt her face go warm, but she refused to look away. *Let him see me, sticky hands, stray hairs, and all. I don't care.*

"You work here?" he asked Annie, his voice low enough for only her to hear.

"Sometimes," she said, not trusting herself to say more.

"That's good work you're doing," he said, nodding at the pile of peeled apples in the bucket.

"Thanks," she replied, looking down at the apples. *They're just apples.*

"You got a name?"

"Annie," she replied. *Why is he asking? Don't expect me to ask for your name, mister. Why should I? Who are you anyway?*

Hazel stood up. "I'll leave you two to get acquainted." She jumped off the porch and ran towards home.

"Thanks a lot, Hazel." She watched Hazel disappear into the distance. *I wish you had stayed. You didn't need to leave me here with this stranger.*

Mrs. MacGregor returned with a box of groceries. She chatted with the man for a few minutes, but Annie did not pay attention to what they were saying. She finished peeling the last of the Gravensteins and scooped up the peels on the floor and dumped them into a paper bag. One peel slipped through her fingers and landed on her shoe. Even though her shoes were worn out, she tried to keep them clean. They were the only shoes she had. She liked the style, how the laces went all the way above her ankles, but picking the sticky apple peels out from between the laces was annoying to no end.

Chapter 2

The next several days passed with the same sunbaked monotony. Annie watched for the stranger each time she sat on the old pine bench and worked the apple peeler or shucked peas. She looked for his figure in the road, his hat among the crowd. An unfamiliar face always sent a ripple through the town's tight current, and she guessed it was only a matter of time before she found out who he was.

Annie didn't see him again until a week later, when he was about a block away. The miners' pay had come in the night before, and the men of Rocky Bar were up early to spend what they hadn't already lost to gambling or opium from the Chinese miners up on Steel Creek. Annie watched the man step through the batwing doors of the Gold Nugget Saloon down the road and disappear inside.

She pulled the crate of apples to where she could reach in and worked the peeler with mechanical precision. She read the label stenciled on the end of the wooden crate. *Nice. I get Jonathans today. Emmet Valley Fruits, Product of U.S.A. One bushel by volume.* The sweet, tart scent of apples filled the air, mingling with the musty smell of old wood from the crate. She liked the smoothness of the apple skin as it slid through her hands. The thin, wet curls dropped onto the floor, coiling like worms. Sometimes the peeler cut too deeply, and a sliver of fruit would fall to the floor. Depending on where it landed, she would reach down and pop it into her mouth. *Worms have protein, right?* Each time the door of the mercantile swung open, she looked up, but it was only the usual tide of men or children or the occasional dog. *Why am I watching for him?*

At noon, he emerged from the saloon and walked over to the mercantile. He stopped in the middle of the street, right in front like last time, squinting straight at Annie, not hiding that she was the center of his attention. "You got a minute?"

She took her hand off the crank. "I'm working."

The man grinned. "Then I'll keep it brief."

A slight wind drifted up the road, carrying the scent of pine trees and the ever-present horse manure. He tilted his head toward the upturned empty apple crate near the porch edge. "Mind if I . . . ?" Before Annie could answer, he sat down.

He smiled, his teeth showing beneath his bushy moustache. "I'm Thomas Morrow. Most folks just call me Morrow."

For a long moment, Annie sat there with her sticky hand hovering over the partially peeled apple, every muscle in her arm strung tight with suspicion. She had expected him to snicker or ask for a discount on the apples, or for a favor of the kind men usually want. *I don't trust you, mister.*

Thomas sat on the steps, planted his elbows on his knees, and watched her with a steady, unblinking patience that made Annie uneasy. She watched a big black beetle crawl across the porch between her shoes and decided not to step on it. *Morrow, Thomas Morrow. Never heard of him.*

When she looked up, daring to meet his eyes, she found him gazing at her. The apple slipped off the peeler, landed with a thud, and rolled towards Thomas. He snatched it up.

"Looking for this?" He held it out to her. She reached over and took it from his hand. Their fingers brushed against each other, creating a tingling sensation inside her. She didn't know what to say, but her mind was racing. *Who is he? Why is he lookin' at me like that? What does he want? I should get up, go inside, and pretend I have some chores to do. That would end the conversation. Or maybe I should stay put just to see what happens. I could refuse to talk to him, and then he might get the message and leave me alone.*

It was too late.

"Mr. MacGregor run you ragged?" he blurted out without warning, nodding toward the front door of the mercantile behind them.

"More like his old lady does," Annie replied, lips twitching toward a smile she refused to give him. *I can be nice if I feel like it. Maybe this is some game he plays, teasing girls. Bring it on, buster.*

He made a low rumble in his throat. "Always figured Rocky Bar ran on the money from drunken miners."

"That so?" she said, eyebrows arching. "Y'all don't get drunk?"

"I don't drink before noon unless it's a holiday."

"Really? I saw y'all walk out of the Gold Nugget Saloon this mornin'. Explain that."

"Simple. That was business. I was negotiating a purchase of beer for the boys at the mine. Any other questions?"

"Nope." She peeled another apple.

For a while, they sat there, Annie on the bench and Thomas on the porch steps as the breeze tossed dust up the road and then back down the road. The only sounds were the incessant banging of the stamp mills. The sweet smell of freshly peeled apples was a pleasant contrast as it wafted between them. They both took pleasure in it. Thomas rested his hands palm-down on his thighs, his scarred fingers splayed out.

"Where y'all from?" Annie asked before she could help herself.

He paused for a moment, considering his words. "All over, I guess. Idaho City, mostly. Worked in the gold mines, sometimes on a dredge. My feet don't much like to stay planted. I tried farm life once in Illinois. Then the rumors of gold got louder than the cornfields, so here I am. There's no future as a dirt farmer."

Annie tilted her head, curious. "And how's that workin' out for ya here?"

He chuckled. "Well, it keeps me busy if nothing else. The prospect of hitting pay dirt keeps me moving, keeps me hoping for something better."

She nodded, watching him with a sidelong glance. "Y'all got a wife out there, or children?"

Thomas shook his head. "Had a wife. She . . . uh . . . ." He shifted his gaze to the mountains in the distance.

So, he used to be married. I wonder what he did to her. Divorce is a really serious business. She raised her eyebrows. "What's next for ya?"

Thomas looked thoughtful, keeping his gaze in the distance. "Guess I'll keep chasing gold, or whatever else catches my fancy. Life's like that, ain't it? One step at a time."

Annie sighed, with a hint of approval in her voice. "Yeah, suppose it is."

It felt too honest. Annie felt herself shrink from it. People didn't talk like that to strangers in Rocky Bar, not unless they were three whiskeys deep. She shifted in her seat and began peeling the next apple with renewed concentration, unsure if she wanted to continue the conversation.

"Your folks around?" Thomas asked, turning back towards Annie.

"Yeah, Pa was a miner. He worked at the big mines. The Elmore, and the Ophir after that." *Don't ask me where he is now, buster. I'm not gonna talk about how Pa was shot and killed in a street fight two years ago.* She kept her eyes on the apple in her hand, refusing to meet his gaze. "Ma does . . . other stuff." Annie had no respect for her mother. The man who was having an affair with her mother murdered her father, and her mother invited the killer to move in with them. *How revolting. I'll never get over that, not ever.*

She waited for him to ask what "other stuff" meant. That question usually came next, or if not the question, then a certain look, the raised brow, or knowing nod, or a smirk. Neither spoke for several minutes. Annie realized she had offered a piece of herself for inspection, and the man sitting across from her was weighing it, maybe picking it apart the way miners will go through piles of ore tailings for the one speck of gold they might have missed. She disliked that this stranger made her feel so exposed. She would refuse to say anything more about her mother or her father. This man Thomas would hear about it from some busybody in town anyhow.

His presence unnerved her. He did not fill the air with the usual squawks and bravado she had grown to expect from his type. Instead, he sat on the porch steps, elbows propped, hands dangling between his knees, and watched her work as if she were the finest entertainment Rocky Bar offered. Occasionally, she would steal a glance at him and then look away, hoping to break his eye contact, but it didn't work. Every time she looked up at him, he was still watching her and obviously enjoying it. She did not enjoy it.

Annie was not sure what to do, so she leaned over and grabbed another apple. A tangle of her loose hair fell across her eyes. *If I brush it away, he'll think I care about how I look to him, but if I ignore it, I'll look stupid. I should've worn braids.* She hooked the escaped strands behind her ear, cheeks showing a little red, as if the hair had been a more intimate part of her, and pressed her lips hard together. She looked up, expecting some crack or lewd smirk, but Thomas's gaze remained steady and unreadable. Either he had not noticed, or he was polite enough to pretend he hadn't noticed. She did not trust people she could not read.

Without warning, a board creaked on the porch, and a customer bounded down the rickety steps right between them and over to the hitching post where he had tied his Appaloosa horse. This startled Thomas right out of his daydreaming, if that was what he was doing. He rolled his hat between his hands and tapped the brim against his knee, then looked over at Annie through that narrowing squint of his, as if he had been mulling something over and decided on the words.

"Mining is hard work."

Annie rolled her eyes and shook her head. She was close to throwing an apple peel at him. "Ha. Tell me somethin' I don't know."

"I didn't mean to pry," he said, his voice gentler now. "Just figured we both got a little too much time for thinkin'. You know how it is."

Annie wasn't sure what to do with that remark. She wanted to snap at him, tell him to mind his own business, but she only stared at the mountains in the distance.

"Yeah, I suppose," she replied, her voice a whisper. "I spend a lotta time thinkin' 'bout stuff."

He nodded. "Exactly. Sometimes thoughts get a hold of you, refusing to let go."

She sighed, her gaze still fixed on the horizon. "I guess we're just tryin' to deal with 'em." An image flashed in her mind's eye of how happy her father looked when she opened the gift that he had given her on her eleventh birthday. It was a tiny sewing kit, the last gift he gave her before James killed him.

Annie glanced at him. "Maybe talking 'bout stuff ain't so bad after all." Her father's image faded away. "Why'd you come here anyway?" she blurted out. The question surprised them both.

He looked at her, his brown eyes wide open and searching. For a second, Annie got the uneasy sense that he wanted her to know his feelings. "I wanted to see if it felt any different here."

"Different from what?"

His gaze drifted past her shoulder, out toward the ragged line of rooftops and the jagged mountaintops beyond. "Every town is the same, far as I can tell. Same miners, same dusty streets, same dead-end mines, same talk about the mother lode and big strikes that never pay off. Only things that change are the names of the saloons and how long folks last before they give up and call it quits. But I hear Rocky Bar is different. Figured I'd come and see for myself."

"Is it? Does it feel different here?"

His laugh was a broken thing, not much above a cough. "Maybe—maybe not. Don't know yet. We'll see." He traced the grain of the apple crate with a thumbnail, head bowed so the brim of his hat made a shadow over his entire face. "Some days I'd like to think I could start over. Walk into a place and not already be the story other folks tell about me." The words came out so quietly that Annie wasn't sure she heard them right.

Is he looking for sympathy? Lots of men were, especially the broken-down old-timers who never struck it rich. But this was different. He's not giving me some sob story.

14

From inside the mercantile, she heard Mrs. MacGregor talking to someone in her thick Irish accent, then the creak of the porch as another tired customer came in and went out a few minutes later. The day had drifted into that still hour before evening, when the exhausted miners dragged themselves out of the mine shafts. The air would fill with laughter and shouting and the stink of cigar smoke and whisky. She glanced over at Thomas, still as a statue, shoulders hunched. He looked weary, not just in body but in the way he held himself.

A tantalizing pause hung in the air between them, thick with unspoken words, until he rose, meticulously dusting the soil from his trousers with a measured grace. "Thanks for the seat, Annie." Her name slipped from his lips like a cherished secret, imbued with unique importance. "Maybe I'll see you around," he continued, his voice laced with intrigue and the promise of what could become, leaving the moment charged with unspoken possibilities.

Annie considered his comment. *What's that supposed to mean? He wants to see me again? Why? What does he want? I've heard about those road agents out scouting for their next victim.*

Thomas walked off down rut-filled Rocky Bar Road, boots thumping in a steady, unhurried rhythm, patting the backs of a few horses along the way. She watched him go for a few moments until he disappeared from sight.

Chapter 3

From the next morning on, Annie watched for him. She tried to convince herself it was nothing, just the lingering curiosity of an idle girl in a town where fresh faces were more rare than rain. But she watched for him, all the same. She found excuses to step out onto the porch: to collect deliveries that had not arrived, sweep away already-swept dust, or stand with her arms folded pretending to look for stray dogs up and down the road.

Some days she didn't see him at all, and on those days, she felt an odd disappointment settle in her heart. On other mornings, he appeared like clockwork, walking with the same measured stride, never in a hurry but always sure of where he was headed. Sometimes he disappeared around the corner toward the assay office or the blacksmith shop, and Annie counted the minutes before he emerged again.

It bothered her how often she thought of him. The more she tried to put him out of her mind, the more she built a mental tally of his habits and patterns. *Was this a good thing, to think about him all the time? It's nice to have his attention, to be noticed, I suppose.* She learned which days he carted ore samples from the stamp mill, and which afternoons he would disappear into the Gold Nugget Saloon. Annie never asked anyone about him because people would think that she was interested in him. She never slipped his name into conversations with Mrs. MacGregor or Hazel, who would have made a joke out of it.

In the evenings, after the mercantile closed, with the road emptied of all but the worst drunks and wildest children, Annie sometimes caught herself replaying their last conversation on the mercantile porch. She would remember the exact sound of his voice, its ragged edge softened by weariness, and the brief, unguarded way he looked at her. Annie liked to hear him say her name, but she didn't know how he made it sound so melodious. She thought about how their banter flowed easily between them, but other times it felt awkward, and she would get confused all over again, for reasons that never made sense. *I hate feeling confused. Can you like something and not like something at the same time?*

If Thomas noticed her watching for him, he didn't let on. He never tipped his hat, never winked or grinned or made any show of recognizing her some days. He passed by, day after day, a silent fact of the road like the piles of broken whiskey bottles that littered both sides. Sometimes Annie imagined catching up to him, starting another conversation, saying something clever, or at least something that would unsettle him the way he unsettled her. But every time she pictured it, the words soured in her mind before she could even form them.

* * *

They didn't speak again for weeks. Every so often, their gazes met across the street, and in those brief moments, the rest of Rocky Bar faded to background noise. Annie broke eye contact first, but it got harder each time. While walking home one evening, she saw someone over at Beaver Creek, crouched low and washing his hands. *Is that Thomas? Could be.* She wasn't sure, as his back was turned to her.

What should I do? I've never approached Thomas. It was always he who came up to the mercantile to talk to me. If I walk over to him, he'll know I'm interested in him, and I don't know if that's a good idea or not. I could ignore him and keep walking, but then I'll never know what could have happened, and I might regret that. Annie stood in the middle of the street, motionless. She didn't even budge when an old man riding by on a horse almost knocked her over. She was stuck, and she hated being stuck, not knowing which way to turn. *Is he acting like bait, tryin' to lure me over? Was there a hook inside that bait? Something tells me this is a big decision.* "Hell with it!" she said out loud and marched towards Thomas. Halfway across the road, she tripped on a rut and almost fell over. *Damn it!* She regained her balance, but her confidence was shaken.

Thomas was hunched over at the edge of the water, scrubbing at his hands like he was banishing the day from his skin. He looked up at Annie as she approached, and the beginnings of a sly grin tugged at the creases around his mouth. "Back for another round of talk?" he asked, not moving to get up. He blinked at the sun as he pinched his tin canteen between his knees and twisted off the battered cap.

Annie opened her mouth to say something, but she just watched him fill the canteen. She couldn't think of anything to say. Thomas waited for her to answer. For several minutes, the only motion was the murky reflection of them both, side by side in the creek, her hair wild and loose, his shirt rolled up past sunburned forearms. *He must think I'm an idiot.*

"You always this shy, Miss McIntyre?" he asked while capping the canteen with a jerk and setting it aside. Annie kicked a pebble with the toe of her shoe and watched it arc into the creek.

"Nope, only with men who think they know everything." The words snapped out, but as soon as they left her mouth, she heard a lilt in them she hadn't planned. *Now he knows I'm an idiot. What a stupid thing to say!* For a second, she braced for a comeback, some off-color quip or veiled sneer, but Thomas only grinned at her.

"I've been called worse," he said, wiping his wet hands on his thighs. "And by folks with a lot more spit than you, Miss McIntyre."

Annie smirked but didn't look away. *Nobody calls me Miss McIntyre, but it sounds kinda nice. What is it with this guy?* Stepping into a shallow spot in the water, she noticed it swirled past her high lace shoes. She stood above him without uttering a word. She shifted her weight from one leg to the other and pushed her hair away from her face. *This is strange, talking to an older man, and not just any man, but the one I know nothing about.*

Thomas fished a battered tobacco tin from his pocket but didn't open it. Instead, he turned it over and over in his palms. "You ever think about leaving?" he asked, not looking at her, but beyond her, up at the mountains. "All this?" He flicked his chin toward the huddle of town, roofs sunken and walls patched with rusty sheets of tin. "Starting someplace where folks haven't already made up their minds that they don't like you?"

She wanted to scoff, to say something about how Rocky Bar was the only place worth knowing, but the question found a crack in her usual self-confidence. She thought about it for longer than she admitted, longer than it took for a yellow aspen tree leaf to float downstream and vanish around a curve.

Annie narrowed her eyes against the blinding sunlight, then turned to Thomas, as if grappling with the bewildering weight of his question. "I'm only fourteen," she declared, hands on her hips, her voice laced with determination, challenging him to dispute her truth. "And this is my home. I've been here since I was five. I survived the God-awful journey on the Oregon Trail all the way to Boise City, and then on a pack train here. Some folks died along the way, but I made it." Her words were edged with a raw, unwavering conviction, leaving no space for denial.

"You could pass for sixteen, you know. You look old for your age and more grown up than you give yourself credit for."

She blinked. *Nobody ever said that to me before.* She fidgeted with her hands for a moment and then forged ahead with her words. "And anyway, it ain't so bad here. The winters are mighty fierce, with winds and snowstorms that'll knock y'all flat on your back. My pa said that only fools run away from their own story."

"And what does that mean?"

She glared at him. "It means bein' honest with yourself and acceptin' who ya really are an' makin' the most of it." She narrowed her eyes at him. "Do I need to draw you a picture?"

"That won't be necessary, Miss McIntyre."

She didn't know why she was talking so much, and why she wanted this scruffy man to know anything about her. It didn't sit well with her, the way he could ask a question and make it feel like she had offered herself up for inspection. She clenched her fists and made her voice brittle. "If y'all are looking for a runaway, mister, try the next town over."

She risked a glance at Thomas, expecting him to laugh or call her a baby for getting defensive, but he listened, his face again unreadable. If she amused him, he hid it under a thick layer of respect. So she went on, softer now. "My ma says there ain't nothin' good left here. Most of the stamp mills have shut down, and high-grade ore is gettin' harder and harder to find. Placer mining's a joke. Says we'll end up as ghosts with no place to haunt. But still, Rocky Bar is my home, for now, anyway." The words surprised her as they came out, and for a second, she blushed.

She cocked her chin, defiant, even as her voice cracked. "Y'all think that sounds stupid?"

Thomas let out a low whistle, like she had recited scripture. "You're better than this place, Annie."

She flushed, angry at herself for letting the subtle compliment strike her. "What makes y'all so sure I'd be any better off someplace else?"

He smiled again, but there was no mock in it. "I don't. But some folks, they got eyes that don't fit the scenery, if you know what I mean, Miss McIntyre." For a second, he let that hang in the air, then pinched the tobacco tin open, rolling thin smoke with shaking fingers. "Guess I'm saying you're one of them."

Annie watched the roll of tobacco take shape in Thomas's hands. She wanted to test him, to get beneath the calm, so she tilted her head a little and said, "Y'all talk like a preacher, or maybe one of them fast-talking gamblers who thinks he can win at the poker table just by his words." She let the accusation hang and waited to see if he would blink.

He didn't. He stuck the rolled smoke between his teeth and eyed her sidelong, the flame from his match painting his face gold for a blink in time. "Maybe so. But at least with a gambler, you can see when you've lost. A preacher will have folks handing over coins for years, thinking

20

they're buying a place in heaven. I would rather sit at the faro table than in a pew."

"Ha, me too."

"You're a curious one, Miss McIntyre. Most girls your age think gamblers are scoundrels."

"Even scoundrels have a good side," Annie shot back, crossing her arms and fixing him with the same stare she used on the out-of-towners who tried to shortchange her at the mercantile counter. "I'd prefer a gambler over a preacher any day," she added. "At least they don't promise ya something they can't give, and you know the risks you're takin'."

Thomas laughed, not a soft chuckle but a sharp crack that startled a couple of sparrows from the pine tree above them. "That's the spirit," he said. "You ever play?"

She rolled her eyes again. "Pa taught me good when I was six. Said every hand is a way of seein' if the world's still a cheatin' on ya."

Thomas nodded his head, looking impressed. "Well, if you ever decide to try your hand, you come find me. Might be the only honest game in town. Sometimes I deal at the Gold Nugget." He flicked the spent match into the water, where it sizzled for a moment before floating away.

Annie wanted to say something clever, to poke at him the way he poked at her, as she watched the match drift out of sight. "Y'all still didn't say why you're here."

He exhaled, the smoke trailing a thin blue line between them. "Figured I'd find something worth the trouble—a lode of high-grade ore, a job, a friend, or a reason to keep waking up." He shrugged. "Rocky Bar's worth a try. Don't worry. I'm harmless." He scooped a palmful of water and let it drizzle through his fingers. "Most folks are, if you ask me."

Thomas continued to talk about random topics, like how an old-timer up at Steel Creek fell in last week, netting some trout, and how the storekeeper's wife kept a bottle of Old Crow 86 proof whiskey in her dress at church, hidden from the preacher.

After a while, Annie knelt by the creek, scooped up a handful of water, and splashed it across her wrists. The coolness penetrated her skin, leaving a refreshing sensation in its wake. Her fingers felt the chill of the water as it flowed between them. She poked at a purple-colored pebble with her forefinger.

"You like to sit around Beaver Creek and wait for people to show up?" she asked, keeping her tone even, smiling behind the words.

Thomas rolled his broad shoulders, the movement lazy and deliberate, and looked at Annie with an expression that wavered between a dare and a plea for honesty. "Only when I want to see you." This time, he didn't dress it up in banter. She wondered if he saw the flush gather under her skin, blooming up from the collarbone and across her cheeks.

He didn't press. He sat there, content to let her flounder through her own thoughts. Thomas remained silent, dragging the back of one hand across his chin, under his handlebar moustache, making a low noise in his throat like he was tempted to apologize or to say it again, louder.

"Didn't mean to catch you off guard," he said, his voice softer. "You strike me as the type of person with an answer for everything." He tapped a stick against his knee, breaking off the tip and tossing it into the creek. The twig spun in the current, caught a little eddy, then vanished around a bend.

"I'm a might tired," Annie said as she stood. "Long day." She meant it as a rebuke, but it landed with no effect on him. She felt young, ridiculous, her usual armor of attitude scraped thin by his disarming words.

"Fair enough." He tilted his head, appraising her with those odd, patient eyes. "You're allowed to let your guard down, Annie. Nobody's keeping score but you."

Annie kicked at the mud, digging the toe of her shoe in deeper. *He has an answer for everything.* "Y'all say things so blunt all the time?" she asked, her voice small but sharp, "or just with me?" She didn't know why she said it. Annie wanted him to admit to a trick, to call it a joke, and let her off the hook. She wanted to know if it was anywhere near true.

Thomas considered this, rolling the question over like a gold nugget in his palm. "I spent a lot of years talking but avoiding the topics that matter.

Got me nowhere but old before my time. Figured I'd try something different." He met her gaze. "With you, seems worth it."

She swallowed, not knowing what to think. She shifted her weight from one foot to the other while rubbing the back of her neck. *This is getting personal.* Annie felt the urge to flee, to turn and bolt for home, but her body stayed rooted in place, like whatever held her here was more stubborn than her own pride. For a while, neither of them said anything. The creek kept up its soft gurgling, and the mosquitoes thickened, as they do in the evenings. A small fish jumped out of the water and plopped back in. Annie sensed Thomas watching her from the side, respectful of the distance but leaving the door open just a crack. It was the first time in months that she had been alone with a grown-up and not felt like she was about to be told off, bossed around, or pitied. It was tantalizing.

"Do you ever wonder what it's like beyond Rocky Bar?" Thomas asked, breaking the silence.

Annie hesitated, her heart fluttering at the unexpected question. "Sometimes," she admitted. "I dream about it . . . but I don't think I'd fit in anywhere else."

He turned to face her more fully, a flicker of intensity sparking in his brown eyes. "You would. Definitely. You're stronger than you think you are."

She felt warmth rise to her cheeks at his words. "What about you? What do you want?"

Thomas paused for a moment, searching for the right words as if they were buried deep within him. "To build something better for myself," he said as he rose and stood beside her.

Annie studied him closely, caught between skepticism and curiosity. He looked so earnest then, and she couldn't help but wonder if there was truth behind that charming facade. She wished the moment would stretch out longer, embarrassed but also a little greedy for it. Annie would never admit it, but it felt good to be paid attention to without having to perform, without having to be tougher or meaner or smarter than the rest. She stared at the horizon again for a long time, then let herself smile a little.

They stood together by the creek, neither moving toward nor away from the other, and the urge to run away subsided. The hush of water and wind filled the space between them, and it dawned on her that she liked his company.

Despite how she felt, she said, "gotta go," and turned back up the trail towards town. "Ma will string me up if I'm late for supper."

"Wait a second."

She stopped without turning around but tensed her shoulders so he would know she heard him. She kept her chin up and waited for whatever came next, bracing for a joke or a warning or some last-minute confession. To her surprise, she only heard his boots crunching the packed dirt as he got closer.

He reached her but paused one step away. They both stood like two statues in the dusk. "I mean, don't go yet. I'm not done talking." He laughed awkwardly, as if he'd never vied for anyone's time before. "Not that I want to keep you from your ma's supper, but—"

"But what?" Annie interrupted, turning to see his face. He looked earnest in the evening light. *What are y'all tryin' to say?*

Thomas scratched his neck. "Most folks don't talk straight to me. I like that you do." He shrugged.

Annie blinked. "Y'all like talkin' straight?"

He considered this, then nodded once, slowly. "Guess I do. With you, at least."

The honesty hung between them with so much suspense that it made her nervous. She had to look away, kicking at a flat stone with her shoe, then turned to face him.

"Fine," she muttered. "If y'all got something else to say, say it."

Thomas hesitated, searching her face for a sign. "You don't have to go it alone all the time. You ain't the only one lost out here—"

"I ain't lost!" She wanted to yell at him, or laugh, or run. Instead, she stood there, arms crossed, eyes fixed on him. "I'll think about it," she muttered as she spun around and walked away.

24

* * *

For the next few weeks, Annie perched herself on the front porch of the mercantile each morning, elbows propped on her knees, eyes fixed on the rutted road that wound past town like a dusty ribbon. At first, she expected Thomas to appear at any moment—striding in from the claims, leading a horse, or stopping to jaw with the miners heading toward the saloon. But he never did.

As September bled into October, the air cooled, sharpening the sounds of the stamp mills. Hammer strikes from the blacksmith carried farther; wagon wheels clattered louder over hardening earth.

The cottonwoods along the creek turned a bright, brittle gold, their leaves whispering like paper whenever the wind swept down from the mountains. Annie sat on the porch, wrapped in her blue sweater, rubbing her chilled hands together as she watched the leaves fall in slow spirals, scattering across the porch. Still, there was no sign of him.

By November, the last of the color had drained from the trees, and frost glazed the edges of the windowpanes each morning. Annie's breath puffed white in the air as she waited, gently rocking on the mercantile's old bench, its wooden slats creaking beneath her. The sour-sweet scent of fermenting apples from a nearby barrel mingled with the sharp smell of wood smoke rising from chimneys down the road. But day after day, the road remained empty of the one figure she ached to see.

The weeks stretched thin, then stretched farther, and before she realized it, months had slipped past—months filled with rustling leaves, biting winds, and the hollow thud of disappointment settling deeper in her chest. Thomas did not appear, not once.

He must have left for the winter. Can't pan for gold under two feet of snow. No miner in their right mind would voluntarily stay in Rocky Bar in the winter. I wonder if he lost interest in me. I hope not. What happened, Thomas? Where are you?

Chapter 4

The McIntyre house was a ramshackle box of pine logs and a shake roof, perched at the edge of Rocky Bar, close enough for Annie to catch the afternoon rowdiness of the saloons when the wind shifted right. Inside, the aroma of stewed beans, stale bread, and boiled pork mingled with the damp reek of mining clothes hung up to dry above the stove. The house never aired out. Every surface, from the cracked enamel basin to the patched burlap curtains, was a reminder of their awful past. She could not remember a time when it didn't feel like a borrowed shell, though sometimes she let herself believe that when Pa was alive, it had been different.

The family gathered around the decrepit dinner table as usual one chilly October evening. At one end of the table sat Marcella, her dark hair scraped back so tight it seemed to pull her entire face up into a mask of unearned dignity. The look on her face was one of disappointment. It seemed like she was always annoyed at something or someone. She never smiled. Whenever Annie returned home, Marcella would glare at her for no reason that Annie could ever figure out. Across from Marcella was George, who had turned eleven but was big for his age. He was a well-behaved boy, but he was clueless most of the time about the tension that pervaded every dinnertime. Across the table from Annie sat James Roberts. He had a perpetual scowl planted on his face, but at least he shaved and kept his hair cut short. It seemed to Annie that whenever he looked at her, he was looking at a fool. James was the only enemy that Annie had in Rocky Bar. She hated him. She loathed the feeling of hate, but she couldn't help it. He murdered her father. He never asked to be called Pa. Annie would have refused anyway.

Tonight was pork night. The only way Annie could tell it from any other night was the fleck of gristle floating on top of her tin bowl. They ate in silence, as usual, with only the distant hooting of an owl breaking the oppressive silence. Annie's braid brushed against her shoulder as she bent to her bowl; her left arm rested on her lap, and her mind formed a barrier against any stray word that might slip out and ruin the fragile peace.

She ate slowly, to savor what little flavor there was, but her mind kept circling, never landing. Every night, it was the same: the annoying scrape of Marcella's spoon against her soup bowl, the way James chewed with his mouth open so you could see the half-chewed food rolling over his tongue. He sounded like a pig. It was revolting. She hated every part of him, from the mole on the side of his jaw to the way he wiped his beard with the back of his hand and then ran that hand through his hair, like he was proud of spreading his filth all over his head. But most of all, she hated that she had to sit at the same table as the man who murdered her father. *Seems like Ma cares more about her lover than her own children.*

Tonight, for the first time in weeks, Marcella broke the silence. Usually, it was James with some announcement about something that never came to pass. "George," she said, voice brittle as a snapped twig, "did you get the firewood like I asked?"

George looked up, startled, the question catching him mid-bite. He nodded, then wiped his mouth on the sleeve of his shirt, leaving a brownish smear across his cheek. "I did, Ma," he said, glancing toward Annie, to check if he'd answered correctly. "Stacked it right outside the door."

"Good boy." She let the word settle, then turned to James, her voice softening a notch. "How was work at the mine today?"

James shrugged, his gaze fixed on the table. "Same story as always. More worthless rock than gold," he muttered, fingers tapping a slow rhythm that betrayed his simmering frustration. "Maybe things will turn around next week. They're talking about putting up a new stamp mill."

George looked at Marcella, then James, then back at Marcella, ignoring Annie, his confusion, a tangible thing in the space between their words.

"Will you get to work there, Mr. Roberts?" George asked, and then, catching himself, "I mean—Pa."

"Doubt it," he said, but there was pride in his voice. "That's for the old-timers." He grinned, and for a second his teeth showed, uneven and yellowed but somehow still functional. "But if I do work there, they should make me a foreman. I got the know-how." He leaned back in his chair and crossed his arms, as if he felt proud of himself.

Annie wanted to call out the lie, but she kept her jaw locked. *Everybody knows the stamp mills are shutting down one by one for lack of good ore. A few years ago, six stamp mills operated. Now there's only one left. What a liar. I hate liars.*

James's voice dropped into a growl as he continued, his jaw tightening and his hands curling into fists on the table. "Problem is, the mine owners keep bringing in those Chinamen because they'll work themselves to death for next to nothin'. It's not fair to us Americans."

Annie leaned forward, planting her elbows on the table, her eyes narrowing. "You know they don't got much choice," she said, her fingers lacing together. "They're tryin' to survive like everyone else," she countered, her tone firm yet tinged with empathy.

He tossed his head back with a bitter laugh. Irritation flickered across his features as he jabbed a finger at his empty plate. "Survive? They're taking food out of our mouths."

Annie sat up straighter, her shoulders stiffening. She readied herself for another confrontation. "That ain't true," she shot back, her voice rising. Her hands spread out in a gesture of appeal, then clenched into fists. "They're grateful for any work they get, and they work hard too!"

James's eyes blazed with anger. He slammed his palm on the table, making the saltshaker jump. "Hardworking or not, they're undercutting us!"

Annie flinched but didn't back down. Her spine stayed rigid, her chin lifted. "It's not their fault they're paid less," she insisted, her voice trembling as emotion welled up. "Blame the mine owners who hire 'em as cheap labor instead of payin' fair wages."

She hesitated, her lips parted, but no words came. Her gaze dropped for a beat before rising again, searching his face, too afraid to continue speaking. She knew what was coming.

Marcella smiled with one of her forced smiles. The lines around her mouth eased, and she reached for James's hand across the table. He let her take it, but his eyes didn't move from his bowl. Annie watched the whole thing, the slow, practiced choreography of fake affection, and felt something twist inside her, anger or envy for the way her mother pretended that everything was okay. She couldn't understand why her mother was like this. *What does she see in him? All I see is a killer who will stop at nothing to get what he wants.*

George changed the subject. "Ma," he said, fidgeting with the spoon, "didn't Pa used to say he'd make foreman, too?"

A silence fell, sharper than the cold that crept under the front door. Marcella's hand remained atop James's. She glared at Annie, daring her not to speak.

Annie ignored it. The old burn rose in her chest, and tonight she was too tired to smother it. "He did," she said, looking at James. "Said he'd strike it rich, buy us a proper house. Not this—" she gestured at the cracked window, the sopping rags stuffed in the frame, "not this broken down shed."

James bristled, his shoulders tensing under the threadbare flannel as he shot an icy stare at Annie. "He talked plenty. Didn't work much."

Marcella glanced nervously over at him, but he went on, his voice rising. "That's the problem with dreamers. They talk themselves right out of a job." He continued to stare at Annie. "That's not how the world works, girl. Dreams don't put food on the table."

Annie felt her cheeks flush with shame and anger, the two so tangled she couldn't tell which was stronger. Her heart raced. "He worked harder than you," she said, low but clear. "He died working for us." The last word hung there, like a nail hammered into the night.

James' eyes filled with anger. The air between them taut as a wire. "He died because he was a fool."

Marcella reached for his arm, squeezing tight, her voice steady but urgent. "Enough," she said, like she'd said a hundred times before. "Let it be."

The words came out of Annie like blood from a wound, thick and unstoppable, and the moment they left her lips, she knew there was no taking them back. "He died because of you!" she screamed at him. "You gunned him down. In the street. Like a dog." She leaned forward, all the years spent swallowing her grief and bitterness erupting in one instant. Every syllable was a stone hurled at James. "You didn't have to kill him!"

Marcella's face drained of color.

James laid his spoon down. He wiped his hands on his trousers, then folded his arms. "You don't know what you're talking about," he said, but his voice was thin, strangled, laced with a tremor that wasn't there a moment before. He shot a look at Marcella. "You going to let her talk to me like that? You want her turning out like *him*?"

Marcella opened her mouth, then closed it.

He continued, "Your pa was nothing but a drunk and a cheat and a liar," he hissed, each word spat with venom. "He tried to steal my claim, and everyone in Rocky Bar knew it. I did what was necessary."

Annie could not contain herself anymore. All those years of silent dinners, of watching her mother and James play-act kindness for the sake of appearances, had culminated in this moment. She wanted to hurt him. "Tell it true for once," she said, her voice raw. "He wasn't armed, and you knew it." Her voice cracked. "But you shot him anyway. *Three times!*" She blinked tears out of her eyes, angry at herself for betraying weakness.

James sneered at Annie. "I guess you didn't get the message. The verdict at my trial was 'not guilty' by reason of self-defense. Chew on that one, Missy."

Annie knew that. She was at the trial. *The testimony in favor of James Roberts was a pack of lies. It was sickening.*

"You probably bribed your witnesses," Annie muttered under her breath. Marcella gasped. George stopped breathing.

"You've got some mouth on you, girl," he sneered. "Just like your old man. Why, I oughta—"

James sprang to his feet. The chair tipped over and crashed to the floor with a bang. He slammed his fists onto the table, leaning in so close that she could feel his hot, smelly breath on her face. "That's enough!" he growled. "Keep running that mouth of yours, and I'll give you something real to cry about."

Annie didn't flinch. She locked eyes with him, her heart thumping, but her voice remained steady as a rock. "Go on, then. Show Ma who she chose over Pa. *I dare you!*"

James's jaw flexed, a muscle jumping under the skin, and his face turned red. For a second, Annie thought he might hit her, right there at the dinner table, but he just breathed harder, then shoved away from the table. He flung the door open and cursed all the way to the street.

In the silence that followed, George cried, soft sobs that he muffled with his hands. Annie looked at him. The fire drained out of her, leaving her empty. She reached across the table, touching his arm, but he pulled away, shaking his head.

"Why'd you do that?" he whispered, voice shredded by tears. "Why can't you stop it?" He covered his ears and rocked back and forth in his chair.

George was miserable, and she didn't have an answer. She watched her mother get up and close the front door, then gather up the dishes with slow, deliberate motions. Marcella's hands were steady, her face set in stone, but Annie saw the faint quiver in her jaw, the sadness in her eyes she would never admit to. Marcella spoke without turning, her back rigid as she scraped the bowls. "You'll have to leave us someday, Annie. If you can't get along, you'll have to go." The words were brief, but they hit harder than any slap from James. *My own mother wants to get rid of me.*

Annie sat at the table, paralyzed. George's sobs faded to sniffles. Marcella finished washing the dishes and then disappeared. Annie couldn't think straight. Her mind was a tangle of questions, doubts, and confusion. The evening cold eventually drove her up to the narrow, lumpy bed she shared with her brother in the attic. She lay awake long after the house went quiet, watching the moonlight crawl across the cracked plaster, counting the seconds between each slow, deliberate breath in the dark. *Would Pa recognize who I've become? Can I ever forgive Ma?*

Somewhere deep down, where the heat of anger met the chill of loneliness, Annie wondered if she would find a way to leave before she lost her mind. *If I leave on my own, then Ma won't have the pleasure of kicking me out. That would show her who I am. I'm old enough to run away; some girls do that, but is that what I really want? I just don't know. What can I do? Where would I go?* For now, she listened to the slow, steady breathing of her brother and let herself believe she could protect him.

Chapter 5

The fight at dinner last night bothered Annie. Despite their many arguments, it was then that Annie first thought James might become violent. *He shot a man to death, so hitting a girl wouldn't bother him at all. He was looking for an excuse to give me a thrashing. I gotta do something, but what? I can't live like this. It's not fair, but I have nowhere to go.*

Lost in thought, Annie wandered up and down Rocky Bar Road for hours. The November chill had produced the first frost of the season. She was halfway past a stinky outhouse when she heard it: a muffled sniffling, a stuttered breath like a wounded dog trying to keep quiet. At first, she thought it was an old miner sleeping off an all-nighter, or maybe one of the Bannister twins hiding from their mother's switch. But the sound was too soft, too desperate. It stopped Annie cold.

She walked over towards the back door of the mercantile. Down in the dirt between stacks of empty apple crates, she saw a small shape curled tight, knees hugged up close, bare feet scratched and dirty. It took her a second to realize who it was. She put her hands over her chest and gasped.

Meng Yao. The Chinese girl. Nobody knew how old she was. She looked like she was seven or eight. Around town, she was almost invisible, flitting in and out of shadows, doing errands for the Chinese miners or running messages between their shacks in Chinatown. Annie had only heard her speak once before, and it was a whisper, thick with an accent that made the words a pain to understand.

Annie stood above her, watching the way the girl's back shook with each shuddering breath. She was shivering.

Annie crouched, elbows on her knees, and tried to catch the girl's eye. "Hey," she whispered.

Meng Yao didn't move. Annie saw the raw pink of her knuckles where she'd been biting them. A line of snot streaked down the side of her mouth. Her hair was tangled, black and slick, plastered to her face and neck. The hem of her garment was torn and crusted brown with dirt.

Annie waited. When the girl still didn't look up, Annie dug in her pocket for the scrap of muslin she used as a handkerchief, ragged and stained from a hundred uses. She rolled it up and tossed it into the dirt next to Meng Yao's bare feet. "Y'all can use that. It ain't clean, but it's better than your sleeve."

A minute passed before a scrawny little hand darted out and snatched the cloth, pulling it back into the darkness between the apple crates. Annie watched as the girl dabbed at her eyes, then at her nose. She made no sound. Annie noticed that the girl's wrists were so thin you could break them with a hard squeeze.

After a while, Annie settled back on her heels, chewing at the inside of her cheek. *You're a long way from Chinatown, little one. I can't just walk away, but what can I do to help you?* "You hungry? Mrs. MacGregor made biscuits this morning. I can fetch you one."

For a long time, there was no response, and Annie was about to give up, but then the girl shook her head, a single jerk.

"No want," Meng Yao said, voice so small Annie almost missed it.

Annie frowned, unsure whether the girl meant the food or her company. She tried again, softer this time. "What happened?" She was going to ask, *did someone hurt you?* She stopped herself because it was obvious: girls like her were always hurt and abused, one way or another. *The Chinamen treated girls like slaves, even though they were supposed to be indentured servants, whatever that meant.* Annie had seen the looks the other children gave the Chinese girls, the way even the grown-ups in town crossed to the other side of the street rather than risk the shame of being seen near one of them. *Why do people have to be so mean?*

The girl didn't answer. She wiped her eyes with the cloth, then balled it in her fist. Annie wanted to reach out to pat her on the shoulder the way Hazel sometimes did with the smaller children, but she didn't. So, she did what she did best—she sat, and she waited, and she watched. *What can I do for this poor thing? I heard that parents in China sold their daughters to smugglers for a few bags of rice. Girls had little value in China. They would be sent by sailing ship to San Francisco, where they would be auctioned off to the highest bidder, always a Chinaman with money. From there, they could be taken to God-knows-where as part of the Chinaman's concubine or as a prostitute, where they were held captive in filthy shacks called cribs. If they complained, they were given opium to keep them in a daze. When they got older, or sick, or pregnant, they would be locked in their crib with a small bowl of rice for several days. The owner would come by and see if they were still alive. They wouldn't be, of course, but that was the plan. The girl would have either starved to death or committed suicide, only to be discarded like trash.*

Annie gave Meng Yao a long look. She couldn't bear the thought of this happening to this innocent little girl, right here in Rocky Bar. Tears welled up in her eyes. She wanted to help, to rescue her. *What can I do? Nothing. It's so unfair.*

A few minutes later, Meng Yao uncoiled a little, peeking up at Annie through a curtain of dirty hair. Her eyes were enormous, black and shiny like spilled ink, and ringed in purple shadows that made her look even younger than she was. Annie smiled, but it felt awkward on her face. "You're safe now," she said gently, knowing the words were false as soon as she spoke them. *This girl is anything but safe. No doubt her master will come looking for her. Who knows what he will do to her?*

The girl blinked. She looked at Annie as if weighing the truth of it, then wiped her nose again and pushed herself upright, like a frightened little fawn. She did not speak, but the trembling had stopped, and she no longer looked like she was trying to melt into the ground. Annie reached over and brushed a loose strand of hair away from Meng Yao's cheek. The touch startled the girl, but she didn't pull back. Instead, she leaned into it, as if the simple act of being touched with tenderness was something she had never experienced. Annie left her hand there a second longer than necessary, then pulled it back. "If you want to talk or sit, that's fine," she said. "But I gotta go soon. They'll miss me at the counter."

Meng Yao nodded, her chin dipping once, and then she did something that surprised Annie. She reached out and gripped Annie's sleeve, clutching the faded blue fabric like a lifeline. The strength of her grasp was surprising. They stayed like that for several minutes, two girls in the dim light behind the mercantile, linked by nothing but a shared feeling of what it meant to be small in a world that did not care about them.

When the church bell tolled eleven o'clock, Annie stood. She hesitated, then squeezed the girl's hand once before letting go. "See you around," she said, pretending their encounter had not shaken her.

Meng Yao looked up at Annie. She did not smile, but her grip loosened, and she nodded again and, with much effort, rose to her feet. Meng Yao was so frail that the act of standing up was difficult for her. She turned toward Chinatown, took a few tiny steps, then stopped and looked over her shoulder at Annie. A tiny smile crept across her dirty little face. A moment later, it vanished as she started on the trail to Chinatown. After taking a few steps, she stopped again. She started to turn around but hesitated, as if she wanted to say something, then resumed walking up the trail.

The heaviness in Annie's heart grew. *How pitiful is the life of this little girl? And there is nothing I can do about it. She doesn't deserve a life like this. It's so unfair.* She stood there, then took a deep breath, regained her composure, and headed to the mercantile to begin her duties for the day. Off and on throughout the day, she could feel the small, steady pull at her sleeve, a reminder that sometimes, you didn't have to say a word for someone to know you were there for them. At least she could do that for little Meng Yao.

Chapter 6

The next two winters were uneventful, except for the avalanches that blocked the road to Alanta for weeks at a time. One avalanche killed a mail carrier on Bald Mountain. The first rainstorm of the spring came in from the southwest, flinging wet grit against the windows and turning the Rocky Bar Road into a river of mud and horse dung. It was the kind of day that kept everyone inside except the unlucky, the unwanted, and the desperate. Annie was all three, and she relished the way the town belonged to her alone on days like this.

She did not expect to see the stagecoach lurching up from the valley that morning, its battered black body slung low on its springs, horses slick with rain and foaming at the bridle. It had been months since anyone worth the trip had come off that coach. Annie slowed, then stopped, the sharp twist of curiosity drawing her toward the covered stoop of the assay office, where she could watch without being seen.

The coach clattered to a halt, and the driver yelled something towards the door of the Alturas Hotel. Annie watched as the door to the coach swung open, and a man unfolded himself from the shadows inside. Tall, broad in the shoulders, with deliberate steps. For a moment, she thought it couldn't be him. Then he stepped down, and she saw the face beneath the battered hat and the handlebar moustache. *Thomas Morrow!*

He looked older. There was a hollowness to his cheeks now, a weariness in the way he stood for a moment in the rain, letting it soak him like he needed to be reminded he was still alive. He looked around, taking stock of the town, and for a heartbeat, Annie thought he might leave again without even noticing her. *What if he doesn't see me?*

Thomas spotted her, and his face twisted in a wry smile. He did not wave, did not call out. He walked over to her, boots splashing through the cold brown soup of the street, until he stood close enough that Annie could smell his wet denim jacket.

"Hello to you too, Annie," he said, voice softer than the memory of it.

"Where've you been? I ain't seen you for a year and a half."

"Boise City. Got a job at a warehouse."

For a long moment, they stared at each other, the spring rain coming down hard enough to drown any more words worth saying. Annie wanted to reach for him, to make sure he was real and not some trick of her own imagination. She held back, shoving her hands deep in the pockets of her dress.

"What happened to your face?" she asked, noticing the scabbed-over cut above his eyebrow and the new line scored deep into his skin.

He shrugged. "Some saddle tramp in a saloon wanted to pick a fight. I didn't want to fight, but he insisted, so I let him have it." His eyes flicked past her to the empty street, the dark windows of the saloon, the ridge of snow on the mountains far above. "Looks like nothing here changed much while I was gone."

Annie shook her head. "Some things changed," she said. "I'm sixteen now." She had let her hair grow out past her shoulders. She wore it loose or sometimes up and knotted in a bun. There were days when she looked in the cracked mirror behind the counter at the mercantile and couldn't help but notice her developing figure. Her voice, too, had changed, deeper and less likely to crack with nerves. She did not mention the things that had changed for the worse: the slow shrinking of the town as claim after claim went bust and the stamp mills shut down. She did not mention Meng

Yao either, who still orbited the fringes of Rocky Bar, more as a ghost than a girl.

Thomas gave her a long, searching look, like he was mapping the places she'd grown. "I missed you," he said, not like a confession, but a fact. "Didn't think I would. But I did."

Annie felt the old ache inside her again, the part of her that was braced for disappointment. "Y'all never wrote to me," she said, trying to sound cold, but her voice tripped on the words. "Not even once."

He nodded, as if he had expected this. "Didn't think you'd want me to." He paused, and when he spoke again, the words were heavier. "Didn't think I deserved to write to someone as good as you."

She could not think of a response to that. The rain eased up a little, leaving a hush broken only by the slap of a stray horse's tail somewhere up the block. Thomas shifted his weight, then jerked his chin toward the Gold Nugget Saloon. "Buy you a drink?" he asked. "Or is that still against the rules?"

Annie smiled. "Ha. There ain't no rules here," and for the first time, realized how true it was. They were free to do anything they wanted.

They ducked under the awning and slipped into the half-empty saloon. The place smelled of sour beer and wet sawdust, but the wood stove provided more than enough warmth. The oil lamp over the bar cast a yellow, comforting light. Annie found a seat in the back, away from the windows, and watched as Thomas strolled over to the bar to order drinks. She studied his back, the way the fabric of his jacket pulled across his shoulders, the patch on one sleeve, the line of his neck. She felt foolish for the nights she had lain awake imagining this exact scene, rehearsing her lines as if she were in a play.

When Thomas returned, he slid a glass across the table to her and kept the other for himself. "To the old times," he said.

She picked up the glass, knocked it against his. "And to the new ones." This was not her first drink, but it still burned all the way down.

They sat in silence for a while, the kind that pressed warm and awkward between them. The saloon hummed with the low rumble of men swapping

39

stories about finding the motherlode or bragging about how much gold they had found.

Every so often, their eyes met. Annie broke eye contact first, but each time, the pull of his gaze lingered longer, tugging at her like a thread caught on a nail. Her stomach fluttered every time she caught him watching her, slow and steady, as if he were reacquainting himself with every angle of her face after eighteen long months.

She studied him: the way Thomas lifted his glass, turning it a little before bringing it to his lips, how he paused a heartbeat between each sip, as though measuring his words before he even spoke them. The lamplight caught the line of his jaw and the faint scar above his brow that she remembered so well. She wondered if he could hear how fast her heart was beating.

She suddenly felt self-conscious about her hands, which were wrapped around her whiskey glass, as if she didn't know what to do with them. Thomas was staring at them. She reached up and smoothed the sleeves of her blue-and-white gingham dress, tugging at the fabric as if it needed adjusting. Finally, she blurted, "Do you . . . do you like my dress?"

Thomas's eyes softened in that slow, familiar way that made her feel both cherished and skittish. "It's beautiful," he said, leaning in. His voice dipped low, "just like you."

Annie held her breath. Heat crept from her neck to her cheeks. She took a small sip just for something to do, the whiskey burning warm as it slid down her throat. "So, what now?" she asked, forcing her voice to steady. "Y'all planning on stayin' or just passin' through?"

Thomas rested his arms on the table, his fingers brushing close to hers—close enough she felt the warmth of him, though they didn't quite touch. He took a long drink; his gaze fixed on her over the rim of his glass. "Don't know," he said slowly. "Reckon I could stay . . . if you want me to."

Annie dropped her eyes to the table, tracing the swirls and knots in the grain as if she could disappear into them. She counted three knots before trusting her voice. "And why would I want that?" she said, looking down at her whiskey glass.

Thomas smiled, small but knowing, and tilted his head. "Don't know," he murmured. "But your hinting that it does *not* matter to you . . . makes me think that it *does*."

His fingers crept closer. Annie swallowed, her pulse throbbing under her skin. She looked away again, pretending to study the colorful whiskey bottles behind the bar. However, her senses stayed fixed on him—his nearness, his voice, his steady patience, and the possibilities she had been trying and failing to forget for the last year and a half.

Thomas leaned back, a crooked smile on his lips. "You're not a good liar, Annie."

She looked right into his eyes. "Okay, you caught me. I hope you will stay. There, I said it." She looked down at her hands. "I missed you." Annie surprised herself with her confession. *Why did I say that?*

Thomas gleamed. "I missed you too, Annie."

Annie felt the words hanging between them, fragile but impossibly heavy. She hadn't meant to let them spill out—not here, not now, not with him watching her like he could read every unspoken thought she tried to hide.

Thomas's smile softened, losing its teasing edge. He shifted closer—not touching, but close enough that the space between them warmed. "You don't have to look so bewildered," he murmured. "It's just me."

"I'm not trying to make this complicated. I just want to be honest for once. When you left town eighteen months ago, I—it wasn't easy."

Thomas inhaled slowly, as if her words hit harder than he expected. "It wasn't easy for me either."

She glanced up, searching his face for the lie, but there wasn't one. Only truth. Only him.

Thomas's fingers—those same fingers that had crept toward hers—finally closed the distance. He brushed the back of her hand with a touch so faint she almost wondered if she imagined it.

She didn't pull away.

He tilted his head, studying her with the same patient intensity he'd always had. "You want me to stay," he said softly. "But what do you want that to mean?"

"I . . . don't know," she admitted. "But I don't want tonight to be the last time I see you again." For the first time in a year and a half, Annie let herself believe in the possibility she'd spent so long trying to forget.

* * *

The following months passed in a haze. Thomas found work at the only stamp mill still operating in Rocky Bar, and sometimes he hauled supplies for the boarding houses and hotels. He always found her in the hours between dusk and dark, by Beaver Creek or along the narrow paths behind stores where nobody could see them. At first, it was talking, long walks, and awkward silences, each figuring out the shape of the other after so much time apart. When Thomas placed a hand at her waist, it felt like a warm embrace, a sense of belonging she hadn't felt in a long time. As they walked, often their hands would brush against each other, sometimes unintentionally, sometimes deliberately. Each time, their touch sent tingles up her arm. Once, in the shade behind the blacksmith shop, Thomas bent close and kissed the corner of her mouth so quickly that she almost missed it. Annie did not know what to do with the unfamiliar feelings that followed.

It was on a sunny July afternoon, sitting on the mossy log beside Beaver Creek, when Thomas took her hand in both of his, running a thumb along the tiny scar at her wrist. "You ain't scared of anything, are you?"

Annie shrugged, not sure if it was a compliment. "Ain't scared of you, if that's what y'all mean."

He laughed, shaking his head. "Maybe you should be," he said. "People say I'm nothing but trouble."

She smiled. "People say a lot of things. That don't make 'em true. Anyway, I might like a little trouble now and then," she said as she slid over until their legs were touching. He put his arm around her shoulders and gave her a light squeeze.

They spent the summer that way, living in the grey zone between their conscience and desire. Annie did not tell anyone about Thomas, not even

Hazel, during their frequent chats on the banks of Beaver Creek. It felt better to keep it hidden, a treasure too precious for the eyes of others. She did not want anyone to interfere with what was growing between them. Often the boys in town yelled at her from across the street, "hey Annie, how's your boyfriend Thomas?"

She ignored them. "He's doing mighty fine," she would whisper to herself, "and so am I."

She learned the rhythm of Thomas's heart, the way his body fit against hers, the soft words he whispered into her hair when the night was thick. For the first time in her life, she felt something like peace and the possibility of genuine happiness. She saw a way to escape the torture of living with James and her heartless mother.

By autumn, the rumors had started about the wild teenage girl and the man twice her age, about what they did in the dark after most people were asleep. Annie pretended not to care, but she heard the whispers, saw the way the men on the porches leered at her as she walked by. She ignored them, but there were days when the weight of their attention annoyed her. *Why can't people mind their own business? Ma and James are clueless about Thomas and me. If they knew, they wouldn't care anyway.*

One night, after a long silence, Thomas said, "I see how people look at us. If you want me to leave, say so. I know it must not be easy for you."

Annie shook her head. "I never asked for an easy life. I know what I want, and it's you."

Thomas touched her face, his palm rough and steady. "Then I'm not going anywhere," he promised.

They sealed it with a kiss, slow and certain, in the doorway of an abandoned stamp mill. Annie knew then, with the certainty that surprised her, that whatever happened next, she would face it with Thomas by her side.

Chapter 7

Rocky Bar made it through another winter. Annie and Hazel were eager to resume their afternoon chats on the old mossy log. Hazel was already there on this spring day, perched on the log with her peach-colored dress hiked up to keep the hem dry, feet dangling above the swirling current. Her blonde hair, worked into two braids with purple ribbons at the ends, was immaculate, as usual. They swung in rhythm with the motion of her head as she scanned the water for signs of fish.

Annie approached, her shoes sinking in the wet grass, and for a moment she wished she had worn something nicer. She hadn't seen Hazel in weeks and wondered if Hazel even remembered what they used to talk about before everything became about boys, money, and the prospect of adulthood.

Hazel didn't look up right away. She waited until Annie was almost beside her before she said, "You like to sneak up on people, or just me?" Her voice was light, but there was a thread of something hard beneath it.

Annie shrugged, settling onto the log beside her. She felt the dampness of the wet moss through her dress but didn't mind. "Only you," she said, forcing a smile. "You are the only one worth the trouble."

Hazel laughed, her nose wrinkling. "That's a lie, and you know it. I'm not the only one." She kicked her heels, the toes of her shoes grazing the water. For a while, they sat in silence, listening to the rush of the creek and the sharp, distant call of a hawk somewhere up in the treetops.

Annie stole a glance at Hazel, noticing for the first time how her friend had changed. She was taller now, her face thinner and more angular, the freckles on her nose having faded over the winter. But it was her eyes that were most different, still blue, but ringed with a gravity that made her look older than seventeen. Annie felt an unfamiliar pang of envy.

"I hear you've been spending a lot of time with Thomas," Hazel said, her tone casual but her hands tight around her knees.

Annie tilted her head. "Who told ya that? Mrs. Bannister? She don't like me."

Hazel shook her head. "Don't matter. Word gets around." She turned, fixing Annie with a stare that was both worried and exasperated. "You know people talk, right? About what you two are up to when you think nobody's watching."

Annie lowered her gaze picked at the log's splintered tree bark beneath her fingers. "Let 'em talk. They got nothin' better to do."

Hazel's braids swung as she shook her head, disbelief painted plain on her face. "You can't just—" she stopped, searching for the right word, "—act like you're different from the rest of us. And Thomas . . . he's not the man you think he is."

Annie bristled, her entire body tensing like a tightly coiled spring. "And what's that supposed to mean?" she demanded, her voice dropping to a low growl. "You think you know him better than I do?"

Hazel's expression softened, but her gaze remained unwavering. "I don't know him like you do. But I know what men like him want." Her words lingered in the air.

Annie struggled to keep her voice from shaking. "He's not like the others." Desperation clung to her words; she needed Hazel to believe her, to understand. "He listens. He treats me like I'm somebody. Ma and James don't do that."

Hazel let out a sharp, humorless cough that cut through the air. "That's what they do in the beginning. They sweet-talk you until you can't see straight. " Her fingers twisted the hem of her dress with a restless intensity; her eyes locked onto the creek with a hollow gaze. "I'm afraid that he's going to leave you. Maybe not today, maybe not this year, but he will. And when that time comes, you'll be the one left alone to pick up the pieces. I don't trust him. You're only sixteen, and he's what, thirty years old?"

"He's twenty-nine."

"Annie, think about what you're getting yourself into. I don't like it."

"Ma was only fifteen when she had me."

"Right. And how did that turn out for you. From what I've seen she ain't no good as a mother."

"But Thomas—"

Hazel reached over and took Annie's hands in her own. "I can tell you're in love with him. Love makes people do stupid things, I mean *really* stupid things. They say love is the most powerful force in the universe. When you're in love, you lose control. Common sense goes out the window. I'm worried about you. Don't let him take control of you, *please*. I'm telling you this because I care about you, Annie. Can't you see that?"

Annie wanted to stand, to storm away, to call Hazel jealous or small or plain mean, but she sat planted on the log like her body was fused to it, her hands pressed white-knuckled in her lap. The echo of Hazel's words spiraled around her head like a swarm of gnats. "I want to be in love, Hazel, and I want a man that's in love with me. I want a husband, a family, and children. I want a life worth living. Thomas can give that to me. Can't you understand?"

Hazel twisted around, fixing Annie with an earnest stare. "I understand what you want, and I want that too. But I don't think Thomas is the answer." Her voice softened. "You should want better for yourself. You're worth more than some tired man with mud on his boots and nothing good in his pockets." Hazel reached out, hesitated, then put her hand on Annie's knee. "Don't let him own you."

Annie stared at the ground and the log. It should have burned, the truth of it, but all she felt was a dull, formless ache. *What if it's true? What if he is like the others? I hate being wrong. Thomas doesn't have much, but he's lived more life than a girl in Rocky Bar could ever hope to match. Maybe he will leave me. Maybe not. Who knows?*

Annie brushed a strand of hair out of her face. She stared at the way the current rippled around the rocks, the water too fast for anything to hold its place for long. She wanted to argue, to tell Hazel she was mistaken, but the words tasted too bitter in her mouth to speak.

Hazel's voice dropped to a softer, imploring tone. "Look at me, Annie. You're my best friend. I don't want to see you get hurt. I care about you more than you know."

Annie's throat tightened as she struggled to suppress the tears threatening to surface. "I'm not a child, Hazel," she said, her voice wavering, caught between defiance and doubt. "I can take care of myself."

Hazel sighed, her eyes filled with concern. "I know you can, but sometimes being strong means asking for help. Please let me be there for you. I'll do anything for you. You know I will."

Annie hesitated, her defenses wavering. "I don't want to be a burden to you." Her gaze dropped to the ground.

"You're never a burden to me. We're in this together, no matter what."

"Oh, Hazel, what am I to do?" She fingered the hem of her dress as she stared into the water.

For a while, neither of them spoke. The sun climbed higher, bathing the surrounding riverbank in a golden light. Annie felt the warmth on her face and arms, but inside she was worried. She trusted Hazel, but she loved Thomas.

"You know, Annie, I saw you one time walking out from behind that old, abandoned stamp mill. Is that where you meet Thomas?"

Annie looked down at her hands clasped together on her lap and picked at one of her fingernails. She found a loose thread on her dress and pulled on it, breaking it off. She threw it towards the creek, but it landed back on her dress. She picked it up and let it fall into the dirt.

"Okay, you don't have to answer that, but be careful. Thomas is not the only thing that worries me. I've heard about creepy things going on in that place, like grinding noises and things falling for no reason. Whatever you do, don't you ever go into one of those tunnels. There's Tommyknockers in there."

"What?"

"You know, Tommyknockers. Deep in those tunnels, the miners say they hear knocking sounds when nobody else is around besides their crew. I'd be scared to death if I ever heard something like that."

"I don't believe in that stuff, Hazel, and I don't see why you do."

"Some things don't have an explanation. Please promise me you'll stay out of those tunnels."

"I promise." *Tommyknockers are the least of my concerns. Thomas would protect me anyway.*

They sat there and let the slight breeze envelop them.

Hazel broke the silence, her tone resigned. "If you ever need me, you know where to find me." She reached over and squeezed Annie's hand before letting go. The gesture felt like both a promise and a goodbye.

Annie nodded, unable to trust herself to speak. She watched Hazel stand, brush off her dress, and head back toward town.

Annie remained on the mossy log. She couldn't make up her mind if she wanted to stay there or walk home.

Hazel's words echoed, *he's going to leave you.* It sounded like a curse as much as a warning, and no matter how she tried to shake them loose, they clung to her heart with tenacity. She imagined hearing Thomas's voice, teasing and sweet: *Nothing can break you, Annie, not even this whole town trying.* She drew solace from it, but beneath the comfort was a tremor of doubt.

Was Hazel right? Am I a fool, attracted to the very thing that might ruin me? The thought both ignited her fury and stirred a deep unease within her. Anger flared, sudden and hot, and she wrapped her arms around her knees as if to hold herself together. Her fingers dug into the fabric of her skirt, twisting it until her knuckles ached. With a sharp, wordless cry of frustration, she seized a stone and hurled it into the rushing water. It splashed, and the ripples slowly spread out. She reached down and dug a bigger stone out of the gravel and threw it into the water with all her might. *Damn it! What am I supposed to do?*

She remembered the days when they had been as close as sisters. Memories of laughing under the covers, whispering dreams and secrets as if they would conquer the future side by side, surged back. She never imagined then that love could be the force that drove them apart rather than the glue that held them together.

Chapter 8

The old stamp mill at the edge of Rocky Bar had stood empty for as long as Annie could remember, its massive timbers blackened by years of smoke and laced with rusted nuts and bolts the size of her fist. *Nobody goes in there anymore except trespassers, a stray animal, or children stupid enough to risk tetanus and a beating from their parents. That makes it perfect, for us.*

The August evening air felt cool as Annie ducked through the side doorway, careful not to snag her dress on the wood splinters or rusty nails. The cavernous building was dimly lit, as the only sources of light were holes in the roof and a few small windows. The air inside was dusty, and she imagined the machinery pounding away at thousands of tons of gold-bearing quartz being ground to dust and the echoes of men who'd lost their fingers to the hungry teeth of the mill. Gigantic rusty gears, pulleys, and pipes were everywhere. Massive wooden beams that once supported heavy machinery littered the ground. Bird droppings and cobwebs covered everything that remained. She liked the way the space dwarfed her, how it swallowed sound and light, made her feel invisible.

Annie was early. She picked her way along the concrete and rusty steel troughs, her shoes crunching through piles of dirty, white quartz and gravel, until she found the spot they chose as their meeting place: a little pocket behind the main stamp battery, shielded from the side door by a wall of huge rusty ore bins.

She leaned against a monstrous vertical beam, careful to avoid the splinters. Annie felt comforted by the seclusion that the structure provided. She imagined Hazel somewhere warm, sewing or reading a dime novel, and for a second, she felt a flicker of guilt. It vanished as soon as it arrived. *This is okay. Different people want different things. Hazel wouldn't be caught dead in here, but for me, this is exciting. It's an adventure, hoping but not knowing what's gonna happen next. Suppose I am in love with Thomas. How could that be so wrong?* She couldn't go five minutes without thinking about him, about the sweet things he told her, and imagining what he would say the next time they met. She wanted nothing more than to be near him, to savor the sound of his voice, the feelings that stirred when he said her name, and how he touched her like nobody else ever had. *Is this what love is like?*

When Thomas slipped in, he was a shadow at first, then a body: broad and solid. He wore his work coat, patched at the elbows, and his hair was wild from the wind. He saw her, and his face broke open into that grin that she loved to see.

"You're early," he said as he adjusted his coat.

"Didn't have anything better to do."

He hopped over a few pieces of rusty machinery and stood in front of her. For a minute, neither of them uttered a word. They stood inches apart, breathing in each other's air, with electricity flowing between them.

Thomas leaned in slowly at first, giving her time to move or signal no. Annie didn't. She closed the gap, hands clinging to his jacket, and let herself be kissed. The heat of it was invigorating, a jolt that ran from her mouth to the tips of her toes. She'd thought about this, dreamed about it, replayed the almost-kisses of the past, but nothing prepared her for the way the sensation consumed her, leaving her breathless.

She returned the passion. His hands were big and sure, holding her waist, pulling her closer. She let herself go soft for a moment, amazed at the way their bodies fit together perfectly. She lost the ability to think. Everything was a magnificent swirl of feelings, desires, and sensations. She was under his spell, and she was about to lose what remained of her self-control. Her fingers tangled in his hair, pulling him closer as his big arms enveloped her waist.

"Want to know something, Annie?"

"What?"

"I like squeezing you."

They might have stayed that way forever, but the noise came first as a scuffle of boots, then the unmistakable snickering of boys who thought they were invisible. Annie broke the kiss, heart hammering, and turned just in time to see a cluster of little boys, three or four, peering through a crack between the ore bins, wide-eyed with their mouths wide open.

Thomas looked at them, then at Annie, and shrugged. "Guess the secret's out," he said, not sounding the least bit concerned.

Annie's cheeks burned, but she forced herself not to hide. She squared her shoulders, shot the boys a glare that promised retribution, and then turned back to Thomas. For a moment, she considered pretending nothing had happened. Instead, she reached up and brushed a few cobwebs out of his hair and straightened the collar of his jacket. As an act of defiance, she reached up and kissed Thomas again while looking directly at the boys.

"Hey, boys, next time pick a better hiding spot," she yelled.

They took the hint and scattered, their laughter echoing in the hollow guts of the mill. Annie and Thomas stood there, facing each other, watching the birds fly in and out through the holes in the roof.

"You okay?" Thomas asked.

Annie nodded. "Better than okay." She felt something new bloom inside her, a kind of defiant pride. *I don't care who knows, not anymore. I know what I want.*

They walked out together, with Thomas leading her by the hand. Annie glanced at Thomas, and he grinned, squeezing her hand before letting go. As they stepped outside into the light, she caught their reflection in a cracked dust-covered window.

"Hey Thomas, look at that." She pulled him over to the window, and they stood in front of it, side by side. The reflection was a portrait of a girl and a man, like a faded work of art. *What a masterpiece.* Annie and Thomas had never had the chance to look at their own reflection side by side in a mirror before. She grinned. *I sure look happy. So does Thomas.*

Thomas turned and faced her. He searched her face as if looking for something that would vanish if he blinked. "You know what I think, my dear?"

She gazed up into his eyes. "What?"

His lips twitched, but he didn't smile. "We should get married."

The machinery of her thoughts seized. She made a noise, something between a gasp and a cough, and then blinked at him several times. Her heart raced.

"You're . . . serious?"

He shrugged, but the movement was careful. "Why not? I love you," and quietly, as if it was something precious that would break if spoken too loudly, "and you love me, don't you?"

Thomas turned and placed his hands firmly on Annie's shoulders. "Listen to me. How old was your mother when she got married and had you?"

"Fifteen."

"And how old are you?"

"Seventeen."

"So, what's the problem?"

"There ain't none."

"Okay, my sweet, what's your answer?"

She thought of Hazel, of her warnings, of loss and risk, and how things went wrong for girls who reached too high or wanted too much. Then she looked back at Thomas and saw the man and the future he was offering: a lifetime of love and happiness, a family, and an exciting life. He was a way she could leave behind, once and for all, her disgusting stepfather and her good-for-nothing mother.

"Yes!" She jumped up and threw her arms around his neck.

53

"We'll do it next month. Why wait?"

His words interrupted her elation. *Why wait? Why so quick? I heard that when people get engaged, they set the wedding date together. You didn't ask me about it. You decided by yourself.* She drew back. "Do we need to do it so soon? I mean, I want to get married, of course, but this is a big decision. Can't we talk about it?"

"What's there to talk about? We're in love, and that's the only thing that matters, my dear."

"Okay, if you say so." *If I don't go along with him, he might change his mind and not want to marry me. That would be awful.*

Thomas placed his hands on her shoulders again. "Do you want to know a secret?"

"What?"

"The first time I laid eyes on you, you were sitting on the porch of the Rocky Bar Mercantile, working that apple peeler like there was no tomorrow. You looked so serious. I'd never seen a girl work so hard at anything like that before. That's what got me interested in you. Later, I asked some men at the mine, 'Who's that girl who sits on the porch of MacGregor's Mercantile?' They said, 'Oh, that's Annie McIntyre. Ain't she a real looker? She's the prettiest girl in Rocky Bar.' That's what people say about you, Annie. Fact is, you *are* the prettiest girl in Rocky Bar, and now you're mine."

Annie blushed, and as much as she tried, she couldn't hide it. "You have a way with words, Thomas."

"There's more to me than just my words." He cupped her face in his hands. "Soon you'll be my bride, and my wife. I love you, Annie McIntyre."

"I love you too, Thomas."

Chapter 9

The stagecoach ride from Rocky Bar to Boise City was uncomfortable. It was not because of the endless bumps and jolts from the rough road. It was the tension in the air. Marcella looked down at her hands the whole time, and James kept his gaze focused on the passing scenery. George sat helplessly, as if he didn't understand what was happening. Thomas sat expressionless except for an occasional grin, as if he was amusing himself with silent jokes. The only bright spot was Hazel. Thomas had not wanted her to come, but Annie insisted.

The morning light slanted in through the grimy windows of the two-room building near the center of Boise City. Annie was not sure if the building was a meeting hall or if it had been built for some other purpose. A ceremony at a church was out of the question, as Thomas wouldn't hear of it.

Annie sat on the varnished wood bench near the doorway that separated the entryway from the main room, hands folded tightly in her lap. She wore a white dress, borrowed from Mrs. MacGregor, who had to bring it in to fit Annie's slender figure. She had washed her face three times and pinned her hair back with a blue ribbon she'd found under the counter at the mercantile. There were no flowers, no veil, and no music. The only sound was the far-off scrape of the judge's boots on the wooden floor as he paced back and forth in the main room, but Annie did not care.

She took a silent inventory of the people with her. Marcella perched beside James on a straight-backed chair, and her lips formed a thin, pale line. She wore a black dress, as if in mourning, but her hair was brushed, and her face washed clean of any emotion except the faintest flicker of annoyance. James, for his part, looked as though he would rather be anywhere else, his eyes fixed on a point above Annie's head, jaw clenched tight. Annie felt an odd satisfaction at their discomfort. She would be free of them soon.

Annie sat next to George. Hazel sat on the opposite bench, her dress neat and pressed, her blonde hair in the usual two braids with purple ribbons. That made her look younger than she was. Annie reached over and squeezed George's hand now and then. George shifted constantly, tugging at the collar of his shirt as if it was choking him. His eyes darted around the room as if he expected to be called out for some crime he didn't remember committing. Annie caught his gaze once, and he had a feeble smile before dropping his eyes again. Thomas was nowhere to be seen.

Hazel got up and sat down next to Annie, her braids brushing Annie's shoulder like a loose thread unraveling the tension between them, and whispered, "You look like you're about to jump out a window."

Annie's lips twitched despite herself. It would have stung from anyone else, but from Hazel it was a small kindness, a break in the tight, breathless knot that bound her chest. She glanced sideways and pretended to scowl, her brows pulling together with mock offense, but her eyes shimmered with something too soft to be anger. She wanted to laugh, or maybe cry. Instead, she slipped her hand into Hazel's under the edge of the bench with the briefest squeeze.

Hazel's warm fingers curled around hers. She leaned in again, closer this time, her lips barely moving near Annie's ear. "You know I was against this whole thing in the beginning, but if you're going to go through with it, I'll support you all the way."

Annie almost laughed then, but she bit down on the urge. "I want this," she said. The words tumbled out, surprising her with their rawness. *I want this. I want Thomas. I wanted a future that isn't a story someone else told about me. I want out of the oppression from James and Ma.*

Annie was locked in a tug-of-war with a persistent, yet scarcely audible uncertainty about the impending moments that promised to redefine her existence. *This was going to change everything. Children? Having children with this man? How many? How come we never talked about these things? I feel like I'm standing on the edge of a cliff. If I step forward, there's no turning back. I'll fall into the abyss, never to return. If I step back from the edge, I'll be safe and secure.* Just when she thought she was resolute and sure in her decision, a shadow of hesitation loomed, like an unwelcome intruder that wouldn't go away. *Is this really happening? If marriage was so great, why do people get so nervous? This is the biggest decision of my life. That's scary. It's too late to turn back now. Or is it? Let's get on with it, judge.*

Annie bit her lip. *What if Thomas has changed his mind? What if he heard stories people were telling about me and decided I'm not worth the trouble? If he never shows up, well, that would be the end of it. He said he hated waiting rooms, so he's probably out front smoking a cigar.*

She had pictured the future she had chosen for herself, but now it was blurry, shifting, impossible to pin down. All she knew was that in a few minutes she would be a wife, and nothing would change that.

The judge, an older man with wire-rimmed glasses and a wispy grey mustache, poked his head into the entryway and called out, "We're ready for you." Annie stood, nauseous, legs trembling, and smoothed the skirt of her dress with both hands. She tried to steady her breathing, to quiet the thumping of her heart, but it was no use.

She walked to the front of the room, feeling every pair of eyes on her. The miners in the back smirked and elbowed each other; the women whispered behind gloved hands. She refused to let their stares unnerve her. *Who are these people? I don't recognize any of them. They must be*

Thomas's friends. She quickly searched the crowd for Hazel and found her in the back of the room. Hazel was the only person wearing a smile.

When Thomas entered the room, everyone's eyes fixated on him. He wore his only suit, a gray wool jacket, so worn it had polished to a shine at the elbows, and a white shirt with a frayed collar. He looked like a man prepared for his own funeral, but he smiled at Annie, and in that moment, she forgot about the rest of the world.

The judge recited the vows, his voice flat and nasal, as if reading from a bookkeeping ledger.

"I, Thomas Morrow, take you, Anna McIntyre, to be my lawfully wedded wife. I pledge to stand by you in times of hardship and in times of plenty, to give you my labor, my protection, and my steadfast heart. I will be faithful to you as long as we both shall live."

"I, Anna McIntyre, take you, Thomas Morrow, to be my lawfully wedded husband. I promise to walk beside you through trial and triumph, to give you my care, my trust, and my devotion. I will be true to you for all the days granted us."

"By the authority vested in me by the Territory of Idaho, I now proclaim you husband and wife."

For a moment, everything was silent. Annie looked over at Marcella, who returned her gaze with an expressionless face. James sat motionless, looking bored, hands folded on his knees, refusing to meet anyone's eyes. Hazel beamed, her entire face lit up with pride, and even George managed a crooked grin.

The judge dated the marriage certificate August 27, 1876, signed it with a flourish and handed it to Thomas, and stepped back. Thomas reached for Annie's hand, his grip warm and steady, and together they walked out into the bright morning sunlight. The small crowd followed, some lingering on the steps, others drifting off to resume their daily routines.

Annie felt the wind pick up, scattering a flurry of leaves around their feet. Thomas offered his arm, and she took it, her hand fitting into the crook of his elbow as if it had always belonged there. She glanced back once, just for a second, and caught sight of Hazel, still standing inside the doorway. Annie smiled at her, and Hazel nodded back and waved.

They walked down the steps together, husband and wife, the leaves swirling in their wake. For the first time in her life, Annie felt the weight of the future settle on her shoulders, not as a burden, but as a promise.

The tension vanished during the ride back to Rocky Bar, allowing the banter to flow easily between everyone.

Chapter 10

The wedding glow did not last for more than a few weeks. By the first day of October, Annie was doing her best to conform to Thomas's idea of what it meant to be a wife. She made breakfast for him every day at seven o'clock. He liked bacon and eggs, sometimes with reheated beans. She swept the pine floor of their tiny house daily and kept the kitchen organized. The bed was theirs now, even if the old mattress still had the depressions that the previous occupants left behind. Some nights, when Thomas was in a good mood, Annie let herself believe that this was what happiness felt like: his arm draped heavily across her chest, the safe cocoon of his breathing, the way his hand found her waist even in sleep.

In the second week of October, the air was sharp with the tail end of an early freeze. Annie hunched at the battered pine table, fingers cold from the wash bucket, re-braiding her long brown hair so it would stay put through the day. She heard his boots on the floor before she saw him: heavy, confident, the walk of a man who never worried about waking anyone up.

He poured himself a cup of strong coffee and sat across from her with a grunt. She waited. Thomas did not say anything for a few minutes, which made Annie feel uncomfortable. He was a man who liked to wind up to his announcements, and Annie had learned not to disrupt his game by jumping in first.

He threw back two long swigs, each gulp loud in the silence, then set the cup on the table. "We're leaving in three weeks."

His tone was flat and clipped, like he had announced the time of day. The phrase floated in the air between them—too brutal, too sudden for her brain to catch its meaning.

Her hand froze mid-motion, tangled in her hair. "Leaving what?" she whispered, her breath caught in her throat.

He didn't bother to look up. His eyes stayed fixed on the grain of the scarred table. "This dump. Rocky Bar. We're heading to Boise City."

His words fell like stones into a dry well.

"Why?"

Thomas's stare remained locked on the table, knuckles white where his hand gripped the edge. "Opportunities are in Boise City. I've lined up contacts with men who know how to run a profitable business. We need to climb. Can't do that in this town. Don't you see?"

Annie's heart thundered, echoing in her ears like distant hoofbeats. "But—" She hated how small she sounded, how young. "All I know is here." She swallowed and steadied her voice. "What about my brother? And Ma?"

A cold twist curled one corner of his lips. "Your Ma'll manage. And George can visit once we settle in."

She reached beneath the table, clutching a leg for balance. "I—I don't wanna go," she stammered. Fear rose in her chest as she realized how powerless her words were. The muscles in her throat tightened. She wanted to protest with more conviction, but the desire to do so wilted.

At last, he lifted his gaze. "You're my wife now. Where I go, you go."

The words struck her like a fist, making her head spin. She blinked at him, struggling to focus; her mouth opened but no words came. *I'm not Annie McIntyre from the Rocky Bar Mercantile anymore. I'm Mrs. Morrow, and Mrs. Morrow speaks only when spoken to.* A wave of nausea rolled through her, rising hot in her throat.

"I wanna stay in Rocky Bar," she pleaded.

His jaw muscles clenched, and his nostrils flared. "You want to spend your life in a shack?" he snapped, his voice rising with a sudden, seething energy. "You want our children born into this squalor?" He swept his arm at the peeling wallpaper, the broken chair in the corner, the lifeless floorboards coated in dust. "We're through here. I said so."

She swallowed again, tears stinging behind her eyes. "I grew up here. I like it. Why can't—"

His fist came down on the table with a sickening crack, the sound cutting through the room like a gunshot. She flinched, recoiling from the blow even though it hadn't touched her.

"Enough," he growled. His eyes were cold iron, unblinking. "I'm not debating this with a child. Get used to it, Annie. We are leaving next month. It's for the best. You'll see."

And with that, he stood, drained the last of his coffee, and walked out the front door, leaving her alone at the table, hands still clenched so tight around the legs of the table that her fingers cramped.

She sat there for a long time, letting the ache in her heart settle in. She wanted to cry, to break something, but if she let herself loose, she wouldn't be able to stop. Instead, she sat watching the morning light creep across the table, unable to move. *So, this is what marriage is like. I don't understand.*

It wasn't until hours later, after she'd washed and re-braided her long hair for the third time, scrubbed the table clean, and started a pot of beans for supper, that she let herself cry. *Married life isn't supposed to be like this. He's the head of the household, but I'm his wife. Doesn't that mean anything? I guess not.*

* * *

Three days passed before she worked up the nerve to visit Hazel. She dreaded the conversation they were going to have. It made her sick thinking about it.

She found Hazel on the porch of the old Anderson place, barefoot and cross-legged on a sagging rocker, darning a pair of stockings with such ferocity it was a wonder the needle didn't snap. The creak of the chair matched the rhythm of her stitching: sharp and precise. Hazel's blonde hair was loose today, falling in tangled waves past her shoulders, catching the sun like strands of gold straw. It made her look younger.

When she saw Annie coming, her whole face lit up. Hazel's eyes softened, and her hands paused mid-stitch.

"Why, Mrs. Morrow," Hazel teased, her voice warm and low like worn flannel. "You here to gloat at getting hitched before me or to borrow sugar?"

Annie managed a smile, but it barely lifted her cheeks. Her eyes were heavy, rimmed with red. She stepped up onto the porch. The wood creaked beneath her, and she sat on the step, letting her dress bunch at the knees.

She stared at the ground. "He's making us leave." The words came out. "He says we're moving to Boise City."

The warmth drained from Hazel's face. Her brows drew together; her jaw dropped.

"What?" Hazel was incredulous. "Why on earth would he do that?"

Annie nodded, lips pressed tight. She looked at her hands in her lap, fingers knotted together so tightly her knuckles ached.

With a frustrated huff, Hazel tossed the half-mended sock aside and scooted closer to Annie. The scent of sun-warmed cotton and wood smoke clung to her clothes. She leaned in, her voice dropping so no passing neighbor would hear over the distant sounds of the neighbor's barking dog and the blacksmith's hammering down the road.

"He can't haul you off like some—" She caught herself, biting the edge off her anger, her jaw tight. "What about your Ma? Or George?"

Annie shook her head; the motion was limp. "He doesn't care. Says it's for the best." She sniffled and wiped her nose with the back of her hand and looked away, cheeks flushing with shame.

Hazel reached for her without hesitation, wrapped her arm around Annie's shoulders, and pulled her close. The cotton of her sleeve was soft, and the gesture was firm. She squeezed tight, cheek resting against Annie's forehead.

"You're not going alone," Hazel said, her voice fierce but steady. "I'll come after you if I have to. You know I will."

Annie nodded, but it felt like a lie as she leaned into her and relaxed. *There's no way Hazel would make it all the way to Boise City, not with her father's debts and her own brothers to watch over.* Still, she was grateful for the words, for the warmth in her friend's touch. They sat in silence for a while, watching the clouds build over the mountaintops. Hazel was the only person Annie had ever told about the dark moods that gripped Thomas some nights, the way his voice would turn to ice and his hands would linger too long on her wrists. Hazel had never said, "I told you so." She never judged; she listened and promised always to be there. Annie didn't know what she would do without her.

Hazel's beautiful blue eyes, which usually danced with a spark of mischief or blazed with the fire of defiance against the harshness of their world, were now softened by a desperate sincerity that Annie had rarely seen before.

"Annie," Hazel implored, reaching out instinctively, her fingers brushing against Annie's arm with a warmth that seeped into Annie's chilled resolve. "Please don't let him take you away like this. You and I, we can figure something out. We're not without options. There's Mountain Home," she urged, her hands moving like birds weaving patterns in flight, gestures full of fervent promise. "You could stay there for a while. Or even Idaho City! I know people in both places who'd help us, no questions asked." She paused. "My Aunt Ruth," Hazel continued, her tone shifting to one of certainty that anchored them both amidst the swirling doubts. "She'd take you in without a second thought."

The idea of fleeing beckoned. For a fleeting moment, she imagined it: the two of them side by side on a stagecoach, dust swirling around them as they laughed breathlessly into the wind. The taste of freedom was a tantalizing prospect that shimmered on the edge of fantasy, only to slip away like morning mist.

But reality was a relentless tide pulling her back to shore. "Oh, Hazel," she sighed, lightening her tone as though dismissing childish fairy tales. "Running away . . . that's for people who can't face reality. It's not the answer." She cast a sidelong glance at Hazel's hopeful expression and squeezed her friend's hand. "You know, I wish it was that simple," Annie continued, her voice softening. "Just pack up and leave, start anew somewhere far away. But then I remember, life isn't a storybook. I'm married. We have to face what's here, make the best of it, even when it's hard."

Annie looked at Hazel and noticed a tear on her cheek. "Besides," she continued with fragile resolve, "Thomas wouldn't let go. He'd hunt me down across mountains and prairies until he caught me. It's only Boise City," she added after a silent moment. "It's only another place on the map."

Chapter 11

Two days later, Hazel showed up on Annie's porch, the bottom of her green and white gingham dress splattered with mud stains. She walked right in, face red and hair wild, voice pitched so loud it startled Thomas.

"This isn't right, and you know it," Hazel said, marching right up to Thomas with her hands planted on her hips. She glared into his eyes. "Annie's not a piece of baggage; you can't pack her off every time you get bored with a town."

Annie, who was peeling potatoes at the counter, froze. Thomas set down his newspaper, his face going blank. "I don't believe we invited you in," he intoned.

Hazel was undeterred. "I'm not here for tea, Mr. Morrow. You're hurting her, and you know it. What's so great about Boise City, anyway?" She pointed a finger at him, fierce as any preacher. "If you were decent for once, she'd want to follow you."

Thomas stood, slow and deliberate, and stepped between the two girls. His mouth twitched, and for a second Annie thought he might slap Hazel.

"This is none of your business," he said, voice like a knife's edge. "You can run your own life how you like, but my wife goes where I go."

Hazel stared him down, blue eyes blazing. "She's not your property."

Thomas narrowed his eyes, voice dropping to a cold, deadly calm. "If you want to end up in a ditch, keep talking."

Hazel held the stare for a long moment, then broke away, muttering something under her breath. She shot Annie a look of desperation, then backed out of the cabin, slamming the door behind her. For a minute, the only sound in the house was Annie's panicked breathing.

Thomas turned to Annie, his face dark. "Don't you ever bring your little friend here again," he said. "We don't need the whole damned town knowing our business."

She nodded, hung her head down, her eyes fixed on the floor. He stalked out of the room and slammed the bedroom door, causing the windows to rattle. Annie stood by the sink, hands trembling, listening to the echo of Hazel's voice in her mind. She wanted to run after her, to scream at Thomas, to do anything but stand there like a scared little girl. She set down the potato peeler, folded her arms across her chest, and stared at the closed bedroom door. The sound of Hazel's words lingered. *She's not your property.*

That night, after the house had gone quiet and Thomas was snoring in the next room, Annie crept out onto the front porch. The sky was clear, the stars sharp and close, and she let herself breathe deeply for the first time all day.

I miss Hazel already, and I miss Ma. That's ironic considering her bad feelings about me. I ran to escape one cage, only to land in another. But there was something in her still that refused to go quiet, a stubborn spark that Thomas had not snuffed out yet. She promised herself, right then and there, that even if she had to follow him to the ends of the Idaho Territory, she would never let him take complete control over her. *Let him have Boise City. I can survive it. I can survive anything.* She looked up at the stars until her neck ached, then wiped her face and went back inside, closing the door quietly so he wouldn't hear her coming back inside.

* * *

Boise City was nothing like the world Annie had known. From the moment they stepped off the stagecoach, she felt overwhelmed and out of place. People swarmed in every direction, weaving around her in hurried knots—men in tailored coats with shiny watch chains, women with parasols bobbing like colored sails, and Chinese laborers with pointy hats pushing handcarts.

Annie had never seen so many horses. They were everywhere. Some shone with polished leather harnesses and well-groomed manes, the pride of wealthy merchants or stage lines; others were skinny, sway-backed creatures whose dull eyes spoke of long, punishing miles. They tugged freight wagons piled with crates and carried scruffy-looking cowboys who slouched in their saddles.

The air throbbed with snorts and the sharp crack of whips. The stench of sweat, manure, and old hay wrapped around Annie like a filthy blanket. She tasted it on the back of her tongue. Stray dogs zigzagged between wagons, barking, nipping at each other. One bumped her leg as it shot past. She jumped, startled by the sudden press of fur and the yelp that followed.

Voices rose and collided in a constant, dizzying roar. Street peddlers shouted over one another—"Hot pies! Fresh bread!"—"Tobacco, finest in the Territory!"—their cries blending with the clang of a blacksmith's hammer and the clatter of wagon wheels. Every sound felt too close, too oppressive, as though the city was drowning her.

The air felt thick enough to chew. Coal smoke oozed from chimneys and drifted across the streets, turning the sun into a dull yellow splotch in the sky. The haze curled around her face and seeped into her clothes, mingling with the dust kicked up by a thousand restless hooves. Annie glanced over at Thomas. None of this bothered him. He was smiling.

Even though mountains surrounded the city, they did not seem as friendly as those in Rocky Bar. *In Rocky Bar, the mountains wrapped around the town like a great cradle. Here, I don't feel protected by them.*

Even the mud felt different under her feet. Boise City mud was rich and dark, clinging like soft dough to the soles of her shoes. It didn't crack and crumble into dusty cakes the way Rocky Bar's earth did. It felt cultivated, like everything else in this place.

In the distance, beyond the edge of the city, stretching out east and west, were farms with orchards, neat rows of potatoes, wheat, sugar beets, red barns, and windmills spinning lazily in the wind. Annie had never seen anything like this. *In Rocky Bar, the only things that grow are weeds and trees.*

Within a few months of settling into their new life in Boise City, Annie discovered she was with child. The realization dawned on her as she found herself overwhelmed with waves of inexplicable nausea each morning. Seeking confirmation and guidance, she visited a doctor whose practice was a few blocks away. The doctor's office was a quaint yet sterile room, filled with the faint scent of antiseptic and the clutter of medical gadgets. He offered her a list of remedies that seemed more like a list of old-world curiosities: mercury, opium, turpentine, even bloodletting.

Each of your suggestions sound more absurd and dangerous than the last. No thanks, doctor. I'd rather endure the nausea than risk poisoning myself with such strange concoctions.

Attached to one wall, Annie saw a shelf of patent medicines.

Dr. Werner's L & L Friable Tablets - Lead and Laudanum
Mayr's System Regulator and Tonic - 10% alcohol
Gelatin Coated Corrosive Sublimate - Parke, Davis & Co
Piso's Tablets - For the Diseases of Women
Micajah's Medicated Uterine Wafers
Dr. Kilmer's Swamp Root - A Diuretic to the Kidneys and Mild Laxative.

Pretending to talk to herself, but loud enough for the doctor to hear, she muttered, "I'd rather be constipated than take anything named Swamp Root."

The doctor coughed and said, "I wasn't going to recommend that for you."

She said goodbye and headed home, choosing a more traditional remedy: a sip of whiskey now and then to ease her queasy stomach.

Annie hoped Thomas would lose interest in her now that she was sick most of the time. But every night he came to bed, smelling of the whiskey and sweat that clung to him even after a bath. At first, she thought of it as something to endure, a duty to go limp for, eyes fixed on the cracked plaster of the ceiling. But some nights, when Thomas was gentle, and the house was still, she almost liked the weight of him, the way his hands would cup the small of her back and draw her tight.

The baby arrived in the summer of 1877. Her labor lasted less than a day, but the hours twisted and stretched until Annie lost track of time. She refused to let Thomas in the room; she didn't want him to see her in pain or to hear the words she might scream. Instead, it was the elderly neighbor lady, Mrs. Byrne, who wiped her brow, gripped her thighs with a fist like a blacksmith's clamp, and told her to "push, girl, push!" The world contracted to the agony in her lower back and the stink of unfamiliar bodily fluids.

At dawn, Mrs. Byrne handed Annie a red, squealing thing wrapped in a towel. The baby's head was crowned with dark, spiky hair, her fists balled tight. Thomas hovered at the door, wild-eyed and pale, but Annie ignored him and pulled the child close. "Welcome to the world, Anna Eliza," she whispered, and the baby's mouth puckered in reply.

After that, the days blurred together. She spent hours walking the tiny parlor or rocking Anna Eliza in her arms in the creaky old chair, humming wordless lullabies that came to her from nowhere, except for the ones that she knew the words for.

> "Rock a bye baby, on the tree top,
> When the wind blows, the cradle will rock.
> When the bough breaks, the cradle will fall,
> And down will come baby, cradle and all.

Rock a bye baby, gently you swing,
Over the cradle, Mother will sing.
Sweet is the lullaby over your nest
That tenderly sings my baby to rest."

After singing this several times, Annie paused to consider the words. *What kind of mother would put her baby's cradle up in a tree? What a horrid idea, especially on a windy day, when the mother knows full well that the branch might break. Some people are unfit to be parents. I'll never put you up in a tree, Anna Eliza. Don't you worry about that, my little one. I will always take care of you. I'll love you forever.* She let the baby's tiny fingers curl around one of her braids with a gentle tug.

She hung blankets over the windows to keep out the sun, but the light found its way in, dust motes swirling in golden halos around the crib. When Annie wasn't singing *Rock a Bye Baby* or humming another song, sometimes she talked, narrating the trivialities of her new life: how the cat from two houses down had scratched at the kitchen door, how the milkman had shorted them again, and how the neighbor boys had played ball in the street and spoiled Anna Eliza's nap.

There were newspapers in Boise City, and Thomas brought home *The Idaho Tri-Weekly Statesman* regularly. There were no newspapers in Rocky Bar, and she had never looked at any from Boise City that found their way to the checkout counter at the Rocky Bar Mercantile. Besides, she had only learned to read two years ago, and she did not want to embarrass herself by stumbling over big words that she couldn't understand, even if she was alone. It was different here. She practiced by reading aloud articles that looked interesting.

One day, she found one. Chief Joseph had surrendered in Montana on October 5, 1877. The US Cavalry had been chasing them and caught up with the chief and his Nez Perce people. Some people called him the Red Napoleon. *Who was this Napoleon? Never heard of him.*

The chief made a speech, and it was printed on page 4.

I am tired of fighting. Our chiefs are killed. Looking Glass is dead. Toohoolhoolzoote is dead. The old men are all dead. It is the young men who say, "Yes" or "No." He who led the young men is dead. It is cold, and we have no blankets. The little children are freezing to death. My people, some of them, have run away to the hills and have no blankets, no food. No one knows where they are—perhaps freezing to death. I want to have time to look for my children and see how many of them I can find. Maybe I shall find them among the dead. Hear me, my chiefs! I am tired. My heart is sick and sad. From where the sun now stands, I will fight no more forever.

Annie read a few more articles about the Nez Perce war. Hundreds of people were killed or wounded. Deaths among US Cavalry soldiers and Indian warriors were understandable, but on the Indian side, casualties included women and children. *That doesn't make sense. Why did soldiers kill women and children? What's wrong with them? That's not war; that's murder. This is how my government operates? It should be a crime. Shame on them!* From that day forward, Annie refused to read anything about war or politics and stuck to local events and business news.

Thomas was gone more often than not. He'd found work in the city, first as a warehouseman, then as the manager at a dry goods wholesaler, in addition to his mining interests in Pine Grove. He came home late, sometimes with a bottle tucked under his arm, and his moods grew as variable as the weather. Some nights he swept Anna Eliza into his arms, bounced her on his knee, and told stories about the wildness of his youth, the gold strikes, and the blizzards and the men who died in the mines. Other times, he'd sit in silence, brooding over a mug of beer until he slumped asleep in his chair.

Annie knew better than to press him. She kept the house clean and learned to bake bread, make biscuits and johnnycakes. Annie ignored the way the world shrank around her and the way the neighbors' voices grew softer whenever she walked by with the baby under her arm. It was in the pale-yellow nursery, the one Thomas had painted himself, that she realized she was pregnant a second time. Anna Eliza was two years old, not yet walking, but Annie already felt the heavy pull in her belly and the same aches and queasiness as before. She kept it from Thomas. She wanted to see if he would notice, if he had put the pieces together without her having to say the words.

He did a few weeks later, and the only sign was the way his jaw set, a flicker of disappointment that passed through his eyes and was gone before she could call it out.

"Better be a boy this time," he said without even looking at her.

* * *

The second baby, John William, arrived at the end of winter in 1879. This time she let Thomas stay in the room, but only because she knew he would stand in the corner, hands balled in his pockets, too tense to do more than watch. With the help of Mrs. Byrne, the delivery was quicker, but messier; for a while, she thought she might bleed out because there was blood everywhere. John William arrived howling and furious, fists even tinier than Anna Eliza's had been.

Mrs. Byrne wrapped the baby in a patchwork quilt, the one she had made for Annie as a housewarming. Anna Eliza, now toddling and mischievous, constantly peeked over the edge of the crib and stroked her brother's face with curious, clumsy hands. Annie let them share every nap, pressed together like two halves of a single creature. She told herself she would never let them feel alone, the way she sometimes did.

It was the winter after John William's birth that things turned ugly. Thomas came home later and later, sometimes not at all. There were nights when Annie sat at the kitchen table until the oil lamp burned out, heart thumping with dread, not sure if she wanted him to come through the door or if she wished he would freeze to death in a gutter. When he arrived, it was often with a foul temper, reeking of whiskey and bitter about the world's refusal to reward what he considered to be his genius. He would talk about moving again, about "getting out from under the city's thumb," about opening a store of his own, but nothing ever came of it. He spent entire nights staring at the fire, jaw set, hands twitching with unspent rage.

One night in January, he stumbled in just before midnight, tracking snow across the parlor rug. Annie was nursing John William in the rocking chair, with her nightgown loose and long hair unbraided. She saw at once that he was drunk, the dangerous kind of drunk that could snap from love to violence with the wrong word.

This night, Thomas teetered on the edge of fury, his eyes narrowing into slits that cut through the dimly lit room. The red in his eyes mirrored the bitterness that had curdled his spirit, and he directed its full force at Annie. "Why do you always look at me like that?" he spat, his words dragging with the weight of alcohol and resentment. "What, you think you're better than me? Just waiting for me to mess up, huh?"

Annie kept her head down, focusing steadfastly on the infant cradled in her arms. The baby nursed rhythmically, oblivious to the storm brewing around him. She counted each heartbeat as if it were a lullaby, willing herself to remain composed, not daring to meet the accusation she felt boring into her skin.

Thomas stumbled forward, closing the distance between them with an unsteady gait. His voice reeked of bad decisions and hollow dreams. "You think I don't see it? You think I'm blind? You're just waiting for me to fall apart so you can say, 'I told you so,' aren't you? Admit it, woman!"

Annie's heart quickened beneath her calm exterior, but she fought to maintain an even tone as she replied, "You're tired, Thomas. Come to bed. It's late." The plea hung in the air like a fragile peace offering, but Thomas was not in the mood for peace. He lashed out with sudden violence. His hand met the mantel with a resounding crash that sent tremors through Annie's makeshift collection of teacups, a testament to small joys salvaged from other people's discards. They rattled precariously before settling back into uneasy stillness.

"Don't talk down to me!" he shouted, his voice echoing through the house with a volume that seemed poised to shatter both glass and nerves alike. His reddened face and the veins bulging in his neck were terrifying. "You think I'm nothing? A joke to you? Say it, Annie! Admit you can't stand me!" It was louder than Annie had ever heard him yell before.

The sudden noise startled John William from his feeding, jerking him back from the comfort of his mother's breast. The baby startled, pulling free, milk dribbling down his chin. Without thinking, Annie stood and bounced John William, whispering nonsense to calm him.

Thomas watched her, the anger draining away, replaced by a strange, raw sadness. He slumped onto the nearest chair, cradling his head in his hands. "I'm sorry," he muttered, voice thick with self-pity. "I hate it when I get like that."

Anger rose within her, but she smothered it, the way she'd learned to smother everything else. She waited until his breathing slowed, until she was sure he wouldn't lash out, and then she set the baby in the crib and tiptoed past him to the bedroom.

Early the next morning, she discovered him in the dimly lit kitchen, hunched over the worn wooden table, his gaze fixed on a chipped cup as if he were divining the future from the intricate network of cracks. The silence hung heavily between them when she entered; without uttering a single word, he reached for her hand, the skin rough and calloused from years of labor, and squeezed it. She looked at him, and beneath the layers of time and hardship, she saw the boy he must have been a lifetime ago, now isolated and seething with anger at the world. For a fleeting moment, a tempest of emotions surged within her; she felt the urge to hate him, to scream or flee, or even to hurl the fragile cup at his stubborn, obstinate face. Instead, she squeezed back.

Annie continued like this because she could not see any other options. She prepared meals, mended his clothes, changed and washed diapers, nursed the children through coughs and fevers, and endured the mind-numbing boredom of winter after winter. She read every scrap of newspaper she could find, devoured old dime novels when she could borrow them, and sometimes, late at night, she'd write long letters to Hazel, even though the mail between Idaho's towns was slow and unreliable. Hazel's replies always brought a smile to her face, at least for a minute. Hazel wrote about the scandals in Rocky Bar, about a wild new preacher who'd come to town, about her own impossible dreams. She never said, "I told you so," and for that, Annie loved her more than ever. *Hazel is gold.*

Sometimes, after Thomas had gone to bed and the house was silent, Annie would sit in the pale-yellow nursery and watch her children sleep. She stroked Anna Eliza's dark curls, traced the curve of John William's tiny fingers, and wondered if this was all that life had in store for her.

One morning, a few months after John William's second birthday, Thomas woke her before dawn. He was sober, calm, and gentle. "Let's take the children to the river. I want them to see the water."

They walked, the four of them, along the muddy banks of the Boise River, Thomas swinging Anna Eliza onto his shoulders while Annie cradled John William against her hip. For an hour, they watched the birds fly, float, and dive into the water. Thomas's knowledge of birds surprised Annie. He pointed out Mallards with their green heads, huge Canadian Geese, Cormorants, and even an elegant Great Blue Heron off in the distance. Annie let herself forget, just for a while, that she was his prisoner.

When they returned home, Thomas built a fire, then sat the children in his lap and read to them from a battered Old Farmer's Almanac, making up stories about the pictures. Annie watched him, a strange warmth blooming in her chest. For a minute, she believed things would be all right, that the man she had married might someday be a good husband and father. But when she put the children to bed, she found the bruise on her wrist from the day before, when Thomas yanked her out of bed. She massaged it, trying to make it go away. It didn't.

Chapter 12

The third baby arrived in the bitter winter of 1880, when the Boise River had frozen into black glass, and the streets in Boise City crunched under a sheath of brittle ice and snow. Annie had grown adept at hiding her pregnancies. There was no one left in town who cared to gossip about her anymore, and Thomas's friends were from the circles where a man's virility was measured in the number of mouths he had to feed. Annie wore thick shawls and loose dresses, did the laundry, cooked the meals, and patched the children's pants with a brisk, efficient fury that left her hands sore and her mind numb.

This birth was a difficult one. Thomas had been gone two days, off chasing some scheme or opportunity, and Annie had no one but little Anna Eliza to call for help. The girl was only three, still soft-cheeked and unsure on her feet, but Annie had no choice. Gritting her teeth against a rising contraction that twisted through her like a hot wire, she pressed a trembling kiss to her daughter's forehead and sent her toddler into the cold to fetch Mrs. Byrne.

The pain began around midnight, low and insistent, like a knife dragged across the base of her spine. Outside, the wind howled against the windows, rattling the panes in their loose frames, and the fire in the hearth had burned low, casting long, flickering shadows that danced across the walls like ghosts.

By the time Mrs. Byrne arrived, breathless and wrapped in a faded wool shawl, Annie had already soaked her nightdress with sweat. The labor did not break into manageable waves; it came in a relentless tide, dragging her under again and again. The room swam in and out of focus. Candles scattered around the room burned low, their wax pooling in the holders. Annie gripped the edge of the iron bedframe until her knuckles cracked, her cries hoarse, echoing off the cracked plaster walls. At times, she fell silent, her lips parted in a grimace of pain so deep it took her voice.

Mrs. Byrne worked with practiced, brutal efficiency, shouting commands, wiping Annie's brow with a damp cloth, and muttering prayers under her breath. "Come on, girl," she growled through clenched teeth, her hands slick with Annie's sweat. "You hold on. Breathe! You ain't done yet."

At some point, Annie slipped into a fever dream. Her body trembled, drenched in cold sweat. She saw snow falling through the ceiling, a baby's wail carried on the wind, and Thomas laughing somewhere far away. She believed she might die, that she would never see the baby's face. When the boy came, just as the sky outside turned the color of old ash, he was blue and motionless, his limbs limp as rags. For a moment, everything stopped. No sound but Annie's shallow, shuddering breath.

But Mrs. Byrne wasn't done. With the grit of a woman who'd delivered more babies than some doctors, she seized him, turned him upside down, and slapped his back, once, twice, three times, with a force that shook the silence. Nothing. Then she dribbled whisky into his tiny mouth, the sharp scent cutting through the blood and sweat like fire through fog. Another slap.

Finally, a thin gurgling cry burst from the boy's chest like a spark catching dry kindling. Annie wept at the sound, choking on it, her whole body shivering with relief and exhaustion as the baby's wail grew stronger, more defiant. Annie held him to her breast, her arms trembling, tears dribbling down her cheeks as she kissed the crown of his damp head. He was red-faced now, angry but alive, and against the odds, so was she. She named him John Henry.

Annie lined the crib with old flannel and tucked John Henry in every night, humming him the same lullabies her own mother had sung when she was a child. Sometimes, in the dark, Annie ran her hands over the wood window sills and imagined the world outside, the distant but sharp ridges of the mountains off to the northeast, the deep, endless hush of snow, and thought about how far she had come from the carefree girl in Rocky Bar.

By the time John Henry was weaned, Anna Eliza was old enough to help with the laundry, and John William spent whole days in the garden, digging tunnels and building mud castles for his army of stick soldiers. After Annie finished her daily chores, her preferred pastime activity was to sit on the back porch, look out over the landscape, and daydream. Her favorite was that she was an honored mother, one of the fine women on the east side of town who prided themselves on immaculate parlors and perfect children. But it never lasted. There was always a cough, a fever, a sudden blow-up from Thomas that ruined any pretense of peace.

The spring of 1882 arrived in Boise City like a breath of fresh air. She had the sewing out that day, with shirts to mend, a dress to let out for Anna Eliza, and a pair of cheap canvas shoes that needed patching if John Henry was to make it through another season without splitting them wide open. She worked at the little table by the window, needles and thread scattered in front of her, eyes half-closed against the bright sunlit yard outside. The coolness of the room, the high walls, and the faint lingering of last year's pine garland almost let her pretend she was somewhere else.

Thomas came in just before noon, slamming the screen door behind him so hard that John William, asleep on the sofa, jerked upright and cried. Thomas ignored the boy, crossed the room in three strides, and dropped a folded newspaper onto the table. The motion was quick and deliberate, as if he wanted the sound of the paper hitting wood to be attention-getting.

Annie ignored it. She didn't look up right away. She finished the seam, trimmed the thread, and only then slid her eyes over the top of her work.

Thomas stood with his arms crossed, jaw clenched, sweat darkening the collar of his shirt. "It's done," he said. "Congress did what they should've done years ago. No more of their kind stepping foot on this land."

She knew at once what he meant: the Chinese. The headline of the May 7, 1882, edition of the paper screamed across the top of the front page.

PRESIDENT SIGNS EXCLUSION ACT!

Annie felt her stomach knot. She did not concern herself with politics, but she knew what would come next.

"They work harder than any white man I've ever seen," Annie declared, her voice carrying a mix of defiance. She set the sewing aside with deliberate care, her fingers lingering on the fabric as if seeking reassurance. "All they want is a chance to feed their families."

"You have no idea what you're talking about, woman. They're changing everything for the rest of us. Taking jobs. Dragging wages through the mud." He snatched the paper again, jabbing at the headline with a thick finger, though his conviction wavered. "They're not even meant to be citizens. Why should we foot the bill for their children in the schools or let them own businesses?"

Annie braced her elbows on the table, fingers interlocked, concealing their slight tremor. "They deserve the same rights as any man. They work the hardest, and they endure the worst. You yourself once said the Chinamen crew at the mine put every white man to shame."

His eyes flashed with anger. "That was before they outnumbered us two to one. Do you want our children growing up with them as neighbors? Do you want our daughter to marry one? Can you imagine that?"

She looked past him to the tangle of children on the rug. Anna Eliza was reading to John William, her words slow and careful, her mouth barely moving. John Henry, now two years old, had curled up again, thumb in mouth, his cheek pressed against the rug. They appeared so small, so perfectly themselves, so pure and innocent.

"I want them to live in a place where decency matters," she said, her voice tinged with longing and uncertainty. "Where they don't have to hate people just because they look different."

Thomas's hands clenched into fists, but his steps faltered as he paced back and forth across the room. "That's not how the world works," he said, his voice a low rumble, caught between a growl and a plea. "It's us or them, woman. It always has been."

She stood up carefully, so the ache in her back would not be revealed. She tucked the needle into the cuff of her sleeve, a habit from the Rocky Bar days. "It's only like that because men like you keep saying so," she said. "Justice shouldn't depend on your race. Or by who can shout the loudest."

He stopped pacing and spun to face her. The heat in his eyes was almost unbearable. "You think you're so much better than everyone here," he said, voice low and ugly. "You think you're smarter, you think—"

"I don't think anything, Thomas," she snapped, louder than she meant to. "I don't want my children growing up to be cruel."

Thomas snatched up the paper, crumpling it in his hands with a frustrated energy before hurling it into the corner of the room. He strode over to the front door, gripped the handle, and flung it open. Annie waited until the door slammed, then slumped into her chair, the last of her anger leaking out with every slow, measured breath. She glanced at the children. Anna Eliza was watching her, eyes wide and solemn. Annie tried to smile, but her face wouldn't obey. Instead, she reached for her sewing, found the place in the hem, and resumed her stitching.

* * *

Two years later, when labor pains started for the next child, Annie begged Thomas to get Mrs. Byrne. He pretended not to hear her.

Raising her voice, she said, "Thomas, fetch Mrs. Byrne, I tell you!"

"I'll get her when you need her," and he left the room.

"Thomas, I beg you. Get Mrs. Byrne right now. I feel something's wrong!"

He poked his head back into the room. "Alright, crybaby. I'll get her."

After what felt like an eternity, Mrs. Byrne barged in and ran over to Annie. "What the hell, Thomas? Why didn't you come get me sooner? Annie's bleeding like crazy."

Another contraction hit. The pain was excruciating.

"Push Annie! Push!" The baby slid out and landed on top of a mass of blood-soaked bedsheets. Dizziness swept over Annie, and everything went dark.

Annie regained consciousness to the sound of the baby wailing on her chest. Mrs. Byrne hovered over her. "You did it, girl! You're a fighter if I ever saw one. I'm mighty proud of you," as she wiped the sweat off Annie's forehead with a wet cloth. "How are you feeling? You lost a lot of blood."

Annie moaned, "my whole body hurts." After resting for a few minutes, she looked down and whispered, "hello, Susan Margaret, my sweet baby." She latched onto Annie's breast and screamed at anyone who moved her. Susan Margaret was frail, but Annie concealed her concern. She worried that the baby girl might not survive her first winter, but Susan Margaret clung to life.

Soon after Susan Margaret arrived, Thomas stopped making any effort to hide his temper. He still worked long hours at the wholesale business on some days. On other days, he made the hundred-mile trip on horseback to the mines at Pine Grove and came back a couple of days later, usually late at night. There were some good nights, when he brought home scraps of candy for the children or lifted John Henry and spun him around until he shrieked with laughter. But more often, he was dark and silent, brooding next to the fireplace with a bottle of Old Crow in his lap, hands trembling as if he were barely keeping himself together.

Violence became a part of Annie's life. At first, it was a tight grip on her arm, enough to leave a ring of purple bruises that took a week to fade. She told herself it was a fluke, a mistake, and when he apologized the next morning, tears in his eyes, hands shaking, she let herself believe it. The second time, it was a shove. The third was a fist to her shoulder when she stood between him and the boys, who'd been fighting over a broken toy and refused to quiet down. After that, Annie learned to keep the children upstairs when Thomas was in one of his moods.

She lost her ability to forgive him for his outbursts after the night he broke John Henry's arm. It happened so fast that Annie could not remember the details. Thomas had come home drunk, yelling about a missing wage packet that Annie had never seen. John Henry was under the table, playing with scraps of wood, and Thomas tripped over him. The crack of the bone was sickening—a wet snap. The boy didn't even scream; he just went limp and turned white. Annie bit her tongue to keep from collapsing. She spent the night by her son's bed, applying cold rags and splints, whispering that it was a "terrible accident," that Papa hadn't meant it. In the morning, Thomas brought home a sack of penny candy and apologized, over and over. Annie wanted to slap him just to make him stop.

After that, she began hiding money around the house. Annie saved every spare coin, sewed them into the hems of her dresses, and tucked them into the folds of old towels and pillowcases. She thought about running, but she didn't know where to go. Hazel's last letter had come months ago, and Rocky Bar was a world away. Besides, Annie couldn't imagine surviving with four children and no job, no support, nothing but her own stubborn will, but she had to do something.

Chapter 13

In the spring of 1885, Thomas acquired a mercantile business from an older couple that wanted to retire and move to Salt Lake City. The first thing he did was rename it Morrow's Mercantile. The business was a world of numbers, and Annie learned to live by them. It started with small things: taking inventory in the cellar, memorizing the price of sugar and beans, tallying the receipts for each month on a slate behind the counter. But as the years pressed on, the business grew, and so did Annie's responsibilities.

Annie knew well that most people in Boise City despised the city tax collector and avoided him like the plague, but Annie's attitude was different. She saw an opportunity. She befriended him, and because of this relationship, he taught her the basics of bookkeeping. He had to explain three times why assets minus liabilities equals equity, but Annie finally understood. Before long, she was comfortable discussing whether a store fixture should be classified as a current asset or a long-term asset, the difference between preferred and common stock, and how company dividends should be recorded in the ledger. She knew how to record debits and credits in order to make balanced transactions. She could put all that together and make an income statement and a balance sheet. By 1886, she was running the books for their business, with an accuracy that impressed even the tax collector. She allowed herself to feel a little pride. *This was something I can do, and I think I'm pretty good at it.*

Occasionally, Annie rode with Thomas on the supply runs, while Mrs. Byrne watched the children. They rode up and down the wild mountain roads between Boise City, the distant diggings at Pine Grove, and Idaho City. One trip took them all the way to Placerville, an especially rowdy mining camp. Thomas mentioned to her after they had finished their business in there that it used to be known as Hangtown because of the frequency of vigilante hangings.

In the dry heat of summer, the trails kicked up so much dust that it left her mouth tasting like grit for days; in winter, the snow came down so fast that horses had a hard time plodding through the snowdrifts. They traveled light, with only a saddlebag of ledgers, a pouch of paper currency, and gold coins for purchasing supplies. Nights in the mining camps were brutal. Almost every night she overheard arguments between the miners and drunken brawls in the streets. The first time she heard gunshots, it startled her right out of her chair, but Thomas didn't even flinch.

Their mercantile business was profitable. Annie managed the inventory: flour and salt pork, bolts of calico, gingham, wool, and cotton prints, as well as boots, shirts, hats, patent medicines, and even small luxuries like peppermint sticks. Boise City was booming, with every month bringing fresh faces, new mouths to feed, and new competition. Annie spent her days behind the counter, her hands never still. If she was not grinding coffee beans, measuring yard goods, or managing the credit accounts, then she was wrangling the children, all four of them. It was a respite from the horrors of their turbulent home life, as Thomas's drinking got worse every year.

She did most of the bookkeeping by candlelight, double-checking every line, her fingers smudged with ink by the end of each night before she headed home. The flame wavered with every small draft, throwing soft golden halos over the ledger pages and casting long, quivering shadows across the counters and shelves. The air held the faint scent of paraffin and the day's lingering aromas—coffee beans from the burlap sacks, sawdust from the floorboards, and the faint medicinal sharpness of the liniment bottles.

She grew fond of those tranquil hours after the mercantile closed, when the rest of the world slept, and the windows reflected only her own silhouette. Outside, the wind sometimes rattled the windows, and once in a while a horse clopped lazily down the road, but mostly she heard only the steady, comforting scratch of her fountain pen as it traveled across the page. That sound—delicate, rhythmic—was soothing. The bookkeeping became more than work; it became a refuge, a place where her mind moved unchained, where she belonged to no one but herself.

Once home, her shoulders loosened from the stress of each day as night deepened. Her breath settled. In the hush, she could almost forget the bruises that Thomas left on her arms so often. Here, alone in the soft glow, she felt something inside her unfurl, and relax. Annie craved the regular evening solitude. In those moments, she almost felt free—a small but fierce spark of freedom, fragile yet real.

The quality of Annie's work did not escape Thomas's notice. He leaned on her more and more as the months wore on, sending her to negotiate with suppliers and to settle disputes with local farmers or the freight companies. At first, he hovered close, ready to step in if she faltered, but it soon became clear she never did. Annie had a way of reading a man's character before he finished his first sentence, and she used it to her advantage. She learned to spot the liars, the gamblers, the desperate, the grifters. Annie even caught a few con men before they could pull their trick. She learned to walk the line between kindness and ruthlessness, to smile enough to get what she wanted.

She built a network of trust, small but resilient: the young lawyer who handled their taxes, the blacksmith's wife who swapped gossip for dime novels, the nuns at St. Mary's who ran the soup kitchen and knew which families needed help in the coldest months. Annie kept the business open late for them, even when Thomas grumbled about "giving away the profits." She knew that kindness cost less than a lost customer, and besides, she enjoyed feeling needed and helping others.

During one dinner in May 1887, Thomas cleared his throat and announced, "more gold's been discovered in Pine Grove, and the mines are opening up. There will be some excellent business opportunities. We're moving next month."

Annie had become accustomed to life in Boise City, and she dreaded the prospect of moving to some rough-and-tumble mining camp, but there was no point in objecting. She continued chewing on a slice of sourdough bread.

By the time the family arrived in Pine Grove, there were already over two hundred miners there and several profitable mining operations. Thomas gained interest in two of the mines. This generated a steady income for the family.

One day, while Thomas was off to meet with a mine foreman, Annie wandered out to the edge of the South Fork of the Boise River, which ran east of town. She spotted a small group of Chinamen working alongside the river.

They hunched over a long wooden sluice box, where gravel mixed with water sloshing through it. A stout man with a thick German accent spotted Annie. Without introducing himself, he explained that since gold is sixteen times heavier than water, it will sink and collect in the little ridges in the sluice box.

The laborers did not look up as she passed by. The foreman added that the Chinamen were going to "pick this spot clean," and that no white miner can compete with their tenacity. Chinamen were only allowed to work in gravel beds that white miners had already worked, since they were prohibited from owning their own claims. Annie watched the men for a while, admiring the steady rhythm of their hands, the silent way they communicated with sounds and words she did not understand. She found a seat on a log near the water and watched for about an hour.

"What are you doing out here?" Thomas sounded irritated as he walked up behind her.

Annie rose, brushing dirt and twigs from the fabric of her dress with deliberate care. Her fingers lingered on the rough weave, grounding herself in its familiar texture. "Just looking," she replied, her tone light yet laced with an undercurrent of defiance. She gestured toward the swirling waters where men toiled.

He glanced at the Chinamen, his gaze hardening. "You spend too much time watching them," he said gruffly. "Did you hear what happened on the Snake River up towards Lewiston? A bunch of Chinamen were killed, thirty-four, I heard. They're nothing but troublemakers. They're calling it the Hell's Canyon Massacre. A bunch of yahoos from Oregon did it and then took off with their gold. There's only so much gold to be had, and in this country, it belongs to us Americans."

She met his eyes before turning away again, unable to help herself from observing the relentless rhythm of work happening around them. "You're disgusting," she whispered. She felt like saying it again louder, but she didn't want to start another fight. *Why did people give the Chinese such a hard time? They're only human. And the Indians, for that matter? For gold, that's why. Because of greed and gold, and men who can't think of anything but themselves. They all want to get rich, and powerful, the rest of the world be damned.*

As they walked back toward the town together, Thomas grumbled about schedules and orders while Annie remained silent beside him. Inwardly, she steeled herself for what lay ahead: a future as unpredictable and unforgiving as any mountain wagon road they had ever traveled.

A few months after they moved to Pine Grove, Thomas sold Morrow's Mercantile in Boise City and purchased another mercantile in Pine Grove. He told Annie there was more potential and less competition. Annie continued for the next two years running the Pine Grove Mercantile, keeping the books, raising the children, and holding her world together with the force of her own will. Thomas grew heavier, more settled in his ways. He still grumbled about the money Annie spent on seasonal decorations for the mercantile, and birthday gifts for the children, but he never challenged her decisions in public. The townsfolk treated her as the head of the business. When the suppliers stopped by on their regular rounds presenting their new products, with increasing frequency they preferred to speak with Annie, even when Thomas was present. The first few times this happened Thomas glared at them from the back of the mercantile, but it eventually stopped bothering him. The priest at St. Mary's addressed his letters to *Mrs. A. Morrow, Proprietress*. That made her smile.

* * *

As the months slid by, Annie felt a restlessness growing inside her, something sharp and unwavering that would not let her sleep peacefully. Some nights, she sat by the back window after the children were in bed, listening to the incessant pounding of the town's stamp mills. *One day, I'll find something more than this. I don't know how, but I will, even if it's the last thing I do on this Earth. I owe it to myself. This is not the life I wanted.*

The fifth child, Ethyl Frances, came as a surprise during their third year in Pine Grove. Annie had long since stopped keeping track of her periods when her belly swelled again. *Not again. I don't need this! I'm not in my twenties anymore. I don't know if I can handle this.* This pregnancy was the hardest yet. The morning sickness never let up, and some days she couldn't stand without feeling dizzy and seeing black spots swimming before her eyes. The children learned to care for each other. Sometimes, when Annie couldn't bear to get out of bed, Anna Eliza would bring her cold water or stroke her forehead and whisper in her ear, "it's all right, Mama, don't worry, we're fine. We love you."

Ethyl Frances was born in late spring, a tiny thing with pale hair and an ear-piercing scream. Thomas was sober for once, and he held the baby with a gentleness that surprised Annie. He talked about how they would start fresh, how this time he'd be better, that he would stop drinking. He stayed home the whole first week and shocked Annie the first time he brought her herb tea in bed. Annie looked up at him, and their eyes met. There was sadness in her eyes. *I want to believe you, Thomas, but I can't. Words are cheap. Change would be too hard for you. I know it. I wish you could change. I wish you would be like the man I grew to love, sitting by me at Beaver Creek. Why can't you be like that? That's the man I loved, not what you've become. You hurt me, Thomas, and I don't know if I can forgive you. What's the point of forgiveness, anyway? You'll just keep doing what you've been doing.*

The good days never lasted. He always slipped back into the old routines: the late nights at the saloon, the sour stink of whiskey on his clothes, and the clink of poker chips echoing in his pockets when he stumbled home. Rage simmered under his skin, waiting for the slightest excuse to erupt.

Once she recovered, Annie resumed her routine of scrubbing the floors until her knees ached, keeping the children quiet as ghosts, and cooking meals even when the cupboards were practically empty. But it was never enough. There was always something to set him off. It could be a spilled cup of milk, a sock left on the floor, or a letter from his mother left unopened on the kitchen table.

One morning, after a brutal winter storm had knocked down the backyard fence, Annie came out of the bedroom with Ethyl Frances on her hip and saw him standing in the kitchen. The woodstove was cold. The air inside the house smelled of damp clothes.

He was staring at the broken pantry door, which hung crooked on its hinges, the latch torn clean off.

"I can fix it today, just need to find the hammer," she said.

He didn't move. Didn't blink. He stood there, still as stone, eyes dark and unreadable.

"You hear me?" she asked again, a little louder.

Annie's breath caught. Ethyl Frances whimpered, and she rocked her, keeping her voice steady. "I've done all I can, Thomas. The roof held. The stove's working now. The children are warm. We're—"

He turned toward her, eyes hollow, jaw twitching. His voice was low and bitter. "You think warm children make up for this?" He nodded toward the pantry. "For the damn mess everything's become?"

Her spine stiffened. "What mess? The pantry door's broken, not the world." She set the baby down in her crib, then faced him. "You want to yell at me, go ahead. But don't pretend the door is the problem."

"I work all day," he snapped, stepping toward her, "and I come home to this—this dump. This broken-down shack and a wife who lets everything fall apart!"

"I *keep* everything from falling apart," she shot back, eyes narrowing. "While you're out drinking your pay and pissing away the rent money!"

His eyes narrowed. A muscle jumped in his cheek. He leaned forward, right into her face. "Don't start."

For a moment, neither of them budged. This was not the first time they had a standoff like this. Annie clenched her fists and stared back at him as if she was going to explode. Ethyl Frances stirred in the crib. The wind moaned around the eaves.

He turned and slammed the pantry door shut with such force that the wood cracked down the center. The sound echoed through the kitchen like a gunshot. Without another word, he stormed out the back door, boots thudding against the frozen porch. Annie stared at the splintered wood, her breath fogging in the freezing air. The tension drained out of her body. Then she turned, picked up the baby, and held her close.

"I'll fix it myself," she whispered.

That night, he dragged her out of bed by the arm and hissed in her ear that she was making a fool of him, that everyone in town could see she didn't respect him. She yanked her arm away, and he grabbed her again, fingers digging deep into her skin. She bit his hand with all her might, and for a second, he looked at her with genuine fear. He let go, staggered backwards, and left the house, slamming the door behind him.

Annie stood there trembling, her arm already swelling with pain. She waited until the children were asleep, then went into the kitchen, poured some bourbon into a small tin cup, and stared at the crescent moon through the frost-covered window. She pressed her bruised arm to the cold cup, letting the pain clear her head. *That does it. I can't take this anymore. I'm going to leave him. Our marriage is over. If this keeps going, he might kill me, or I might kill him.* Annie froze. The thought that she might kill him horrified her. She felt sick to her stomach. *I'm not a killer, but what can I do? As terrible as he is, I could never kill him.* Her tears flowed.

An image formed in her mind of her and Thomas in the midst of a heated argument. He pushed her, and she pushed back. He pushed her again with so much force that she fell backwards and slammed her head on the stone fireplace. She saw herself laying on the floor unconscious, with a pool of blood forming under her head, as her life slipped away.

I have to escape! The thought rose with sudden clarity, as sharp as a gasp after being held under water. But it was followed at once by another, heavier truth that crushed the breath from her lungs. *What about my children?* The question circled her mind relentlessly. She pressed her palm to her mouth, as if she might silence it, but there was no stopping it now. *I can't leave them here—alone, defenseless, trapped with a man whose temper already sought me as its target. If I flee without them, I know his rage would target them next.* The image made her stomach twist. *I can't trade my own freedom for their suffering.*

Somehow, we must escape together. Yet no path revealed itself—only locked doors and dead ends. The weight of it all bore down on her until her shoulders sagged. She poured another cup of bourbon and drank it too quickly, the burn offering no relief. She refilled it again and again. Each swallow felt less like comfort and more like punishment.

When the bottle was finally empty, she set it down with a dull thud and stared at it as though it had failed her. Her chest ached with exhaustion and grief. Dragging herself from the chair, she moved toward the bedroom, each step heavy and deliberate, as if the floor itself resisted her. She collapsed onto the bed fully clothed; the mattress sagging beneath her weight. Staring into the darkness, she let the tears come once again, her body curled inward around a single, unyielding truth: she would endure anything, suffer any blow, before she abandoned her children to his cruelty.

* * *

The next morning, she packed a bag with a change of clothes for the children. She hid the bag under the bed, telling herself she would only use it when she had to. For the next several weeks, she moved through her days like a sleepwalker. She said nothing to the children about her plans. She kept a close eye on Thomas, assessing her distance from the door, and watched for the first signs of anger or hatred.

One afternoon, after he'd left for work, Annie took the children out to the backyard. She set Ethyl Frances on a blanket and watched Anna Eliza and John William chase each other around an apple tree. For a moment, she let herself believe that the world could be different, that she might find a way out.

Then she heard footsteps behind her and turned to see Thomas standing in the doorway, watching them with an unreadable expression. He said nothing. He stood there, eyes moving from Annie to the children and back again. She stared at him, meeting his gaze. For the first time, she felt no fear. No hope either. She turned back to the children, calling them in for supper. As they tumbled through the kitchen door, she caught Thomas's eye one last time. He looked away first, which scared her because it gave no hint about what he might do next. Nothing happened, this time.

That night, after tucking the children in, Annie sat at the table, clutching a mug of tea as if it were a lifeline. She gazed at the moon rising over the city, its cold silver light casting shadows across the floor. Her mind raced with thoughts of escape, of Rocky Bar, of Hazel's Aunt Ruth, and the hope that once fueled her dreams. Yet, the faces of her children, so bright and trusting, haunted her. Their future was precarious, teetering on the edge of disaster. She wrestled with herself, torn between the urge to flee and the pull of responsibility. In a whisper, she made a promise to herself and to them. *We will not be trapped here forever.* Yet, a part of her questioned whether she had the strength to break free, to find a way out, and what that would cost her.

Thomas took to sleeping in the front room, claiming the baby's howling kept him from getting a decent night's rest. He was home even less than before, and when he came through the door, it was usually with a bottle in one hand and the day's tension already bristling across his shoulders.

Annie kept up the routine: morning oatmeal, lessons at the kitchen table, chores, errands in the afternoon, and an hour at the business ledgers every evening. But the smallest slip, burnt porridge, a missed bill, a stain on the tablecloth, was enough to ignite Thomas's temper. It had gotten worse since Ethyl Frances was born. His outbursts no longer needed a reason, and sometimes he struck her before he even spoke.

Yet, faced with it all, she remained determined and composed, her actions deliberate and purposeful as she wrote her letter to George. The flickering light of the lamp and the warmth of the stove provided slight comfort amid the chaos.

> Dear Brother,
> I am desperate and have no one else to turn to.
> We have spoken little these past years, but I
> need you now more than ever. Thomas is not
> just a threat to me; he is a danger to the children
> as well. I am pleading with you; if there is any
> space for us in Mountain Home, please tell me. I
> will work tirelessly, do anything to pay our way. I
> implore you, keep this confidential.

She paused, staring at the words, the ache in her chest almost suffocating. Then she added:

> I am not safe. Please answer quick.
> AM

She initialed it and carefully blotted the ink.

Annie sealed the envelope, addressed it with a trembling hand, and sat at the window until the sky paled over the mountains. She bundled Ethyl Frances in a shawl and slipped out the back door to the post office down the street. The city was still asleep, with the only sound coming from the hollow clop of her shoes on the frozen mud.

She carried the baby back home, crawled into the narrow bed with the other children, and slept until noon.

The next morning, instead of getting up, she let her thoughts drift. *What had happened to the man who used to walk up to the porch at the Rocky Bar Mercantile just to get a good look at me, and for the opportunity to exchange a few words? Was this the same man who made me giggle while sitting side by side on the banks of Beaver Creek? Where was he? How could someone who showered me with love and affection in the abandoned stamp mill now just as fervently hit me? Who was this monster that replaced him?* She resigned herself to lying there for the next hour.

Two weeks later, the mail carrier arrived at their front door. Annie peeked through the curtains as the man knocked, handed a single envelope to Susan Margaret, and tipped his hat before leaving. Susan brought the letter inside, eyes wide. "Who is it from, Mama?"

Annie took it with shaking hands. "It's from your uncle George. Let's keep this a secret just between us, okay? Don't tell Papa." She didn't open it at first. She tucked it into her apron pocket, finished the day's chores, bathed the baby, and waited until the house was quiet before unsealing it at the kitchen table. Annie sat there, gripping the letter with trembling hands. She read it twice, then a third time, each word sinking deep into her heart.

> Dearest Sister,
> Of course you can come here. The children too.
> Tell me when, and I'll come for you myself if
> needed. I can get you work at the hotel. You're
> not alone.
> Your Brother, George

Tears welled up in her eyes, tears she'd suppressed for years, and they spilled down her cheeks and dripped onto the letter, smudging the ink. The relief was intense, and a glimmer of hope flickered within her. She moved to the old cast-iron stove and placed the letter inside. As the flames licked at the paper, she watched the edges curl and turn black, until the letter was nothing but ashes. She swept the remains into a small dustpan and carried them outside. In the garden, she scattered the ashes among the rose bushes, ensuring that the children playing nearby would never stumble upon them.

That night, she made plans. Thomas was on a business trip to Boise City and was not supposed to return for three days, so this would be the best time to leave. She had visited the stagecoach office the day before and paid an extra twenty dollars for a special run to Mountain Home. The driver promised there would be no other passengers on the stagecoach.

Just as the sun set, she rounded up the children. They slipped out the back door, shadows in the soft gray light. The dirt streets stretched out before them as they embarked on the ten-minute walk to the stagecoach office. Anna Eliza and John William shouldered the weight of the trunk between them, their steps synchronized in the cool evening air. Little John Henry, with his tousled hair, clung to Susan Margaret's hand, their fingers intertwined like a lifeline. Annie cradled Ethyl Frances against her chest, feeling the warmth of the tiny body through her clothing as they moved forward, a determined family desperate to escape.

Anna Eliza, who was now twelve years old, asked, "Where are we going, Mama?"

"We're going to visit your uncle George in Mountain Home."

"Why isn't Papa coming with us?"

"Papa is busy with work, so it's just us."

Susan Margaret, who was six, said, "I'm cold. Mama, can we go back home?"

"I'm sorry, Suzie. You'll be warmer once we get into the stagecoach. I promise."

The six of them climbed in, and Annie closed her eyes until the driver yelled at the horses. The coach jerked and rattled and began the ten-hour journey to Mountain Home. Annie imagined how happy she would be when she and the children reached the safety of her brother's home. She fingered the rolled-up bundle of hundred-dollar bills she had sewn into the hem of her dress. Thomas would not notice anything missing since she did the bookkeeping.

Chapter 14

The coach rolled along at a steady pace for the first hour, but after the horses tired and the driver lost his nerve on the ruts, the rhythm of escape slowed to a crawl. They were only five miles out of the city limits before the driver braked at every gopher mound, every cow skull, every suspicious shadow that flicked across the road. Annie did not blame him. She understood the fear of what might wait in the dark, especially for the easily spooked horses.

By midnight, the dirt road had vanished in a swirl of sage and darkness. The youngest two children huddled together on the threadbare seat, their breath fogging in the musty air. The older ones sprawled and twitched in a shallow, exhausted sleep. Every so often, the stagecoach jolted, which added to Annie's nervousness.

She imagined Thomas coming home to the empty house and pictured the shock and rage on his face when he realized the children's shoes were gone, the beds still made. Annie could see the way his hands would clench on the doorframe, and then the storm as he tore through the kitchen for any clue of where they had gone. She imagined the violence in the air as he upended drawers, the vicious stomp of his boots on the creaking floors.

The image burned so bright that Annie barely noticed when the coach slowed to a stop. The driver announced, "Gonna walk the horses a stretch. Too dark to push 'em any harder."

I wish you wouldn't slow down. We need to hurry. We need to get to Mountain Home as fast as possible! I told you this before we started. The children whimpered, reaching for each other. Annie wrapped her arms around Ethyl Frances, tucking the girl's wild blonde hair under her own shawl. It was cold inside the stagecoach because of the constant influx of outside air. They were built without glass in the windows because glass would have shattered due to the jolts suffered along Idaho's rugged wagon roads. The leather shades that flapped in the windows were useless.

The children slept in shifts, waking only to the bump of wheels over a rut or a rock. Annie envied them. She wished she could sleep like them, but every time she drifted off, the image of Thomas appeared behind them, like a demon. Sometimes he wore his old suit and the red necktie she had made him for their first Christmas together. Sometimes he wore nothing at all, only the black fur of a wolf stretched over his bones, baring his fangs.

She woke from one of these dreams with Ethyl Frances's small arms wrapped around her neck. The stagecoach had stopped again. Someone was yelling at the driver. Then a heavy fist hammered on the side of the coach three times. Annie's heart shuddered.

The driver's voice, trembling, said, "Ma'am, there's a man out here— says he's your husband."

A chill ran up Annie's spine. Annie shook her head, mouthing, "No, no, no!" A wave of nausea welled up inside her, and she broke out into a cold sweat.

The door flung open, and there stood Thomas, glaring at her, as if he were the devil himself. He held his pistol in his right hand, barrel down, but ready. "Get out!" he sneered.

Annie climbed out of the coach, and with all the courage she could muster, stood right in front of Thomas, inches from his hate-filled face. "Let the children go! Take me if you want but leave them alone!"

"No!"

He glared at the driver, who hid behind the horses, ashen with fright. "Turn this thing around," Thomas barked. "Back to Pine Grove. Now!"

The driver obeyed, scrambling into the seat and snapping the reins. The coach lurched, made an awkward turn around, and began its retreat down the dusty road. Annie stood where she was with her hands coiled into tight fists at her sides. She could see Anna Eliza leaning out a window. For a second, she thought the girl would leap out of the stagecoach and run back to her. But she only stared, her eyes wild with terror.

When the coach was gone, silence swallowed the road.

Thomas remained behind, watching Annie, his hand on the pistol. *He might shoot me and leave me for dead alongside the road in the middle of nowhere and claim it was an accident. Is he waiting for the coach to get far enough away so that the children won't hear the gunshot?* Annie met his gaze but did not move. She knew what happened to prey that ran from a predator.

"I should have known." His voice was low, oozing with spite. "You never were any good at hiding your lies. You're a damn fool. Didn't you think I knew that you'd run to your brother?" He shoved her with so much force that she fell backwards into the dirt. Afraid to move, she froze as Thomas stood over her, clutching the pistol at his side. He raised it up, bent over her, and pointed it right at her chest, his finger on the trigger.

"I could kill you for what you've done to me," he said as he spat in her face.

Annie's mind froze, and she lay there paralyzed. She shut her eyes, dreading what was to come, and let out a muffled whimper, with tears in her eyes. Nothing happened. *What are you waiting for? Are you going to shoot me? Damn you to hell, Thomas!*

She heard boots scuffing in the dirt. She squinted her eyes to see what was happening. Thomas had stood up and was towering over her, looking like he was about to explode in fury. She knew that look only too well.

"You'll never see your children again!"

He backed away towards his horse, never turning his back, and mounted up. He swung it around and galloped after the coach, leaving Annie lying in the dirt, in the dark, alone, abandoned. She couldn't move. Her children were the most cherished part of her life, and Thomas stole them from her.

Annie saw her children's faces in her mind's eye, the way they looked when they were sleeping, the way Anna Eliza blinked at her before bed, the way John William pressed his cheek to her palm and closed his eyes like a cute puppy.

She struggled to hold on to those memories, but every time she tried, all she could see was Anna Eliza leaning out of the window of the stagecoach, terrified. Annie curled into a ball, arms clamped over her ears. She rocked back and forth, not knowing what else to do, sobbing into her knees, not knowing if she would ever move again. *Maybe I'll freeze to death.*

Annie dragged her legs out in front of her, every joint aching as if the bones inside had been hammered. The motion scraped her torn dress over the frozen ground. She let herself collapse backward. The ground met her spine with a brutal jolt—frozen, uneven, studded with sharp bits of sticks and rocks that pressed through her dress, beneath her shoulder blades, digging into her spine, another into the back of her head. The earth was as merciless as everything else in her life, unyielding and uninterested in the broken woman splayed across it. The chill seeped through her coat in a minute, stealing the little warmth her body had left. The air knifed into her lungs with every shallow breath, tasting of dust and smelling of sage.

Above her, the night sky stretched in all directions, a vast and pitiless vault arching over the empty land, a black sheet pricked with a million frozen stars. The cold made them seem sharper, crueler, like tiny chips of broken glass scattered across an endless void. They stared down like silent witnesses to her death, distant, merciless, and uncaring. A faint wind hissed through the dry grass at the roadside, stirring it enough to whisper against her ears, like voices too far away to help.

People talked about constellations, about finding pictures in the stars. Bulls, bears, warriors, and swans. But I don't see anything. No shapes. No stories. No guiding lines: only lifeless specks scattered across the empty blackness.

Her bruises pulsed in slow, vicious waves—dull, deep aches along her sides; a hot, stinging throb at her cheek where skin was bleeding. Her fingers, numb and clumsy, curled into the dirt, gathering only grit and brittle grass. The sound of the wind moving through the empty landscape was thin and lonely, as if it were mourning her. A distant coyote yipped once, twice, then fell silent. Even that animal sought to abandon her. There was no comfort to be found in the heavens, only the cruel reminder that she was alone, abandoned beside a road in the middle of nowhere.

When she finally stood, it was only because she could not bear to lie on the freezing ground any longer. It was sucking the life out of her body. She staggered a few paces down the road, then collapsed again, sobbing so hard she could not see. *Maybe I can wish myself dead,* but that thought was pushed away by another one.

Don't give up, Annie.

It was more than just a thought. It sounded as if it had a voice, a familiar voice, but she couldn't place it. *Is that my imagination?* She couldn't tell if it was real or not.

Annie forced her lifeless body to get up again and take a few more steps. She could hardly see the road in the darkness, and what she could see was only because of the faint light from the crescent moon overhead. *Maybe a pack of wolves will finish me off. Maybe I'll freeze to death.* Annie lost her desire to move. She huddled by the side of the road and remained there for what must have been hours. *What's the point of trying? I might as well die right here.*

She did not notice the rider until he was almost upon her. The hoofbeats, steady and even, were not like those of Thomas's wild charge. When the horse and rider crested the rise, Annie looked up. She knew the man at once, though his face was fuller now, and his hair touched with gray. It was George.

He reined in hard, hooves sliding in the dirt. For a second, he stared at her, like she was a ghost. He was off his horse in an instant, stumbling toward her with hands half-raised.

"Annie?" His voice was soft, the way it used to be when he would wake her after a nightmare. "God, Annie. What happened?"

She couldn't utter a word. Annie collapsed into his arms. She leaned into him, shuddering, and for a moment she felt safe. He held her that way for a long time. When she pulled away, she saw tears in his eyes. She wiped them with a shaking hand.

"Where are the children?" he asked, his voice small.

She pressed her face to his shoulder and sobbed, the grief as fresh as if it had just happened. He waited, letting her spend it all, then led her to the side of the road and sat with her next to a sagebrush. He pulled out a flask and handed it to her.

Once she could speak, she spilled out the story between sobs: the stagecoach, the chase, the gun, Thomas's face. "He said I'll . . . I'll never see my . . . my children again!"

George listened without a word, his expression never shifting. When Annie couldn't speak any further, he said, "He'll pay for this. I swear to you, Annie. He will pay, even if it's the last thing I ever do. I oughta get my gun and—"

"No, George. Don't even think that." She leaned against him, feeling the tension in his muscles as he sat beside her. The air between them was thick with unsaid words, a fragile silence that threatened to crack under the weight of their shared anger and sorrow. Her voice, when it came, was a whisper. "You can't go after him." Each word was laced with fear she could not hide. "He'll kill you."

George's gaze dropped to the ground, wrestling with words he could not yet find. His breath came in short bursts, visible in the night's chill. "He's just a man, Annie," he said, his voice gruff with conviction and no small measure of hatred. "A man who bleeds like any other. He can be stopped."

Her heart twisted painfully at his defiance. She could feel the tremor in her hand as she reached out, fingers curling around his with a desperation born of love and fear. She squeezed with all her remaining strength. "Promise me," she breathed, each word imbued with urgency, "promise me you won't do anything stupid."

There was a long pause. George's eyes searched hers, looking for something unsaid. He gave a slow nod, a gesture that promised nothing but tired acquiescence. Yet Annie knew well enough the fury burning behind his calm facade to recognize it for what it was: a battle held at bay by sheer will. He nodded again, more firmly this time, though his lips remained set in a grim line that spoke louder than words of promises he couldn't keep.

They sat together in silence, his arm wrapped around her shoulder, on the desolate road where time itself seemed to stand still, interrupted only by the distant howls of a lone coyote echoing across the vastness of the desolate land surrounding them.

Chapter 15

George helped Annie to her feet and guided her toward his horse tied up nearby. He lifted her onto the saddle before swinging up behind her with ease borne from years spent on horseback. He wrapped his arms around her and held her tight. As they began their journey toward Mountain Home under the moon's pale glow spilling across their path, an unspoken bond formed anew in their shared adversity. He steered in rhythm with hers; two bodies moving as one beneath starlit skies.

"We can't go to my place," he said. "First thing Thomas'll do is come looking for you there. He knows where I live. And if he doesn't, his friends will tell him."

Annie nodded. "He'll never stop. Not until he has me back. Or I'm dead."

"Stay at my friend Edith's place. You met her once or twice. She's a midwife, and she can take care of you. You'll be safe there."

"Okay."

They rode into the night all the way to Mountain Home. George led Annie by the hand up to the front door of Edith's house just as dawn was showing its colors in the east. After a few minutes, the door swung open to reveal Edith standing there in her long white nightgown.

"Lord have mercy! What on earth happened to you?" she said, pulling Annie inside. "You poor little scrap of humanity. I remember you. You're Annie Morrow, aren't you?"

George spoke to Edith so quietly that Annie could not make out what he said, but she didn't care. She was alive, even though she had died inside. Edith nodded, ushering Annie to a chair by the stove and wrapping her in a thick quilt. She heated some beef broth, forcing Annie to sip it, and then set about cleaning the dirt and blood from her arms and face. Annie let her, grateful for the rough kindness.

"You poor thing. Stay here as long as you need. No one will find you. I got a Colt .45 and a dog meaner than a rattlesnake."

George lingered by the door, his hat twisting in his hands. "I'll come by when it's safe," he said. "And I'll watch for the children."

Annie reached for him. "Thank you, George," she whispered.

He squeezed her hand. "Anything for you, Annie. I'll do anything."

When he was gone, Annie let herself collapse into the chair. Edith covered her with another quilt and sat across from her, darning a pair of socks with silent efficiency. The only light came from the stove, warm and golden. Annie let herself close her eyes and rest.

She dreamed of the children. They were running to her on a sunny day through tall grass, laughing, their arms outstretched toward her. At the very moment they would embrace, the dream ended, and she would awaken. Her heart felt as heavy as lead.

Edith's house was small but sturdy, the walls chinked tight against winter, and the floor was kept swept. The bed was soft, the quilts warm, and the kitchen full of the sharp, medicinal smells of dried herbs and boiled roots. Annie spent the first days in a fever, drifting in and out of sleep as Edith nursed her with barley tea and ladled beef broth between her lips.

* * *

After the fever broke, Annie woke up, surprised to find herself in a bed. A warm shaft of sunlight shone through the thin curtains, casting golden stripes across the faded bedspread. The air in the room was thick with the rich, yeasty scent of sourdough bread baking.

She tried to rise, but every muscle in her back shrieked with pain. A gasp escaped her lips, and she sank back onto the pillow, teeth clenched. Her limbs felt heavy, swollen with exhaustion, and her throat burned.

Edith appeared in the doorway, her shoes scuffing against the floor. She had pulled her auburn hair into a messy twist, wisps escaping to frame her weathered face. Edith was a sturdy woman with a kind demeanor and beautiful brown eyes. She was like the mother Annie never had, full of compassion, understanding, tenderness, and most of all, a heart filled with love. In one hand, she carried a white plate stacked with thick slices of buttered sourdough bread, steam curling upward from the golden crust. In the other, a mug of something dark and savory, like beef broth.

She gave a curt nod when she saw Annie's eyes open. "Thought I'd lost you there for a minute. You got a constitution like a miner's mule."

Annie tried to smile, but even that tugged at the raw edges of her skin. "Thank you," she whispered, her voice ragged.

Edith grunted, a sound somewhere between agreement and impatience. "Eat," she ordered, crossing the room with sure, heavy steps and setting the tray down on the bedside table with a soft clunk. The steam from the bread and mug rose between them, carrying warmth and a hint of butter. "You got to build up your strength if you want to outlive that bastard."

Annie's eyes fluttered at that. She reached for a piece of bread, fingers trembling from the effort.

"Edith is a pretty name."

The older woman blinked, surprised, and turned away for a moment, busying herself with straightening a wrinkled towel on the washstand.

"It's a variation of the Old English name Ead, which means 'prosperous' or 'blessed'," she said at last, offhandedly. "I looked it up once."

Annie smiled, faint but genuine, her hand still curled around the warm bread. "Very appropriate." She let the tranquility of the room envelop her mind. She could not remember the last time she felt this peaceful.

Edith sighed, and her cheeks flushed a little, betraying the compliment's impact. She busied herself again, saying something about checking the stove, but her pace had slowed, a touch gentler than before.

Annie forced down the bread, grateful for the taste of anything other than her own terror. After a while, Edith helped her sit up and unbuttoned the back of her dress to check the wounds. She pressed Annie's skin up and down her back and along the sides of her spine.

"As far as I can tell, you ain't got any broken ribs, but we should have the doctor take a look at you. Men who do this to a woman oughta have their hands chopped off. I'd gladly do the honor myself if I could." Edith softly hummed the melody to a lullaby as she dabbed the wounds with vinegar and covered them with bandages. "But the world don't work like that. So we women get by, and we help each other."

"I really appreciate your taking me in, Edith. I can pay for room and board. I have money. Our business in Pine Grove was profitable."

"Horsefeathers! You'll do no such thing, Annie. You're here because I care about you, and you need some caring in your life. Keep your money."

Over the following weeks, Edith taught Annie how to tend the chickens, how to split kindling without tearing up her palms, and how to make a poultice. Edith showed her how to measure out remedies by the pinch and the grain.

The chores were never-ending and consumed Annie's every reserve of energy, leaving her too weary to dwell on the tragedy that loomed over her thoughts like a dark storm. Each moment unoccupied by toil was an invitation for grief to rise and swallow her whole. The emptiness left by her children's absence was a cavernous void in her soul. *Will I ever see my babies again? Children should never have to grow up without their mother's love. Ethyl Francis is barely a year old. Will she remember me when she grows up? What if she forgets about me? What if we run into each other in the street years from now and she doesn't even recognize me? What if I don't recognize her, my own daughter? That must be what hell is like.*

When the unrelenting memories drew tears from her eyes without warning, Edith would sit beside her, not out of pity but solidarity, and offer only silent companionship. Edith brushed Annie's hair when the memories grew unbearable. Annie would close her eyes and imagine that Edith's gentle brushing was cleansing her of her wounds. Annie savored Edith's loving touch and the way her voice soothed her even when she wasn't paying attention to what she was saying. Occasionally Edith hummed a lullaby, as if Annie was once again a little girl. That alone would bring tears to her eyes. Annie would let her mind drift away, visiting memories of her sitting in her father's lap in their backyard, pointing out animals in the clouds and feeling the warmth of the sun's rays on her face.

Edith talked little about her own past. She said only that she'd once been a miner's wife but left him after he spent her dowry on a worthless claim and then tried to drown her in the river when she called him a fool. She had no children, but plenty of stories, most of them about the women she'd helped to bring their babies into the world, or the time she knocked a man's teeth out with a skillet for beating his pregnant wife.

* * *

After a month, Annie could walk to the nearby stream by herself, and she did so every day, letting the cold water numb the scars on her legs and arms. She learned to read the weather from the shape of the clouds and the direction of the wind.

The nights were the worst. She dreamed of her children, their faces peering out the stagecoach windows, their hands reaching for her as the stagecoach rolled away. She woke some mornings with the sheets twisted into ropes. Edith would find her, sit on the edge of the bed, and let her sob into the soft wool of her dress. She never told Annie to hush or that everything would be okay. Edith would hold her close and wait for the storm to pass.

Before long, Edith asked Annie to help with the midwifery. "You got gentle hands. Better than mine ever were. The women trust you, and you're not squeamish. You're a good soul, Annie. I can see that, plain as day."

Often Annie awakened in the middle of the night to ride with Edith to distant farms, helping women through labor, washing newborns, coaxing breath into purple mouths. She learned to tie off a cord, to cut and stitch, to clean blood from blankets and from her own hands. Sometimes, she saw men at the bedsides: fathers, brothers, husbands, and the sight of them would make her heart clench with old fear. But most of the time, it was only the women, with breathless anticipation before a new life entered the world.

Annie became known in Mountain Home and the neighboring towns as the best assistant a midwife could have. She was quick, smart, and never shied from the mess. Women sent for her even when Edith was unavailable, and sometimes Annie went alone, riding out into the night with nothing but a carpetbag and a lantern. After every birth, every life she helped deliver, Annie would sit for a while by the new mother's side, watching the rise and fall of the baby's chest, and wonder where her own children were, and whether they ever thought of her. *I would give anything to hold them again.* The sight of newborns brought back painful memories of her own, not memories of the physical pain of childbirth, but the pain of realizing she will never see them again. *These new mothers have a whole life ahead of them, nurturing their babies with love and raising up their children. I have . . . nothing.*

Annie wrote letters to her children on days she let her daydreaming take over her thoughts. Her letters were an expression of her love, and each letter brought a glimpse of happiness into her life for a brief time. She imagined each child: Anna Eliza, John Henry, Susan Margaret, John William, and especially little Ethyl Frances, opening their envelopes. Annie imagined how their faces would light up as they read the loving words from their mother. She knew she could never mail them, so she always put them in the stove and watched the paper burn until there was nothing left but ashes. She imagined the words floating into the sky, carried by the wind, finding her children wherever they might be, and settling into their hearts. Edith often saw what Annie was doing, but she never asked about the letters.

On the longest summer days, when the sun set late in the evening, Annie and Edith would sit on the back porch, feet propped on the top rail, sipping Annie's own mix of cold cider and whisky, swapping stories. Edith would tell a new one every time: a woman who birthed twins, an argument with the sheriff about a baby's name, a time the sky turned green before a hailstorm. Annie would listen, and sometimes she would relate stories of her happy times with Hazel back in Rocky Bar. They never talked about Thomas or the children.

* * *

One year passed this way. Annie grew strong. The scars faded, though they never disappeared. She learned to laugh without feeling guilty, and to sleep without waking in terror. Annie knew, deep down, that she would never stop missing her children. The ache was part of her now, woven into her soul. But she also knew that she had survived the worst, and that as long as she had work to do and women to serve, she would keep on living. She was a survivor.

One afternoon, while Annie was sitting by the open front door, she heard quite a ruckus outside. She peered out the front door only to see a large crowd in the middle of the street, yelling and hollering and cheering. *What in tarnation's going on?* She listened and tried to discern what they were yelling about. Soon they broke into a chant, "Idaho, Idaho, Idaho," on and on and on.

"Hey Edith, what's all the hullabaloo about?"

"Didn't you hear, Annie? We're a state. Idaho is a state as of July 3rd, 1890. President Harrison just signed the Idaho Statehood Act. We've been a territory for twenty-seven years, and now we're state number forty-three."

"Okay, but I have work to do. Being a state will not make my bread rise any faster."

On a balmy evening in August, as the sun relinquished its hold on the day and the stars emerged from their shrouded slumber, Annie and Edith settled on the porch that had become their haven. The air was filled with the earthy scent of dew settling on grass, a gentle reminder of nature's ceaseless cycles. They sat side by side, each lost in the rhythm of their own thoughts, when Edith reached across the space between them. Her work-worn fingers slipped into Annie's, a wordless gesture that spoke volumes more than language ever could.

"You know," Edith began, her voice carrying a weight that made it remarkable in its rare vulnerability. "You're the best thing that ever happened to me, Annie Morrow, truly." Her words hung in the air like a gentle breeze.

Annie felt an unexpected warmth flood her chest; it was a feeling she hadn't allowed herself to embrace for so long, the comfort of belonging somewhere, to someone. It drew a soft laugh from her lips, one tinged with gratitude. "You saved *my* life," she replied, her voice steady yet laden with emotion born from days too arduous to recount.

Edith let out a long sigh, and there was fondness beneath it. "We saved each other, we really did," she declared with conviction, squeezing Annie's hand with a strength that belied her years.

Annie looked over at Edith. "You saved *me* more than I saved *you*, Edith."

"*Not so*, my dear. I never told you about what happened a few weeks before you showed up at my front door." She bowed her head and stared at her shoes. "Listen to me. A baby died because of me. I'm a midwife. I should've known better. Claire from Glenns Ferry came all the way here to have me deliver her first child. The labor went on for hours, and Claire was in agony. I gave her some concoction from the doctor to help with the pain. It was laudanum. I knew what it was, but I had never used it before on a woman in labor. It's a mixture of opium and alcohol. Her pain subsided, but so did the contractions. They stopped, but then they started up again. Finally, she pushed the baby out, but it wasn't crying. I cut the cord and slapped it a few times, but it lay there limp in my arms. I couldn't get it to breathe. Claire howled at me like a banshee. It was the most bone-chilling scream I've ever heard. I tried everything, but the baby was gone, stillborn. I put the baby on Claire's chest and stroked her hair, trying to calm her down. I didn't know what to do. I felt so helpless. I failed her. I, as a midwife, failed this mother. Pray to God, Annie, that you never have to hold a dead baby in your arms. I found out later that the dosage the doctor gave me was ten times stronger than what was safe. I should have double-checked it. When I read the dosage on the bottle, I thought it was strange to give such a large amount, but I gave it to Claire anyway. I have to live with that for the rest of my days, Annie. Until you came along, my dear, I was going to give up being a midwife. I figured I was incompetent. I was a baby killer. That's the worse fate that a midwife could ever have. You gave me a reason to continue after I had made the biggest blunder of my life. You were someone I could care for, nourish, and heal. You showed me that I can still help another human being. That's how *you* saved *me*, my dear Annie. I can never thank you enough. Do you understand what I'm saying, Annie? If you hadn't shown up on my doorstep half dead, I don't know what would have become of me."

Annie leaned over and put her arm around Edith and rested her head on her shoulder. "You're a remarkable woman, Edith, and I'll always remember what you did for me."

They sat in silence for a while, listening to the wind in the trees. Annie looked up at the stars and wondered what her children were doing, and whether they were looking at the same stars. *I hope they remember how I smiled at them and how I sang to them as I put them to bed. I surely hope so. I miss my children. But for now, I hope this will be enough. I am alive. I have a friend. I have a future.* And for the first time in a long time, fear no longer had a place in her mind.

Chapter 16

Annie continued to assist Edith in her duties. She did not want to become a midwife, even though Edith offered to train her. She learned the importance of empathy and how to make someone feel hopeful when they were discouraged, and how to help women handle pain. Learning to care for and serve another human being was invaluable. Understanding what a person needs while they are suffering and providing it to the best of her ability was something she enjoyed. When not assisting Edith with her patients, there was plenty of cooking, cleaning, and organizing to be done around the house. After a few months, Annie found a one-dollar gold eagle on the table next to her bed. If Edith had given it to her directly, Annie would have refused. She did not need to be paid. Annie considered Edith to be the mother she never had.

It was honest work. Most nights, she fell into bed so tired she didn't even dream. When she did, it was often the same. She found herself on a road out in the desert. She knew it was the road that led to Mountain Home, and when she walked, her feet would sink into the ground. She could keep walking, but with each step, her feet sank deeper and deeper into the ground, eventually forcing her to crawl with tremendous effort. In the mornings, she would go down to the stream and wash her face with cold water so she could get those images out of her mind.

Occasionally, Edith made Annie take days off and sent her to the market in town or out to the hills to gather willow bark and camas root. "You got to let the world remind you who you are, every so often," Edith would say, shooing her away with a slap of a dishtowel. "Else you end up like these other women who think the most important thing in life is the size of their bustle. You got to make something of yourself, Annie. Figure out what you really want."

Excellent question. What do I want? It's not a husband. That was a disaster. I want children. I have children out there somewhere. I have a friend, Edith, and then there's Hazel back in Rocky Bar. It's good to have friends, people who you can trust. I wonder how Hazel is doing these days. What else do I want? To be somebody, to have a purpose, to work at something meaningful, to serve, to be in control of my life, and not beholden to any man. That's what I want. What about love? Everybody wants love, but not everybody gets to have it. I tried with Thomas. I love my children, but if I never get to see them, what good is it? I can't love memories, and that's all my children are to me now.

On the days when Annie's workload was light, she would walk out past the edge of Mountain Home, following the narrow wagon tracks as they snaked east toward Glenns Ferry. She thought about her children every time a stagecoach passed by her, and wondered if Anna Eliza still slept with her hands tucked under her chin, or if John William had stopped biting his nails. It hurt to think of them, but Annie learned not to look away from that pain. Edith said that healing was like lancing a boil: if you didn't face it straight on, it festered.

The idea of going back to Rocky Bar started as a joke. One night after too much homemade blackberry wine, Edith told stories about Idaho's boomtowns, gold rushes, and the time she held a two-ounce gold nugget in her hand. Annie laughed and said she ought to go stake a claim of her own, now that she was free of Thomas. Edith chuckled. "You'd last a day in Rocky Bar before you owned the place," she said, wagging her spoon. "Hell, you could run your own shop—or a saloon—or a restaurant—or even a school, if they'd let you."

School, nope. Everyone in Rocky Bar knows I was illiterate until I was *ten. Saloon, maybe. I like to have a few now and then. Restaurant, yeah.* *Now there's something I could do. Everybody's gotta eat.* Over the following weeks, Annie sketched plans in the margins of her blue book: how she'd run a real kitchen, one that never ran out of steak, bread, or coffee; how she'd treat every man and woman who walked through the door with the respect that she never got.

"Like your restaurant idea the best. I know how to deal with suppliers, I know bookkeeping, I can cook, and I enjoy working with people. I would serve beef, pork, lamb, venison, chicken—the kinds of meat that real men will pay good money for. I could even serve Rocky Mountain Oysters. You know what those are?"

"Never tried one. Aren't those the part of the bull that dangles between its hind legs? That does not appeal to me."

"That's what they are, all right. They're edible if you cook 'em right. Some men consider them aphrodisiacs. It's about supply and demand. If there's a demand, I will supply." She chewed on the end of her pencil. It cracked, causing her to spit out a tiny wooden sliver. She resumed chewing it. "I would have to come up with a catchy name. Any ideas?"

"How about Annie's Kitchen?"

"That might work if I was famous, but I'm not. Not yet anyway."

"How about Boise Basin Beanery?"

"Nope. Sounds cheap."

Edith scratched her chin. "Grubstake Griddle?"

"Now you're talking."

"Tieton Trail Trough?"

"I'm not feeding cattle."

"Sourdough Sally's?"

"Sourdough baking in the oven has a savory aroma. Everyone likes fresh sourdough bread. Sourdough Sally's . . . ."

"Okay, Annie, I'll keep thinking."

"Thanks."

She thought of the money she had saved from her years in Pine Grove, and every twenty-dollar gold eagle now hidden at the bottom of her sewing box and the several one-hundred-dollar bills underneath them. She made a list of supplies she would need to start a restaurant and added new items every time inspiration struck.

One night, as the snow melted into rivulets outside the cabin and the last log burned low in the stove, Annie caught herself staring into the embers for a long time, poking at them with a skinny pine branch. Edith was darning socks, feet propped on a stool.

"If I left," Annie said while gazing into the flames, "would you be okay on your own?"

Edith glanced over at her. "I survived before you; I'll survive after. But if you're asking would I miss you, the answer is absolutely yes." She finished the row of stitches, then set the sock down and looked at Annie square in the face. "Don't stay here on account of me. I'll be fine." Edith stared into the fire for a few minutes. "How old are you?"

"Thirty-two."

"You're a beautiful young woman, Annie. But it's what's on the inside that counts: moral character, and you got it. You have your whole life ahead of you. Like I told you the other day, figure out what you really want. Decide what you want to do with your life. It's a balance between what you want to do and what you're good at doing. They're not always the same. Don't let the past haunt you. Go to Rocky Bar and start fresh. You have my blessing. I believe in you."

Annie was taken aback. "You believe in me? Nobody has ever said that to me before."

"Listen to me, Annie. You've been through the mill. You've had more hurt and pain in your life than anyone I know, and you came through it. Give yourself credit. A lot of folks would have hearts filled with anger, resentment, and hate if they had gone through what you did. I see nothing like that in you. Do you know what I see when I look at you?"

"No."

"A gracious, kind, and generous woman with a heart full of compassion and empathy. That's a rare thing in these parts. That will take you far in this life, Annie, whatever you decide to do. I'll say it again, I believe in you, but you gotta believe in yourself too."

Annie took a deep breath and turned her gaze towards Edith. "Thank you, Edith. It truly moves my heart to hear you say that."

"One more thing, Annie."

"What?"

"Based on what you've told me about her, I bet Hazel would love to see you again."

The image of Annie's wedding popped into her head. Once again she saw Hazel sitting in the back row of the room, smiling at her. Hazel was always there to support her, no matter what. *Hazel is (or was?) my best friend. Either way, I sorely miss her. What would she do if I just showed up on her doorstep one day, unexpectedly? I'm sure she would remember me, of course, after all, we've written each other a few times. Still, I think that would quite a surprise for her. We haven't seen each other in what, fifteen years? I'm not the same person that I was when I left Rocky Bar. Edith is right, I've been through hell, but I survived. Why shouldn't I go back home to Rocky Bar? I'm sure many people would be shocked at my return. And then there's Meng Yao. She may have perished by now. What a sad story. If I go back to Rocky Bar, it won't all be happy reunions.*

* * *

After finishing their coffee the next morning, Annie made the decision to move back to Rocky Bar. She packed what little she owned into a satchel: three dresses, a petticoat, an extra pair of shoes, a bunch of knick-knacks, the blue book with her recipes, and the sewing box with her savings. She wrote a brief letter to George explaining her plans in case he ever came looking for her. She told Edith she'd write as soon as she arrived in Rocky Bar.

The journey to Rocky Bar traversed a toll road. Each time the driver stopped to pay the fees at the tollgates, Annie peered out the coach window at the men sitting on the benches. She knew Thomas couldn't be one of them, but it worried her just the same.

About two-thirds of the way through the trip, the route passed through Pine Grove. *As far as I know, Thomas and the children still live here. I wonder if I could be lucky enough to get a glimpse of them walking down the street. I would give anything just to see them for even a moment. Thomas could be walking down the street, too. If he saw me, he would know that I'm going back to Rocky Bar. I can't let that happen. I could look out the window for my children, or I could hide so Thomas couldn't see me. Should I risk it? Thomas be damned.* She pulled aside the leather shade and scanned the people walking about, but her children were nowhere to be seen. Annie sat back in her seat, closed her eyes, and let out a long sigh.

The wagon road continued to Featherville, and was mostly flat, as it followed the course of the South Fork of the Boise River. Once the stagecoach passed through Featherville, the road climbed up into the mountains. The route was still rough and unmaintained, just as Annie remembered it from her stagecoach journey with Thomas from Rocky Bar to Boise City years ago.

When the stagecoach rounded the last bend, Rocky Bar appeared in front of her, smaller than Annie remembered, as if the buildings had sunk into the ground. Several of the older log cabins had collapsed, and a few others looked abandoned. It looked like the Alturas Hotel was still operating, as were the Newcomer House and the Hoffman House. A few miners wandered down Rocky Bar Road, heads bent, eyes squinting against the glare as they passed by. It was a different place, but it still felt like home.

The driver let her off at the edge of town in front of the Willow House. "If you need work, ask for Mrs. Dunkle," he said. "She's always got something for a woman who ain't afraid to earn her keep."

Annie shouldered her satchel and stood for a long time, watching the street. She felt a strange mix of dread and pride. She was a different person now. Her eyes swept the faces of everyone she passed, looking for any sign of recognition. There were none. She passed by Rocky Bar Mercantile, where she had first seen Thomas walking along the street on that hot

August afternoon. She remembered how giddy he made her feel, and the sweet talk he lavished on her on the banks of Beaver Creek and in the abandoned stamp mill. That felt like a lifetime ago.

Rocky Bar had aged poorly, and so had most of its people. During Annie's first day in town, she took a slow walk down and back up Rocky Bar Road. She saw more vacant lots than she remembered.

She stopped in front of the Rocky Bar Mercantile, expecting to see Mrs. MacGregor still bustling behind the counter. A much younger woman, thin with a baby tied to her chest, manned the cash register. Annie stood outside, thinking she might go in and say hello, but the woman stared at her through the open doorway, uninterested, so Annie drifted on.

At the post office, she inquired about her mother. "Haven't seen her in a decade or more," said the postmaster, a crotchety old man who had the habit of scratching at a scab on his neck. "Last I heard, she was in Boise City, married to somebody named William Floyd, but that was years ago."

"And James Roberts?" Annie asked, bracing for the answer.

The man frowned. "That ne'er-do-well was gone not too long after you disappeared. Up and left your mother in the middle of the night, from what I heard. Where to, I don't know and I don't care. I never liked the rascal. Seemed like he was forever scheming about something. He never came back, and good riddance."

I didn't disappear. I was taken! Stolen. Against my will. I never wanted to leave. Annie nodded. The news did not surprise her. She thanked the man, who went back to sorting mail as if their conversation had never happened.

She found her old house easily enough. The house had been painted a sun-blistered blue, and the yard, not more than a patch of weeds in her childhood, was now crowded with chicken wire and a pair of rabbit hutches. Annie lingered at the edge of the yard, staring at the bedroom window that used to be hers. *I wonder who sleeps there now. I hope their family dinners are better than mine were. That's one thing I don't miss about this place.*

A young boy burst out of the front door, letting it slam on its hinges. He saw Annie and froze, a loaf of bread clutched to his chest.

Annie called out, sounding as cheerful as possible, "Hello."

The boy narrowed his eyes, then called over his shoulder, "Ma! There's a lady out here."

A woman appeared in the doorway, her hair frizzed, and cheeks flushed with heat. She wiped her hands on her skirt and gave Annie a look of curiosity. "Help you?" she asked.

"No, ma'am," Annie said. "Just . . . passing through. Used to live here."

The woman shrugged. "Lots of folks used to live here. You want the boys; they're out yonder that away," she said as she pointed down the road.

Annie shook her head. "No, thank you."

Annie turned away, her shoulders tightening as if bracing against a sudden gust, though the air hung still. She walked faster than before, her shoes crunching over packed earth. She could feel the weight of the woman's eyes lingering between her shoulder blades until she rounded the bend in the road and the house slipped from view behind the pines.

She followed the winding road to where it dipped closer to Beaver Creek. The faint chatter of water reached her first, a soft, familiar rushing that smoothed the edge off her thoughts. The scent of damp earth and sun-warmed mud floated on the breeze, mingling with the scent of pine needles covering the ground. Weeds and tall grass had overgrown the short trail down to the creek. They brushed against her dress as she pushed through, snagging a thread here and there. She swept them aside with the back of her hand.

Standing at the water's edge, she paused and let the soft gurgling of Beaver Creek fill her senses. She remembered how she and Hazel used to come racing down this trail barefoot, shrieking with laughter as mud squished up between their toes. Hazel always ran faster, her braids flying behind her like little blond whips, but she would slow down at the last second so they could leap onto the old log at the same time. Annie could still feel Hazel's hand grabbing hers—warm, calloused from chores, tugging her forward with youthful enthusiasm.

120

The creek shimmered in the afternoon light, rippling gold and slate. And there, rotting away, lay the old moss-covered log, once their throne, their secret lookout, their summer haven. A whole section had collapsed inward, wood puckered and blackened with decay, but part of it still held firm.

Annie stepped onto it carefully, testing it with her weight. A soft groan of old wood answered, but it held. She eased herself down, tucking her dress beneath her, and pulled her feet up onto the log. Drawing her knees to her chest, she wrapped her arms around her shins, her chin resting on her knees. A warm breeze drifted past, carrying the smell of the clean creek water and the faint sweetness of wildflowers. Annie closed her eyes and let the memories come flooding in.

They used to sit side by side, their thighs pressed together for balance, sharing everything they'd scavenged that day: a handful of berries, a shiny pebble, a feather striped in charcoal and cream. Hazel acted as though each treasure was a marvel, her eyes widening, her grin spilling over. Finding a smooth pebble, Hazel would rub it between her fingers and say, *"this one has a good feel to it,"* and that was enough to make Annie believe it too.

On hot days, they'd dunk their feet in the creek, kicking until droplets sparkled in the sun like tiny diamonds. Hazel liked to hum a tune her grandmother taught her, and Annie would hum along because neither of them knew the words. It was something about Mary's little lamb. She would nudge Annie with her shoulder and say, *"You have such a beautiful voice, Annie. You could grow up and be a singer. And because you're so pretty."*

Annie could still taste the huckleberries they used to pick on the hill above the waterline. She savored their perfect blend of sweet and tart flavors. Hazel insisted they should save some for supper, but she usually ended up eating most of hers before they made it home, reddish-blue juice dripping from her chin and fingers. The two of them would sprawl in the grass, sunlight warming their faces while they exchanged grand plans— how they'd build a raft and float all the way to the ocean, or how they'd live in a cabin together someday with a pet raccoon that Hazel swore she could train to gather acorns.

She imagined hearing Hazel's laugh—bright, bubbling, rolling over the murmur of the creek. In her mind's eye, she saw the two of them sitting right here, legs dangling, bumping shoulders whenever one made the other giggle too hard. They would talk about everything and nothing, hour after hour, until their mothers' calls drifted through the trees and broke the spell.

Even their quieter moments glowed in Annie's memory. The two of them sitting back-to-back, staring at the sky through the branches of the pine trees. Hazel enjoyed pointing out shapes in the clouds, finding creatures where Annie only saw smudges of white. A prancing elk. A sleeping cat. Once, Hazel insisted she spotted a dragon, and Annie pretended she saw it too, just to keep Hazel's delight alive.

Annie blinked, her throat tightening as the memory melted away into the present sound of the creek. Those days felt like a lifetime ago. But for a moment, sitting on this old log, she could almost reach out and feel Hazel's arm looped through hers, and hear her whisper, *"We'll always be best friends, no matter what. I promise." Hazel was the best thing that ever happened to me. When I told her my secrets, she never judged or criticized. I should find her tomorrow. I hope she still lives here. Her last letter was some time ago.*

She considered, as she listened to the water gurgling over the stones, what she expected to happen in Rocky Bar. Perhaps she needed to prove to herself that she was still Annie Morrow, that she was a survivor, that she never gave up, no matter what happened to her. *Life in Boise City was a living hell, but I survived. I made it back here. Maybe I can prove to myself that I'm somebody, that I got what it takes to make something of myself. I should start a business, a restaurant maybe. Watch out, Rocky Bar, Annie Morrow is back!*

She lingered beside the creek for hours, lost in thought. When the sun dropped behind the ridge and took its warmth with it, she strolled back into town. Annie found the Willow House without trouble. Mrs. Dunkle, red-haired, heavy-set, and loud as a storm, gave her a room on the second floor for a week's rent in advance. "You got family here?" Mrs. Dunkle asked.

"Not anymore." *You don't know who I am? I don't remember you either.* She carried her satchel up the narrow stairs of the boarding house, the wood creaking beneath her steps.

Her room was small, but the bed was clean, and a pitcher of water had been placed on the stand. She set her things down, took off her shoes, and lay back on the quilt with her arms folded behind her head. A boarding house. Everyone knows what that means. Sure, there are some actual boarders, some locals, some out-of-towners, but the rooms in the back serve another purpose. Most boarding houses and saloons in mining camps were like this. The townsfolk didn't like to use the word *prostitute*. Instead, they called them *soiled doves, fallen angels, scarlet ladies, sporting women,* or *upstairs girls.*

Annie sat on the edge of the bed, grappling with a tangle of thoughts that pulled her in conflicting directions. The idea of Mrs. Dunkle operating a boarding house with hidden undertones was unsettling to her core, but she felt an odd sense of acceptance seep into her bones. Laws were more like suggestions, a set of rules that bent and twisted as the circumstances required. Law enforcement operated with a lackadaisical attitude as long as the right pockets were lined at the right times. Women were scarce and men's desires abundant, so there was money to be made.

Annie studied the patterns in the ceiling, pondering over how lonely the miners must feel, their nights cold and hollow without companionship. A thought came to her as if whispered from somewhere deep within. *Were these girls not another way to provide what men need?* Yet, beneath this rationalization lay a deeper discomfort, a recognition of the desperation that fueled such transactions. It was something she would neither condone nor condemn.

Yet despite this internal conflict, Annie saw an opportunity in the shadows of moral ambiguity. A business opportunity indeed, a chance to make her mark in Rocky Bar beyond any past reputation that lingered. Women in mining towns had limited opportunities. *I can't deny Mrs. Dunkle's tenacity and shrewdness in running the boarding house. I'm sure she's had to deal with the scornful looks from self-righteous womenfolk. If*

Mrs. Dunkle thought it acceptable to manage such an establishment under uncertain legality, who am I to pass judgement? Perhaps this was precisely what Rocky Bar needed: someone who could walk the fine line between practicality and principle. I could do that.

Still sitting on the bed, she shifted her gaze around the small room, her mind weighing options while seeking clarity amidst confusion. Outside, the sounds of Rocky Bar drifted up through the open window: a pair of men arguing in the street, the metallic clatter of an iron pot in somebody's kitchen, horses protesting their bridles, and the wild laughter of children running somewhere in the twilight. Annie listened, letting the sounds fill up the space inside her that had been empty for so long. She could start over here, in the ruins of her old life, and she'd do it on her own terms. Edith's words popped into her head: *I believe in you, but got you believe in yourself.*

Chapter 17

Annie spent her second morning in Rocky Bar walking the length of town a second time, looking for familiar faces.

"Is that you?" a low-pitched female voice called out from behind her. "Is that you, Annie Morrow?"

She whirled around. "Mrs. MacGregor?"

"Heavens to Betsy! It is you!" She marched over to Annie and gave a big bear hug. "Dear me, I thought I'd never see you again. Look at you! When you left, you were just a girl, and now . . . now you're a full-grown woman, as pretty as ever. What brings you back to this dust-bucket of a town? It ain't what it used to be."

"It's a long story. I'll tell you about it another time."

"Fiddlesticks!" Mrs. MacGregor said briskly as she grabbed Annie's hand. "Come along."

They walked over to the porch of a boarded-up business and sat next to each other on the bench.

Annie folded her hands in her lap, her fingers intertwined. "I didn't plan to run into you," she said softly. "I thought—well, I thought perhaps you'd be moved away by now."

"And miss seeing you walk back into Rocky Bar?" Mrs. MacGregor snorted. "Not likely. Now start talking."

Annie drew a breath. "I never wanted to leave, but Thomas insisted. He always got his way. He wasn't the man he pretended to be," Annie said at last. "Not after the wedding. It got worse over the years, the abuse, I mean."

Mrs. MacGregor's mouth tightened. "But you stayed."

"I stayed for my children, until I couldn't bear it any longer." Annie said, her voice barely audible. "I stayed because I was trapped. Afraid of what he'd do if I ran. Afraid of what he'd do if I stayed."

"How did you get away?" Mrs. MacGregor asked finally.

Annie stared at the mountains off in the distance. "He was on a business trip to Boise City. I hired a stage to take me and the children in the middle of the night to my brother George's house in Mountain Home."

"And?" Mrs. MacGregor prompted.

Annie looked down at her hands. Her fingers tightened into fists. "He caught up with us . . . and . . . ."

"The children?" A look of pain swept across Mrs. MacGregor's face. "Stop, Annie. I know the look of a mother's grief when I see it. No need to talk about it now. Some other time."

Mrs. MacGregor studied her for a long moment, then nodded. "You were a good worker," she said, "and a decent girl. Whatever you had to do to survive is between you and the Lord. The rest of us can mind our own business."

Annie let out a shaky breath she hadn't realized she was holding. "Thank you."

Mrs. MacGregor stood, peering out at the dusty street. "Rocky Bar isn't what it was," she said, echoing her earlier words. "But it still remembers its own. You'll have to answer questions, Annie Morrow. Some kind. Some not. Just remember—you don't owe anybody an explanation."

Annie sat in silence and watched a freight wagon rumble down the road, raising a dust cloud as it rolled by.

"Boise City is so different from Rocky Bar. I could never get used to city life. Everything about it was so hurried and fast-paced. It feels good to be back home." Annie finally relaxed and leaned back against the wall.

"Do you have a place to stay? You'd be more than welcome at my house."

"That's very kind of you, but I'm staying over at the Willow House."

"That place? With Mrs. Dunkle? Watch yourself, Annie. People talk about what goes on in there, and it ain't good. Steer clear of those people."

"I appreciate your concern, but I can take care of myself. It was nice to see you again, Mrs. MacGregor. You look as happy and healthy as ever."

"Liar. *You're* the one who's blossomed into a beautiful woman. I'm just . . . getting old."

"Don't be so hard on yourself. We all get old, in our own time."

"You're a dear soul, Annie. Don't let anyone take that away from you."

"I promise."

Annie rose and walked back out into the street and wandered by the post office again and noticed some papers on the bench outside. It was the *Elmore Bulletin*. She flipped through a few pages until a small ad caught her eye. She mouthed the words to herself.

Elmore Restaurant

Rocky Bar, Idaho

Mrs. Shaffer & Co. Props

Now Open

Good Meals at All Hours

Fine Lunches a Specialty

Everything Neat and Clean

And Well Cooked

Give the Ladies a Call

Ice Cream Every Sunday

Below that was an ad for a barbershop, J. A. Brookfield, Prop., opposite the Alturas Hotel. *Don't need a haircut, but I'll have to introduce myself to this Mrs. Shaffer. Gotta make myself known.*

The next two people she encountered on the street shook their heads when she asked if they knew where Hazel lived. The third, a boy with a runny nose, barefoot, and a slingshot in his back pocket, knew at once who she meant.

"Hazel Jackson? She lives over near the old schoolhouse. The house with a tall chimney. Got two brats and a husband who limps, but she's all right."

Annie thanked him and made her way up the hill, her shoes kicking up dust with every step. *That hasn't changed. I wonder what Hazel will think of me now. I hope she got a decent man for a husband. I don't remember any Jacksons in town.* Her mind was a mix of nervousness and anticipation.

She found the house with the tall chimney, heard children laughing, someone calling for a dog, and a woman singing to herself. Hazel was in the yard, bent over a wooden washtub, wrestling a wet sheet into submission. Her sleeves were rolled up to her elbows, and her sun-tanned arms moved with the rhythm of someone who'd done this a thousand times. Her hair was still that beautiful blonde, but now it was in an elegant updo. She was older, and her figure had a fullness. A woman had taken root in the former teenager.

When she looked up and saw Annie standing at the edge of the yard, she froze. Her eyes went wide, and the color drained from her face, then flooded back in a rush.

Annie stood still at the gate, her hand resting on the top rail. Her tongue felt like wood behind her teeth. Hazel moved first, letting the sheet fall onto the grass, marched straight to the gate, and threw it open.

"Is it really you?" Hazel whispered, and in it Annie heard the old music, the laughter in the schoolyard, secrets in the dark.

Annie nodded, swallowing hard. Her voice was fragile but steady. "It's me. It's really me."

And that was all it took. Hazel closed the distance in two strides and pulled her into a fierce, desperate hug. They clung to each other as Annie buried her face in Hazel's shoulder.

Hazel's arms trembled, and Annie felt the way her hands gripped and loosened and gripped again, as if she couldn't believe she wasn't dreaming. Annie clutched her just as hard, squeezing her with all her might. They weren't quite crying, but tears shimmered in their eyes.

"Fifteen years, Annie. It's been fifteen years!" They stared into each other's eyes for the longest time.

"I heard you ran away from Thomas in the middle of the night," Hazel said, her voice was roughened by emotion. "And then I heard you were dead. That broke my heart. I missed you so much! You were the best friend I ever had. Losing someone you love is the worst thing ever. I mourned you, Annie."

Annie leaned back, their hands still clasped between them. "I mourned myself, too," she said, her voice thick. "I almost disappeared from the face of the Earth."

Hazel smiled then, eyes bright with tears. "Well, you're here now. And I swear, if you disappear again, Annie Morrow, I'll chase after you to the ends of the Earth."

Annie smiled. "I'm not going anywhere. Not this time." They stood there face to face, not speaking a word. Instead, they savored each passing moment, as if they satisfied a lifetime of hunger right then and there.

Hazel broke the silence. "Come in and have some tea and meet my little ones, Benjamin and Alma."

Hazel's children, a boy of five and a girl three, were wild and curious, more interested in Annie's high-lace shoes and the strange accent that had crept into her voice than in any of the grown-up stories she and Hazel told each other.

"You look older, but not old," Hazel said, as they cleared the dishes together. "You look like a woman who's done some living. Fifteen years. I can't believe it. That's an awfully long time, Annie." Hazel reached over and tucked a stray hair behind Annie's ear, just as she used to when they were girls.

"We lived in Boise City for eleven years and then Pine Grove for three years. After I left Thomas, I spent a year in Mountain Home. I'll tell you about it someday."

"You left him?'

"I had to."

"I see. We'll have plenty of time to talk now that you're back. Can I show you something interesting?"

"Sure."

Hazel grabbed Annie by the hand and led her over to the back wall of the kitchen. "We got one of those newfangled telephones. The line from Mountain Home came through to Rocky Bar a couple of years ago. It's much more convenient than using the telegraph. Is there anyone you would like to call? All you do is pick up this thingy here and tell the operator who you want to talk to, and then they connect you. It's easy."

"I'd love to call my—" She couldn't say the word children. Her heart grew heavy in an instant, and her chest tightened. Tears came, and she wiped her eyes and regained her composure. *Calling my children is impossible. Thomas would pick up the phone and hang up the second I spoke. I'd give anything to talk to my babies again.* Annie closed her eyes, stood motionless, and let out a long sigh.

"It's okay," Hazel said softly as she put her hand on Annie's shoulder. "Don't speak of it now."

The rest of the afternoon, they walked through town, stopped at two different restaurants for apple pie, and talked about the old days and the new one. They strolled down to the Beaver Creek, where they used to race sticks and invent stories about where the water went once it left town. They found what was left of the old moss-covered log and seated themselves side by side.

"Do you ever wonder if it was a mistake, leaving Rocky Bar?" The silence was interrupted by the tapping of a woodpecker high above them in a tall aspen tree.

Annie pondered the question and allowed her gaze to wander over the hills and mountains covered with pine trees. Their scent brought back memories of the two of them sitting there for hours on end, giggling and poking each other after telling dumb jokes. She took a moment and let the silence settle between. "I had no choice," she began, looking down into the water, her voice carrying both the weight of reminiscence and an undercurrent of determination. "I couldn't say no to him. I tried. Believe me, I tried."

Her voice grew steadier as she spoke more about her past. "It wasn't a mistake," though now there was a steeliness that hadn't been there before, a fierce resolve against any shadow of doubt. "But it certainly wasn't what I'd imagined it would be. I was just a teenager in love, too stupid to know any better." She chuckled, shaking her head at the younger version of herself, who had clung so tightly to Thomas. "You warned me about him. I should have listened to you. You were right. Now I feel like an idiot."

"You're no idiot. You were in love. People in love do crazy things. Don't beat yourself up about it. It's ancient history. You're here now, with me, just like it used to be." Hazel reached over and gave Annie's hands a gentle squeeze.

"That's the thing, Hazel. We're not children anymore. We both got married and have children. You have a family; I don't. You have something that I'll never have."

"Oh, Annie, I'm sorry. I shouldn't have said that."

They both grew silent, with only the sound of the water trickling over the rocks.

"You'll always have me, Annie."

Annie thought about that and took a deep breath of the refreshing mountain air. "Thomas had this way about him," she continued, each word dropping like a stone into a pond, sending ripples through her memory. "He acted as if he owned every part of me, like I was some prize he'd won and could do to me whatever he wanted." Annie swallowed, the bitterness still fresh on her tongue despite the years that had passed. "I couldn't take it anymore, Hazel. Staying would have been the death of me. After I escaped, I ended up staying in Mountain Home with a friend of my brother George. She was a midwife named Edith, one of the most amazing people

I've ever known. One day, we were jabbering on the back porch and the idea came up of me going back to Rocky Bar. That's how I ended up here again."

"What about your children, Annie?"

Annie froze. She opened her mouth to say something. She choked. A tear rolled down her cheek, which she wiped away. "I . . . uh . . . I'm sorry . . . I can't."

"That's okay. You don't have to say anything. Sit here and relax. Breathe. Take a deep breath. That's right. Do that a few more times. Inhale. Exhale. Don't think about anything right now. I'll take care of you, sweetie."

Turning toward Hazel, she allowed vulnerability to seep into her eyes like mist creeping into a valley at dawn. "I missed you so much, Hazel," she confessed, emotions welling up as she extended her arms wide open. They embraced once more beside the creek. The familiarity and warmth wrapped around them like a soft wool blanket.

"Welcome home, Annie."

Chapter 18

The next few weeks fell into a comfortable rhythm. Annie spent her mornings working at the Willow House and had most afternoons free. She and Mrs. Dunkle worked out an agreement in which Annie could stay without paying rent in return for doing chores and handling the bookkeeping. In the afternoons, she would cross town to Hazel's place, where Benjamin and Alma greeted her with shouts and a fresh tangle of questions. Sometimes Hazel would rope her into canning pickles or patching the roof, and sometimes they'd sit on the front porch, feet bare, sharing stories and secrets with a familiarity that felt almost holy. Annie's favorite time was when they lingered on the steps until dusk and the fireflies came out. She loved to watch them dance in and out of the bushes like tiny fairies.

They talked about everything: the pain, the losses, the men they'd loved and hated. Annie told Hazel about Edith's story and how they saved each other's lives. She spoke little about her children, or about Thomas, except in the vaguest terms. She knew Hazel understood and would not press for reciting details that hurt more than they helped.

For the first time since coming back, Annie felt the weight of the past loosening its grip. She could laugh again without feeling the echo of fear in her soul. She could sleep without nightmares, knowing that in the morning she could walk over to Hazel's, where there would be coffee, the sound of children in the yard, and her best friend who knew her down to her bones.

One evening, as the sky went pink and the men wandered out from the mines, Hazel walked Annie to the Willow House. They looked up at the old two-story building. The board-and-batten walls were a sun-bleached grey. They sat down side by side on the bench next to the front door. "You shouldn't stay here. You could stay at my place if you wanted. There's always room for another woman who knows how to cook and keep the peace."

"I appreciate that, but I'm okay here. Wanna know a little secret?"

"What?"

"Someday I'm going to own it. The Willow House is going to be mine."

"What?" Hazel jerked her head and looked Annie in the eyes. "I don't think that's a good idea. You know what goes on here. You can do anything if you put your mind to it, so why this place?"

"It's only a thought. We'll see what happens."

They smiled at each other as Hazel placed her hand on the back of Annie's neck and massaged it for a few minutes. "Turn around. Let me work on your shoulders." Hazel placed both hands on Annie's shoulders and massaged them with a steady rhythm. "Your muscles are so tight. Relax." She worked her way down Annie's arms and back.

Annie let her shoulders drop and her arms go limp. "That feels so good, Hazel. I'll give you an hour to stop."

They watched the sun setting over a mountain ridge. *This is where I need to be, and who I need to be with. I wish I could sit here with you forever, Hazel.*

* * *

A few days later, on a bright sunny morning, Annie knocked on Hazel's door as had become a regular habit.

"Mornin' Annie, come on in, I've got something to show you."

"What? Another one of those fancy telephone things?"

"No, this is much better. Here, have a seat at the table and I'll make us some tea."

Hazel placed the kettle on the stove and disappeared into the back room. After a few minutes, it whistled while she was still absent, so Annie got the kettle and poured the water into the teapot. Next to the teapot, Hazel had placed a square tin of tea. It had red lettering on a yellow background. She picked up the tin and read the label out loud, "Lipton Black Tea. Known All over the World for its Supreme Quality. Orange Pekoe & Pekoe." It had a picture of an English-looking gentleman with a white moustache wearing a ship captain's hat. She said with a chuckle, "Mr. Lipton, I presume?"

She popped off the lid, poured a small amount into the strainer in the teapot, and let it steep.

Hazel returned to the kitchen with a gleam in her eyes and a sly smile, holding a small piece of paper folded in half. "I see you found Mr. Lipton's Tea. It's grown in his own tea gardens in Ceylon."

"That so? Must be good, then."

"Best I've ever had. If the English know one thing, it's how to make tea."

Hazel walked over to the cupboard above the stove and picked up two small ceramic dishes. She set one down in front of Annie and set the other one by her chair. "I made some huckleberry tarts yesterday after you left. Remember how we used to pick huckleberries when we were children?"

Annie sighed, the sound long and weighted. "Those were such wonderful times." She traced a small crack in the dish's glaze with her fingertip. "We didn't know how good we had it. No husbands to answer to. No children to worry over. Just the hills and the Beaver Creek and the lazy summer days."

Annie lifted her eyes, meeting Hazel's across the table. There was gratitude there. "I used to think of those days when things got hard. It helped me get through the bad times," she admitted.

Hazel reached over to the counter, where a half dozen tarts were arranged in a circle on a big plate. She picked up one and placed it on Annie's dish, and then one on her own. "Don't mind my fingers."

"There's nothing wrong with your fingers."

Hazel glanced down at her fingers. One had a smudge of huckleberry juice on it. She licked it off, and smiled at Annie. "You're so sweet."

After they both ate several tarts, Hazel placed her elbows on the table, resting her chin on her interlaced fingers, and peered into Annie's eyes. She cleared her throat and shifted her weight in the chair. She cleared her throat a second time and wiped away a few loose strands of hair from her forehead. "When your letters stopped coming, I feared the worst for you, Annie. Not knowing what happened to you was worse than getting bad news. I used to lie awake at night, so worried about you. Sometimes I couldn't get to sleep for hours. It was awful. I cared about you more than anyone. Life without you was not the same."

She let the words sink in. "So, I wrote a poem about you—well, actually, it was *to* you, more than *about* you. I imagined the day when I would see you again. Would you like to hear it?"

"Of course." Annie shifted in her chair, a little nervous.

"Okay. I feel a little embarrassed. Here goes. I hope you like it." She took a sip from her teacup and cleared her throat again.

My Annie
By Hazel Jackson

The day you left, a brand-new bride,
A dusty road, your groom beside.
I waved until you disappeared,
And let loose the tears I feared.

Your laughter lingers in my mind,
A song the years can't leave behind.
We shared the whispers, dreams, and schemes,
And stitched our hearts with golden seams.

We shared every secret, each dream, every fear,
In the warmth of your presence, the world felt so near.
You married, you moved to a faraway place,

Leaving echoes of joy in this now-empty space.

Oh, Annie, my friend, how I miss your sweet grace,
The sparkle in your eyes, the warmth of your face.
But still I keep a place for you,
Where friendship stays, bright and true.

I dream of the day when our paths cross again,
When laughter and stories will mend all the pain.
We'll sit as we did, with no time to keep,
And our friendship will bloom where heart's roots run deep.

Until then, my Annie, I'll carry you near,
In the songs of the wind, in the stars' gentle cheer.
For though you're far off, in a new life begun,
Our bond is unbroken, forever as one.

I dream we'll meet on some sweet day,
Where time's long miles have slipped away.
And hand in hand, we'll start anew,
My dearest friend, I'm waiting for you.

Tears formed in Annie's eyes and rolled down her cheeks. She tried to smile, but her lips wouldn't allow it. She stood up, bounded around the table and hugged Hazel like she had never hugged anyone before.

Annie stepped back to her chair, wiping her eyes. "That was beautiful, Hazel. Look, you made me cry."

"Wrote what I was feeling. You know, Annie, I learned something through your being gone and then coming back."

"What?"

"You can't experience having a dream fulfilled if you don't have a dream."

Chapter 19

The only thing Annie knew for sure was that Meng Yao still lived somewhere up Steel Creek in Chinatown. Everyone she asked around town couldn't or wouldn't tell her anything. She asked Hazel, who frowned and said, "You shouldn't go up there, not alone. They don't take kindly to our kind, especially now."

"Why now?"

"A Chinaman was found dead in Steel Creek a few weeks ago. They're convinced one of the men from the Elmore Mine did it. Probably true."

Annie shrugged off the warning. "This is something I need to do."

She dressed in her oldest work clothes and walked the length of Rocky Bar Road until she reached the footbridge that crossed into Chinatown. The buildings here were smaller, built tightly together, with faded scraps of red silk nailed above some doorways. Those were the cribs, and everyone knew what went on inside them. Every so often, Annie caught a whiff of something sharp and unfamiliar: spices, or medicines, or perhaps opium.

She started with the Chinese laundry, the same one that had been in business for as long as she could remember. Inside, a man with silver-threaded hair worked a mangle. Annie cleared her throat, but he did not look up. She watched for a moment as he fed wet sheets between the rollers, squeezing out the water. They came out flat and stiff.

"Excuse me," she said. "I'm looking for someone. A girl, Meng Yao."

The man's eyes glanced over to her, cold and unreadable. "No here that name," he said, and returned to his work.

She walked over to the next ramshackle building. It had a small piece of yellow cloth nailed above the door. That was a chow-chow house. Annie walked in, the savory aroma of noodle soup filled her senses. The woman at the counter listened, nodding, and gave a toothless smile. "No Meng Yao," she said, and shooed Annie out with a wave.

At the next building, before Annie said anything, a young girl opened the door, growled at her, and slammed it an instant later. She continued, only to get more looks of disdain. A group of small boys pelted her with sand, shouting words she could not understand. Annie did not flinch as she brushed the sand out of her hair and kept walking.

When she was about to turn back, she passed a narrow alley lined with laundry drying in the breeze. An old woman with long gray hair sat at the entrance of the alley, sewing a patch onto a man's shirt. Annie tried again: "Please, do you know Meng Yao? I want to find Meng Yao, the girl."

The woman did not answer, but her fingers stopped moving. She stared at Annie for a long moment. She raised one hand and pointed with a gnarled finger to a small shack at the far end of the alley.

"Thank you," Annie whispered.

She followed the directions, with her heart pounding. The rundown shack had a scrap of red cloth hanging over the doorway. Dread swept over her. She stood in front of the door, motionless. *I don't know if I should do this. If Meg Yao is in there, will I be able to even look at her, seeing how she's been abused, and . . . used? What if she doesn't want to see me?* She knocked once, then twice. No answer. She knocked again, louder. No answer. *I should leave. But if I turn around now, I'll never come back. I gotta do this, even if it kills me to see what's happened to her.*

She took a deep breath and slowly pushed the creaky door open and stepped inside. It was dark, but she could see a small window covered with rags on the back wall. A young woman sat on a wooden bench, slowly washing her hands in a bowl of water, her scraggly black hair coiled at the base of her neck. She did not turn when Annie entered.

"Hello?" Annie said, uncertain.

The woman turned around, her eyes darting to the open door and then to Annie, then to the ground. She remained motionless.

She looked familiar. She wore a dirty, worn-out dress, and there was a yellow bruise on her wrist. "Meng Yao?"

The young woman stared at her, silent, then motioned for Annie to leave. Her gaze returned to the bowl of water on the bench.

Annie's heart sank. She stood motionless, not knowing what to do. *You don't recognize me? What have they done to you? I'm sure you're Meng Yao.* In spite of that, she said softly, "I'm sorry, you're not who I'm looking for. I'll leave."

With that, the woman paused her hand washing and jerked her head towards Annie. She looked up, confused, as if she was trying to remember something.

"Meng Yao, it's me, Annie. Can't you remember?"

The woman blinked and went back to washing her hands.

"Meg Yao! Please remember me! How can I get through to you? I know you're in there." Annie fumbled around in her pocket and felt a handkerchief. She pulled it out, balled it up and reached over to offer it to Meng Yao. *Maybe she'll remember when we first met behind the mercantile and I gave her a piece of cloth to wipe her nose.*

Meng Yao took the handkerchief and turned it over and over in her hands. She looked up at Annie with a blank expression on her face, and then back at the handkerchief. A moment later she let it slip through her fingers and fall to the floor. Again, she looked up at Annie, squinting her eyes. She opened her mouth, her eyes widened, then narrowed, and without a word, she stood, leapt across the tiny room, and threw her arms around Annie's waist. The embrace was desperate, trembling, and Annie felt a shock of recognition in the way she clung to her: the same tight, breathless grip Meng Yao used when she first tugged on Annie's sleeves so many years ago.

She buried her face in Annie's chest, and for a moment neither of them moved. Then Meng Yao cried, not loudly, but deep, muted sobs that made her whole body shake. Annie stroked her tangled hair, whispering nonsense, the way Edith used to do for her. "It's all right," she said. "It's really me. I came back." They stood that way for a long time, the world outside the shack faded away to nothingness. When Meng Yao let go, she wiped her eyes on her sleeve and gave Annie a sweet little smile.

"You come back," Meng Yao said in her high-pitched little voice. "You alive!"

"Yes. I came back."

Annie looked around the dingy room, noticing the neatness, the careful way every item had been arranged. There was a small altar in the corner, candles melted down to stubs, and a faded drawing of a woman Annie guessed was Meng Yao's mother.

"Are you safe here?" Annie asked, sitting beside her on the bench.

Meng Yao nodded, but then shook her head and pouted. "Better when you here."

Annie smiled. "I'm not much good at saving people, but I can try."

"You good for Meng Yao."

They sat together until the sun moved low in the sky. Meng Yao told her about the years in between, about the man who bought her contract, who then sold it to another man, about the laundry work, about the loneliness and the abuse. Often, Meg Yao struggled to find the right words and broke into unintelligible Chinese. It took effort for Annie to comprehend what Meng Yao was saying with her broken English, but sometimes the girl's expression and tone of voice communicated everything she needed to know when words failed.

"Many men have me." Annie knew what that meant, and she pushed the mental images out of her mind. Annie recalled hearing about a Chinese woman named Polly who was smuggled from China to San Francisco back in 1872. *She was purchased by a Chinaman in Warren, another mining camp about one hundred miles north of Rocky Bar. She was part of his concubine, or maybe was an indentured servant. Somehow, she gained her freedom and lived with a man named Charlie Bemis. I don't know how Polly got her freedom, but it was possible. If it were possible for Polly, it should be possible for Meng Yao.*

When Annie stood to leave, Meng Yao followed her to the door.

"You come more? You see me?" Meng Yao said with shyness in her eyes.

"Yes, I'm not going away this time."

"Shyeh shyeh."

Meng Yao smiled, and for a moment, Annie could see the girl she had first encountered years ago, peeking out from between the empty apple crates in back of the mercantile.

Annie walked back into town as the lamps flickered in the windows. The world felt lighter, less haunted. She'd lost so much in her life, but today, at least, she'd found something worth keeping. Tomorrow, she'd bring Meng Yao some proper food and a little companionship.

Annie retired to her room at the Willow House and thought about Meng Yao and then about her own future in Rocky Bar. *There must be something I can do for Meng Yao; she can't do anything about her situation by herself. No matter how girls like her try to pay off their contract debt to the owner, they keep adding fees and penalties for all kinds of made-up infractions, so the debt can never be paid off. They live like slaves until the day they die. I think her freedom could be finagled somehow. It worked for Polly.*

* * *

A few days later, while Annie and Mrs. Dunkle were finishing up their breakfast of eggs and cornpone, Mrs. Dunkle sat back in her chair and crossed her arms. She looked intently into Annie's eyes. "You got a knack for keeping things straight Annie, you're good with numbers and such. You have hands to do the work, and you're good at preparing the meals for the guests. I can see that. I'm pleased with our agreement of your doing the chores and the bookkeeping in return for your room and board. I think that's worked out pretty good for both of us. However . . . I think it's time for a change."

Annie swallowed. She put down her fork and placed her hands on her lap under the table, and squeezed them together. *Is she going to kick me out? Did I do something wrong? I've always done my best. Is it because I spend too much time with Hazel? Well, it was nice while it lasted.*

"Annie, dear, I'd like you to become the manager of this place. I ain't gettin' any younger, and I don't have the energy I used to. How about it?"

Annie's jaw dropped. "You're not joking, are you? I don't know what to say."

"You should say 'yes.' "

Annie thought for a moment. "Yes, I'd be honored."

"That's the correct answer. You can start right now."

Annie's shock evolved into elation. *This is what I want: more responsibility and authority, a chance to run a business my way.* As soon as they finished breakfast, Annie set about cleaning the place from the attic to the cellar. She tossed out every soiled mattress, painted the front steps, and boiled every linen in the backyard cauldron until the stench of old sweat and mildew was gone for good. Annie was determined to do her absolute best. She was even more thorough with the bookkeeping, refusing to let a single penny go missing, and soon the regulars, miners, salesmen, even the lawyer from Boise City, were telling folks that the new boarding house ran cleaner than any in the territory. Her experience in managing Thomas's businesses in Boise City and Pine Grove gave her the skills and confidence she needed.

Her next goal was saving Meng Yao from a future that was too awful to consider. Annie asked around town, but most places in Rocky Bar wouldn't even think of hiring a Chinese girl, especially one with a past like Meng Yao's. The best offer came from the kitchen at the Alturas Hotel: "We don't mind her, but she don't get to eat at the staff table." Annie declined. Over the next three days, she made multiple trips to Meng Yao's crib in Chinatown, sweet-talking the owner, a hawk-nosed old man named Zhi Peng. He refused every offer she made.

As the manager of Willow House, Annie could hire and fire people as she wished. On the fourth day, she showed up at Zhi Peng's door with a warm loaf of bread and spoke with the simplest English she could muster. "I want Meng Yao work for me at Willow House. She live better with me. I send you part her pay."

Zhi Peng looked her up and down. His muscles tensed, and a sneer crept across his face. He grabbed the loaf of bread and tossed it onto the bench next to Meng Yao. He gave the same response he always did. "Meng Yao, mine! No!"

"Listen to me. What you're doing to her is wrong! You have no right to keep her as your concubine or slave or whatever you think she is. It's not fair just because she's a girl."

He stared back at her. His sneer vanished, replaced with a blank expression. Annie looked around the crib with disgust at the filth on the walls and floor, and then looked at Meng Yao, huddled in the corner, eyes wide and terrified, her hands covering her ears. She was wearing nothing but rags.

"You know about Polly? Polly in Warren. Polly is free. Now Polly free. You . . . free . . . Meng Yao . . . to me."

Zhi Peng folded his arms and stood there, feet spread apart, unmoving and silent. His blank stare morphed into a look of contempt that needed no translation.

She kept at it. "I take Meng Yao. I give you money. I give you half Meng Yao pay. Half pay to you." Now he was frowning with the ugliest frown she had ever seen. *What does it take to get through to this man?* She imagined herself slapping him upside the head. "What's wrong with you? Can't you see I want to give Meng Yao a better life? Don't you care about her?"

Exasperated, she threw up her hands in disgust. "Meng Yao is going to die here because of you. Is that what you want? Damn you to hell!"

She made another attempt. Annie fished a shiny one-dollar gold eagle out of her pocket and held it in front of him. She leaned into him, inches from his face, and stared him in the eyes, the way Thomas used to do to her right before he hit her. She pointed at Meng Yao, then at the gold coin, and then at him. "Understand, you son of a bitch?"

He blinked, and then he blinked a second time.

He reached over to where Meng Yao cowered in the corner and grabbed her by her hair and threw her over to Annie's feet. "One year. One year money. Go!" as he snatched the gold coin.

Annie helped Meng Yao get to her feet, and they rushed out the door and down the alley, fearing that Zhi Peng would change his mind and come running after them, yelling obscenities in Chinese. They made it back to the Willow House.

* * *

Meng Yao was a mess, far worse than Annie had imagined. She looked like she hadn't had a bath in months, her skin hidden beneath layers of filth and dried sweat. Her hair, once sleek and black, hung in thick, matted ropes around her face, crusted with dirt and clumped with something that smelled of mildew. Her broken fingernails were caked with grime, her bare feet so calloused and cracked they looked more like old leather than skin. The air around her reeked of urine. It was all Annie could do to keep from bursting into tears.

She regained her composure and announced, "the first thing we got to do is get you clean." She pumped water from the well, the handle squeaking and clanking with each heavy pull. Cold water splashed into the tub, and Annie poured in kettle after kettle of boiling water from the wood stove until the steam filled the small washroom with a fog that clung to the windows.

Meng Yao stood by the tub, her arms folded across her chest. She flinched when Annie reached for her and didn't lift her gaze. Annie peeled off her clothes. The rags came away stiff with dirt, reeking of smoke, and with spots of dried blood. Annie tossed them straight into the garbage bin. *No amount of washing can save those.*

What she saw beneath made her gasp. "Oh . . . sweetheart," she whispered.

Meng Yao's frail body was a road map of suffering. Bruises bloomed across her ribs, hips, and shoulders in shades of blue, purple, and green, fading into yellow. Thin scratches crisscrossed her forearms and shins, some scabbed over, others raw and weeping. Along her back were welts, long, raised lines, some old and silvery, others fresh and red.

Meng Yao stood there shivering—not from cold, but from something more profound, as if some terror was still lodged inside her.

Annie helped her into the tub, and Meng Yao winced as the warm water met her skin. She didn't cry out, didn't even whimper; she clenched her jaw and lowered herself inch by inch. It took two hours to scrub her clean. The water turned brown and oily. Annie used rag after rag, warm, soapy cloths wiped over bruised limbs and raw patches. The girl did not flinch from what must have been painful scrubbing. *You must be used to pain. I'll try to be more gentle. I can't believe what they've done to you. You don't deserve this.*

Annie struggled with the mats in her hair, soaking and brushing, but the tangles were too deep. Her brush could move only a few inches before getting stuck in a massive knot. At one point, she found a large scab and drew back, horrified. She fetched scissors and knelt behind her.

"I'm sorry, my love," she whispered. "There's no saving this."

With each slow snip, matted clumps of hair fell to the floor. When it was done, the girl's face emerged, gaunt, pale, with eyes too large for her face and hollow cheeks that hadn't seen proper nourishment in months. Skin and bones described her arms and legs, and it was easy to see where her ribs were.

Annie wrapped her in a thick towel, then bundled her into a clean wool blanket. She took Meng Yao by the hand, guided her to a spare bed, and tucked her in with the same care that she had used with her own children. Meng Yao was no longer the child she had first met years ago. She was a woman now, but she was the most skinny and frail human being that she had ever laid eyes on.

Meng Yao blinked as Annie smoothed the blanket over her and tucked it under her chin.

"You're safe now," Annie whispered, brushing a few strands of clean black hair away from her forehead. "You don't have to go back."

Meng Yao blinked a few more times, but did not smile. A single tear slid from the corner of her eye and soaked into the pillow. "*Shyeh shyeh*," she whispered.

Annie reached over and tenderly wiped the tear's trail off her cheek. She sat there for several minutes, her hand resting on Meng Yao's. Then she whispered, "goodnight, my darling." She rose, turned down the oil lamp, and drifted out of the room.

Chapter 20

The next day, Annie moved Meng Yao into an empty room. Annie had borrowed a plain-looking dress from one of the upstairs girls who had a petite figure. She worked tirelessly, cleaning wherever she went. Sometimes, when the Willow House was empty, they sat together in the kitchen, and Meng Yao showed Annie how to shape dumplings or repair a torn seam with a few quick stitches. Annie taught Meng Yao how to cook cornpone, eggs, bacon, and baked beans. They didn't talk much, but they didn't need to. Annie felt more at peace in those silences than she ever did in a crowded parlor in Boise City.

The following morning, Annie sat across the kitchen table from Meng Yao, enjoying some Chinese egg drop soup.

"We need to talk, Meng Yao."

"Okay."

"I want you to understand something," Annie began, settling into her words with gravity. "You'll never have to endure what you did before, not here, not while you work for me." She leaned forward, the wooden chair creaking beneath her as if echoing the weight of their conversation. "I've seen enough of that kind of pain," she continued after a pause, her voice softening yet with resolve. "If any of your former clients show up here, tell me immediately. I know where Mrs. Dunkle keeps her pistol, and I'm not afraid to use it. The girls here make their own choices about how they live. This ain't a brothel and I ain't no madam. What the girls do in their rooms is their business. As long as they pay their rent and don't cause trouble, it's none of my business. And you," she paused to let the weight of the promise sink in, "will never be forced back into that life again." She felt a surge of protective fierceness rising in her chest. "If any of the girls here try to get you into that line of work, I'll kick them out so fast they won't know what hit them."

She wasn't sure whether it was the air in Rocky Bar or something long dormant waking within her, but she felt it: pride in what she was doing. It was raw and invigorating, a new skin still tender with novelty. Protecting Meng Yao wasn't merely an obligation; it had become something deeper and unexpected—a responsibility.

Meng Yao stared back at her, blinking, her mouth hanging open.

"What you say?"

"You heard me. No more men. That's not why you're here."

Meng Yao rose to her feet, walked around the table, and gave Annie the biggest hug her frail body could manage. "You good woman."

"One more thing, Meng Yao. You need to work on your English. I know they don't teach you much in Chinatown, but if you're going to succeed here, you have to know how to communicate. I'll borrow some children's books from the schoolmarm, so you can study when you're done with your chores. Does that sound good?"

"Yes. Sound good." Meng Yao bowed. *"Shyeh shyeh."*

"Tell me, Meng Yao, what does that mean? You say it all the time."

"Shyeh shyeh mean 'thank you'."

"How do you say, 'you're welcome'?"

"Bu ke tsi."

"I'll stick with 'thank you'."

Word spread through Rocky Bar that a Chinese girl was living and working at the Willow House, but Annie didn't care. She earned the respect of the people of Rocky Bar, as much as the manager of a boarding house with upstairs girls could hope to expect.

The business grew. Out-of-towners started requesting upstairs girls by name. Their favorites were Josie, Daisy, and Violet. Each one knew how to use their feminine wiles in their own special way. Travelers from Boise City and beyond wrote letters in advance, asking if "the Chinese girl with the pretty face" could make them egg drop soup on Sundays. Annie made sure they tipped her generously, then sent the cut to Zhi Peng every month, just as promised. She and Meng Yao saved every extra penny in a coffee tin under the floorboards.

Sometimes, late at night, Annie would wake to find Meng Yao sitting by the window, eyes fixed on the moon or the stars, sometimes with a wistful smile, but most of the time expressionless. On rare occasions, she heard Meng Yao singing in Chinese, with melodies that sounded like lullabies. Annie never interrupted; she understood what it meant to long for a faraway place.

Other nights, Annie herself would wake up from a nightmare. The worst dreams were about her children. It was always the same thing. They were running through a grassy meadow on a sun-filled day with their arms outstretched, reaching for her, laughing with delight. When they were just about to embrace, she would wake up with a start. She never got to cuddle them.

By autumn, the boarding house had a waiting list, and Annie made plans for the future, fixed the back porch, and thought about planting a patch of peas or corn come spring. She had more work as the manager than she could handle, and only a few friends she trusted. It wasn't the life she had dreamed of as a girl, but it was hers, and she was in charge.

* * *

It took less than a year for Annie to own the Willow House outright. Mrs. Dunkle had developed a cough that wouldn't quit, and she had a son in Twin Falls who wanted nothing to do with the place. By spring, the cough had hollowed her out so badly she couldn't climb the stairs without stopping to wheeze.

"I'm afraid it might be consumption," she confessed one night, after the boarders were fed, and the kitchen scrubbed spotless. Mrs. Dunkle cornered Annie by the stove. "I want you to take it," she announced. "You pay me what you can. If you can't, I don't care. I just want this place to last. I own the mineral rights to this property and a few others in town. My former husband filed claims here, but never did any mining. If you own a claim, you own anything built on top of it." Mrs. Dunkle paused and thought for a moment. "By the way, Annie, it's a good thing that you're doing for that Chinese woman. You probably saved her life. I don't know of anybody else who would have done that. I'm proud of you. Give yourself some credit."

"That's kind of you to say so, Mrs. Dunkle. It felt like the right thing to do." *Nobody has ever told me they were proud of me before. I suppose I earned it.*

The next morning, after reviewing the paperwork, she signed her name and title: Anna Morrow, Proprietress. The business was profitable and had a quick turnover. The first thing Annie did was change the name. *Willow House? What did a willow tree have to do with anything in Rocky Bar? There weren't any willow trees around here. The name should mean something to the people who live and work here. How about Miner's Refuge, Miner's Lodge, Miner's Paradise—nah, that's too funny, Miner's Heaven—too religious, Miner's Haven. Hmmm, I kinda like the sound of that one. Miner's Haven . . . it would be a haven for the boys in more ways than one, if I keep the girls.*

She did not celebrate her new acquisition; there was too much to do. Annie fixed the broken gutters, patched the roof, and added two new beds on the top floor. She hired a girl from the south end of town to help in the kitchen. Annie's reputation as a hard worker and a hard woman grew with every month. She knew how to keep the men in line, send a drunk packing without leaving a bruise, and make even the hardest-to-please guest walk away satisfied.

The news spread through Rocky Bar faster than wildfire. Within a day, half the town was gossiping about the "lady boss" who had bought the

Willow House. It was the biggest scandal the town had seen in years. The men loved it: they came to see what Annie would do, if she'd pretty up the girls and get rid of the knife fights or burn the place down and build something new. The women, especially the churchgoers, hated it. They called her "that scarlet woman" and said she was no better than the girls who worked upstairs.

Annie remained unfazed by what people said. She treated the upstairs girls there better than any of them had ever been treated, giving them a cut of every drink they poured and letting them keep their own tips. She was not a madam. The girls paid their rent like any other guest, and she did not get involved with what they did on their own.

Business was booming. After several lessons in basic bookkeeping, she let Meng Yao assist with the books, and after a few months, put her in charge of them. Meng Yao's ability to work with numbers surprised Annie. She enjoyed the expressions of shock on customers' faces when made a point of telling them that a *Chinese* girl handled the books. Annie was building a reputation as the town's provocateur, and that gave her something to smile about. Ruffling the feathers of the townsfolk had a strange appeal.

After a busy weekend, Annie was kneading bread dough at the kitchen table, sleeves rolled past her elbows, black strands of hair tucked into a kerchief, when the back door creaked open, and a shadow fell across the floorboards.

An old man stood there, gaunt, sun-worn, with a bristle of gray beard and trousers stained with old mud and pine pitch. His hat was in his hand, pressed flat against his chest like he was walking into church.

"Mrs. Morrow?" he asked, voice raspy like gravel.

Annie didn't look up. "You're trackin' dirt across my clean floor."

"Beg pardon," the bedraggled man said. He took a careful step backward onto the stoop. "Name's Ezra Knox. I was told you is amenable to . . . arrangements."

That got her attention. She studied him. "What arrangements?"

He cleared his throat. "Grubstake. I got a lead—a real one. Quartz with good color about five miles up Beaver Creek. But I need provisions. Tools. Maybe a mule if you can spare one. And I'll give you a quarter of whatever I make."

She wiped her hands on a rag and leaned against the counter, eyeing him like she might a man trying to sell her a hollow log full of snakes.

"Don't hornswoggle me. You're the third clodhopper this summer with a 'real' lead. The other two came back broke, heads full of lice, and smelling like they'd been dead a week. No more loans." She crossed her arms. "What makes you different?"

Ezra stepped in again, lowering his voice. "Because I been up there. I ain't guessin'. Found a quartz vein with gold showin' last fall afore the snow drove me out. I marked the spot—cairn next to a fire-black stump. It's a waitin' for me."

"Then why didn't you stake it last fall?"

"I was sick an' near starved," he admitted. "Couldn't make it back up afore the snows hit. And this spring I been workin' at Miller's livery just to scrape by. I ain't lazy, Mrs. Morrow. Just broke. And gettin' older."

Annie narrowed her eyes. She'd heard sob stories from dozens of different men, most of them too fond of bug juice and too allergic to honest labor. But there was something in Ezra's rueful voice, tired but firm, and not the desperate kind of tired that led men to lies. She stared at him for a long moment before speaking. His eyes met hers with a steady gaze. He didn't flinch or look away.

"I'm no banker, and I don't take kindly to being bamboozled. You fail, I lose it all."

"Yes, ma'am. I ain't no greenhorn."

"I'll want it in writing."

He nodded.

"This ain't no loan. It's an investment. I get thirty-three percent. And if you find anything, anything worth working, you come back here first. Not to anyone else. Understand? And I won't tolerate no foolishness."

"Understood."

A slow grin tugged at Ezra's face, revealing missing teeth and more sincerity than she had seen in a long time. "Thank you, Mrs. Morrow, much obliged."

"Hold your thanks," she muttered, already moving toward the sideboard. She pulled out a small ink bottle, a stub of a pen, and a yellow sheet of paper, which she smoothed across the tabletop. "You can read and write, can't you?"

"'Enough to scratch my name."

She sat and wrote in a small, precise script, her hand steady from years of bookkeeping and purchase orders. The ink soaked into the paper as she penned the agreement:

> I, Anna Morrow, hereby furnish Ezra Knox with
> provisions and tools for the purpose of
> prospecting in the Beaver Creek drainage basin.
> In return, Mr. Knox agrees to deliver thirty-three
> percent of any and all mineral discoveries or
> profits to Anna Morrow, with said findings to be
> reported first to the undersigned. Terms
> accepted in full by both parties.
> Signed and sealed on this, the fourteenth day of
> April, 1891, at Rocky Bar, Idaho.

She slid the paper across the table and handed him the pen. "Sign it."

He leaned over and wrote "Ezra T. Knox", each letter carefully etched in large block letters.

Annie countersigned it, blew on the ink, folded the paper in thirds, and tucked it into a ledger behind the flour tin. "Now you've got two things depending on you makin' good," she said. "Your word, and my money."

He nodded solemnly. "I won't forget it, ma'am."

She waved him off. "Go on. Skedaddle before I change my mind. You'll have your bundle by sun up."

Ezra stepped outside; the door creaked shut behind him. Annie stood a moment in the silence, staring at the folded contract, then turned back to the dough.

Fool woman! One more roll of the dice with someone else's dream. But then again, in a place like this, that's how you build a future: one gamble, one grubstake, one business at a time. He deserves a chance.

This scene repeated itself several times that summer. She didn't mind helping the poor prospectors who were down and out on their luck, with visions of pay dirt filling their heads. She was in a position to help them, so she felt it was something that she ought to do. In fact, it was the right thing to do. Despite this, every once in a while, there was a new insult, a new rumor, a fresh attempt to run her out of town. The churchwomen organized petitions, but they never got too many people to sign them. *What a snooty lot they are. Why can't people believe that the owner of a boarding house with working girls can also have compassion for those in need? Are they that closed-minded and intolerant? To hell with them.*

The sheriff stopped by once a week, on schedule, to deliver a notice of violation and collect the fine. The violations varied, depending on what mood the sheriff was in on the day he made his rounds: keeping a disorderly house, promoting immoral behavior, or causing a public nuisance. In the eyes of the town's womenfolk, he had to make it look like he was enforcing the law. Regardless, he accepted the fines with a wink in his eye and parted with, "Good day, Mrs. Morrow. Till next time." Miner's Haven was an integral part of Rocky Bar's economy, regardless of who disapproved.

Chapter 21

In her second year back in Rocky Bar, Annie hosted a Christmas supper at the Miner's Haven for the miners who couldn't go home for the winter. She cooked for three days straight, making pies, stews, and a turkey that barely fit in the oven. Over fifty people came, including the church ladies, who insisted on bringing their own dishes but ended up eating more of Annie's than they wanted anyone to notice. Afterwards, the entire crowd walked over to the Gold Nugget Saloon for music and dancing, and for one night, nobody cared who owned what or who belonged where. Annie's girls, wearing their most modest outfits, made a brief appearance and left before drawing too much attention to themselves.

After Annie acquired the Willow House and changed the name to Miner's Haven, an opportunity arose for her to get what she wanted the most: her own restaurant. The Elmore Restaurant down the road always looked busy. She broached the subject of buying the place with Mrs. Shaffer, but she wouldn't hear of it. "Not to you, anyway," was her response. There was another one at the other end of town, the Grub Shack. It was pretty run-down, and the food had a reputation for making people sick. There was a saloon next to it, owned by the same person. Rumor had it that the faro dealer was a bunko artist. Nobody trusted him.

She thought about it. *Some folks called the restaurant the Ptomaine Palace. Not sure why. Some days, there were no customers at all, and the owner, Mr. Schmidt, would sit out by the front door and watch people walk by, ignoring him. The customers were mostly people travelling through Rocky Bar, and most locals avoided the place like the plague. The saloon never had more than a few customers. Seems like he never got the message. Maybe the place could be turned around. Worth a try.* She made him an offer, and after wavering back and forth, he reluctantly accepted it. He did not want to accept the fact that his businesses were failures. After the paperwork was done, he left town and was never heard from again.

The name Grub Shack has to go. It's tarnished beyond repair. Like Miner's Haven, the name has to mean something. People should want to stop by based on the name alone, knowing nothing about the food. That's advertising. Annie's mind flooded with names. *Idaho Eats, The Tin Plate, The Cookhouse, The Hungry Prospector, The Chuckwagon—that's too cowboyish. This ain't Texas. Nope, these don't sound appealing enough. It had to feel personal, inviting, and friendly.*

Her mind wandered back to the day she and Edith were tossing around potential names for a restaurant. *What was the one I liked? It was something about bread. The bread box? No. Gingerbread House? No, that's too much like Christmas. Let's see, my favorite bread is . . . sourdough. That was it: Sourdough Sally's. I never knew anyone named Sally, but that didn't matter. The name has a nice ring to it: Sourdough Sally's.* She renamed the saloon next door The Lucky Strike.

I need a cook, a real grub slinger, someone who knows how to make flap-jacks that melt in your mouth or pork chops as tender as butter. The cook can make or break a restaurant.

Annie hired a cook out of Nampa. He had ordered biscuits and gravy one morning and then complained that the biscuits were as hard as rocks and the gravy was too greasy. Annie had challenged him, "you think you can do better?" He replied that he once worked as a cook for a fancy hotel in San Francisco during his younger years. Annie had him in the kitchen the next day. He liked to sing to himself while working the skillets. Pretty soon, Sourdough Sally's earned the reputation as one of the better places to eat in Rocky Bar. People did not come just for the food. Having a saloon right next door was a big draw. Annie provided the best in spirits that she could get a hold of for The Lucky Strike: Old Crow, Four Roses, Old Forester, and her favorite, Old Overholt.

One Friday evening, after she finished her work at Miner's Haven, Annie walked over to The Lucky Strike and found the place packed. *Hmm. Looks like I got the newest hot spot in town.* She took her position behind the bar and wiped up several puddles of spilled beer. Soon an argument broke out between two prospectors disputing the common boundary of their claims. Annie waded in, broke it up with a few choice cuss words, and sent both men home with a warning to take their problems elsewhere.

The next night was going well. The place was packed again, noisy, and full of cigar smoke. *Here come those two dimwits again.* They worked themselves into another heated argument about the same claim boundary. This time it got ugly. One of them picked up his chair and smashed it on the head of the other, knocking him flat on his back. One of her regulars, Little Man, a gorilla-sized hunk of a man who looked like he was seven feet tall and weighed three hundred pounds, saw what was happening. He picked up the guy on the floor by his belt and threw him out the front door. The other guy knew he was next, so he ran out like a scared rabbit.

"Thanks, Little Man. I appreciate that."

"My pleasure, Annie," he said as he wiped his hand off on his shirt.

When the last customer left, Annie wiped down the counter, counted the till, and locked the doors. She did everything herself, trusting no one but Meng Yao, who sometimes helped out on the busiest nights at the restaurant and saloon after she had finished her chores at Miner's Haven.

Next Monday morning, on her way from Miner's Haven to Sourdough Sally's, she thought about last night. *It was nice to have Little Man around when things got too hot, but I don't want to depend on a man for my welfare, not even Little Man.*

She made a slight detour to one of the town's mercantiles, walked in, and told the shopkeeper, Mr. Bevelander, "I need me a gun. What do you have?"

"You ever heard of Wyatt Earp?"

"The outlaw?"

"One and the same, but sometimes he was a lawman. Ever hear of the shootout at the OK Corral in Tombstone, Arizona?"

"Sounds familiar. What of it?"

"That's where Wyatt Earp and Doc Holiday shot and killed three cattle rustlers in October 1881. After that, they formed a posse and killed three of them from the same group. Did you know that a few years ago, Wyatt Earp and his wife Sadie lived in Eagle City? It's about forty miles east of Coeur d'Alene. They ran a dance hall, a saloon called The White Elephant, and they had a few mining claims. At some point, he even got a job as a deputy sheriff of Kootenai County. Go figure. But that didn't last too long, and they eventually left town. The reason I mention this is that the Colt .45 was his weapon of choice. I don't have any of those in stock, but I have one of these."

He reached under the counter and produced a brand new, shiny Colt .44. "This," he said, "is the Colt Frontier Six-Shooter. Officially, it's a Colt Army Model M1860. It was designed for the US Army, so it should be good enough for you. It's a single-action, six-shot revolver accurate up to a hundred yards. It has a lot of firepower for four pounds and four ounces. Single action means you got to pull back the hammer before you pull the trigger. That rotates the cylinder and puts the next round in position. You'll need these lead bullets, gunpowder, and caps. I like it a lot more than the Remington Model 1858, which I have in stock. Personal preference. It won't make you as good as Calamity Jane, but it'll stop a man dead in his tracks, if you know what I mean." He demonstrated how to measure the powder with the metal tube, pour it into each chamber, add the bullets and the caps.

"I'll take it."

As Mr. Bevelander went into the back room to get something, a well-dressed young woman and her son walked into the mercantile and went over to a shelf where several rows of shiny new dinner plates were on display. She studied them. Her son pointed to one in particular, which had little red roses painted around the edge.

"Hey, Ma, that one's pretty."

She reached over and picked it up. "I wonder what it's made of?"

Annie glanced over her shoulder at the woman. "It's a new kind of synthetic ceramic. Invented in Paris, I think."

"Oh my, I've never heard of that. It's beautiful."

Annie tried hard to suppress a chuckle. *I love making things up. Synthetic ceramic? That's a good one.*

Mr. Bevelander returned to the counter with a wooden box for the gun and placed it inside.

"Here you go, Mrs. Morrow. Have fun with it."

"I'm sure I will. I'll take the holster too."

She winked at the boy on her way out the door. The boy looked up at her, confused.

A few days later, the two quarrelsome prospectors showed up again at The Lucky Strike, but this time, Little Man was off somewhere else. *Not a problem, not with my friend Mr. Colt by my side. We'll see what happens.* After a few drinks, they started arguing again. *These two rock jockeys must be nuts! Why don't they go their separate ways? Something must be wrong with their heads.* The language got louder and more colorful, but this time she would not wait for them to break the furniture.

She pulled out the Colt .44, aimed it at a spot above their heads, and yelled at the top of her voice, "Hey fellas! Look what I got." She pulled the trigger. *BANG!*

Everyone froze. "Get the hell out of here! Next time I won't miss!" They fell over each other as they raced to the door. *That was fun. I don't mind a bullet hole in the wall.*

At closing, Annie counted the cash, checked the receipts, locked up The Lucky Strike, and repeated the procedure at Sourdough Sally's next door. She crossed the street, checked in at Miner's Haven, and found everything in order. The boarders were asleep; the maid had finished her work. Meng Yao was sitting at the kitchen table, reading a children's book.

"What are you reading?"

"Meng Yao looked up. "It's about a girl named Alice, by . . . let's see, Mr. Lewis Carroll . . . published 1865. She follows a rabbit down a big hole. It's unbelievable what happens to her, but I don't understand some words, and do Cheshire cats really smile?"

Annie smiled at her. "No, Meng Yao, it's just a story, but I do know some people that smile like a Cheshire cat. Be careful if you ever meet someone like that."

Annie sat at her desk, added up the day's profits, and made a note to order more beer and whiskey. A few customers had requested Heidelberg, so she decided she would order a barrel. She smiled, pleased with the numbers, pleased with herself. It hadn't been easy, but she'd done it. She was the proud owner of three profitable businesses. She poured herself a last drink of Old Overholt, stood at the window, listening to Meng Yao quietly reading aloud to herself, and watched the moon rise over Rocky Bar Road.

Chapter 22

A few days later, while Annie was deep in thought in the parlor of Miner's Haven, the sound of wagon wheels crunching over the packed dirt of the road startled her. The sound stopped, and the horse whined.

Hazel, who was sitting in a chair on the other side of the parlor, got up and peered out the front window. "Who's that?"

Annie got up and stood in the open doorway. Hazel joined her. The man who stepped down from the wagon was tall, with a thin moustache, spectacles, and dressed in a dark suit that had the faint shine of much travel. Behind him, lashed into the bed of the wagon, were several large travel trunks and a small black box.

"Looks like another salesman. Lord knows I don't need more Yankee notions, tinware, elixirs, or patent medicines."

The man approached and stopped at the foot of the stairs. "Good morning, ladies, my name's Alfred Winslow, travelling photographer out of Twin Falls. I'm on my way to Atlanta to take some photographs for the owners of the Monarch Mine, and I've been told Rocky Bar has some of the comeliest ladies in Elmore County. I'd be honored to take your portraits, Miss . . . ?"

"*Mrs*. Morrow," Annie said. *Why do men assume I'm single?* "I'm not much for sittin' in front of one of those fancy cameras."

Hazel's eyes lit up. "Annie, think of it—a photograph for Miner's Haven. You could put it in one of those fancy wood carved picture frames like they have at the mercantile. It would look so nice hanging on the pretty wallpaper in the parlor, maybe even have it made into postcards to send out. That's what they call marketing."

"I'm not one for fuss, and those contraptions take forever."

"Forever's a small price for a bit of polish," Hazel said. "Besides, he's here now. You'll regret it if you pass it up."

It took another ten minutes of Hazel's wheedling, plus the assurance from Mr. Winslow that the entire process could be finished in under an hour, before Annie relented and let the man inside.

Mr. Winslow carried in his pride and joy, a Folding Rochester view camera. "This is the new self-casing bellows camera that is the talk of professional photographers everywhere. This model isn't like those cumbersome old-style view cameras. The case itself becomes the camera's support when I open it up, and when folded shut it locks tight, protecting the ground glass screen and lenses from the dust and jolts of travel. The best part is that it uses dry plate negatives, not the messy wet plate negatives."

Mr. Winslow set it on a polished wooden tripod in the parlor, where the morning light spilled in through the front windows. "This design makes my work a great deal easier, and it's perfect for five by seven negatives. It has a high grade symmetrical lens, which will cut the field of view clear and sharp with full opening. The ground glass screen is spring actuated, so it's aways in the correct position when the film holder is inserted or removed."

"Sounds nice, but that doesn't mean anything to me," Annie blurted out.

Unfazed, Mr. Winslow continued and explained with a trace of pride as he unfolded the camera. "Please have a seat on that chair next to the table, Mrs. Morrow." He pulled a thin white cloth out of a satchel and hung it over the window. "Diffused sidelight is the best if you want to get the Rembrandt lighting," he said.

"The what?" asked Hazel with raised eyebrows.

"Rembrandt lighting. You know, the famous artist who lived in Amsterdam in the sixteen hundreds. He used a soft light from one side to produce a delicate balance between light and shadows on the subject's face. Photographers can learn much from the Old Masters." He studied Annie's face. "Turn your chin a touch towards the window, Mrs. Morrow . . . yes, just so, and tilt your head ever so slightly to your left. Now rest your right arm on the table and let your hand drape over the end of the table. Place your left hand on your lap and relax, and I'll adjust the aperture and the focus."

Hazel jumped in and adjusted the white bow at the top of Annie's dress, straightened out her black choker, and gave her long black hair, parted down the middle, a quick once-over with her brush. "You're a natural beauty, Annie." She stepped back to admire her work.

Mr. Winslow examined the image on the ground-glass screen on the back of the camera. "Very nice, Mrs. Morrow. If you don't mind, me saying so, you're quite a sight for the eyes."

Hazel glanced at Mr. Winslow. "Back when Annie was a teenager, people said she was the prettiest girl in Rocky Bar."

"Yes, I can see why."

"Get on with it, please. Quit your jabbering, Hazel."

Mr. Winslow adjusted the focus.

"Can I look?" Hazel blurted out.

"Sure."

"Look at the back of the camera, right here."

"Mr. Photographer—something's wrong! Annie's upside down, and backwards."

Mr. Winslow chuckled. "Not to worry, miss. That's how cameras work. When I make the print, everything is reversed, so there's no problem."

"Oh," said Hazel sheepishly. "I knew that. You're sure pretty, Annie, even upside down and backwards."

Annie gave Hazel a faint, wry smile, which quickly disappeared.

"When you hear the click, hold your breath and try not to move." He pulled the dark slide from the holder, cocked the brass shutter, and counted, "One . . . two . . . three . . . ." *Click.* "Very good, Mrs. Morrow. You're an excellent subject." He carefully placed the negative into a black bag.

"I will come back tomorrow with your prints, Mrs. Morrow. I'll give you one large one that you can frame, and one small one for yourself."

Mr. Winslow arrived the next morning at ten o'clock with a large brown paper envelope. Hazel saw him coming and opened the door before he could knock.

"Come right in, Mr. Photographer," Hazel said with excitement, clutching her hands together to her chest. "Let's see the pictures."

Mr. Winslow gave the envelope to Annie. "Subject gets the first look."

Annie withdrew the large photograph from the envelope and studied it for a few moments. "Looks all right," she sighed, and handed it to Hazel.

"It's a wonderful picture, Annie, but you don't look too happy, kind of sad, even. But you're still pretty. This is going to hang right above the front desk. Folks will know they're in a fine house the minute they walk in and see the beautiful proprietress."

Annie studied the picture again for a long moment before giving a reluctant nod. "Reckon it's not so bad. It's who I am."

* * *

A week went by, and one afternoon, Hazel and Annie found themselves once again sitting side by side on the old moss-covered log on Beaver Creek. Hazel placed her hand on Annie's shoulder. "Annie, I need to talk to you about something," she said, hesitating, her eyes betraying a mix of reluctance and urgency. "It's about . . . us."

Hazel shifted her weight from side to side. She kept her eyes on the ground where the flowing water met the pebbles beneath her feet. She swung her feet back and forth.

"Out with it. What's gnawin' at you?"

"Annie . . . it ain't me, you understand. It's . . . it's my husband, Aaron."

"Your husband's got some quarrel with me now? I can't imagine what for."

"He says . . . he says it doesn't look right—our keeping company with each other. He aims to be well-regarded in this town, as people are gossiping about the friends that his wife keeps."

Annie's smile vanished as she wrinkled her forehead. Her voice sharpened.

"Because of Miner's Haven? Because of who I rent to on the second floor? That's what he means?"

"He says that no decent woman ought to sit at your table or walk beside you in public."

Annie pressed her lips together and bit down on her tongue. She crossed her arms and clenched her fists.

"I can't believe it! And what do you say, Hazel? Is that how you see me?"

Hazel whirled around to stare at Annie. "No! Lord help me, no! You've been more sister to me than anyone in this town. I don't care what you do to keep a roof overhead or food on the table. But—" her voice broke, "—he's my husband. I swore myself to him. And he says if I don't put distance between you and me, there'll be hell to pay at home."

Annie's shoulders slumped, and she stared at the ground, as though the weight of Hazel's words was too much to bear. A heaviness settled on her heart, and a painful knot formed in her stomach.

"So that's it, then. The good men of this town get to tell us women who we get to have as friends."

"Don't think I want it this way. My heart aches something fierce just speaking the words. I'll miss you every day, Annie."

Annie turned her face aside, tears slipping down her cheeks, though her voice tried to hold steady.

"You'll miss me? I'll be here, sitting on this mossy log alone from now on? It ain't fair. Women have no rights. Men decide everything for us."

Hazel covered her mouth to keep from sobbing, but it didn't work. She burst into tears and put her head in her hands.

"Go on, Hazel. Go tend to your husband. Leave me with my girls. I'm not angry with you. I'm angry with the way the world treats us, like we're second-class citizens."

Hazel sniffled and wiped the tears from her eyes. She couldn't bring herself to look at Annie. "I'm so sorry."

Annie looked over at her. "So, this is the last time we will ever see each other? I will not say goodbye. I do not accept this. This is not right! Aaron be damned!"

They sat in silence for several minutes.

"Hazel."

"What?"

Annie looked at the ground. "Never mind."

Hazel stood, turned around, and ran away as fast as she could. Annie watched as Hazel tripped on something in the road. She hit the ground hard, scraping her knees, her palms slapping against the dirt. For a moment, she stayed there, stunned, small as a wounded fawn. When she finally lifted her head and looked back, Annie caught a glimpse of her face. Hazel was crying. It was the most pitiful thing Annie had ever seen.

Go to her, her heart begged. *Help her! Hold her! Don't let this be how it ends!* Annie's legs refused to move. They felt rooted in the earth, heavy with the knowledge of what she was losing. An ache welled in her chest, rising so sharply she thought she would choke on it.

Hazel tried to push herself upright. Her arms trembled. She sagged back down. The little sob that escaped Hazel was so weak that it barely reached Annie's ears, yet it pierced her heart like a knife.

Annie couldn't bear to watch for another second. She turned away and stared down into the dark ribbon of water beneath her feet. The creek did not care. It murmured along its crooked path as though nothing in the world had happened, oblivious to the shattering of their hearts.

Behind her, Hazel's whimpers sputtered and faded. Annie listened, every muscle locked, waiting—for what? A few footsteps followed, uneven, unsteady. Then . . . nothing.

Annie shut her eyes, her breath shallow, knowing with a terrible certainty that she had let her best friend walk out of her life forever—and she was now cursed to carry the weight of that moment for the rest of her days.

This is the world men have built for us. A world where a man's word shackles a woman tighter than iron chains. Hazel never had a choice. I had no choice with Thomas when he forced me to leave Rocky Bar and go to Boise City. None of us do. We bend, or we break, or we die.

She remained motionless on the log and looked down at the spot next to her. The moss was still pressed down where Hazel had been sitting moments before. *A man stole my children from me, and now a man has stolen my best friend from me. Why? I don't understand. I don't deserve this. Thomas broke my heart, and now Aaron has too. I might as well shoot myself.*

Annie stood and turned around, attempting to get one last glimpse of Hazel, but she was gone.

Don't give up, Annie.

Chapter 23

A year had passed since Annie last saw Hazel, except for the one time when she saw a woman several blocks away who might have been Hazel, but she wasn't sure. She thought of her almost every day. The most painful thoughts came whenever she sat on the old mossy log by Beaver Creek. *This used to be our favorite spot to meet, but now it's just a reminder of what I lost. I should stop torturing myself. Why do I keep coming here?*

That was when she decided she needed to get out of Rocky Bar. Her excuse was that she wanted to expand her business into Atlanta, but that wasn't the real reason. The fire that gutted half the town back in 1892 did more than destroy buildings; it broke the spirit of Rocky Bar. Some businesses recovered, but the future of Annie's town was bleak. Her chief concern was Meng Yao. *I trust her to manage Miner's Haven and Sourdough Sally's, but I'm afraid people will take advantage of her. She's still working on her English and might not be able to handle some smooth-talking city slicker from Boise City. But I could always make the trip from Atlanta back to Rocky Bar if I needed to, but people tell me that road is the devil's playground.*

A few days later, her stagecoach finished its bone-jarring fifteen-mile trek on James Creek Road, which ran from Rocky Bar to where it connected to Middlefork Road and then into Atlanta. The old wagon road crossed the flanks of Bald Mountain and had several steep sections and hairpin turns. The rough and poorly maintained road caused the passengers to endure many bumps and jolts. The first stop was on Pine Street at the edge of town. Two scrappy young men, who were obviously miners, got out. Annie remained seated.

Spring had only barely arrived in the Idaho high country, but Atlanta already buzzed with the raw, dangerous optimism of a mining camp riding its latest boom. Every building between the livery and the huge Monarch Stamp Mill visible in the distance looked thrown up in a hurry, with walls covered with a memory of paint. Atlanta was more spread out than Rocky Bar, with several side streets. Rocky Bar was a one-street town.

Atlanta is an odd name for a mining town in Idaho. I heard it was Southerners who mistakenly believed that the South had won the Battle of Atlanta during the Civil War. This turned out to be false, but the name stuck anyway.

This reminded her of the dispute between the northern and southern miners in another mining camp, Leesburg, up north by the Montana border. *I remember hearing that the miners from the south wanted to name the town Leesburg after General Robert E. Lee. Miners from the north wouldn't hear of it, so they built their own mining camp up the road and named it Grantsville, after General Ulysses S. Grant. Men fight about the dumbest things. What a bunch of knuckleheads. I guess the Yankees gave up, since the name Leesburg stuck. What is it with men? If women are the weaker sex, then men are the stupider sex.*

The stagecoach made a second stop in the center of town, at the intersection of Main Street and Quartz Street. Annie climbed out of the stagecoach with her carpetbag in one hand while lifting her bright blue dress up so it wouldn't drag in the mud.

She passed the first saloon, a single-story board-and-batten building with "Golden Rule Saloon" painted over the door in orange letters big enough for a blind man to read, and made a mental note to take a look at it when the time was right. Through the open door came a wave of cigar smoke and the flat thwack of cards on a table. Next came a restaurant advertising pie at all hours, then a dry goods store, then two more saloons, both claiming to have the best faro game in Idaho. Beyond that was a boarding house, with ROOMS painted by hand on a front window.

She'd read about Atlanta in the Elmore Bulletin and even heard some of the older miners in Rocky Bar talk about it. There was gold here, they said, gold and silver and a stamp mill running so loud it rattled your teeth if you were close enough to it. Annie thought about what she knew about the town. *The Atlanta Lode was discovered in 1864 and sparked the biggest gold rush the territory had ever seen. It had stamp mills that ran day and night. Most of them shut down after a few years, after all the good ore was processed, and what was still in the ground wasn't worth the cost of mining and milling. They didn't expect it to last forever, did they? Atlanta, like Rocky Bar, was a fine example of a boom-and-bust town. Anyway, people still lived here, and that meant a business opportunity. It had more life than Rocky Bar. Plenty of lonely miners here. This looks promising.*

She walked south on Quartz Street two blocks and found what she had heard was the "Doll House" area. There were working girls in their petticoats peeking out of the windows. She turned back toward the center of town and turned left on Main Street, and she saw what she was after—a long board nailed to the side of a two-story building that read Hoffman Hotel. *Rocky Bar has the Hoffman House. Hmm, must be related. This one is bigger. It has two floors with lots of windows, and two dormers above them. Lights on in the dormers must mean business is good.*

She adjusted her hat, which was a little too nice for the occasion but suited her face, and pushed ahead. Several oil lamps illuminated the main room of the Hoffman Hotel. It doubled as the hotel lobby and a saloon. A woman whose dress looked two sizes too small tended the bar at the end of the room, while a row of unvarnished tables, mostly empty, ran down one wall. She wore her hair up, her expression locked between boredom and suspicion. When Annie stepped in, the woman ignored her.

Annie set her carpetbag at the foot of the bar and gave her best smile. "I'm looking for a room. Just for myself. One week."

The woman behind the bar looked tired and worn out, with streaks of grey in her otherwise brunette hair. She gave Annie a quick once-over.

"Five dollars," she said, voice flat and nasal, "payable up front. No men after midnight, no fighting, no drinks in your room. If you need hot water, ask for Billy." She waited, hands on the bar, for a reply.

Annie counted out the one-dollar eagles. "I'm Annie. I'll take a corner room if one's open."

The woman squinted, as if trying to remember if she recognized her name. "I'm Susan," she said. "We're pretty full, but I'll make it work. Breakfast is eggs and bread; supper's an extra dime." She slid a tarnished key across the counter and gestured at the narrow staircase to the left.

Upstairs, the hallway's greenish wallpaper had a pattern of faded red roses in bouquets. Annie's room was at the end, and the window overlooked the back alley, where a plot of dirt served as the hotel's private backyard. She tossed her bag onto the thin iron-framed bed and sat, letting the squeaky springs adjust to her weight.

Annie heard muffled voices from the next room over of two or three women. She could not discern what they were talking about, but judging by the tone of their voices, it was nothing serious. Someone in another room coughed, a hacking, phlegmy sound, then the room fell quiet. The only sound afterwards was the endless hammering of the Monarch Stamp Mill down the street.

Annie took off her coat and shoes, rubbed the ache from her feet, then strolled barefoot to the window. The alley below was empty, save for a stray cat stalking something near the privy. From this height, she could see the backs of the brothels and the kitchen doors propped open for air, the yellow gaslight spilling out like gold. She watched for a while, then closed the thin lace curtains.

She thought about her old life, the one she'd left behind in Rocky Bar. Annie thought about Hazel and Edith, and the years spent running from one invisible cage to another. She wondered if anyone here would care who she was, or what she'd done to get this far. No, she decided. Atlanta was full of people like her, people wishing for their first big break.

Annie lay down and folded her hands behind her head. She did not feel tired enough to go to sleep, and even less willing to stay penned up in a small room on her first night in town. She went downstairs and out onto the street. It wasn't cold, but the air held a bite from the snow still melting in the mountains. She needed a drink, and the obvious choice, a saloon named Whiskey Gulch, was a short distance ahead.

The wooden batwing doors of the saloon swung shut behind her as she stepped inside, blinking against the haze of tobacco smoke and the sudden wash of light and noise. The air was warm and heavy, thick with the aroma of whiskey, beer, and the odor of too many unwashed men in one room.

She hesitated past the threshold; the din pressed against her like a wave. Rough laughter cracked through the saloon like pistol shots, mingling with the jangling plunk of a piano in the corner that was missing keys. Boots scraped against the floor, cards slapped tables, chairs dragged, and voices hollered over each other in a dozen overlapping conversations, none of which sounded very polite.

The room was wide, with a low ceiling covered in embossed tin tiles. The sawdust on the floor was fulfilling its purpose of absorbing spent chewing tobacco that missed the spittoons, spilled beer, and a few spots of blood. A long, battered bar stretched the length of the right wall, stained dark by years of spilled whiskey and tobacco stains. Several brass spittoons were lined up on the floor beside the foot rail that ran from one end of the bar to the other. Behind it stood a lean barkeep with sleeves rolled up to his elbows. A row of cloudy mirror panes hung behind him, half reflecting the crowd in warped silver light. An enormous pair of antlers hung crooked over the bar, either from a deer or an elk.

Oil lamps hung from the ceiling on chains, their yellow light flickering against the stained walls, casting shadows that swayed with the crowd. A few lamps were attached to the walls, with crude paintings of women with exaggerated curves hung between them.

Annie moved along the wall, careful not to brush against the more boisterous men. A man with blackened fingernails and a beard matted with crumbs slapped another miner on the back, howling with laughter as cards spilled across the table between them. Another staggered past her, reeking of sweat and whiskey. He belched out loud and said, "Sorry, scuse me, ma'am," and almost fell over.

A woman in scarlet lace, clearly a working girl, leaned over a miner's lap at the far table, her painted lips close to his ear, while his hand wandered up her inner thigh with little attempt at subtlety. *Get a room, people.*

She found a narrow open space at the far end of the bar. She planted one shoe on the foot rail and scanned the room for familiar faces or threats. The barkeep noticed her and raised a brow.

"What'll it be?" he asked, his voice cutting through the din.

"Old Overholt, if you got any."

He gave her a once-over, then he nodded and moved over, returning with the bottle and a glass. He set both down on the bar in front of her. "Here you go."

Annie poured the shot, took a sip, and then a deep breath. This was a different world from the boarding houses and the dirt streets of Rocky Bar. This was a place of risk and hunger, where fortunes were lost and made over cards, drink, a pistol, or a woman's smile.

So, these are the people of Atlanta. They're a rowdy bunch, for sure. She looked over the tumultuous crowd. *Some of these muck shovelers could be my future customers once I get my business up and running. What kind of business, I'm not sure, but I'll figure something out.* When Annie had had her fill of cigar smoke and whiskey breath, she downed the last of the whiskey and headed out the door into the night, and back to her room at the Hoffman House.

The next night, Annie walked past the Whiskey Gulch and over to the Silver Moon Dance Hall. Even from the street, Annie heard the racket: a piano banging away, men's voices already gone hoarse from yelling, and somewhere under all that, the raucous laugh of a woman having the time of her life.

She stepped inside, letting the noise envelop her. The air was so thick with cigar smoke she had to blink to clear her eyes. A bar ran the length of the front room, lined with men who drank as if the next gold rush was already on its way. The place was crowded. About a dozen couples were doing their best to prance around to the music's rhythm. The girls in their flashy dresses were moving gracefully, but most of the men had obviously never taken dancing lessons. That made her chuckle.

A girl standing in the corner with hair so red that it looked painted on belted out "Sweet Betsy from Pike," her voice careening off the notes like a runaway wagon. Annie closed her eyes and listened.

> Did you ever hear tell of Sweet Betsy from Pike,
> Who crossed the wide mountains with her lover Ike,
> Two yoke of cattle, a large yeller dog,
> A tall Shanghai rooster, and a one-spotted hog.
> Singing too-ra-li-oo-ra-li-oo-ra-li-ay.
>
> They swam the wide rivers and crossed the tall peaks,
> And camped on the prairie for weeks upon weeks.
> Starvation and cholera, hard work and slaughter—
> They reached California 'spite of hell and high water.
> Singing too-ra-li-oo-ra-li-oo-ra-li-ay.
>
> One evening quite early they camped on the Platte,
> 'Twas near by the road on a green shady flat.
> Betsy, sore-footed, lay down to repose—
> With wonder Ike gazed on that Pike County rose.
> Singing too-ra-li-oo-ra-li-oo-ra-li-ay.
>
> Out on the prairie one bright starry night,
> They broke out the whiskey and Betsy got tight.
> She sang and she shouted and danced o'er the plain
> And showed her bare arse to the whole wagon train.
> Singing too-ra-li-oo-ra-li-oo-ra-li-ay.

The piano man, covered with scraggly gray hair and a crumpled shirt, kept his head down, fingers banging the keys with a vengeance.

175

Annie made her way past the bar, careful not to brush up against anyone unless she had to. She didn't bother ordering a drink, found a spot near the corner of the room, and leaned against a varnished post, arms crossed, eyes working the crowd. She liked the way the floor moved under her, boards flexing with every stomp and dance. The entire building felt alive. It reminded her of the old days with Hazel in Rocky Bar, when they sneaked into the miners' dances and stole a turn around the floor before anyone noticed two girls their age weren't supposed to be there. She remembered the way Hazel grabbed her hand, spinning her until the world blurred, then laughed so hard she had to double over to breathe.

This place was nothing like the saloons in Rocky Bar. The dance hall girls here had a practiced look, their smiles as sharp and precise as the cut of their corsets. They danced for tips, or for the sheer pleasure of being the brightest thing in a room full of desperate men. Annie observed them; watching the way they moved, the way they calculated every swing of the hips and toss of the hair for maximum effect. She could see the hunger in the eyes of the men, not just for a body, but for the promise of something sweeter, something that made them forget their endless toil, if only for the length of a song.

The set ended in a scatter of applause and hollers; the singer took a bow so deep it looked like she would fold in half. The piano man coughed and wiped his brow with the sleeve of his coat, then fumbled in his pocket for a silver flask. Men at the bar banged on their glasses, calling for another tune, but the girl grinned and vanished through a bead curtain into the back.

That was Annie's cue. She picked her way over to the bar and found the man who seemed in charge of the place. He was easy to spot: a stout man, going bald, with a walrus mustache and a thick cigar hanging out of his mouth. He stood at the end of the bar, surveying the dance hall with a look of satisfaction.

"You looking for work, or a place to rest your elbows?" he asked as soon as she got within speaking range.

Annie didn't flinch. "I can dance. Used to work the floor at the Newcomer House in Rocky Bar." *That's a stretch. I only danced there three times before me and Hazel got kicked out, but it was fun while it lasted.* "Figured I'd see if there was an opening here."

The man looked at her from head to toe. "You ever danced for a crowd like this? It gets mighty rowdy here on Saturday nights."

"I've danced for worse," she said, her voice nonchalant. *That's another stretch. Keep it honest, girl.*

He grunted, lips twitching as if he might smile. "You got a name?"

"Annie Morrow."

"Well, Annie Morrow, you're in luck. Lost a girl last week to laudanum. Had to let her go. I run a respectable establishment. You start tomorrow, seven sharp. Costumes are in the back. You'll be in there with five other girls. Take your meals in the kitchen. Half your ticket sales and tips go to the house. You got a problem with that, keep walkin'." He smashed his cigar into an ashtray.

Annie shook her head. "No problem. I'm not here to get rich."

"Good," the man said, "because you won't."

"I know what I'm doing."

He lit another cigar, took a long drag, and exhaled right into her face, then turned to start a conversation with an old man standing next to him.

The smoke stung her eyes, and she took that as her cue to leave and headed for the door. On her way out, she nearly collided with the piano man, who had followed her. Up close, he looked even older, his fingers permanently curled from years of pounding out ragtime for men who never learned to dance.

"You gonna dance here?" he said with his raspy voice.

"Looks that way."

"Well, remember, they all want the same thing."

"And what's that?" she asked, genuinely curious.

He leaned in towards her, lowering his voice. "Somethin' to break the drudgery of livin' half your damn life underground. It don't take much to make these fellas happy, and from the looks of you, I'd say you're gonna be good at it. You're right pretty, if you don't mind me sayin' so."

Annie gave him a quick smile. "Thank you."

"The name's Elmer."

"I'm Annie."

"Well, Annie, I believe we'll get along fine, like two peas in a pod. I seen a lot of girls come and go from this place, but I have a good feeling about you." With that, he shuffled off toward the kitchen in the back.

As she left the Silver Moon Dance Hall, the music started up again behind her. This time it was Camptown Races. Once outside, she walked at a slow pace so she could hear the woman's words even as they grew fainter with every passing step.

> Camptown ladies sing this song, Doo-dah! doo-dah!
> Camptown race-track five miles long, Oh, doo-dah day!
> I come down here with my hat caved in, Doo-dah! doo-dah!
> I go back home with a pocket full of tin, Oh, doo-dah day!
>
> Gonna run all night!
> Gonna run all day!
> I'll bet my money on the bob-tail nag,
> Somebody bet on the bay.
>
> The long tail filly and the big black horse, Doo-dah! doo-dah!
> They fly the track and they both cut across, Oh, doo-dah-day!
> The blind horse stricken in a big mudhole, Doo-dah! doo-dah!
> Can't touch bottom with a ten-foot pole, Oh, doo-dah day!
>
> Gonna run all night!
> Gonna run all day!
> I'll bet my money on the bob-tail nag,
> Somebody bet on the bay.
>
> Old muley cow come on to the track, Doo-dah! doo-dah!
> The bob-tail fling her over his back, Oh, doo-dah-day!

Then fly along like a rail-road car, Doo-dah! doo-dah!
Runnin' a race with a shootin' star, Oh, doo-dah-day!

Gonna run all night!
Gonna run all day!
I'll bet my money on the bob-tail nag,
Somebody bet on the bay.

Back at the Hoffman Hotel, she paused at the front door, took a long breath of the chilly mountain air, and let it clear her head. *Tomorrow I will dance. I've loved dancing ever since Pa taught me when I was little. Now it can earn some money with it. I like that idea. How hard can it be?*

Annie pushed open the front door, the warmth spilling over her, and climbed the stairs to her room. She heard Susan downstairs singing to herself as she cleaned up for the night. It was the same old tune, a little off-key, but familiar in a way that made Annie long for something she couldn't name.

Chapter 24

The first rule of the dance hall dressing room was that nobody knocked, and nobody cared what you looked like half-dressed. Annie learned right away that the room behind the crimson curtain was less of a dressing room and more like a cattle chute: one long bench, three cracked mirrors, and the raw, living tangle of five girls wiggling into their evening best.

She arrived early because she didn't want everyone to stare at her when she entered the room full of girls for the first time. The air in the dressing room already simmered with yesterday's stale perfume and hair tonic, the floor littered with the day's mail and last week's feathers. Annie set her carpetbag on the bench, unwrapped the blue sequined dress the Boss Man had handed her, and held it up to the lamp. It was heavier than she expected, festooned with sequins that sparkled from every light in the room. She ran her thumb along the hem and tried not to imagine who had worn it before.

The low amber glow of oil lamps flickered against the pink plaster walls. Beneath a long mirror hung crooked on the wall, the dance hall girls drifted in one by one and readied themselves for the night's work.

"Welcome, new girl, I'm Ruby," said the first one to enter, wearing a genuine smile.

"I'm Annie." Ruby looked to be about thirty and was the unofficial den mother of the group. She sat on an upturned whiskey crate, carefully rolling her chestnut hair into a smooth pompadour, then pinning the rest into an elegant Gibson tuck. Her face was heart-shaped, with high cheekbones and sharp green eyes that seemed to glow with mischief. She carried with her an air of authority. A constellation of freckles dotted her nose, visible beneath the powder. She had a tall, rather muscular figure, broad-shouldered, with long legs and generous curves that filled out her crimson satin dress like it had been stitched just for her. The gown hugged her waist and flared enough to hint at a scandal, with black lace trim at the hem and neckline.

Ruby glanced in the mirror, then over her shoulder and smirked at the next girl who had walked in and sat down. "Millie, if you dab any more rouge on those cheeks, you're liable to scare the boys clean outta their boots."

Millie laughed, dimples appearing in her full, rosy cheeks as she repeatedly batted her eyelashes in the mirror. "I hardly used any. Don't be so persnickety." She looked like the youngest of the bunch, probably still a teenager. She had the air of a hard-working farm girl. Her face was round and soft, with warm hazel eyes and a button nose. Her figure was petite but curvy, with a high, bouncing bust and a narrow waist that vanished beneath a lavender corset with mother-of-pearl buttons. Her skirt flounced with tulle and ribbon, and her hair, golden-blonde and thick as hay in August, had been pinned high, with a few playful ringlets left to dangle at her neck.

Next to Millie, another girl sat down and leaned into the mirror, lining her almond-shaped eyes with soot-darkened powder. She had the quiet grace of someone who knew how to move without overdoing it. Her porcelain skin made her thick lashes, arched brows, and naturally red lips stand out. She wore her inky-black hair in a braided crown wrapped around her head like a halo, with ringlets dangling beside her ears. She was slim and willowy, almost ethereal in her sea-green velvet dress, which shimmered with tiny hand-sewn beads. "I heard that new piano player's got a sweetheart back in Omaha," she said, glancing sideways. "But he was lookin' at you last night, Ruby, like he wanted somethin' only you could give."

Ruby scoffed. "Let him look, Pearl. That don't cost nothin'."

Next to Pearl was an Italian-looking girl who fought with a stubborn comb, trying to tame her wild curls into something resembling order. She had a sun-kissed complexion and amber-brown eyes that gleamed. Her mouth was wide, with a natural pout that made men lean in when she spoke. She had a full, hourglass figure, busty and broad-hipped, with a graceful swing in her step. Her dress was a burst of sunshine, gold satin with cream-colored ruffles that caught the lamplight and made her coppery curls glow.

"Damn thing's got a mind of its own," she muttered, yanking at the comb.

"Oh, quit your complaining," Lottie, someone said.

Pearl looked over at Lottie. "Try wetting the teeth of the comb. Mama used to do that for me when I was little."

Lottie sighed. "If this thing yanks out one more curl, I'll go out there bald."

The girls broke into laughter, the kind that made the room feel warmer. Outside, the piano tinkled its way through *Turkey in the Straw,* signaling that the first patrons had come in. Boots clomped on the saloon floor beyond the curtain.

Sitting next to Annie on the bench, another girl about her age was also getting ready. She wore her thick and glossy brown hair, loose in tumbling waves down her back, with a velvet ribbon around it for flair. The curls framed a face that was both sharp and beautiful: high, sculpted cheekbones, a straight nose, and full, deep-colored lips that rarely gave away what she was thinking. Her eyes were her most arresting feature—a vivid, penetrating green that missed nothing. They had a catlike quality, bold and unblinking, which could shift in an instant from playful mischief to cold calculation. Under the warm lamplight of the dressing room, her eyes sparkled, giving her an otherworldly allure. She had a slender figure and wore a small cameo brooch on a thin gold chain. Her complexion was clear, and there were a few light freckles sprinkled across her cheeks. *You don't need to put on so much makeup. You're a natural beauty, girl, but that isn't what most of the men want now, is it?*

She glanced at Annie in the mirror, then turned and flashed a crooked, lipstick-stained smile. "Don't worry, it looks better on than off," she said, nodding at Annie's dress. Her voice was warm and friendly, pitched low so the others wouldn't hear.

Annie shrugged. "I've worn worse."

"You must be the one from Rocky Bar," she said. "I hear that the girls over there make their dresses out of used feed sacks."

"Only on Tuesdays," Annie replied deadpan, "and we wash them first," not sure if it was meant as a joke or an insult.

They grinned at each other, and for a second Annie felt a prickle of nervous friendship, the kind she remembered from schoolhouse days with Hazel. Just like Hazel, this girl had a smile in her eyes. It was the kind of smile you can't fake.

The dressing room was alive with the buzz of women preparing for the night. The air was thick with the tang of hot metal from the curling irons hissing in their stands, mingled with the powdery sweetness of cheap perfume dabbed on necks and wrists. Someone swore under her breath, and someone else giggled in response.

Annie stood near the cracked mirror propped against the wall, working her dress down over her head with a twist of her shoulders. The fabric whispered as it settled into place, catching the gaslight in a shimmer of sequins and beads that clung to her hips like water droplets. She reached behind to cinch the waist tight, exhaling, tugging, then tying off with a grunt of effort, until the corset hugged her ribs like a second skin. *I didn't know a corset could do this for a girl's figure.*

She turned side to side, letting the skirt swish around her legs in a ripple of satin and glitter. It sparkled, all right, gaudy and proud, exactly as it should. Her reflection in the mirror was warped at the edges, but the woman staring back was still quite striking, she thought. *I don't look that bad.*

She lifted her brush and ran it through her black hair in gentle strokes; the bristles caught lightly on the ringlets she had already set. The soft, crisp scent of hair pomade clung to each wave. She tapped at her cheeks with her fingertips, checking for shine, then leaned in close to the mirror and pressed her lips together with a soft smacking sound, smoothing the crimson lipstick into a perfect bow. Annie allowed herself a small, satisfied smile, not vain, just grateful. She had always taken care with her appearance, not for the sake of vanity, but because it reminded her she could still turn heads.

The girl who sat next to her sidled over and started fussing with Annie's hair, pulling it back and twisting a piece into a little bun. "You got a delicate face," she said, her hands quick and gentle. "Makes the rest of us look like stray cats."

Annie rolled her eyes. "Is that a compliment, or you got something against stray cats?"

"A compliment," the girl said, dead serious. "You got presence, and the men will pay for that. Even if you don't show 'em nothin'. I'm Emma, but everyone around here calls me Dutch Em. When I first got here, I told the girls I was from Deutschland, trying to be cute. They thought I was Dutch, from The Netherlands. They speak Dutch there. I told them that *Deutschland* is how you say 'Germany' in German. That's where my parents are from, but I was born back east. And *Deutsch* is how you say 'German' in German. *Deutch* became 'Dutch'. Anyway, the name stuck. There you have it."

"I'm Annie. How bout I call you Em?"

"Sure," was the reply as Em stood up and tucked into her own dress, a deep red outfit with black lace at the sleeves, and started lacing herself up. She was pretty, and she had an attractive figure, but she was not as tall as Annie. Em dressed like a woman who refused to fade into the background. Her bodice had rich colors—crimson, midnight blue, and emerald—which clung to her slender waist, while her satin skirt swished around her legs with every step. A silver choker adorned her neck.

Despite her glamour, there was something unmistakably hardened about Em—a steel beneath the silk. A faint white scar along her forearm, visible only when her sleeve slipped, hinted at a past full of close calls. She carried herself with the poised readiness of someone who had long ago learned to rely on her wits and her aim more than anyone's protection.

"First night's always the worst, but you get through it. You danced before?"

"Some, in Rocky Bar, but not for a crowd like this."

Em laughed, then looked Annie dead in the eye. "Silly. It's not how well you dance that matters, girl. It's how you look when you're doing it. These miners, they're like dogs. Show 'em a little skin, and they'll start drooling." She winked. "They pay a dollar for every dance, and half goes to Boss Man. On a busy night, you can make forty dollars."

"So how does it work here?" Annie said, keeping her voice low. "We dance with the men, and that's it?"

"Well . . . mostly."

One of the other girls snickered.

"Shut up, Pearl. I didn't ask for your opinion," Em yelled over at her. "Don't mind her. Pearl never did learn to mind her own business."

Em turned on the bench and faced Annie. "The job's simple. The men buy tickets at the bar. One ticket is good for one dance per set, and not necessarily with just one girl. We get passed around all the time. You work the floor, get the men to buy both of you drinks, and you get a cut for every drink they buy. You'll get a drink too, but yours is just tea, but they don't know that. The barkeep knows what to do. Got to keep your wits about you, ya know. When they ask you to dance, you say 'yes', and they give you their ticket. They can buy as many as they like. If they want more than a dance, you talk to Dolly in the back. But nobody's gonna make you. Only if you want to. At the end of the day, give your tickets to Boss Man and you get fifty cents for each one, plus half of the drinks and half of the tips."

"I see."

"And one more thing. Don't let anyone give you a scrap of paper with 'free dance' written on it. They're ain't no free dances here. This happened to Millie on her first night. Some young sodbuster from out of town told her he got it as a gift. She didn't know any better. Here, take a look at this."

Em handed her a dance ticket printed with black letters on orange paper.

Silver Moon Dance Hall
Atlanta, Idaho

DANCE TICKET

Good for One Dance
Price $1

Annie examined it. The corners were tattered, and the bottom had a small tear. "Looks like these things get used over and over."

"They're as good as money here." Em smiled with her entire face. "I love dancing," she said as she stood up, spread her arms and twirled around. "Keeps me from thinking too much." She tilted her head over and fiddled with a dangling earring, a bright glass bead that caught the lamplight. "But a girl's gotta eat, ya know? Sometimes a dance becomes more than just a dance and turns into a visit upstairs. Depends on the man. And my mood."

What? An upstairs girl? That's what you are? The room fell quiet for a second. Annie noticed the other girls listening in, pretending not to, but hanging on Em's every word.

Ruby was the first to break the silence. "Don't let her fool you," she said, rubbing her cheeks with a vengeance. "Em here used to play piano and her fiddle thing in a fancy house back east. Genuine talent, I heard. She could've had a different life, but she chose this."

Em shrugged. "Fancy houses pay less than you think. Besides, I like it here. No one pretends to be something they're not."

When the other girls squabbled about who would get picked first on the dance floor, Em reached under the bench and pulled out a battered rectangular wooden case. She opened it to reveal something Annie had never seen before. It was a bizarre-looking wooden instrument shaped like a thick fiddle, painted green, with a curved metal crank at the bottom and a row of levers along the neck sticking out from under a wooden cover. There were strings like a fiddle had, but there were many more of them.

"What on earth is that?"

Em grinned, with pride in her eyes. "It's a hurdy-gurdy. It's mine. My mother taught me to play when we lived back east. People either love it or hate it." Em cradled it as if it was a baby, gazing down at it, running her fingers over the levers. "Sometimes, when the room gets slow, I play a tune. The men love it, especially the men who remember the old country. Let me show you how it works." She put it on her lap and turned the crank. A wheel under the strings turned, rubbing against the strings."

"It sounds like a cross between a scratchy fiddle and a bagpipe," Annie said.

"You see," Em continued, "with a fiddle, you have a bow that goes back and forth over the strings. Instead of a bow, a hurdy-gurdy has this wheel under the strings. When I turn this crank, it turns the wheel, which rubs against the strings. These levers over here change the notes."

"Well, I'll be damned," was all Annie could say. She reached over and ran her hand over the wood. The green paint was worn off in a few spots, exposing the light-colored wood beneath. "You ever tire of this? Not your gurdy thing, but the noise, the dancing, and the men?"

Em didn't answer right away. "You can tire of anything, if you let yourself. But it beats starving, and it beats being owned by a man with fists instead of words."

Ouch! The last time Thomas hit me, he almost broke my nose. "I know what you mean."

Em packed the instrument away and then turned to Annie. "Ya got a story? You don't have to tell it now, but I like to know who I'm workin' with."

Yikes. That's a hard question. Where would I begin? She knows nothing about me. My life is complicated. "I got a story, sure. But I'm just looking for new opportunities now. I'll tell you someday."

Em was satisfied with that. She patted Annie on the shoulder, then called out, "Let's go, girls! The boys are hungry for us!"

Someone else shouted, "More like they're starving." Everyone giggled.

Another voice proclaimed, "Even dogs have a right to eat." The giggles multiplied.

A third voice asked, "Does that mean we're dog food?"

Em yelled out, "If we're dog food, then I'm the world's biggest, juiciest T-bone steak, smothered in spicy hot sauce." The giggles turned into laughter. The room became a whirlwind of last fixes: stockings tugged, powder patted, and dresses adjusted to perfection.

The thick mass of men packed the Silver Moon Dance Hall wall-to-wall. The atmosphere was full of anticipation and spillover from the saloon next door. The piano man began his jangling melody, a cascade of shivering keys that signaled the start of the night's work. Annie recognized the tune as *Red River Valley*, but nobody was singing along. The room erupted into a cacophony of sounds as boots shuffled against the wooden floor, chairs scraped back, and glasses clinked together in anticipation. Murmurs rippled through the crowd full of miners, storekeepers, drifters, and the occasional gambler with polished city shoes. They turned in unison to watch the girls make their entrance. The dance floor had been swept clean of sawdust, only to reveal dozens of tobacco and whiskey stains. As Annie and the other girls stepped onto the dance floor, the hollers, whistles, and catcalls began. One girl yelled, "louder, boys, we can't hear you!"

Men crowded against one wall, poking at each other as they pointed out their favorites. The air was heavy, but beneath it, a faint hint of sweet perfume wafted from the girls as they floated across the dance floor. The girls' dresses, some more revealing than others, brushed against the eager men as they pranced by, circling closer and closer to where the men waited with anticipation.

The girls were like colorful bouquets of flowers, each one positioned just right to showcase their unique beauty. Pearl, the star of the show, glimmered in the spotlight. Ruby, stoic and serene, moved with a grace that mesmerized the onlookers, her crimson dress a burst of sunshine in the dimly lit room. Millie, the youngest and most playful, twirled and skipped like a sprite, her ringlets flying behind her in wild abandon. And then there was Em, dancing for no one but herself, her body a vessel for the music as she moved with sensuality, enthralling the men who watched. Em was the sort of girl the miners whispered about, admired, feared, and dreamed of—an untamable spirit wrapped in beauty, stepping lightly through the smoke and piano music as if she owned every pair of eyes that followed her.

Annie hung back for a beat, watching. She thought of her own daughters, somewhere out there, asleep or curled up by the stove, and for a flash Annie felt a shame so strong she almost turned and ran. But then she looked at Em, who caught her eye and gave an approving nod, like a secret handshake. The piano man switched to something waltz-like, off-tempo but familiar. Annie had never worn an outfit so garish, but in the swirl of the other dancers, the shock of color and glitter made her fit right in.

Em had told her in the dressing room not to let the men corner her on the first dance, and if one gets too handsy, step to the left, and another girl will cut in. The girls worked as a team, one step ahead of the hunters, teasing with a smile or a touch of their hand before darting off. Right away, Annie learned to spot the men who had paid their dollar and thought it bought them for the whole evening. Those men got passed around the fastest, tired out, and left by the wall with their hands empty.

Em found Annie in the swirl, linking pinkies with her and spinning her in a wide circle. "You're a natural," Em mouthed, the words lost in the music but clear in her smile. Annie felt a giddiness she hadn't known since she was a child. The two of them made a game of out dancing the rest of the girls.

By the time the next tune started, a fresh round of partners was chosen with a snap and a grab, with each man in a race to latch onto the prettiest or the newest. Annie braced herself. The first partner of this set, an old-timer with a beard like a snowdrift, asked, "May I?" She let him. His grip was tight but not cruel, his steps careful so he would not step on her toes. Soon they were spinning, the entire room alive and swimming with bodies in motion.

Throughout the room, Annie saw the same ritual repeat: men getting bolder, girls cackling and slapping away hands that got too fresh, the bouncer wading in only when it looked like things might turn ugly. It was exhilarating, and it moved in undulating patterns. The girls traded off, swapped partners, snuck breaks behind the curtains when the crowd was distracted. In the corner, Boss Man fingered the money and sent shots of whiskey over to the biggest spenders.

Annie danced with a middle-aged schoolteacher who claimed to have walked thirty miles through snow to get here. *Yeah right. And while it was snowing too?* She danced with a young guy from the upper canyon who was afraid to speak but gave her a perfect waltz. *Looks like you took lessons.* She danced with a banker's son, who was so nervous that he kept tripping over his own feet. *Must be a first-timer. Relax, boy. We're only dancing. This ain't courtship.*

In a rare pause between the racket of the piano and the thump of boots, Em meandered over to Annie with a half-full glass that was not tea and handed it to her. "How's it going?" she said, nudging Annie with her elbow.

Annie blinked, swiped a strand of hair off her sweaty forehead. "I think my legs are ready to quit." Out of habit or stubbornness, she straightened her spine, squared her shoulders. "But I'll survive," she declared, but the words came out with a lightness that surprised even her. Her face was warm, not from the whiskey, but the rough-and-tumble joy of being watched and wanted.

Em's sly smile deepened as she gave Annie a gentle shove. "First night's not so bad, is it?"

Annie took stock of herself: her dress, heavy and scratchy with sweat; her shoes, already pinching her toes; her heart, thudding against her ribs. She couldn't deny it. This was fun, but it was also work, the men rough, and the air a soup of smoke and perfume.

Em laughed, "you'll do great here."

A commotion erupted behind them as Pearl and Lottie climbed up onto the bar and started an impromptu high-kick contest, with coins flying as miners placed bets and yelled out the girls' names. From across the room, the old piano man began pounding out a lively polka. Pearl and Lottie timed their kicks to match the two-step rhythm.

Annie and Em exchanged a look. "Ready for more?" Em asked.

"As ready as I'll ever be."

The girls fell into the old routine, pairing off with whoever grabbed them first. As Annie slid among the groping arms and stomping feet, she realized she enjoyed the chaos, the way everyone collided, separated, and collided again, like a living, sweaty kaleidoscope of humanity. She spun away from a lecherous businessman and into the arms of a shy boy, who blushed when she touched his hand. She was passed from man to man, each one thinking he'd snared her for good, only to be left dizzy and empty-handed as she slipped away.

But as the night deepened, and the drinks flowed, the men got bolder and more aggressive. At the edge of the floor, Annie caught sight of Em, who danced with unmatched enthusiasm, keeping the customers at arm's length while never letting them feel rebuffed. Ruth, meanwhile, absorbed every drunken lunge and crude joke with patience.

As Annie stepped away from the dancers to catch her breath near the bar, a hand shot out of nowhere and clamped around her wrist. The force of it sent a shock through her body so fierce that she froze. She whipped around. A young man stood leering at her. His shirt hung open in filthy tatters, his skin streaked with dust and sweat, and a swollen bruise throbbed like a rotten fruit above one brow. His eyes were the worst— bloodshot, bulging, unfocused, yet burning straight into her. He looked at her the way a starving dog looks at a scrap of meat.

Before she took another breath, he yanked her toward him with a violence that nearly threw her off her feet. She pulled back, but his grip only tightened. Then came his breath—thick, sour, gagging. Rotting tobacco. Warm beer. Something rank and unwashed. It hit her full in the face, and she gagged.

"Let go of me!" she gasped, but the words barely escaped from her throat.

The piano man hammered away, oblivious to her plight. The notes twisted and warped in her ears like the shriek of nails on metal.

She yanked again—harder—but he had already grabbed her waist with his other hand, pulling her up against his chest. The pressure of his fingers digging into her flesh wasn't just uncomfortable—it was familiar.

And suddenly, she wasn't in the dance hall anymore.

She was back in the Boise City cabin, with Thomas's hands locked around her waist. The choke of his whiskey breath invading her lungs. The crushing weight of him pinning her down while she kicked and screamed but could not push him away stormed into her head. Her vision blurred and the dancehall spun around her.

"Stop!" Her voice came out broken, strangled. She gasped for air.

The man's grip tightened. His fingers pressed into her ribs, trapping her arms. She tried to shove him away, but her hands slipped uselessly against fabric slick with sweat. Her mind flooded with blind terror. She couldn't breathe. It felt like an iron band had seized her chest. A thin, high-patched gasp was all she could manage. Panic exploded inside her, shaking her from the inside out. She felt her knees weaken, trembling so that she could hardly stay upright. Her vision returned, narrowed to the man's reeking mouth as his fingers dug deeper into her waist.

"Stop, I tell you! Stop!" she cried—but it came out as a whimper.

She clawed at his hands in desperation. She dug her nails into his skin. He only grunted and pulled her even closer. A wild, primal fear possessed her.

Suddenly Ruth's hand slammed against the man's shoulder with a force that almost knocked him over. Annie flinched as though struck herself.

The man jerked around in disbelief. Ruth was inches from his face, her jaw locked, her eyes sharp enough to cut.

"Hands off, buster. Now! Before I break your damn face!"

He blinked. His hands dropped away from Annie as if scorched. He pretended he wasn't shaken, but all he could do was wobble back to his table and fall into his chair.

Ruth caught Annie before she could collapse. The crowd blurred around her in a swirl of noise and color. Her chest ached with every breath.

"Annie! Look at me. Are you hurt?"

Annie blinked. She couldn't stop shaking. Still dizzy, she clung to the edge of the bar with both hands.

Ruth guided her aside, shielding her. "Honey, it's all right. He's gone. You're safe now."

It sounded like Ruth's voice was coming from some faraway place. Annie could still feel the ghost of his hands—Thomas's hands—gripping her waist.

No, Ruth, I'm not safe. Not yet. Not from the past that can reach out and grab me in the middle of a crowded room.

"Ruth, I . . . I need to sit down," Annie managed, her voice thin and trembling. Her knees wobbled beneath her as she staggered toward an empty chair in the corner. She sank into it and immediately shut her eyes, pressing the heels of her palms against them as though she could force the world to stop spinning. But her heart kept hammering, wild and frantic, each beat slamming against her ribs. Her breath came short and fast, scraping tight through her throat. Her fingers curled into fists against her dress, nails digging into her palms.

She had forgotten what it felt like—what *he* had felt like. In an instant, the years peeled away. She was back on the cabin floor. Thomas's shadow blotted out the lamplight. His hands clamped around her wrists so hard she swore the bones would snap. She re-lived the countless times that he threw her to the floor until the world blurred into splinters and the sound of her own begging became pointless. She smelled his breath reeking of stale beer and whiskey. She felt the sting of his hand slapping her face.

The drunken man's grip was nothing compared to Thomas's brutality, and yet her body didn't know the difference. It only remembered fear. It remembered helplessness. It remembered pain. And now it trembled, unable to distinguish past from present.

She wrapped her arms around herself, trying to steady the shaking. Her shoulders hunched forward, shrinking in on themselves, as if she could make her body too small to be grabbed again. A thin sheen of sweat gathered on her forehead, cool against the warm haze of the dance hall.

The piano man churned through the next tune, bright and lively, feeling horribly out of place. Annie felt pinned to the chair, her legs refusing to obey her. She could not move, not yet. The song had to end. The world had to right itself. Her heart had to learn it was safe again. She forced herself to breathe—slow, deeper, steady—as she clung to the present with both hands. *You're here. Not back there. You survived him. He's gone.*

So she sat, rigid and trembling, waiting out the music, willing her past to loosen its grip long enough for her to stand again. Only when the final note faded into the clatter of voices did she feel her lungs begin to thaw enough for her to piece herself back together. With all the resolve she could muster, Annie stood up, brushed the hair out of her face, straightened out her sleeves, and brushed at a few wrinkles in her dress. *I can make it here. I'm Annie Morrow, and I'm somebody. I don't give up!*

Every girl here had survived by learning fast and sticking together when the miners got mean or desperate. Annie understood that now, and when the following set ended, she returned to the dressing room with the other girls, her hair wild, and skin wet with sweat. Finally, her heart stopped racing.

Ruth, applying more rouge, glanced over. "You did good, Annie."

In the mirror, Annie caught her own reflection. She looked flushed, messy, eyeliner running. Annie saw Em in the reflection, standing behind her, arms folded and eyes soft. She glanced over at Ruth. "Thanks for what you did, Ruth. You saved me."

"We look out for each other here."

"You did good," Em said. "You made them notice." There was no envy in her voice, only the satisfaction of watching something catch fire for the first time. Em reached down and tucked an errant strand of hair behind Annie's ear, her fingers cool and deft, lingering long enough to make it an act of kindness. Annie had braced for a joke, a nudge, or even a jab about their dancing like camptown ladies. Instead, Em gave her the unguarded warmth of another woman who had decided, without asking, that Annie belonged.

"Careful, Em," Millie called from across the dressing room, "or Annie here will end up out dancing us all." The other girls cackled, slapping their fishnet stocking-covered thighs, but Em gave Annie a wink as if they shared a secret.

Annie leaned back on the bench, letting the sweat on her neck chill her skin. She wasn't sure what to say. She let herself be seen, let herself take up space in the room. The piano music started up once again, signaling the next set. Annie squared her shoulders, pushed down the churning in her belly, and followed the others out. *Here we go again. Get ready, boys!*

The crowd swelled, with miners coming off shifts, men gathering around the faro tables, and a few old-timers. The air was so hot now that Annie's hair stuck to her neck. Her dress itched, but she ignored it, focusing instead on the quick exchanges of dance tickets and cash, the safe passage from one corner of the floor to the next. She saw how the regulars policed the rowdies, how a nod from Ruth could silence even the loudest drunk, how Em's glare could stop a hand mid-reach. There was a girl's code here.

She finished the last dance, did her bow, and hurried back to the dressing room, her head buzzing with the noise and the blur of it all. The girls collapsed onto the bench, yanking off shoes, wiping sweat from their faces with whatever came to hand.

Boss Man appeared in the dressing room doorway, with the same cigar still hanging from his mouth. He gave Annie the once-over and handed her a folded bill. "For the new girl," he said, loud enough for the others to hear. "You keep this. Call it a bonus." Annie took the ten-dollar bill and slipped it into her pocket.

Em flopped down beside her, pulled a metal flask from somewhere in her dress, and offered it without a word. Annie took a sip. It burned her throat but steadied her nerves. "Was I good?" she asked.

Em shook her head, smiling. "You were better than good. You were amazing. You look like you belong out there."

Since they had finished the last set, Em and Annie changed out of their dresses, trading gossip and funny lyrics from the songs they'd mangled on the dance floor. Em showed off a few bruises from the day before, then offered to walk Annie back to the Hoffman Hotel. The streets were quiet at this hour, with most of the men sleeping off their night or wandering home with a girl on each arm. They said their goodnights at the hotel's front door, and Annie went inside.

When she got back to her room, she counted the night's earnings. *Thirty-six dollars. Not bad for the first night. The schoolmarm in Rocky Bar gets paid twenty-five dollars in a month. That's not fair. On the other hand, there's not much stopping a schoolmarm from becoming a dance hall girl, if she wanted to, and if her husband allowed it, that is.* She set the coins and bills in a neat stack on the dresser, then sat by the open window and listened to the faint echo of laughter coming up the street.

Chapter 25

By the summer of 1895, Annie had gone from the new girl to the unofficial Queen of the Silver Moon Dance Hall. She had learned to read every face in the crowd, to know which miners were flush with gold and which were bluffing, which man would tip big, and which one needed a sharp word to keep his hands to himself. Annie was so popular that her earnings enabled her to buy a small cabin at the edge of town, right off the road that led to Rocky Bar.

Tonight would be busier than most, being a payday. The bar at the dance hall was three-deep with men, the tables full of raucous laughter and cigar smoke. Em moved through the crowd with a tray of brandy, her dress a deep plum color. Annie watched her work, admiring how Em's bubbly personality made it a pleasure for the men to interact with her. She had that effect on people.

"Hey, Annie! Over here!" Joey, one of the regulars, called out. She liked him because he was the perfect gentleman. She slid past the bar, balancing two drinks, and handed one to him.

"How's your claim producing, Joey?" she asked, grinning as he tipped his glass.

"Better now, sweetheart," he said. "But the genuine gold's right in front of me. You know I'm talkin' 'bout you, right? You're the prettiest girl in this boomtown, don't ya know?" He winked at her, and Annie gave him a coy smile, kissed him on his cheek, lingered longer than she needed to, letting him enjoy the flirt before moving on.

Em circled back, her tray empty, and they met near the edge of the dance floor.

"You ever tire of this?" Annie asked, once again.

Em shrugged. "It's like milking a cow. You know how to handle them and out comes the gold."

They both laughed, and Annie took a moment to breathe, looking out over the sea of faces. She recognized almost everyone except for a few new drifters. *Some of these boys could be more than customers. They could be my friends.*

Boss Man watched the room from behind the bar. He nodded once at Annie, then jerked his head towards a man sitting near the faro table. The look on his face said, "that one's got money to burn."

Annie spotted him—tall, well-dressed, carrying himself like he'd never once had to rush for anything in his life. A wealthy man trying his luck in a rough camp like Atlanta drew attention. Annie observed him for a minute. Something in his confidence tugged at her curiosity. She sauntered toward him with a dancer's easy sway, her dress brushing her shoes in a whisper of fabric, but stopped before reaching his table. Her smile curled slowly, deliberately, as though she were allowing it only for him.

"Well now," she said, tilting her chin enough to catch the lamplight across her cheekbones, "you look like a man who wandered into the wrong sort of place. Shouldn't you be somewhere fancy—where the chairs don't wobble and the beer is cold?"

The man blinked, startled that such a direct greeting came wrapped in a velvet voice. "I reckon I'm right where I meant to be, in the place where you work," he replied, though she caught the half-second he needed to prepare his response.

Annie laughed, soft and low. She let her fingertips trail along the edge of a nearby table, moving in a slow arc that led her closer. "Careful with words like that, sir. A girl might think you came to see her."

"Maybe I did," he said. He smiled. "You're Annie, aren't you? Heard about you all the way from Boise City."

She hid her surprise. "Nice things, I hope."

"Best things. Seems like you've made quite a name for yourself here."

Her eyebrows lifted, amused, impressed by the compliment. She dipped one shoulder coyly, as if the weight of his attention warmed her more than she planned to admit. "Is that so? Then you ought to tell me your name, mister. I can't flirt properly with a stranger."

He touched the brim of his hat in a small, polite bow. "Jacob Ellington."

"Ellington?" She whistled softly. "Sounds like money." Leaning in just close enough for him to catch the scent of lilac powder in her hair, she added, "Don't worry—I only charge extra if you brag about it."

His laugh broke free before he could stifle it.

She stepped back with a triumphant grin, hands resting lightly on her hips. *Annie one, Jacob zero.* "There now, Jacob Ellington. That's better. A man ought to smile when he walks into a place like this. Makes the whole room feel less lonesome."

He studied her, taking in the spark in her dark eyes, the way she tilted her head as though waiting for a secret to fall out of him. "What about you?" he asked. "You look like you belong somewhere better."

A faint blush bloomed across her chest and up her throat, but she hid it with a practiced toss of her hair. "Oh, Jacob, a place is only as good as the company you find in it."

Then she extended her right hand, palm up, fingers slightly curled, an invitation as old as dance itself. "Come on, Jacob. Let's see if you can keep up. I don't waste my time on men with two left feet."

He took her hand, warm and steady, and Annie's smile softened—not coy, not calculated, but unexpectedly real.

"Lucky for you," he murmured, "I can't stand to disappoint a lady." He paused. "But I don't have a dance ticket."

"Not to worry. This one's on the house."

As the piano man struck up another reel, Annie's laughter rang bright over the room, drawing curious glances. She didn't notice them—not tonight. Tonight, she had a new partner, and she meant to enjoy every second of his surprise at just how bold a dance hall girl like her could be.

The reel ended in a whirl of skirts and boot heels. Annie let him hold her hand all the way back to their table, which he appreciated. She could tell by the way his thumb grazed across her knuckles, as though memorizing the shape of her hand.

"Well," she said, pretending to catch her breath, "you dance better than you look."

He blinked. "Is that a compliment?"

She grinned. "I'll let you figure that out yourself." She tilted her head. "Or buy me a drink, Jacob Ellington, and maybe I'll tell you what I meant."

Annie watched him as he sat, folding his long frame into the chair with a smoothness that didn't fit the grit and noise around them. The lamps overhead cast a warm amber glow, soft enough to blur the rough edges of the saloon, but not soft enough to make Jacob look like he belonged there. Once he had caught the attention of the barkeep and ordered two whiskeys, Annie spun her chair around backwards and straddled it, her arms folded across the top, chin resting on her interlaced fingers. It was a bold pose, one that blurred the line between playful and intimate. Jacob shifted in his chair, as if the gesture caught him off guard. *Reel him in, girl.*

Now that Jacob was across the table from her, Annie took time to study him. His dark coat was finely cut, tailored in a way she'd never seen in Atlanta. The fabric held its shape despite the dust in the air, and when he shifted, the lapels caught the lamplight with a faint sheen. His vest was a deep blue, embroidered along the edges, and his crisp white shirt made him appear luminous against the smoke-blurred room. Even his boots were polished, the leather supple and high-quality, a stark contrast to the scuffed and battered footwear around them.

But it was his face that held her gaze, with its clean, deliberate lines. He had a well-shaven jaw, strong but not harsh. Although his dark hair was neatly combed, a stray lock had fallen free at his temple, softening his otherwise businesslike appearance. His eyes were cool gray, observant and steady, with a warmth beneath that surfaced only when he smiled. And he did smile, shy at times, as if he wasn't used to letting his guard down.

"You all right?" he asked, voice low and even, while watching her with that careful attentiveness.

Annie lifted her glass, pretending to study the amber liquid instead of him. "I'm fine," she said softly, though her pulse betrayed her. She stole another glance at him through her glass.

He sat with perfect posture. His shoulders were squared but relaxed, his hands folded loosely on the table. He had the manners of a man who'd been taught exactly how to behave in polite company, yet his eyes roamed the saloon with curiosity. Every now and then, he adjusted his gold cufflinks. It was a small, almost unconscious gesture that told her he was used to better places than this one. He looked out of place, but he didn't seem uncomfortable. And that intrigued her more than it should have.

Annie felt heat rise in her cheeks as she let herself really see him. The breadth of his shoulders. The subtle strength in his wrists and hands. The gentle way he leaned toward her, as though trying to hear her better over the clatter of glasses and piano music. He smelled faintly of cedar and clean soap, nothing like the sweat-and-whiskey haze of most men.

She found herself leaning in too, drawn by something she couldn't name. Her breath caught when his eyes met hers, and she didn't look away. Jacob smiled, just a slight curve of his lips, but it lit up his entire face. "You're staring at me," he murmured, amusement flickering in his eyes.

"And you look like you stepped out of a banker's office," Annie shot back, flustered but unable to stop smiling. "What are you doing in a place like this, anyway?"

He chuckled softly, the sound warm and genuine. "I needed a change of scenery."

Annie looked down at her drink, trying to steady herself, but her gaze drifted upward again and again, drawn back to him like a moth to lamplight. *I know trouble when I see it. I know longing, too. Be careful, Annie.* As she took a slow sip of her non-whiskey drink, she wondered how much longer she could pretend she didn't feel the pull of him across the table.

"You always sit so rigidly?" she asked. "Like you're fixin' to be painted for a portrait?"

He laughed under his breath. "I suppose I do."

"You don't need to with me." She shifted, letting one foot stretch out until the toe of her shoe touched the side of his. It was a brush, light as a whisper.

He looked down, startled, then back up at her. She winked. *He's easy. I like this guy.*

The barkeep returned with a second round of drinks, and Annie slid one glass toward herself, but rather than take a sip, she leaned forward, resting her cheek on the back of her hand. Her eyes softened, warm and assessing.

Placing her elbows on the table, she set her chin once again on her interlaced fingers and looked at him with a steady gaze. She allowed their eyes to meet again, and she sensed he enjoyed the sight before him. Annie liked what she saw, too. From the grin on his face, she knew he was savoring every moment. She twirled one of her ringlets with a finger, slowly so he would not miss the slightest movement. That made his big brown eyes sparkle. *It's nice to be appreciated, and to give someone a little happiness by sitting here and doing nothing, but I shouldn't tease him, even though I like to. Or maybe I should tease him. I think he likes it. I know I do.*

"The name's Annie."

"You already told me that. You've hardly touched your drink. Not to your liking?"

Annie felt self-conscious for a moment. *He already knows my name. Careful, girl.* "I never drink more than half. Leaves a gentleman wondering if I'm delicate or just cautious.

"You're different from the usual crowd," she murmured. "You look like a man who thinks too much."

"Is that a bad thing?"

"Not if you think about the right things." She brushed a loose strand of hair away from her face without breaking eye contact. "What are you thinkin' about now, Jacob?" *Let's see how you answer that one, sir.*

He hesitated, and she caught it instantly. Her grin widened. *You're so transparent. You'd make a lousy poker player.* "Ahh, now that's interesting. A smart man usually finds a ready answer. You . . . you paused. Makes me wonder what's goin' on in that head of yours."

Jacob picked up his glass to steady himself, taking a small sip. Annie watched the movement, her gaze tracking the line of his throat, slow and appreciative. It rattled him enough that he nearly set the glass down too hard.

"Well, I'll be damned," she said with a low laugh. "Are you nervous?"

He cleared his throat. "I'm not nervous. I'm just not used to . . . this sort of thing."

She stretched again, letting her foot nudge his boot with a subtle pressure, this time more deliberate. "And exactly is 'this sort of thing' that you refer to?"

"Sharing a drink with a pretty girl I just met."

"Really? I find that hard to believe, Mr. Ellington. I bet you've spent time with many pretty girls."

"Not as many as you might think."

That answer softened something in her expression, though she covered it with a playful hum. "Well, I believe you're in the right place at the right time. I like a man who sticks around long enough to see what trouble he's getting himself into."

Annie reached across the table, picked up his glass, and brought it up to his lips. "Drink."

He took a sip and said, "are you using your feminine wiles on me, Miss Annie?"

"I have no idea what you're talking about, sir."

Jacob swallowed hard. "All right, I admit you make me a little nervous, but just a little, mind you. You're pretty good at what you do."

"And exactly what is it that you think I do here?"

"Do I need to spell it out for you?"

"Humor me."

Annie folded her hands on the table and leaned forward. "Careful, sir. A man can lose his fortune chasing answers from a girl like me."

"You charm men like me into having a good time. Like I said, you're pretty good at it. Job well done, Miss Annie." His words struck deeper than they should have.

"Just so you know, Mr. Ellington, it's not just a job."

She let the silence stretch. It was comfortable for her, breathless for him, as she traced the rim of his glass with a finger. Annie had played this role of smiling, teasing, dangling winks and words like bait on a hook dozens of times. *Jacob doesn't leer at me the way most men do. His gaze is penetrating. I love those eyes of his. This feels different. He's different. He makes me feel different.*

Her heart betrayed her. It quickened, as if believing him against her will. She remembered another man, another night, the promises Thomas whispered in her ear before the hand that caressed her became the hand that struck her. *I swore never again. Yet here I am, flirting with him. Cool it, girl. I feel like I'm standing on the edge of a cliff again, like those moments right before I married Thomas. If I step forward, I could fall in love with you, sir. If I step back, I'll be safe. Why can't feelings be simple and easy to understand? You're a good man, Jacob. What am I getting myself into?*

"You're fun, Jacob," she murmured. "I think I might keep you around a while."

The way she said it felt like both a promise and a dare. She stood and put her hands on the table, leaning over Jacob. "It's been a long night, Jacob. I best be going. Thank you for the drinks, and I hope I'll see you in here more often. I'll always treat you right." She stepped back from the table.

"Okay. I'll be in town for a few days on business. Till next time. Good night, Miss Annie."

"Good night, Jacob."

Annie walked into the dressing room to find Em sitting in front of the mirror, wiping off her lipstick. Without looking up, Em said, "So who's Mr. Moneybags you're flirting with?"

"Who's flirting?"

"You were. Don't kid yourself. You were falling all over him. I seen ya."

"His name's Jacob."

"Jacob who?"

"Ellington."

"Well, that's a rich man's name if I've ever heard one. Did he buy a lot of drinks?"

"He did." Annie unfastened her choker.

"And . . . ."

"And what?"

Em put down the cloth she was using and turned to face Annie. "There's something you're not telling me, sister."

"He's good-looking."

"And . . . ."

"He has money."

"And . . . ."

"He dresses like a gentleman."

"Annie! Out with it. What are you not telling me? You know what I mean."

Annie studied herself in the mirror and began wiping off her eyeliner with gentle strokes. Next, she worked on her lipstick with long, slow strokes, pausing between each one.

"Annie!"

"What?'

"Do I have to beat it out of you?

Annie froze. "That's not funny!"

"Sorry."

"Okay, already. I like him. What of it?"

"Like him? Are you nuts? Flirting is part of the job, dearie, but once you get feelings for the men, you're in deep shit. You can't go and fall for every handsome dude that comes walking into this place. The next thing you know, you'll fall in love with him. I seen it happen. Right here. Boss Man don't like it. Since I started workin' here, I seen three girls run off with the man of their dreams. Don't let that happen to you."

"I just said I like him. I'm not in love with him, and I have no plans to go running off with anybody. Not yet anyway."

"So, you admit it's possible?"

"That's not what I meant. Don't put words in my mouth." She started working on her rouge.

"I'm just sayin' Annie, be careful. I don't need to remind you of what happened between you and Thomas."

Annie turned and glared directly at Em.

"Sorry. I'm just looking out for you."

"I don't need anyone lookin' out for me. You're my best friend, Em, so I appreciate your concern, but you don't need to worry about it."

"Okay. Gotta go. See you tomorrow. Good night, Annie."

"Good night, Em."

*　*　*

Jacob returned a few nights later and sat at the same table, "their table", although Annie refused to let herself call it that. Annie felt his arrival before she even saw him; the faint lift in her chest betrayed her. She glanced over at Boss Man as if seeking instructions, but she knew the routine. She knew what was expected. She played her part.

The same routine happened the next night, and the night after that. Each time she saw him, the warmth inside her grew a little brighter, a little braver. Tonight, when she finally met his eyes, something inside her tightened.

Men stay gentle only as long as they feel like it. I learned that lesson the hard way, with bruises to prove it. Jacob's unwavering eyes penetrated into the bruised places in her soul, stirring a longing she had buried so deep she had believed it dead. *Trusting him means opening a door I nailed shut*

206

years ago. And yet—a tiny part of me wants to pry that door open. Just a crack, to see what happens.

After several minutes of their usual easy banter, Jacob leaned forward, clearing his throat as if gathering courage.

"I'd like to spend more time with you," he said.

The air inside her chest collapsed. *He's serious.* Fear, sharp and cold, rippled down her spine. *I know where this road leads.*

"But you hardly know me," she said, her voice thinner than she intended.

"You're better than this place, Annie."

She stopped breathing. *No! Don't say that! Those were Thomas's words the day he first wrapped my heart in promises. And look what that turned into: fourteen years of torture.* The memory slammed into her. She blinked hard and looked down at her glass. Sweat gathered in her palms.

"Did I say something wrong?" Jacob asked. He laid his hands atop hers, his thumb brushing gently across her fingers.

"No," she whispered. "It's not you. It's me. It just . . . brought back a memory." She hated how her voice felt so weak.

"Do you want to talk about it?" he offered. "You don't have to. I just . . . want to help, if I can."

She lifted her eyes to his. They were wet, and she didn't bother to hide it. "I was married once. Years ago. I have five children." She paused and took a deep breath.

He was stunned. "You have five children?"

"Yes. The marriage felt so good at first—too good. I was young and hopeful, and I loved him with everything I had. But it didn't stay good." Her throat tightened. "I suffered for fourteen years before I had to leave him and my children."

"You left your children?" he gasped, pained. "I can't imagine . . . ." He squeezed her hands. Then, with surprising tenderness, he reached across the table and brushed the tears from her face. "If it would help, I'd apologize for the entire male half of the human race."

She gave a small, broken laugh. "Thank you, Jacob, truly. But apologies don't erase scars." She swallowed hard. "I won't give you the details. You don't need to know them. My heaven turned into hell so fast, and so completely, I barely made it out alive. Some days, I wish I hadn't."

His eyebrows drew together in genuine sorrow. Her pain became his.

She drew in a trembling breath. "Jacob . . . I have to tell you something. I don't want to say it, but I have to." She paused for a long moment and began to tremble. "I can't allow myself to fall for you." The words scraped out of her like broken glass. "And I can see it happening. I can feel it. I'm not saying you'd ever hurt me—not like he did—but I can't take that chance. Not again. I'm too afraid. And it kills me to say it, but we have to stop whatever this is before it goes any further."

Her voice faltered. She forced the rest out anyway. "I'm sorry. I never meant to mislead you. Please forgive me."

Jacob stared at her in disbelief, then lowered his gaze to his hands. The warmth in his eyes faded, and it hurt to watch it happen. "If that's how you feel," he whispered, pulling his hands away. He leaned back and folded his arms, as though bracing himself.

"Yes, Jacob," she whispered. "It's for the best. Truly. I . . . I hope you'll still come by when you're in town. You're always welcome here."

"We'll see. I know when I'm not wanted." His voice was flat now, guarded. He pushed his chair back and stood.

"That's not it, Jacob! I want you, I really do, but I can't. Please understand. It's not you. It's me."

He walked toward the door. Just before he stepped out, panic seized her chest.

"Jacob," she called out.

He paused, and without looking back, he walked out the door.

Annie sat frozen, unable to breathe. The noise of the saloon blurred into a distant roar.

What did I just do? Did I push away my last chance for love? At having a husband again? At not growing old alone? Why can't I let him in?

The answer was immediate. *Because of Thomas.*

Tears welled again, burning hot.

Damn you, Thomas! You still reach for me. Even after all these years. You ruin me from a distance. I wish I had never met you. I hate you!

Her chest convulsed, but no sound came. She sat there, hollowed out, the weight of her choice settling like cold iron inside her. *This reminds me of that night when Thomas abandoned me in the middle of nowhere on the road to Mountain Home. This feels the same, except that this time it's all my fault. I'm the one who pushed away.*

For several minutes after Jacob disappeared through the door, Annie remained utterly still, hands resting uselessly on the table. It was as if her body had forgotten how to move. Someone walked past her table; she didn't look up. The room, bright and noisy as ever, felt impossibly far away, like she was watching it through a window thick with frost.

What have I done?

The realization struck not like a single blow but like a tightening band around her ribs, slow and merciless. *I had pushed away the one man in years who had looked at me with something more than hunger or pity. A man who had listened. A man whose gentleness frightened me.* She blinked repeatedly, willing the tears to be held back, but they slipped free anyway, warm streaks rolling down the sides of her cheeks. She brushed them away with frustrated fingers, but more followed.

Boss Man shot her a concerned glance from across the room; she turned away before he could approach her. *I can handle drunks, catcalls, wandering hands—but not questions. Not now.*

She rose unsteadily, her chair scraping across the floorboards. Her legs felt hollow. Every step back toward the dressing room felt heavier than the last. When she finally closed the door behind her, the dull thump of it shutting echoed inside her head.

The tiny room smelled of powder, soap, and old perfume. Usually, the familiar scents soothed her. Tonight, they pressed in tight, reminding her she had no one waiting for her at home.

Chapter 26

Annie found Em in the dressing room, organizing her tips into little piles.

"Are you okay, Annie? You look like hell. Was it Jacob? You sat with him a long time tonight, and then he just up and left."

Annie sat down and removed her earrings and the bows from her hair. She unclasped her choker and set it on the counter and began wiping off her lipstick.

"Annie?"

Annie finished with the lipstick and started on the rouge.

"Annie."

She finished the rouge and started brushing her hair with a deliberate, slow motion.

"Annie, I'm talking to you."

Annie picked up her brush and began pulling it through her hair in slow, deliberate strokes—too slow, really, more ritual than grooming. The bristles gently scraped her scalp, giving her a steady, familiar point to hold on to.

"Anna McIntyre Morrow!"

"What?"

"Something happened between you and Jacob. I know it."

Annie paused and stared at her reflection in the mirror. Sadness was written all over her face. Her frown grew with each passing moment.

"I may never see him again." Her eyes grew wet.

"It's better that way. You'll see."

"Really? If that's true, then why do I feel so miserable?"

"Come here." Em pulled her over and wrapped her arms around her. "Us girls, we got to stick together. I'm here for you, Annie."

"I'll be okay," she answered as she let out a big sigh. *What a damn lie. I'm anything but okay. I may have said goodbye to the man of my dreams.*

To lighten the tone of their conversation, Em held up the wad of bills and jingled a handful of gold coins. "We did good tonight."

They poured a pair of shots from the last open bottle of bourbon, clinked glasses, and drank.

"To the Queen of the Silver Moon Dance Hall," Em said, her eyes shining.

Annie replied sarcastically, "and to making big mistakes."

* * *

Back in her room at the James Hotel, Annie flopped down face-first onto her bed. She sank onto it, burying her face in her hands. Her last moments with Jacob flooded back into her mind.

He'll never come back. Why should he?

She knew it with a certainty that made her stomach twist. *Men don't wait around with wounded hearts. They don't circle back after being told no. He will leave on the next stage, ride out of my life as fast as he'd ridden into it.*

"This was my chance," she whispered to no one. "My last chance."

She hadn't spoken those words aloud before. Doing so made them unbearable. She pressed her fist to her mouth to smother a sob. The memory of Jacob's face—soft with concern, hope flickering just behind his eyes—stabbed through her. She had watched that hope dim, watched it shutter itself as he walked away.

And I had caused it. I'm an idiot.

A chill ran through her body. Her skin prickled as though the floorboards were radiating winter air. She curled onto her side, pulling a thin blanket over herself even though she wasn't sure she could feel its warmth.

You did the right thing, she tried to convince herself. *Losing love hurts worse than any beating.* She had lived that truth. She bore its scars.

The night dragged on. She could not sleep. She did not take off her dress, nor wash her face, nor unpin her hair. She lay stiff upon the bed as though movement itself might undo her, staring at the dim wall where the lantern cast its weak, wavering glow. Each flicker seemed to measure time not in minutes, but in missed words. She waited for exhaustion to claim her, but her mind refused to quiet.

When the flame finally guttered and died, the room fell into a deeper darkness, and something inside her collapsed with it. The silence pressed close, thick and suffocating. In the absence of light, her thoughts grew sharper, heavier, more relentless. She envisioned Thomas standing at the door with his back turned towards her, unresponsive as she had called out to him. She had wanted to be brave. Instead, she had safety.

She pressed her palms against her forehead, as if she might still the ache by force. She told herself she had acted wisely, that restraint was its own form of strength—but the words rang hollow in the dark. She turned her face toward the wall, eyes burning, breath shallow, and lay there as the night consumed her—mourning not only the man she had lost, but the life she had allowed herself to imagine.

A hollow ache spread through her chest—an ache she recognized all too well. The same emptiness she had carried when she fled Thomas. But tonight, it was sharper, more cruel, laced with regret she could not swallow. The darkness whispered.

You'll never see Jacob again.

You're nothing but a ghost to him.

You'll be alone forever.

No children to run back to.

No husband who loves you.

You don't deserve love.

Her tears spilled again, soaking into the pillow. She didn't bother wiping them away. *What was the point? How many years had she spent building walls? Jacob had been the first man to look over those walls in fifteen long years.* She curled up tighter and tried to banish those thoughts.

"I'm so tired," she whispered back at the darkness, her voice breaking. "So tired of being afraid." She pictured herself as a lost soul, wandering aimlessly in the desolate nether gloom, helpless to know which way to turn or what to do.

A different whisper surfaced. *Don't give up, Annie.*

* * *

The next morning, Annie awoke to the muffled sound of voices in the hallway. She was still in her clothes. She hadn't even taken off her shoes from the night before. She stared at the ceiling.

Jacob. I wonder if he's awake yet. Probably. Should I find out where he's staying and catch him before he leaves? What could I say if I found him? Would he even want to see me? Probably not, after the way I let him go. Biggest mistake of my life, or was it? Maybe Em's right. Or maybe I'm a fool. Who knows?

Annie lay there for hours. She had no desire to get up.

Why does it hurt so much? I wasn't in love with Jacob. Sure, I liked him a lot, but I wasn't in love, not really. I let the possibility of having a lifetime of happiness slip through my fingers. That hurts.

Once again, she heard voices in the hallway. Two men were arguing over whether they should leave town because they had heard about job openings at a mine in Silver City.

Annie sat up, looked out the window, and noticed that the sun was shining.

I don't have to be at the Silver Moon until four o'clock, so it's a good time for a walk outside. I need some fresh air.

Annie spent the rest of the morning and well into the afternoon wandering the dusty lanes of Atlanta with no particular destination in mind, with only the repetition of her own thoughts for company. The sun had climbed high enough to warm her face and the tops of her shoulders, loosening the tension she hadn't realized she carried in her neck. Each time a breeze brushed through town, it lifted a faint sweetness into the air—the unmistakable aroma of bread baking somewhere nearby. The scent tugged at an old memory of the days when she worked the apple peeler on the porch of the Rocky Bar Mercantile, with the same aroma of bread baking wafting up the road.

Without meaning to, she found herself drifting toward the older parts of town, where the cabins stood a little farther apart, and the cottonwoods had had time to grow tall. She paused when a thread of birdsong rose above the hum of the town. She shaded her eyes, peering up into the branches, trying to catch sight of the little musicians, but they were nowhere to be seen. She recalled being ten years old, squatting in the dirt beside Hazel, her best friend in the world, whispering the same question: *Where do they hide? How do they vanish like that?*

Hazel had claimed she could speak "bird," and would press her lips together and whistle a few clumsy chirps, grinning wide when Annie giggled. Then the two of them would chase each other between the log cabins, pretending to follow invisible birds. Annie could almost hear Hazel's voice now—clear, ringing, unbroken by any of life's cruelties.

A burst of laughter pulled Annie back to the present. A little girl dashed past, her braids flying behind her, followed by a small boy determined to catch her. Their joy brushed Annie like a warm hand, tugging at something tender and almost forgotten. For a moment, she felt a pang—not of sorrow, but a bittersweet yearning for the simplicity of those childhood days when friendship cured any loneliness and afternoon games banished the darkest moods.

From the deep recesses of her mind, another memory surfaced. In her mind she saw little John William chasing Anna Eliza around the backyard of their home in Boise City. John William couldn't have been older than seven and Anna Eliza nine. They were laughing so hard. He finally caught up with her and they both tumbled into a patch of weeds, still laughing.

They really loved each other as much as a brother and sister could. *We were so happy then. I was happy too. I wish I could hug them again. I would give anything for that, anything at all.*

But behind the laughter, beneath every comforting scent and happy memory, thudded the incessant pounding of the Monarch Stamp Mill. The metallic rhythm reverberated through the ground and the air—a reminder of the present, heavy and unavoidable.

Annie found a sunny spot at the base of a large pine tree beside the road, sat down, leaned back, and closed her eyes. She let the gentle breeze blow her hair across her face and let it stay there and imagined the warmth of the sun's healing rays penetrating deep into her soul. *Sunshine feels so good, like the universe is smiling at me.* For a moment, she imagined Hazel beside her again, whispering some silly joke, poking her with her elbow like she used to do, insisting everything would turn out right in the end. The images softened her expression, loosening something tight in her chest. *I miss you so much, Hazel. I wish you were here with me.* For a moment she was back again at the Rocky Bar Mercantile, working the apple peeler, with Hazel sitting beside her. She remembered words that Hazel had spoken: *"You're amazing, Annie. You can do anything you set your mind to."*

A noisy horse-drawn wagon rolled by and yanked her out of her daydream. She opened her eyes. *Memories are like jewels in my heart. I cherish them. I should be grateful. I should appreciate them. They're mine forever. Whatever happens now.*

She stood up, arched her back, and stretched out her arms. *Back to reality, girl. Jacob is gone, but I'm still here. I'll remember those moments with him until the day I die. And with Hazel, and Edith, and my dear children.* Accompanied by those lingering thoughts, Annie made her way over to the Silver Moon Dance Hall.

Chapter 27

Back in the dressing room, Em turned to Annie with a devilish grin. "You know, Annie, there's a way to keep more of that money right where it belongs, in your pocket, and even double it," she whispered, her eyes glinting with a dangerous allure.

Annie's eyebrows shot up, a mix of curiosity and caution flickering in her gaze. "Oh? And how's that?"

Em leaned in closer, her voice dropping to a conspiratorial hush. "It's not the nightmare everyone thinks it is. Being a soiled dove, I mean. You call the shots; the pay is damn good. Plus, I've got the right connections. I could introduce you, show you the ropes."

Annie was taken aback, the shadows of her past clawing at her resolve. "I don't think so, Em. I've never done anything like that."

"Think about it," Em urged, her tone dripping with persuasion. "You could reign as Queen of the Dance Hall every night, with more than just a little cash to your name. We'd be unstoppable together, you and me."

Em leaned back in her chair, legs crossed, with one shoe dangling from her foot. She tilted her head to one side, with a coy grin playing on her lips. "You've been dancing your ass off. You're running yourself into the ground."

"I don't know, Em, I'm not like you. I'm . . . not . . . that kind of girl. Everyone knows what you do after hours."

Em chuckled. "What kind of girl do you think I am? A scarlet lady? Fallen angel? Soiled dove? Painted cat? Sporting woman? Or there's my favorite, what the Froggies call a *Nymph du Prairie*? That one has class. Dearie, I make more in a single night than you do in a week, and I got silk bloomers in my trunk to prove it. I admit it, Annie—I'm reckless, I take chances, but my life is exciting. Yours can be too."

"I'm not judging you, Em. I just . . . I don't know if I could do what you do."

Em leaned over towards Annie as their eyes met. "You don't give yourself to every man. You play a part. You learn how to hold the reins. You're in charge. This place ain't no crib like the Chinamen run. Take Ruby and Millie; they're just here for the dancing, nothing more. As far as me, Pearl, and Lottie, well, let's say we're here for more than the dancing. The point is, you get to choose; you do what you want to do. Boss Man is okay with that. His main interest is selling drinks. I heard he charges ten times more than what they cost him."

Em was an expert at beguiling men, and she never hesitated to use her feminine wiles to lure hapless miners under her spell. *I don't want to be like that.* Her voice rose with emotion. "I've already lost so much. My husband, my children, my best friend. The life I thought I'd have. If I give up my body, what's left of me?"

"What's left is survival. Control. Money in your pocket and a roof over your head that ain't leaking. You think that a preacher's wife sleeps better at night than I do? Maybe. But she don't get to decide what happens to her. I do."

Annie sighed, "I used to dream of a little cabin. A proper husband, children, a cozy home, and a garden full of flowers. Now all I got are men looking me over like I'm a piece of meat at the market. If I do this . . . that dream dies for good."

Em looked into Annie's eyes. "That dream died the minute Thomas took you away from Rocky Bar, and don't expect Jacob to show his face here anymore. But it don't mean you can't build a new one. A better one. You ain't giving yourself up, Annie, you're choosing to live. You still get to decide what your life's worth. Ain't that better than letting the world decide for you? No one's expecting anything from you tonight. You take it all in. This ain't some cattle auction; you still own yourself."

The next night, after most of the customers had left, they climbed the stairs to the second floor and reached a door at the end of the hall. Em opened it to reveal a modest but tidy room, decorated with lace curtains, a dressing table with a silver brush, a worn velvet chair, and a wide bed draped in a faded but clean white quilt.

"This one's mine. Not bad, huh?"

Annie stepped inside and looked around. "It's . . . nicer than I thought your room would be. I figured it'd be dark, full of shadows. Is this where you . . . work? But it feels like someone lives here."

Em sat down on the bed, patting the space beside her. "That's because I do live here. This ain't only a place for men to come and go. This is where I rest, where I cry if I need to, where I count my silver and gold and plan my escape if ever I want one."

"How do you do it, Em? How do you smile and talk sweet when every part of you must be screaming to run?"

"You learn to wear the smile like a dress; you put it on, you take it off. Some nights, I pretend I'm actin' on a stage. Other nights, I grit my teeth and count the minutes. But then there're moments . . . when I remember I ain't hungry anymore. I ain't begging no one for nothing. I call the shots. And that power, that's what keeps me going."

Em stood up and walked over to the vanity and picked up a small tin of rouge. She turned and held it out to Annie. "Want to try it on? Just for fun. Might help you see the girl in the mirror a little differently."

Annie took the tin with trembling hands, with a weak smile. "Alright. Just for fun . . . but I'm not ready."

Em walked over and placed a hand on her shoulder. "Then don't. Not tonight. Maybe never. You don't owe anyone your body. I'll fight anyone who says otherwise."

"I don't know Em. What would my children think of me if they ever found out?"

"Don't worry about it. That's on them. No matter what you do, you're still their mother, and nothing can ever take that away."

"But someone did take that away. You know what happened between me and Thomas."

"Well then, you got nothing to lose. This ain't all-or-nothing. You decide what you want to do. I'm not pushing you. I just want you to know your options. You *do* have options, Annie."

Em walked to the door, opened it, then paused on the threshold. She looked back with a sad, almost pleading softness Annie had never seen in her eyes before. "I'll give you an hour," she said quietly. "Use my room. If you don't come downstairs within an hour, I'll send up your first trick. It's your choice." She closed the door.

Annie sat rigidly on the edge of the bed, her hands clenched in her lap. Her heartbeat thudded so hard she thought the men downstairs might hear it. Heat gathered on her forehead, a sheen of sweat born of fear, not from the warm lamplight on the table beside her. *An hour. I have an hour to decide who I am, or who I will become.* She stared at the door. *I could leave. I could stand up, turn that knob, and walk right out of this room. But if I do that, I will never come back here. I don't believe what Em said, that this isn't all-or-nothing. Either I am or I'm not. It is all-or-nothing. There's no in between.* Another bitter thought crept in. *Maybe I'm already too far gone. How can I even consider this? What's wrong with me? Just because Em does it doesn't mean I should.*

The music from downstairs seeped up through the floor, but it was so muffled that she could not tell what song was playing. A floorboard creaked somewhere in the hallway. She jumped up. *I'm not ready for this!* She sat down, so nervous that she could not sit still. She noticed a few wrinkles in the bedspread, so she smoothed them out.

She must have sat there the full hour—frozen, numb, unable to choose, yet choosing to do nothing was a choice in itself. She heard a timid knock at the door. She stopped breathing. *This is it*, as her throat tightened painfully. *I'm gonna be sick.*

Annie forced herself to take a deep breath, hold it, then let it escape slowly through pursed lips. Somehow, she managed to whisper, "Come in."

The knock on the door repeated.

"Come in," she said louder.

The door opened. A young man stepped inside—mid-twenties, hat clutched in both hands, eyes lowered in a kind of embarrassed respect. Clean-shaven, smelling faintly of soap and whiskey. Not cruel-looking. Just tired. He didn't smile. He simply nodded.

"Evening, ma'am," he mumbled.

"Evening," Annie answered, though the word scraped out of her like something forced past a closed door.

The silence stretched between them. It was a hollow, aching stillness. *What on earth am I doing?*

He shut the door quietly behind him and took a hesitant step toward the dresser, keeping a respectful distance, as if he already sensed her anxiety.

"You're new here?" he asked, his voice low.

Annie swallowed. "Yeah." The word felt like a stone dropping into dark water, sending ripples through everything she had ever believed herself to be.

"Um . . . " he murmured gently, shifting his weight, "you don't have to be worried. I won't do anything you don't want. I can leave if you'd rather."

Leave?

For some reason, it sounded ridiculous. *Leave?* She swallowed, her throat tight as a knot. *So many things don't make sense.* "No. You can stay. But . . . give me a moment."

He nodded and moved to the bed, still not lifting his gaze. He perched on the edge as if afraid to ruffle the bedspread.

Poor guy, Annie thought, and the thought surprised her. *He looks as frightened as I am. So, this is what Em does. Right here. In this bed.* The bedspread looked too bright under lamplight, too aware, as if it held the memories of every woman and man who had lain there before.

This is the point of no return.

The memory of her wedding day with Thomas rose from some dark corner of her mind—unpleasant, uninvited, and unwanted. She was back in the courthouse's front room, clutching Hazel's hand, feeling the world tilt beneath her feet. Once again in her mind's eye, she stood on the edge of a cliff, the wind howling up from a bottomless drop. One step forward and she'd fall into the abyss forever; one step back and she'd be safe. She had stepped forward the last time.

Here I am again. It can't be that bad, can it?

Thomas had been a monster in bed—hands rough, breath sour, no concern for anything but himself. *This guy's just a kid.* His shoulders were narrow, his posture timid. *This isn't the same. This is my choice . . . isn't it?*

She could feel him waiting. The weight of his nervous silence pressed on her more than any touch.

Get on with it!

Her body moved before her heart could protest. She stood, fingers trembling as she reached for the laces of her dress. The first knot slipped free. Then the next. Fabric loosened around her ribs. She let the dress fall like something dead, pooling at her feet. Her petticoats resisted for a moment before sliding down her legs. With each layer shed, her thoughts tangled tighter—shame and dread blurring together until she couldn't tell one from the other.

Right or wrong . . . I can't tell anymore.

Annie lay flat on her back on the bed. She stared at the tin ceiling tiles, looking for patterns. She saw circles, diamond shapes, leaves, and flower petals, but nothing was interesting. The ceiling tiles were all the same, dirty, and tarnished tin. She closed her eyes, steadied her breath, and waited for it to be over.

When he finished, he hesitated and then pulled his boots back on, as if uncertain of what to do next.

He turned towards her, his voice low with concern. "You okay?"

Annie forced the word out, hollow and small. "Yeah."

But she felt as if she were tumbling helplessly over the edge of that old cliff, the wind rushing up to swallow her whole. *I'm done for!*

He placed three one-dollar gold eagles on the table, nodded, and left without another word. The door clicked shut. Annie got up and rambled over to the mirror. Her hair was messed up, and her ringlets were out of place. Her cheeks are still pink from the rouge; her eyes looked older, and there was a sadness in them. She spoke to her own reflection. "What the hell have you done?"

She picked up one coin and studied the front. It was heavy. Solid gold. There was a profile of a woman with long hair that was curled as it flowed down the back of her neck. She wore a crown with a row of flowers sticking out of the top. The crown had the word "Liberty" in tiny letters on the side. Around the edge of the coin were the words "United States of America". She turned it over in her fingers. On the back, in the center, was "1 Dollar 1854" framed by a wreath of wheat stalks, corn, and leaves. She put the coin back on the dresser next to the others.

I'm worth three dollars? The thought shocked her. *How can you put a price on a living, breathing person?* The three coins mocked the tumultuous whirlwind of emotions that roared within her chest, a storm she was desperately trying to subdue. It felt as though her soul was being squeezed, pressed into some mold that neither fit nor offered any comfort. *Is this another bad decision that would end up as a disaster, like getting married to Thomas?*

A wave of nausea rose within her, a bitter tide that surged up but receded before reaching its peak, leaving a sour aftertaste of disappointment mingled with self-reproach. *What have I done? Am I nothing more than a soiled dove now, like those other girls? Like Em?* Anger bubbled beneath the surface of her skin. *This is not how it's supposed to be. This is not part of my plan. I shouldn't have to put my body up for sale.*

She put her petticoat, dress, stockings, and shoes back on, brushed her hair, and headed for the door. She walked down the hallway in a daze. Em was waiting at the bottom of the stairs.

"How was it?" Em asked with sympathy in her voice. "It was Billy that I sent up. He's a nice kid. One of my regulars."

Annie choked. "I did not need to know that."

With effort, she regained her composure. She took a deep breath. "Well, it was a lot nicer than the last few times I had to do it with Thomas. He used to beat me if I didn't do everything he demanded in bed."

"You'll be okay, Annie, I promise."

Afterwards, they cleaned the place up, Em humming, Annie sweeping, doing her best to block out of her mind what had just happened. They both got a little drunk, but not enough to lose control. When the dance hall was spotless, they stepped outside into the chilly mountain air.

They walked down the deserted road. The whole town was quiet except for a stray dog yelping off in the distance. Annie looked up at the sky, counted the stars she could see, and wondered if her children were out there somewhere, looking at the same night, at the same stars. She wondered if they missed her. She wished she could hug all of them at once. *Thank goodness they can't see what I just did.*

Back in her room at the Hoffman Hotel, Annie set her earnings on the nightstand, then fell into bed, still wearing the gold-trimmed dress. She closed her eyes and listened to the silence, letting it fill her until there was no room left for regret. Tomorrow will bring a busy night with another round of dancing, drinks, and men.

Chapter 28

After Annie's initiation, the nightly activity evolved into business as usual for the next few weeks. Em invited Annie up to her room one afternoon while everything downstairs was quiet.

The late morning sun spilled through the lace curtains hung on the window of Em's room above the dance hall, painting soft gold over the bare wood floor. She watched as Em, barefoot and flushed with excitement, tore through the twine and brown wrapping paper of a flat parcel.

"Let me show you what a traveler from the East Coast gave me last night."

"You'd think he gave you a diamond ring, the way you're tearing into that," Annie said, sipping her lukewarm coffee.

"He might as well have," Em breathed, her fingers trembling as she unfolded the paper. "You have to see these."

Out spilled three pristine issues of *Life* magazine from the previous year, as neat and crisp as the day they were printed. Em laid them out on the coverlet with the reverence of a priest arranging relics. "Look at this issue from November 15, 1894." Em turned to the page she had already memorized from peeking earlier. It was a pen and ink sketch of two high-class women sitting on one side of a circular sofa peeking at a gentleman sitting on the other side. The caption read:

"Do you know that Chollie actually gives evidence of
possessing intelligence at times."
"Oh, nonsense."
"Fact—he has learned to look both ways for approaching cable
cars in crossing Broadway."

"It's hilarious how the women make the men look like fools. These are
Gibson Girls."

"Who?"

"You don't know about Gibson Girls?

"Sorry, I have no idea what you're talking about."

"Annie, look here! Have you ever seen such a creature?"

Annie leaned over and squinted at the picture. "Hmm. Pretty lady, all
right. But she don't look like any woman I've ever met. Who is she
supposed to be?"

"Not a real woman, at least not one in particular. She's a Gibson Girl.
Charles Dana Gibson, the illustrator, draws them. They've taken New York
City by storm! Every issue of *Life* has folks swooning over them. Every
girl in New York City dreams of being a Gibson Girl."

Annie raised an eyebrow. "A Gibson Girl? That sounds mighty fanciful.
What makes her so special?"

Em held up the magazine in front of Annie. "It's the way she looks. She's
tall, graceful, has spirit, with that swan's neck and big hair piled high. She's
the ideal American woman."

Annie inspected the illustration. "Spirit, eh? She don't look like she's
ever hauled a bucket of water from a well, or scrubbed a shirt in creek
water.

"That's not the point. She ain't no pioneer woman. Imagine Manhattan
streets lined with carriages, ballrooms glittering with chandeliers, dresses
cut from silk that cost more than this whole town's worth of calico. Gibson
Girls glide through that world, heads high, every man turning to look.

"And you'd like to be one of 'em, would you?"

Em hugged the magazine to her chest. "Yes! More than anything! I'd travel clear to New York City, sit in a studio, and Mr. Gibson himself would sketch me and turn me into one of his Gibson Girls. Folks would open a magazine and say, 'There's Emma von Losch, living the life of high society.' Wouldn't that be grand?"

"You? In silk gloves and pearls? How much whiskey have you drunk today? I can scarce picture it. You'd have to give up your sass."

"Oh, I reckon I'd keep the sass. That's part of the Gibson Girl charm. She ain't no wallflower. She's clever and bold and holds her own against any man. Look, here's another illustration. Look at her hair swept up like that. It's magnificent. Here, look at this one," she said, tapping one with her fingernail.

Annie leaned closer. A full-page illustration showed another one of Gibson's famous girls. She was a tall, confident woman with an impossibly slender waist, elaborately upswept hair, and an expression of cool wit and self-possession. She wore a high-collared blouse, gloves, and a knowing smile that made her both untouchable and alluring.

"I admit she is pretty," Annie said.

"She's everything," Em replied, eyes wide with wonder. "She's a Gibson Girl. She's like a queen who doesn't need a king. She could walk into the fanciest New York parlor and turn every head without showing an inch of stocking or batting an eye. Look, here's another one."

"You realize it's just a drawing, right? They're not real people."

Em was not finished. "Here, look at the cover of this one. *Life* magazine, Volume XXIV - New York, July 5, 1894 - Number 601. See the drawing of the Gibson Girl holding her head high with the young man sitting in a chair behind her with his hand on his chin thinkin? Read the caption."

If He is a Man
He: I could hypnotize you so that within an hour you would throw your arms around my neck.
She: I could hypnotize you with that effect in five minutes.

"You can do that already, Em, that is, if the man has had too much to drink. You don't need to be a Gibson Girl to pull that off."

Em ignored the teasing. She flipped to another issue and spread it open. "I want to be her," Em said, almost whispering. "I want to wear a walking suit and carry a parasol down Fifth Avenue. Gibson Girls represent the new woman—a woman of position, status, style, and poise. I want to be drawn by Charles Gibson himself. Gibson Girls are real people. He makes these illustrations from models."

Annie shrugged. "You think Charles Gibson is going to come all the way to Idaho to sketch a hurdy-gurdy girl in Atlanta?"

"No, silly," Em said with a defiant lift of her chin. "I'm going to go to *him*. I'm going to *New York City*."

Annie's jaw dropped. "No."

"Yes! Ever since I saw that first sketch in this magazine. I don't want to dance in stinky dance halls my whole life. I want to be more than some miner's late-night distraction. I want to be seen. Not just for what's under my petticoats, but for something else."

"Like what?"

Em thought for a long moment. "For style. For elegance. For making men and women alike stop and stare and say, 'there's Emma von Losch, living the life of high society'."

"That's the second time you said that. Miss von Losch." Annie studied her friend and noted the gleam in her eyes, the way her fingers traced the lines of the drawings. Em's enthusiasm was undeniable, and she did not want to quench it.

"You'd make a damn fine Gibson Girl."

Em beamed. "You really think so?"

"Sure. You've got the hair for it. And the face. And the attitude."

"And the waist," Em added, twisting side to side.

Annie rolled her eyes. "I'll believe your New York City dream when I see a train ticket in your hand."

Em grinned and wrapped up the magazines, one by one, like precious china. "One of these days, I'll be standing in a studio in Manhattan, all cinched up and perfectly coiffed, with Mr. Gibson sketching me from behind his easel. And you know what?"

"What?"

"I'll still remember every damn two-step I learned right here, in a dance hall in the frontier of Idaho."

They both laughed. In a place unknown to the rest of the world, Em's dreams appeared impossible.

"This," Em muttered, glaring at her hairdo reflection in the mirror, "is a disaster."

"You said that ten minutes ago."

Em huffed and turned towards Annie, revealing the latest failed attempt at a Gibson Girl pompadour. Her hair, wound too tight, sat lopsided. One stubborn coil sprang sideways.

"Well, I ain't giving up," Em declared, tugging it all down again. "Every magazine in that last freight wagon said this look is what every woman wants. Smart, confident, statuesque, like a woman who could run her own newspaper and still break hearts for fun."

"You run your mouth and break hearts just fine without the hairdo," Annie teased.

Em shot her a look and tried again. She pulled her hair into a high twist, piled it up with shaking fingers, then shoved a comb in to hold it. The entire structure sagged to the left.

"Oh, hell's bells," she groaned, pulling out the comb. "Why doesn't it look like the pictures?"

"Because those pictures are lies," Annie said with a grin. "Or witchcraft. You pick."

Em flopped onto the stool, exasperated, arms dangling. "I swear, if I don't get this right, I'll be the only girl in the dance hall that looks like a schoolmarm from Kansas."

"You couldn't look like a schoolmarm from Kansas even if Boss Man paid you. Schoolmarms don't have a lick of sensuality, and you got more than your fair share, I might add. And nobody's gonna care what your hair's doing if you wink at 'em the way you winked at that rancher last week."

"That man thought I was offering him a free dance. Nearly broke my toe. Remind me to never dance with a rancher with those sharp thingies on their heels."

"They're called spurs, for making the horse run faster. They don't work on people, though."

They both burst out laughing, Em doubling over as her hair fell all over her face.

"Alright. Sit still. Let me try."

Em perked up. "You? Since when do you know how to do a Gibson Girl look?"

"Never said I did," Annie said, grabbing the comb and some of the scattered pins. "But I've watched you mess it up five times now, and I figure my odds are just as good."

Em stuck her tongue out but sat facing the mirror. That reminded Annie of the time Hazel stuck her tongue out at her while they were sitting on the porch of the Rocky Bar Mercantile. Annie jerked her head and banished the thought.

She gathered Em's thick hair and began twisting, fingers careful but not too delicate. "What is it about this look that's got you so fired up, anyhow?"

Em shrugged. "I dunno. Just . . . tired of feelin' like a dance hall girl sometimes. Like the kind the men throw coins at but never remember the name of. Those Gibson Girls, they look like they'd throw a drink in a man's face and still get asked to dance."

Annie paused, then smiled. "Ha. You did that one time, don't you remember? He still wanted to dance with you."

Em grinned. "Come to think of it, you're right. But the bum deserved it. Anyway, it'd be nice to look like I belong in one of those fancy sketches. Just once."

Annie twisted the last strand and jammed a pin in triumphantly. "There. Don't move."

Em leaned forward and gasped. The effect wasn't perfect; it was a little crooked, and one tendril curled down like a rebellious vine, but it was close. She tilted her head, smiled, and her eyes sparkled.

"Well, I'll be damned," she said. "I look respectable."

"Don't let it go to your head," Annie warned. "You're still in Idaho."

"Okay." Em smoothed her skirts and stood up, tall and proud. "Now help me with my corset. If I'm gonna to be a Gibson Girl, I might as well suffer like one."

They laughed again, two friends in a room above the noise and grit of Atlanta, preparing to descend once more into the dance hall din. But tonight, Em would descend with her head held high, a pin-studded pompadour on her head, and with a dash of New York City elegance.

Chapter 29

The next few weeks flew by. Annie continued to service the men of Atlanta at the Silver Moon Dance Hall, with each time becoming less nerve-wracking. She was aware of her reputation as word got around that she was quite the lady of the night. *If I'm going to do this, I might as well be the best. Funny how a sense of pride can afflict your judgement. Besides, the money turned out to be much better than I thought.*

Annie never saw Jacob again. Now that she was giving herself to so many men in the most intimate ways, remembering how she had come close to falling in love with Jacob made her cringe every time she thought about it. *We could have been married, had children, and lived a life of luxury. Jacob was a successful businessman, but I threw all that away, for what? If I had allowed myself to leave Atlanta with him, I wouldn't be in the sisterhood. What would he think if he saw me now, with what I do every night? Maybe that's why he never came back. Probably heard about me. Oh, what could have been. Letting Jacob go was the biggest mistake of my life. What was I afraid of? Jacob was no Thomas. He was already a successful businessman. Thomas was nothing but a brute who could sweet-talk. Jacob was the man for me. I'm an idiot. I traded love for money. Stupid me.*

Annie was pleased that she had accumulated enough money to finally open a boarding house, despite her misgivings about the way she earned it. It was an existing establishment known as the James Hotel, but the wild nights in Atlanta were too much for the owners, so they were only too happy to sell.

After signing the paperwork, she stood in the middle of the street to admire her purchase. It was one of the largest buildings in Atlanta, except for the stamp mills. The exterior walls were board-and-batten construction. It had three floors and a second-floor balcony that spanned the front of the building. *That balcony would be the perfect spot for the girls to flaunt their stuff for the boys walking down the main street of town.* Two additions, each with its own front door, were built on the right side. The parlor and the rooms had classic floral-patterned wallpaper.

On this particular morning, she brushed the sawdust from the hallway rug, checked the ink in the inkwell, and unlocked the front door just as her first boarders arrived. Two young men, miners from the new strike up at Big Boy, their faces gray with fatigue and dust, stood inside the threshold, hats in hand.

Annie sized them up, then smiled. "Welcome to the James Hotel, boys. Rooms are five dollars a week, breakfast included, supper if you want it. No gambling, no fighting, and you clean up after yourselves in the washroom. You got a problem with any of that, try your luck at the place down the road."

The taller of the two grinned, showing crooked teeth. "No problem, ma'am. Just need a bed and a roof."

"You'll have both. Come on in."

She led them down the hall, past the freshly dusted parlor, and up the stairs to their rooms. The beds were made, the sheets clean. She pointed out the privy and the water pump, gave them each a towel, and left them to unpack.

Downstairs, she found the maid she'd hired last week. Jessie was a plain-looking girl from Caldwell, quick with a mop and quicker with gossip, and she was already sweeping the kitchen floor. "After you're done with the floors, make up rooms three, four, and five for the next arrivals. And put on another pot of Arbuckles."

"Yes, ma'am." She nodded, smiled, and got to work.

In the weeks that followed, Annie took her morning coffee in the parlor while she reviewed the week's expenses. *This is a useful way to kill time on cold, rainy mornings. I'm already ahead of where I thought I would be. I should make a note to buy more Arbuckles, soap, and some more bedsheets.* She was proud of the business skills she had learned from working with Thomas at his mercantile business and mining claims. *I can balance the books as well as any man.*

Around this time, she heard it. Something or someone was poking around outside the back of the boarding house, behind the kitchen. *Racoon? Bear? Another beggar?* She opened the door a crack and peeked through. She saw nothing, but she heard it again, this time clearer. This was no bear. Off to the side of the back porch, she saw it. Two sorrowful brown eyes blinked up at her from beneath a curtain of black and white fur. Not a bear. But the size of a bear cub. It was a Newfoundland dog, soaked to the bone and shivering.

"Well, I'll be damned." Annie crouched. "Where'd you come from, fella?"

The dog whined again and tried to stand, but its legs trembled. With a groan of effort and a deep sigh, it sank to the ground, head low in submission. Annie hesitated only a moment before stepping forward. "Ain't no call letting a creature like you freeze to death out here." She reached out and ran a rough hand over the dog's sodden coat. It didn't flinch or growl.

"Alright," she muttered, standing. "Come on in."

With a grunt and a bit of awkward maneuvering, she lifted the heavy dog into her arms. It was all bones and fur, and limp as a sack of beans. She carried it through the back door into the kitchen, setting it down near the crackling cast-iron stove. It let out a long sigh and looked up at her with sorrowful eyes.

Annie searched through a pile of dirty dishes by the washbasin and found several chunks of leftover roast beef and some biscuits. The dog looked up but didn't lunge; it waited until she placed the plate in front of him along with a bowl of water. The dog ate ravenously, gulping down everything on the plate. He licked the plate clean and then rested his head on his paws and looked up at her.

Annie crouched beside him again, brushing a clump of wet fur from the dog's face. "You're a big old boy," she said with a smile. "Can't just call you 'Dog' now, can I?"

She thought for a moment, scratching the top of his head.

"You know what? You look like a Jack. Will that suit you?"

The dog thumped his tail once against the floorboards, and Annie chuckled.

"Alright then, Jack. Looks like you found yourself a home."

She tossed another log into the stove, banked it well, and settled into the rocking chair near the warmth. Jack, with a belly full, no longer shivering, stretched out across the rug.

At noon, the new boarders filed into the dining room, hats off, hands washed. Annie served up bread and beans, ham from the smokehouse, and a jug of cold cider. She listened to their stories and complaints about the mine boss and the price of boots. She liked the tranquility of the place when the men were gone or asleep. The ticking of the mantel clock, the sun spilling through the window, and the smell of bread rising created a homey atmosphere. Sometimes in those moments, she wondered if this was how her life was supposed to turn out. *No, not without my children.*

In her own room, Annie sat at her window, looking out over the darkened street, lost in thought. She could see the lights of the Silver Moon Dance Hall down the block, hear the faintest echo of music and laughter drifting through the night. She smiled, thinking of Em holding court at the dance hall, and felt a pang of pride.

Later on, as the wind carried the scent of pine trees and chimney smoke through the town, Annie stood on the front porch of the James Hotel, just as twilight started. Atlanta had been peaceful for the past few weeks, with nobody getting shot and no street brawls, but she knew it wouldn't last for long. Summer was coming, and with it, hundreds of desperate men.

* * *

The next morning brought something new. Annie studied the three girls standing in the parlor in a nervous row before her. *Time to hire some ladies. The James Hotel will be Atlanta's newest brothel, but it will keep the same name.*

The youngest looked like she'd been scooped off a farm not three weeks past. Her frizzy brown hair was tied back with a strip of calico, though half of it had worked free and frizzed around her ears like she'd been caught in a storm. She couldn't have been over eighteen. Her face was pale beneath a dusting of freckles, and her eyes, big, gray, uncertain, shifted from Annie to the floor and back again without ever settling. She gripped a worn carpetbag with tenacity. Her cotton dress, wrinkled from too many hours sitting in a stagecoach, sagged at the shoulders, and her shoes were too big.

Next to her stood a redhead, with her legs set apart as if someone braced for a fight. Her hair was the color of autumn fire, bright red and scraped back into a rough twist at the nape of her neck, and her jaw had a stubborn angle. Her skin was sun-tanned, and her eyes were amber like whiskey.

"You the madam?" she asked, voice gruff, like she'd smoked or shouted too much in her life. "I'm Clarabelle and the young one here is Betsy. We come together from Pocatello."

"That's a long ways away. Why here?"

"We heard there were opportunities in Atlanta, so here we are."

The next girl in the line stepped forward, letting her hips sway enough to be noticed. She had a dancer's grace and the smug self-awareness of a woman who'd turned plenty of heads. Her hair was long and golden, like spun honey, tumbling in ringlets down her back. She wore a cinched bodice that flattered her curves and a smug little smile that said she knew how pretty she was.

"Name's Ophelia, but you can call me Ophie. I've worked dance halls from Denver to Salt Lake," she purred, her voice syrupy with practice. She flipped a curl over her shoulder and tilted her chin at the right angle. "I know how to keep a man coming back with gold eagles in hand."

"Sounds like you know how things operate, but this ain't a dance hall. You know what we'll do here. If you want to dance, go to the Silver Moon Dance Hall down the street. But you could work both places, I suppose, if you're up to it." Annie studied her for a moment. She appreciated confidence, as long as it didn't turn into drama.

"No question about it," was Ophie's response.

"Keep in mind this ain't no crib like those over in Chinatown," Annie said, her voice low but firm as she paced back and forth across the parlor. "I run a clean house. The men pay before they touch. No drunkards, no beatings, and no thieving from the till, not from the customers, and not from you. Keep your drinking under control. And no opium or laudanum. That's a deal killer. Cavorting with the johns is okay, but don't make too much noise. You'll have clean sheets, two dresses provided, and a cut of every trick you turn. Respect me, respect the house, and you'll do fine."

For a moment, none of the girls said a word. Clarabelle cracked her neck. Betsy swallowed, eyes wide as saucers. Ophie smiled like a cat in a sunbeam.

Betsy looked at her with wide eyes. "And if we want to leave?"

"You leave, but not in the middle of a snowstorm, and not without advance notice. You give me warning. Fair's fair."

Clarabelle looked at the bar at the far end of the room. "And if someone starts trouble?"

Annie reached inside her dress and pulled out her Colt .44. She laid it on the small table beside them. "Then I remind them whose house they're in. I've used this more than once, and I'm not afraid to use it again. Don't you worry about a thing."

Silence settled in for a moment. Clarabelle glanced around the parlor again and let out a low whistle. "I seen some right fancy sporting houses. You got taste, ma'am."

"I got sense," Annie replied. "The boys will spend more for velvet and a soft touch than they will for whiskey and rum."

She led them to the back hallway, where each room bore a fresh coat of paint and a brass number on the door. "You each get one of these. Lock from the inside. Bath on Thursdays. Doctor in Rocky Bar once a month if the pass is open."

They all returned to the parlor. Annie looked at the three of them, this little flock of battered birds, hoping for a better life. "Well?"

Betsy nodded. Clarabelle gave a quick grunt of agreement. Ophie smiled and reached out her hand.

"I believe we got ourselves a deal, Madam Annie."

Annie shook it, firm as a miner with his pickaxe. "Welcome to the James Hotel," she said. "Now get yourselves cleaned up. The boys will be crawling in by dusk."

Annie paused for a moment. "One more thing, girls. There's a hot spring on the east edge of town. You can go there to bathe, but you have to wait until it's dark. The womenfolk of Atlanta have conniption fits every time the girls from the Doll House go there in the daytime. Understand?"

"Yes, ma'am," was their response in unison.

Chapter 30

At noon, a few days later, a miner came in, dusty and desperate, begging for a loan until his next payday. Annie listened to his story, weighed the truth of it, and gave him enough for a hot meal and a pint, but only after he swore on his mother's grave to pay her back. "You keep your word, and next time you can have a tab."

The man nodded. "Much obliged, ma'am."

The first frost had already laced the edges of the pines that loomed above Atlanta like sentinels, and the mornings smelled of wood smoke and snow on the way. Inside the kitchen at the James Hotel, Annie stood, sleeves rolled up, arms dusted with flour, kneading bread dough with practiced rhythm. The girls appreciated fresh-baked bread, even though it was unnecessary for her to cook for them.

She was setting loaves to rise when she heard it: a knock at the back door. Not a confident rap, but a hesitant tap-tap . . . pause . . . tap-tap. Annie wiped her hands on her apron and moved to the door, brushing a wisp of hair from her forehead. She opened it.

Three men stood there, barely more than shadows in the early morning mountain light. Their clothes were torn and filthy, patched with gunnysack and pine pitch. Their faces were hollow, with gaunt cheeks, and droopy eyes dulled with fatigue. One of them, a boy, couldn't have been over sixteen. The oldest one, with a long white beard, had a cough that racked his entire frame.

"Ma'am," the eldest said, doffing a crumpled hat. His voice cracked. "We don't mean no trouble. We ate nothin' but jerky fer three days. We just . . . we heard you might be willin' to spare a piece of bread or coffee. We'll chop wood or haul water. Anythin'."

Annie blinked, heart tightening in her chest. "Poppycock. Come on in before you freeze out there." *What a sorry sight! These guys look half dead. There's nothing worse than a prospector who can't find anything but rocks and gravel. There were stories about men who bet their lives on striking it rich in the gold fields, only to feel like failures when they went back home empty-handed. Last month, the father of one of my customers committed suicide.* She opened the door wide.

They hesitated, exchanging wary glances. The boy looked like he was going to burst into tears.

"I said, 'come in,'" she repeated, more gently this time. "Sit by the stove. I'll fix you some grub. Don't look so bewildered. Just because this is a brothel doesn't mean I don't believe in charity. Mind your manners and Jack won't bite."

They shuffled in like ghosts, removing their hats and holding them in gnarled hands, eyes wide as they took in the warm kitchen filled with the smell of fresh bread, simmering beans, and bacon grease. Annie moved with efficiency, ladling hearty venison stew into bowls, slicing bread thick as her thumb, pouring tin mugs of strong coffee.

The men ate like starving dogs. Jack lay against the wall and watched them, as if he was amused. The boy mumbled a thank-you between every bite. When they finished, the eldest stood and took off his hat again. "Ma'am, I don't got words," he said, voice husky. "Ain't many'd do what you did fer us."

"You got folks?" Annie asked the youngest one.

"Not anymore," he replied. "Atlanta's all we got, and she's been right mean to us lately. No matter how deep we dig, we ain't finding no gold an' no silver. Nothing but worthless quartz."

She gave a soft nod and didn't say a word.

A couple of days later, Annie was peeling potatoes by lantern light when another knock came at the back door. This time it was a single man. He was much older, unshaven, and limping. Same hollow look. Same slow, hopeless voice.

"Ma'am. I hate to ask, but—"

"Come on in." She was already holding the door open. "Don't mind Jack. You can pet him if you like. He's a good boy." It was the same scenario all over again, but she didn't mind. *Nothing wrong with helping the poor souls who are down on their luck. If I can help, that's what I ought to do. It's the right thing to do.*

Word spread, as it does in close-knit mining camps. One by one, the broken and starving began showing up at Annie's back door, never the front door of the brothel. Sometimes one man, sometimes two. Once a widow with soot on her cheeks and three bedraggled children in tow arrived. A young Irishman, whose partner had died of the fever, showed up. They all received the same: a warm meal, a kind word, a place to sit without shame under the watchful eyes of Jack. She never asked for anything in return.

She heard rumors that miners were calling her the Angel of Mercy. Some paid what they could later, like a bundle of kindling, a snared rabbit, a pinch of gold dust. Others never paid. *If they don't pay, it means they can't pay. I'm okay with that. What a sorry bunch of men. I hate to see people suffer.*

The down-and-out came by often, but it was never too much for Annie to handle. Eventually, they began asking for grubstakes. Annie arrived at the county recorder's office just before sunrise, her shoes covered with slush, collar pulled high against the wind. The place was already full of miners waiting to register claims. A clerk sat behind a desk reading the day's news, and a handful of lawyers drank weak coffee and pretended to be busy.

Annie didn't waste time. She had grubstakes in Rocky Bar, so she knew how the system worked. She found her way to the back room, where the actual business happened. A rough-hewn table ran the length of the room, its surface scarred with years of contracts and the occasional knife fight. Three prospectors who had shown up at her back door the previous day waited there, hats in hand, eyes bouncing between the ledger and the door.

"We surely appreciate this, ma'am," said the oldest, a grizzled man with a thumb missing.

Annie set her leather satchel on the table. "As soon as you sign the paperwork, we're in business."

The men nodded, each sliding forward a packet of forms, dated November 3, 1895, signed by them and witnessed, with the claims mapped out in shaky ink. Annie read every line, careful not to miss any details. She'd learned from Thomas and every sharp operator who'd tried to cheat her back in Rocky Bar: trust nobody, and always bring your own pen, never a pencil.

She signed her name, Anna Morrow, in crisp, slanted script, then initialed the addenda. A one-quarter interest, non-negotiable, and first right of refusal on any new claims within fifty yards of the original strike.

The miners looked at each other and grinned. "We got a feelin' about Atlanta," said eldest. "There's gold, sure as anythin'. Just need the right gear to get at it."

Annie shrugged, unimpressed. "You strike it rich, I'll see you in the saloon. You go bust, you can come back and clean my floors."

Once the men had gone, Annie lingered, watching from the window as they disappeared into the dawn mist. She saw the way they hunched against the cold, the way their voices, though muffled, were full of optimism. *I wonder if any of them know that the odds are against them, or if, like most men out here, they believe in nothing but their own luck.*

Annie slid the three signed contracts into her satchel, tucking them behind the ledger she kept for her own reference. It was full now: every page a tally of loans, bets, bar tabs, and every other deal she'd made in the last year. Some women in Atlanta collected ribbons, letters, or pressed flowers. Annie collected contracts, and she liked the way the investments felt more valuable than knickknacks ever could.

The clerk wandered over, surprised at the sight of so much gold changing hands. "That's a lot of risk you're taking, Annie. They say Atlanta's pretty much played out."

Annie shrugged, not bothering to look up from her notes. "Men said the same thing six years ago. There's always more if you dig for it." She closed the ledger, snapped the buckle on her satchel, and slipped a dollar eagle across the table to the clerk. "For your trouble," she said.

He tried to hand it back. "Not necessary, Mrs. Morrow. I'm glad someone's got the backbone to try to keep this town alive."

She left him standing there, coin in hand, and made her way out onto the street. The wind cut sharper than before as she walked over to the Silver Moon Dance Hall. Em had said the day before that she wanted to talk to Annie about something.

Chapter 31

That afternoon, payday had turned the Silver Moon Dance Hall into a riot. The miners were shoulder to shoulder at the bar, barkeeps sloshed cheap whiskey and beer into cracked glasses, and the haze of cigar smoke was so thick you could lose a child in it. Em was sitting at their favorite table in the corner. Even though Annie had a steady income from the James Hotel, she still danced at the Silver Moon Dance Hall occasionally because she loved dancing, and she loved the way the men would fight over her for the first dance of the evening. Other days, like today, instead of dancing, she would sit in the corner and watch the revelry. Sometimes she would sing ballads too, with Em accompanying her on the hurdy-gurdy.

Em slouched opposite her at the table, legs sprawled, hands cradling a drink like it was the last warm thing left on earth. It was her day off, too. Her hair was down, loose over her shoulders, and she'd tied a red ribbon around her wrist that made her look both younger and more reckless than usual. She was on her third glass of bourbon and already making eyes at the foreman of the Monarch Mill crew. "Look at them, Annie," she said, as she leaned in so close that Annie felt Em's breath in her ear. "It's like someone hit a beehive with a shovel. You ever seen so many easy pickin's?"

Annie let out a brief laugh. "Is that all you ever think about?"

"Why not? That's what they're here for, an' I aim to please."

It had been a long, dry winter, both for gold and for men's patience. Half the miners had left town at the first heavy snow. They couldn't work when their claims were buried in the snow. Where they all went, she didn't know. Boise City for a winter job, Nevada, or California, where the weather was mild. There was tension in the air from the way the claims kept coming up short and the way the mine bosses kept squeezing every ounce of labor out of their crews. Tonight, the miners would let loose, loud, mean, and desperate to remember what it felt like to win something, even if only a hand of faro or a dance with a not-so-pretty girl.

"It's too noisy in here, Annie. Let's go over to Whiskey Gulch, where we can hear each other talk. I have something important to talk about."

They got up and walked out of the Silver Moon Dance Hall and down the street to Whiskey Gulch. The room was crowded, more men than air, the tables jammed with prospectors and drifters and the occasional city slicker in a clean shirt who looked uncomfortable at finding himself among a rough crowd. It was noisy, but not as loud as the Silver Moon Dance Hall. They spotted an empty table in the back corner and sat down, each with a glass of Old Overholt.

"Did you hear?" Em said, lowering her voice. "The mines at Rocky Bar have a huge payroll run. Word is, they're bringing in girls out of Boise City just for the weekend. That's how much gold is coming through."

"Rocky Bar is a dump. The only reason anyone goes there is to get away from here."

"Or to get rich," Em replied. "You think it's a joke, but I know at least four girls who made more in one night over there than they do here in a month. You and me, we could clean up. All it'd take is a day or two, and we'd be set for a long time. We should go to Rocky Bar," Em said with a wicked grin on her face. "You know the payroll hits there tomorrow morning. It's only what, ten miles? We could make a killing, Annie. Those boys ain't seen a real woman in months."

"It's fifteen miles, and those ain't easy miles. The James Creek Road is a nightmare even in the summer." She made a show of looking Em up and down. "You even own a coat? Or are you planning to charm the snow into melting?"

"I own several coats," Em replied, pretending to be hurt. "Some of them even have brass buttons. Besides, you owe me a trip. You said yourself last week, 'if the tips keep dropping, we'll have to find a new gold rush.' Well, I found us one. You want to sit here and wait for the next Atlanta gold rush, you do that. But I wanna go where the money is. Rocky Bar."

Annie thought about it. *Rocky Bar is a dump, but it's my old home. I could walk those back alleys blindfolded, and every man in town knows my name, some in ways I'd rather forget. It would be good business if we get there in time.*

"There's one problem," Annie said. "We don't have horses. It's too far to walk, and I'm not riding a mule again. The last time I did that, I was sore for a week. "

Em shrugged. "We could borrow them from the livery."

"Mules?"

"No, silly. Horses."

"What do you mean by 'borrow'?"

"I know the man who works there," Em said. "Or, more accurately, I know a man who owes me a favor. I was really nice to him once, maybe twice."

Annie raised an eyebrow. "How nice?"

"The kind of nice that makes a man forget he's got a wife and three children," Em said, looking smug. "What a night that was . . . did I ever tell you what we did?"

"No, and I don't need to know."

"Are you sure? You wouldn't believe it unless I told you face to face."

"I said 'no', Em."

"Anyway, it's that old coot Brubaker. He keeps two of his own horses at the livery, and the wife doesn't know about them. We could take them, make the run, and bring them back before anyone's the wiser."

"And if we get caught?"

"Then we tell him the truth. They call you the Angel of Mercy, right? Well, the Angel of Mercy can do more than provide a meal in the back of the kitchen. Think of all those poor, lonely men yearning for comfort, wanting nothing more than to have a good time. I heard one of them found a gold nugget as big as his fist. Must be worth a fortune."

Annie stared at her, amazed. "That's incredible!"

"Definitely, except for the part about the gold nugget. I just made that up."

"Girl, don't do that to me! Don't joke about gold. It's serious business."

"Spoilsport," Em shot back.

Annie gave her another look. "You realize going over the pass is suicide, right? It might snow again soon, and the pass is still a mess from the last snowstorm. Last week, a whole mule team froze to death up there."

"Mules are dumb animals. We're smarter than mules. We dress warmly and bring a bottle, or maybe two bottles. You scared?"

Annie wasn't scared, but unease gnawed at her, nudging memories of the last time she was caught in a blizzard. It was two long, uncomfortable days trapped in a root cellar with three filthy prospectors. The stench was unbearable. "I'm not scared," she insisted, though uncertainty crept in. "But I like to know the odds before I risk losing everything."

Em's grin widened, trying to dispel Annie's hesitation. "Odds are better than here, honey. If we get there by tomorrow night, we can clean up before the wives even know we're in town. It's about making more money than we need to just survive here."

Annie's stomach twisted at the thought, but it wasn't hunger that made her feel sick. It was fear.

"There's a risk," Annie said, her voice barely above the sea of conversations that surrounded them. "I feel it in my gut, Em."

Silence fell between them. "I ain't askin' you to do anything I wouldn't do. Hell, I'm going, with or without you. But it'd be easier with you there. We watch each other's backs. Keep warm. Make good money and get out before the snow sets in."

Annie's breath came shallow. *True, the men in Rocky Bar are hungry for more than a meal, and their pockets will be full of gold. Em was always supportive since the first day we met at the Silver Moon. Does she really want to do this? Does she understand the risk? Something tells me this is not a good idea.*

Annie set her empty whisky glass down with a soft thud. "You're sure we'll beat the snow?"

Em nodded. "We leave today at noon. The pass is clear for now, but it won't be for long."

Annie stared into her whiskey glass. *The pass by Bald Mountain is not clear. Yesterday, I overheard two stagecoach drivers complaining about how deep the slush was at the pass and how they struggled to make it through. Why are you so desperate?* Annie's intuition kept prodding at her, a soundless warning buried beneath reason. *This is not a good idea,* popped into her head again. She pushed the thought away, and after a few minutes, she couldn't hear it anymore.

Annie swallowed, forcing her voice to steady. "Alright," she said at last, her voice betraying the uncertainty that still lingered. "Let's do it."

Em's face lit up with relief, unburdened by Annie's doubts. "I knew you'd say yes."

Annie felt uneasy. *You have that effect on people.*

They clinked glasses, sealing it the way they usually finalized their plans. They remained at the Whiskey Gulch and shared drinks for another hour. Annie lost track of how many rounds they ordered. When they stood up, both of them almost fell over. *Whoa. I didn't drink that much.*

They wandered back to Annie's cabin to get Jack. He eagerly joined them.

The road to the livery was uphill, and by the time they reached it, both of them were dizzy. Em had lost her balance twice, and Annie had to catch her both times so she would not fall over. Mr. Brubaker met them at the door with a scowl. A bay horse stood behind him.

"Well," said Mr. Brubaker, "if it isn't the Queen of Atlanta and with her little sidekick, Dutch Ass—I mean Duchess."

Annie disliked him. His reputation as a skin-flint was well deserved. People called him Scrooge behind his back. She forced a smile. *It might be better to rent the horses than steal them.* She cleared her throat and announced, "We need two of your horses, and we need them for the weekend."

Brubaker looked them over, head to toe. "You mean to tell me you're riding out in those ridiculous outfits?" He gestured at their flashy satin and velvet dresses. "Where are you going, the governor's ball?"

Em pouted, "Hey, wait a minute. Why didn't they invite us?"

"There is no governor's ball, you idiots. Floozies like you wouldn't get invited anyway."

Em stepped forward with her brightest smile. "Anyway, we're off to Rocky Bar. Heard they're short on girls and long on money. We'll bring your animals back full of oats and clean as nuns."

Mr. Brubaker spat on the ground, unimpressed. "That's a long ride if you're sober and the weather holds. I seen you two more than once gallivantin' around from saloon to saloon at all hours of the night. You got a reputation, you know, and it ain't a good one. You'd be lucky to make it out of town before you freeze. You're both smashed. You two gutterslugs ain't fit to ride a hobbyhorse, let alone on the pass to Rocky Bar. You even know which end of the horse is the front?"

Em glared at him. "We're not idiots. The front is where the head sticks out, and the rear is where the tail is. See? We're not so dumb."

Annie crossed her arms, hiding how dizzy she was. "You got the stock or not, Mr. Brubaker, sir?"

"Got the stock. But I don't loan to drunks, and I sure as hell don't want to scrape your froze bodies off the pass come thaw."

The refusal cut deep. Annie tried another tactic. "We'll pay double."

Mr. Brubaker grinned, but it was just teeth. "You'll pay triple in advance and sign a note for damages."

Em snorted. "Hell no, we're ain't signin' nothin'. You'll get the horses back, trust us. I promise. Ya got nothin' to worry about." She crossed her arms but had to take a step backwards to keep her balance.

248

"You think I'm some kind of fool? I wouldn't trust you to carry a bucket of horse manure." He turned away, picked up a brush, and worked on the horse's mane. "Didn't you hear about what happened last week up there? A whole mule team froze to death."

Em glared at him. "We're smarted than mules."

"Not by much."

Annie leaned on the stall fence and steadied herself. "We're paying, aren't we? Real money. Gold. Want two horses. Good ones. Strong ones. It's okay if they're ugly. We don't care what they look like."

"The answer is no. Besides, I wouldn't send my wife over that pass in this weather even if my life depended on it."

"We're not your wife," Em shot back, voice steady. "We're professionals. We just need the animals for two days, three at most. Probably. I'm sure of it. Pretty sure, anyway. You can bet on it, Mr. Scrooge. Deal or not?"

Annie jabbed Em with her elbow and gave Mr. Brubaker the biggest smile she could manage.

He held up his hands. "What did you call me? No horses for the two of you. Not tonight. You come back when you're sober, and I'll think about it."

That stopped Annie cold. "You think I can't handle a horse?" she said with genuine indignation.

"I think you can't handle the weather, the road, or yourself," he replied, getting more and more annoyed. "Last time I let a woman out of here in this condition, she barely made it back alive."

Em leaned forward into his face. "But was she dressed as nice as us?"

He shook his head. "You want to die, go dig your own grave. I'm not sending you off to Rocky Bar to get yourselves froze to death. I like getting paid, but I don't need the guilt. I said no. How many times do I have to tell you? Now get out of here, you nitwits!"

Jack growled as he sensed the tension between them. Annie opened her mouth to argue, but Em cut her off. "Come on, Annie. Let's go. We can walk it. I done ten miles in a day and never broke a sweat."

"Yeah, but not in snow, or while you're so hammered you can't walk straight," Mr. Brubaker muttered under his breath, but Annie was already turning for the door.

For a second, Annie thought about slapping him out of frustration. But the logic of doing that vanished. "Fine," she said, her voice gone flat. "We'll walk."

Em did a little curtsy, unsteady, and nearly toppled over. "You'll see, Brubaker," she mumbled. "And you still owe me for the other night. Not everyone's as good as me, and don't you forget it. We'll come back super rich, and you'll wish you'd been nicer to us ladies."

"Good luck with that," he called after them. "Hope you pack a coffin or two."

They stormed out and slammed the door. On the street, the wind hit them again, but neither slowed. After a few minutes, they found themselves sitting at the kitchen table at the James Hotel, each with a glass of whiskey. Annie could not recall how they got there.

"I say we do it," said Annie, voice tight with anger. "I say we walk the whole damn way, just to prove the cheapskate wrong. I heard the pass is still under snow, but this late in the season, it should be crusted over so we can walk on top of it without sinking in, even without snowshoes or skis."

"There's nothing to worry about," said Em, wrinkling her nose. "That man acts like we're invalids. You ever heard of the Donner Party? Back in '47 they crossed the Sierra Mountains in California in the middle of winter. Granted, they ate each other along the way, but that's not the point."

Annie laughed despite herself. "I doubt you'd taste good, Em."

"Oh, honey, I'd be delicious."

"If I didn't know you better, Em, I'd say you're crazy."

"My grandma once said to me, '*Verrückte haben mehr Spass*'. She didn't speak English."

"Do tell, what does that mean?"

"Crazy people have more fun."

"Right. And you aim to prove it?"

"I'm tellin' you, Annie . . . it's not even that far. Someone told me it's more like ten miles. We follow the road and stay ahead of the snow."

Annie leaned over the table and stared Em right in the eyes. "For the second time, Em, it's fifteen miles, not ten. Get that through that thick German skull of yours. You remember what happened to that mail carrier last December? What was his name—Ben Mackay or McIntosh or McGinnis?"

"Who? Ben? He was drunk when he tried to walk over the pass. What a dumbass."

"No, Em, you're confused. Ben was the mail carrier who was killed in an avalanche. You're thinking of that old timer Oscar. He was the drunk dumbass."

Em sat back in her chair and folded her hands behind her head. "Well, if you ask me, they were both dumbasses. You and me, we're smart drunk. Big difference."

"Smart drunk? That's not a real thing. Either way, by avalanche or stupidity, that pass at Bald Mountain has a way of killing people."

Em countered, "We gotta go. I can feel it. We go now, we get there before the next big storm. Couple days' walk, tops. Then we get money. Food. Warm beds. Hopefully, most of the men won't smell like pickled mules."

"And how do you know what a pickled mule smells like?"

"Never said I did. Some men smell as bad as what I figure a pickled mule would smell like if somebody ever tried to pickle a mule. There was this one guy the other night that I'm pretty sure smelled like a pickled mule, and boy he was as hairy as one. It was all over his back. Does that make sense?"

"I don't understand. What did you say?"

"Sheesh, Annie. Forget about it. Now you made me forget what point I was tryin' to make. Anyway, we can get there in a few hours if we start now."

"Or we freeze to death halfway up the switchbacks. Like statues. Two gals sittin' in the snow forever, holdin' hands with icicles in our hair." Annie pretended to shiver.

Em sighed. "Kinda romantic, ain't it?"

"I love you, Em, but not that much. It's dumb. It's the dumbest idea since you dyed your hair with blackberry juice."

"That was a good idea! I just let it set too long," Em said with a big frown.

"You looked like a clown for a week!"

"What do ya got against clowns? I like clowns! Anyway, maybe you'd like to stay in Atlanta. Starve to death in this dump of a town, huddled up in this drafty kitchen of yours with nothin' but cockroaches for company."

"There are *no* cockroaches in *my* kitchen, Dutch Ass!"

"Oh yeah? Then what's that bugger crawling across on the floor towards your left foot?"

Annie looked down and lifted her left foot. "Where? I don't see nothin'."

"That's 'cause you're too drunk to see straight."

"Right, Em, we're in no state of mind to walk to Rocky Bar. You just proved my point. If I go with you, it's only because if I don't, you won't go by yourself, and then you'll be mad at me for the next week."

"Fine. Stay. Freeze here instead. See if I care."

"You do care, Em. You don't like going alone. You want me to come along so I can pull you outta the snow when you fall in a drift and start cryin' like a baby."

"I don't cry like a baby."

"You do too. You cried when my chicken died."

"That chicken had personality. She would cluck at me every time I saw her lay an egg. She was my friend."

"Listen to me, dammit. We're both too juiced for big decisions."

"Nah, it's the best time for 'em, if ya ask me. It's when you're clear-headed that you start doubting everything."

"I am doubting everything." Annie paused and looked down. "Why is the floor moving?"

"That's the whiskey, Annie. Or maybe it's fate. Movin' us forward. Pushin' us to go, now."

"Fate needs to shut the hell up. Besides, it's almost two o'clock. Isn't it too late to start?"

"Annie dear, I'm not stayin' here to rot. I want out. You do too, I know you do.

"I do. I just . . . I don't trust that mountain.

"Then trust me."

"Oh, all right. We'll go. But if I die, I'm haunting your ass."

"Deal. Just don't scare off my customers."

Chapter 32

They walked for half an hour before Em started shivering in earnest. "Do you have anything stronger than this?" she said, holding up a thin flask. "This was supposed to last us to the top of the pass."

Annie grinned. "I thought you'd never ask." From the folds of her dress, she pulled out two more flasks and held them up. "This one's got Old Forrester, and this one's got Old Overholt. Did you know Old Overholt was Doc Holliday's favorite?"

"I didn't know that."

"Doc Holliday and his pal Wyatt Earp shot up a bunch of outlaws at the OK Corral in Tombstone, Arizona. You knew that, right?"

"I'm not much for history, Annie. What's your point?"

"If it's good enough for a real man like Doc Holliday, then it's good enough for us. We deserve the best of the best. That's my point, dearie."

"Wait a minute, how do you know what Doc Holliday drank?"

"Told me hisself. We got drunk together once."

"You were with Doc Holliday? I don't believe you. You never met Doc Holliday!"

"Well, maybe not, but I know for sure it was his favorite. Somebody told me, I just can't remember who. Anyway, I packed for a blizzard, and for you."

Em looked at her with genuine admiration. "I swear, you're the smartest woman in Atlanta, Annie."

"I know," said Annie, pulling the cork and taking a long, burning swallow. "Now let's see how far we can get before we freeze to death."

"That's not funny. You think we'll make it?"

Annie shrugged. "Depends on how many men are in Rocky Bar with full pockets. That's what keeps a girl going."

They laughed, but Annie heard the nervous edge in her own voice. She'd been places, seen things, survived more than she cared to admit, but she still felt the old rush, the hot-cold gamble of putting everything on the line for one more shot at making it big.

Em took a swig. "Something tells me we're going to make history."

Annie glanced over at Em. "What did you say?"

"We'll be famous someday. I know it."

"If you say so."

"*Komm schon, Maedel, heute schiessen wir uns die Lichter richtig aus. Kein Gelaber, einfach voll wegballern.*"

"Are you talkin' German again?"

"I just said let's get drunk."

"I think you said more than that."

"*Spielverderberin.*"

"Stop it!"

By eight o'clock, the world was all blue shadow and moon glow. Each time they crested a hill, another one appeared. The whiskey helped less and less. Em stumbled and went down, hands splaying in the dirty slush.

Annie stopped and turned around so quickly that it made her dizzy. She steadied herself and stared at Em for a long moment. "You alright?"

Em didn't answer. She rocked forward and tried to stand. Annie grabbed her elbow, steady but not gentle. "Maybe you should turn back."

Em pulled away. "I said I was fine."

Annie kept a hold of her. "Look at yourself, Em. You can hardly breathe, you can't walk straight, you're half-froze already."

"So are you," Em snapped, then folded over, coughing.

Annie's temper flared, then vanished, leaving just tiredness. "I can do this alone. I won't tell anyone you chickened out. Hell, I'll say you got hired by a city slicker and left me."

Em shook her head, stubborn as always. "No. I need this. I have to send money home. My grandfather's sick, and he won't make the year without a doctor. I told you that yesterday. I'll visit him after modeling for Mr. Gibson."

"Then we rest," Annie said. "Ten minutes, then we go."

They found a spot behind a boulder, half-sheltered from the wind. Annie gave Em her own scarf, and Jack curled up beside them, warm and cozy.

Em's voice was small. "I'm not a child, Annie."

"Never said you were."

Em looked away, but Annie saw her tears. "If I die up here, will you promise to send my body home?"

Annie stared at the darkness, her breath visible in the moonlight. "What on earth are you talking about? You're not going to die."

"But if I do?"

"All right, I promise."

They sat like that, shivering together, sharing the whiskey in silence. When Em's breathing slowed, Annie stood and kicked at Jack, waking him up. "Let's go."

The stars were out—thousands of glittering points of light. They walked on, as the night swallowed their shadows and the cold settled deeper into their bones. The slush on the road had frozen and now crunched beneath each step.

By the time they hit the fork where the wagon road climbed, the stars disappeared as thick clouds rolled in. The snowflakes drifted down, thin and fluttery. Soon the flakes fattened up, turned heavy, and started sticking to their hair and the fur on Jack's back. Within an hour, the ground was a featureless white, the dirty slush-covered ruts vanished, and every step left a print that filled in before they could look back.

They crunched through the next mile in silence. There was a rhythm to it: ten steps, pause, ten more steps, another pause, and so on. The whiskey helped for the first hour, then made Annie's vision blur. She blinked and pressed forward, fixing on the way the road curved ahead. Each time, a turn presented itself, and the path climbed.

After another mile, Em lagged. She coughed, bent double, and spat into the snow.

"What's wrong, Em?" Annie said, not looking back.

"Just the cold," Em managed, but her voice was thin.

Annie stopped, leaned against a tree, and waited for Em to catch up. "Turn back. I can do this myself."

"I don't want to turn back," Em said. "I just want to catch my breath for a minute."

Jack whined and pawed at the snow, then lifted his leg and made a yellow streak against a tree stump. Annie envied his simplicity. No guilt, no doubts, go where you're pointed and make your mark.

When Em reached her, she was shivering so hard her teeth chattered.

"You look like hell," Annie said, not as an insult, but with concern.

"Thanks," said Em, and wiped her nose with the back of her hand. "So do you."

They slogged on. Annie's feet went numb.

"I should have left you behind," Annie said. "You're too sick for this."

"Stop talking to me like that." Em snapped, but the fight was gone from her. She pulled up the collar of her dress and looked at the ground. "I thought . . . I could keep up. You're always so sure, Annie. Even when you're wrong. I should've worn boots."

"You don't own any," Annie answered. She didn't mean it to sound cruel, but that's how it came out.

The snow deepened, and the trees closed in. The world shrank to the patch of dim white in front of Annie's feet, to the slap of shoes against crust, to the smell of sweat and whiskey. They kept moving, slower and slower with each passing hour.

Annie checked the time and realized they were less than halfway to the pass. She stopped and looked for a place to shelter. There was nothing—just more trees, more snow, more silence.

At the next bend, Em stopped cold. "I can't," she whispered. "I can't go any farther. Can we stop now?"

Annie walked up the road and found a pocket between two huge pine tree roots, sheltered on three sides by the tree trunk and heavy branches above. They crawled in, the cold less savage out of the wind but still biting. Em curled up, knees to her chest, hands under her chin. Jack wedged himself between them.

Annie lay back, arms crossed over her stomach. She was so tired that her whole body ached. She thought about Rocky Bar, about money, about the future, but her mind kept wandering back to Atlanta, to the heat of the kitchen stove and the noise of Whisky Gulch.

Em's voice came out of the dark. "You asleep?"

"No."

"Me neither."

Em's breathing slowed. Annie was aware of the moisture from Em's breath, even though she could not see it in the darkness that enveloped them.

They sat for a while, not talking. Jack's body felt warm even through the snow. Annie could smell his damp fur, and it reminded her of the first dog she had ever owned. It was a mutt that slept at the foot of her childhood bed and once bit a neighbor who made fun of Annie when he found out she was illiterate. Jack was warmer than Em, warmer than Annie, and his steady heartbeat gave Annie something to focus on besides her own fears.

"I'm sorry," Em said, her voice thin and raspy. "If we don't make it."

"Shut up! We'll make it."

"We have a plan," Annie said after a while. "We get to Rocky Bar, make a killing, come back with a boatload of cash. Maybe we'd even get ol' Jack here a girlfriend." She cupped Jack's head in her hands. Her nose touched his. "Jack's a very good boy. Yes, my Jack, you are."

"I'm going to be a Gibson Girl, you know. Once I get enough saved up, my dream is to go to New York City and pose for Mr. Gibson. His models get paid big money."

That brought back a memory. "You know, Em, a good friend once told me, you can't experience having a dream fulfilled if you don't have a dream."

"That makes sense. Smart girl. Who is she?"

"Her name is Hazel. We spent a lot of time together when I lived in Rocky Bar."

"Do you keep in contact with her?"

"I wish, but I can't."

"Why not?"

"Her husband doesn't approve of me."

"Sorry to hear that. What was she like?"

"Hazel? She was the best friend I ever had, until I met you. There was this creek that ran through Rocky Bar—Beaver Creek. We used to sit on this old mossy log for hours on end, talking about everything you could ever think of. She was the best thing about living in Rocky Bar, when we were teenagers and later when I returned after a few years. We were so happy when we were together. Sometimes it feels like a dream. I do have dreams about Hazel once in a while. I miss her so much. She wrote a poem for me once. When she read it to me, I couldn't hold back my tears. I was so moved. They were the most beautiful words I've ever heard."

"Wow, that Hazel sounds amazing. Could I meet her someday? Could you introduce us?"

"Sorry, Em, but that can never happen."

"That's too bad. I bet I would like her. Any friend of yours is a friend of mine."

They sat in silence for several minutes. The only sound was Jack's breathing.

"I don't have a family," Em whispered, "except you. You're all I got in this world, Annie. I don't even know if my parents are still alive. You're everything to me. Could we be friends forever? I wish I could be like Hazel, for you." She took Annie's icy hand in her own stiff hand and held it tight against her cheek for a long time.

Annie felt something twist in her chest. It was a feeling she wasn't used to. She understood for the first time how much compassion she had for this girl snuggled beside her, this Dutch girl who wasn't really Dutch. Annie had no real friends in Atlanta except Em. *You're my best friend, Em. Here we are stuck under a tree in the middle of the night, with each other. Was it fate that brought us together? No, there's no such thing as fate. How could fate give me a marriage to an evil man like Thomas and then take away my children? And let me meet Jacob only to lose him? That made no sense. It's so confusing. What are we doing here?*

They didn't talk after that. They breathed, counting the minutes until morning. The snow piled up outside, sealing them in, muffling the world. Annie closed her eyes and tried to sleep, but every time she drifted off, a memory shoved its way in. Memories of her father, her children, Edith, and Hazel offered little comfort.

Chapter 33

Annie woke the next morning with her face buried in a tangle of hair and pine sap, the taste of blood from her chapped lips in her mouth. She sat up. Every inch of her body was sore. The world was white, where nothing but snow existed, and everything else had been erased. Jack was gone, but he reappeared a minute later, shaking snow from his fur and whining at the patch of sky above them. Em was awake, too, curled in a tight ball, lips with a bluish tint, hands tucked into her armpits. She looked worse than yesterday.

They didn't have a fire, or food, or dry clothes. *Our best hope is just to keep moving, so that exertion beats the cold for a while.* Annie shook Em's shoulder, then yanked her upright. "Come on," she said. "We'll die if we stay put."

She stood, brushed the snow from her dress, and offered Em a hand. "Come on. We'll make it together."

Em took the hand, her grip surprisingly strong. They started again, moving at a snail's pace, with Jack leading the way. The snowfall thickened, but so did their resolve. The snow was now two feet deep, with drifts even higher where the road curved.

Em coughed every few minutes, but Annie ignored it at first. "It's not so bad," she said to convince herself. "If we keep moving, we'll stay warm. Once we hit the pass, it's downhill to Rocky Bar."

"You sure?" Em asked, voice muffled by her scarf.

"I've done it a hundred times."

"On horseback," Em replied, halfway through a cough.

Annie jammed her hands into the pockets of her dress and kept plodding along.

Jack ran ahead, circling back now and then to nip at their heels. His excitement made Annie jealous. He had no idea where they were, or how far they had to go, or what perils might lie ahead. Annie wished she still had that kind of ignorance. After another hour, a sound broke the silence. They heard the swishing rhythm of someone on skis coming up from behind them. Jack perked up, barked, and bounded down the hill, disappearing in the drifts. Annie squinted, then saw a figure moving fast towards them, cutting through the snow.

It was a man, hunched forward on a pair of homemade skis, a pack lashed to his back. He wore a parka stitched from old flour sacks and a battered felt hat pulled down low. The man passed them and then circled back.

He came to a stop in front of them, breathless. "Well, well," he said. "What's a pair of city girls like you doing out here? You got a death wish?"

Annie recognized him: Bill Tate, the mail carrier. She'd seen him in Atlanta, lurking in the bar's corner, ears open, never smiling. She remembered hearing that Bill made the trek up to the pass every other day to exchange mail with the carrier from Rocky Bar.

"We're going to Rocky Bar," she said.

He stared at them. "What? You'll never make it. Bald Mountain Pass is snowed in, maybe worse on the other side. You should turn back now."

Em glared at him. "We don't have that option."

He grunted, looked up the road, then down at them. "I don't have time to argue. I'm on mail duty, gotta meet the Rocky Bar carrier at the summit cabin. If you don't turn around, you'll end up like that jackass from Boise City last winter. Took four men to dig out his frozen carcass come spring."

Bill crouched in the snow, balancing on his skis. "Listen, I've got to get to the summit cabin. The weather's going to sock in by noon, and the Rocky Bar carrier will be there waiting for the hand-off. You two should turn back. There's no sense dying for nothing. But if you get to the cabin, there's a stove and dry blankets. I'll leave the door unlocked for you."

"We'll be fine." Annie didn't believe her own words. "We've got Jack, and we know how to keep warm."

They watched him vanish up the road. Em looked at Annie. "He might be right, you know." There was a hint of fear in her voice.

She grabbed Em's hand, and they started forward again, step after impossible step. The wind picked up, slapping at their faces. Each mile took twice as long as the last, and the world kept shrinking, until it was only two women, a dog, and a blinding, merciless cold.

A dream Annie used to have while she lived in Mountain Home flickered across her mind. It was the dream where she found herself on a road in the desert, and she had trouble walking. Her feet were sinking into the ground with every step, and it became harder and harder to keep going. *So this is what it feels like to have your feet sink into the ground. But this ain't no dream.*

They lost their sense of time. It was replaced by the monotony of lifting one foot, then the other, leaning into the wind, and hoping the drifts wouldn't get deeper. Annie's mind wandered. She remembered the taste of coffee, the squeak of the saloon's floorboards, and the way Em used to sing in the evenings with her hurdy-gurdy. Em did not speak. She kept her head down and plowed forward like a sleepwalker.

At the next curve, Bill reappeared, gliding down the road towards them. He'd dropped his mailbag, his coat open, hair stiff with ice. He skidded to a stop, stared at them both, and swore. "I thought you turned back," he said. He was angry, and there was fear under it. "It's a wonder you two didn't freeze yet."

"Not yet," said Annie, refusing to give him the satisfaction. "You did your mail run?"

He nodded. "Swapped mailbags at the summit cabin."

"We're almost to the pass, right?" Annie said.

He shook his head. "Yeah, but you'll never make it. Not in this. Turn around now, I tell you, or you're dead."

Annie wanted to argue, but her mouth wouldn't work right. She looked at Em, whose lips were cracked and bloody, her breath shallow.

"No," Em whispered. "We can do it."

Bill's eyes narrowed, and he squinted at them. "Don't stop moving," he said. "Listen to me! Don't sleep. If you feel tired, slap each other in the face. You stop, you die. I'm serious."

Annie eyed him. "Why are you telling us this?"

Bill's face softened. "I don't like finding bodies when the spring thaw comes." He looked at Em, and Annie saw what he saw: the bluish corners of her mouth, the tremor in her hands. "You gotta turn back," he said, softer. "It's not worth it, ladies."

Annie wanted to laugh, but it came out as a cough. "We got no reason to turn back. Not anymore."

He shook his head. "You're both insane. But if you change your mind, you better hurry."

With that, he pushed off, skis snapping over the crust, and vanished down the road, taking full advantage of the downhill slope back to Atlanta. Annie watched him go. *Maybe we should turn back, but we've come so far. We can't be that far from the pass, and it's downhill from there.* Em coughed beside her, Jack barked, and the thought faded away.

They pressed on. The world shrank to a tunnel of snow and wind. Now and then she looked back at Em, who was fading, her steps unsteady and her eyes glazed. "You okay?" Annie asked every time she noticed the sound of Em's footsteps ceased.

"I'm fine," Em would say, but it was a lie.

Annie took Em's hand, skin cold as ice, and pulled her forward. They made it another mile. Time lost meaning. When the day faded into twilight, they found another tree with branches heavy enough to block some wind. Jack dug a hole and lay down, head between his paws.

They crawled under the branches, sat together, backs against the trunk, sharing the last inches of whiskey in silence. Em handed the bottle to Annie, her hand shaking so badly she almost dropped it. Annie took a sip, coughed, then looked at Em. Strands of frozen hair hung across her forehead like icicles.

"I know we're gonna make it, Em. Don't worry."

They pressed close, sharing what little warmth they could. The night came fast. The darkness enveloped them, and Annie could no longer see anything. She let herself drift, her mind wandering with random thoughts that made no sense. The cold was worse at night.

Em shivered. Out of the darkness came, "I don't want to die . . . I don't want to die," over and over, like a chant. Sometimes she whispered it, sometimes she choked it out, sometimes she breathed and said nothing at all. Annie held her, but her own arms were numb, her hands little more than pieces of wood. She wiggled out of her dress, wrapped it around Em, and tucked her in next to Jack, who was already curled tight and breathing shallow. *Em's worse off than me. My petticoats will be enough for me. I hope.*

The hours stretched. Em whimpered, remained silent, then whimpered again. Annie drifted, then woke. Drifted again, then woke again. Each time she felt Em's face, her breath was a little weaker. "I don't want to die," Em said again, with her voice fading. "I'm gonna be a Gibson Girl, in New York City. I'll be famous. A Gibson Girl. Gibson Girl Emma von . . . ."

Annie tried to stay awake, but she couldn't.

A shiver woke Annie up. It was still pitch black. She could hear the wind, but she couldn't see anything. Em wasn't shivering.

She nudged Em's shoulder. "Em," she said with a whisper, "how are you doing?

No response.

She nudged her a little harder. "Em. Wake up. We gotta to stay warm." Still nothing.

This time she shouted, "Em! Wake up!" She reached out through the darkness and put her hand on Em's face. Her skin was cold and stiff. Em was not breathing.

She screamed, "Em! Em!" and burst into tears. Annie collapsed onto Em's chest, sobs racking her body uncontrollably. "Oh Em, I'm sorry," she whispered, again and again. "I'm so sorry."

When she reached for Jack, she found a furry ear, but he, too, was gone.

Annie wrapped her arms around both of them, pulled them close, and wailed. She whispered Em's name over and over until her name was too painful to speak. *I wish I was dead.* A voice inside her head said, *don't give up, Annie.* It was the same voice that slipped into her mind years ago when Thomas left her for dead on the road to Mountain Home, and again when Hazel walked out of her life.

"Pa?" she whispered. Annie couldn't tell if it was her imagination or if she really heard it. With those words lingering in the back of her mind, she passed out.

When Annie awoke, she couldn't open her eyes. She reached up to feel them and realized her tears had frozen them shut. Even though she could hardly get her fingers to work, she managed to pick at her eyelashes enough so that she could see. She tried to move her legs. They didn't budge.

"Em, wake up, we gotta go." There was no response. It hit her like a hammer. *Em is dead!*

She struggled to get up, but her feet were nothing more than deadweights. Annie pulled herself forward with her arms, out from under the tree, dragging herself through the snow. She tried to stand, but she fell. She tried again and again, but every time she fell into the snow. The snowfall had stopped, but all she could see in every direction was featureless white.

She crawled, hands numb, elbows burning. Sometimes she blacked out, and when she came back, the world was different: snowing again, or someone singing far away, or the smell of whiskey, or the sound of cards shuffling, or a baby crying. Sometimes she saw her children, sometimes her mother, sometimes Thomas, arms folded, sneering at her.

She saw Em waiting for her up ahead, arms outstretched, but it turned out to be a tree stump. She crawled until she couldn't move another inch.

I'm so tired. I'll lie here for a while, then I'll be okay. I need to rest . . . just for a minute.

She heard skis on the snow behind her and saw a dark shape moving towards her.

"Jesus, Annie, what the hell!" It was Bill, and another man on skis was right behind him.

"We gotta get you to the summit cabin or you'll freeze to death. Let us help you up. When you didn't come back last night, we figured you were in trouble, so we came as soon as it got light." Together, they raised Annie out of the snow and dragged her over to the summit cabin, pulled the door open, and set her on the bench inside.

"Stay put while I go back to Atlanta and get some skis for you. I can't drag you all the way back. We'll be back as fast as we can."

Annie sat there shivering, confused. *Where's Em? Why did Bill leave me here? Why can't I move my legs? What am I supposed to do? Where are you, Em?*

What seemed like a minute later, Bill returned. "I'm back. Let's get you out of here."

Together they struggled to stuff Annie's shoes into the binding of the skis. Once Bill strapped them in, they took off down the snowy road back to Atlanta, with Annie clutching their arms so she wouldn't fall over. Annie was in a daze for the entire trip. Whenever she tried to speak, all she heard was a jumble of words that didn't make sense.

They reached Annie's cabin right before dark. Bill put her in her bed, wrapped her in every blanket he could find, and left a cup of water on the table.

* * *

As Annie regained consciousness the next morning, she noticed a tingling in her feet and legs. At first it was distant, but a moment later, it swelled and felt like pins and needles. She opened her eyes and saw she was in her bed in her cabin in Atlanta. She didn't remember climbing into her bed. Bill was dozing off in the chair across the room. *What's Bill doing in my cabin?*

"Hey Bill, what's going on?"

He awoke with a start. "You almost froze to death on the road to Rocky Bar. We found you Sunday morning, crawling in the snow, delirious and wearing nothing but your petticoats. We brought you back here."

Annie let that sink in, but the pain in her feet was getting worse. She tried to stretch her legs, but her feet would not move. "I can't move my feet, Bill," with a concern in her voice.

"You got frostbite, Annie. Mighty bad frostbite. You couldn't move them even when I stuffed your feet onto the skis."

I don't remember that, so I have to believe him. Bill never lied about anything. I remember asking old man Brubaker for horses, or was it Mr. Johnson? The memory was fuzzy. She tried again to move her feet, but they wouldn't budge. There were two bumps under the blanket at the foot of her bed. *Why can't I move my feet?*

Her mind wandered back to her and Em asking for horses. *I'm sure it was Brubaker at the livery, not Johnson. He refused to give two of his horses to me and—*

"Where's Em?"

Bill stared at the floor and then looked at her, his face expressionless. He turned his head and looked out the window at the empty street that ran next to Annie's cabin.

She raised her voice. "Bill, where the hell is Em?"

Bill rose from his chair and walked over to the foot of Annie's bed. He sat down and put his hands in his lap but didn't say a word.

"Damn it, Bill. You're scaring me! Where's Em?"

He looked at her and frowned. "I'm sorry, Annie. We couldn't find her. I'm afraid Em didn't make it back."

"What? What do you mean she couldn't make it back? You found me, and Em was right beside me!"

"I looked, but there was no sign of her," he said, his voice cracking. "I know what she meant to you."

"You don't know squat. Em was my best friend, and now she's . . . gone?"

Annie couldn't hold back her tears. That brought back the image of her and Em huddled under the tree with Jack, shivering and freezing.

Annie shouted and struggled to sit up. "You gotta go an' get her! We were under a big tree by the road, close to the summit cabin. I promised her . . . ."

"Okay, I'll organize a search party, but don't get your hopes up. That blizzard buried everything up there on that road."

"Find her, Bill, even if that's the last thing you do on this Earth. You gotta find her, please!" Annie felt a new pain in her heart. The aching in her heart was worse than the pain in her legs, realizing that she might never see her Em again.

"I sent notice to Dr. Newkirk in Mountain Home. You need to have him look at your frostbite. It looks mighty bad. It might take him a few days to get here, so in the meantime, I'm afraid you're in for a rough ride."

"Get me a bottle of the good stuff from the James Hotel. It's in a drawer to the left of the sink in the back room."

"Will do."

A moment later, "Do you know Effie Prey? She's educated as a nurse, and her husband, Gilbert, asked her to come over and look after you until Dr. Newkirk gets here. She's only seventeen, but no one else could be found. The bandages on your feet and legs will need to get changed."

"All right, I suppose."

That afternoon, while Annie was alone, Effie walked into the room and sat down on the chair in the corner.

"Good afternoon, Mrs. Morrow, I'm Effie Prey," she said without standing up. "I'll be looking after you until the doctor gets here."

Annie scrutinized the young nurse. She had a round face with full cheeks and wore her brown hair in a rolled bun on the top of her head, with short curls in the front. Effie had a serious look on her face, as if it would be painful for her to smile. She wore a white apron over her dark green dress. A heart-shaped pendant hung down from a thin necklace. Their eyes met.

"Tell me, did they find Em?"

"Yes."

"Yes, what?"

Effie stood up, dragged her chair over to the side of Annie's bed, and sat down. She clasped her hands together and placed them on her lap. She took a deep breath, and a look of sadness swept over her face.

"Yes, they found her . . . body. I'm so sorry, Mrs. Morrow."

The last dregs of Annie's hope that Em was still alive evaporated. "Em was my best friend."

Neither of them spoke for the rest of the afternoon. The weight of Em's death crushed any desire Annie had to speak another word.

When twilight darkened the skies, Annie broke the silence. "Nurses are for sick people. I ain't sick, just injured."

"Gilbert asked me to come over here. It wasn't my idea. I'll leave as soon as I'm not needed."

"Sooner the better. You can skedaddle outta here anytime."

Effie walked over to the table beside the bed, took the bottle of whiskey and set it on the windowsill, out of reach, and replaced it with a tin cup of water. "It's better for you," she said, as if Annie were a child caught with her hand in the cookie jar. Effie turned down the lamp, sat in the straight-backed chair, and started reading her Bible out loud but in a soft voice, loud enough for Annie to hear.

Annie listened, not because she cared for the words, but because Effie's voice was soothing. With each break in Effie's reading, her suppressed thoughts about Em and her children erupted in her mind. Sometimes Annie interrupted with a crude joke to see if Effie would flinch. When that had no effect, Annie let out a string of every curse word she knew. Effie would put down her Bible, glance over and say, "Language," in the same tone of voice that a schoolmarm would use to address an unruly boy.

"Hell with that. I got a reputation to protect."

"And what kind of reputation is that?" Before Annie could answer, Effie added, "Never mind. I don't want to know."

"As if you didn't know already. Don't play dumb with me, girl. I know what you people think of me."

That night, when the pins and needles in her legs got worse for a few minutes, Annie started a fight. "Why are you here?" she asked, picking at the crust on her bandages. "Don't say it's for charity. I know what the town calls me. You think you can fix me up and save my soul before I die?"

Effie didn't look up from her book. "You're not dying. Not today, anyway."

"So, what, then? You want a badge for tending to the worst woman in Atlanta?"

Effie marked her place, set the Bible on the table, and folded her hands. "I'm here because my husband, Gilbert, asked me to be here. I did not volunteer. Be clear about that. You're a human being, Mrs. Morrow, no matter what else you are. The rest is between you and the Lord."

Annie snorted. "I'd rather take it up with the devil. He'd be more fun at parties."

Effie allowed herself the thinnest smile. "You're funny. But you're stuck with me, so you might as well behave."

"Humph," was all that came out of Annie's mouth. On the first day, the pain was annoying, but it was bearable. That changed on the second day. That's when the throbbing and burning sensation started. Each time she shifted her position, it got worse. The third day, she couldn't feel any pain in her feet, but now it was even more intense in her legs. She finished the first bottle of whiskey and ordered Effie to get another from Whiskey Gulch.

She looked up from her book. "I will not set foot into that hell hole," and continued reading.

"Well, then get someone else to do it, Miss Prissy." Effie scowled, stood up, left the room, and came back half an hour later. "It'll be here soon enough," and went back to her reading.

The worst part of the ordeal was when Effie changed the bandages. It felt like she was peeling off the skin, an inch at a time. It was all Annie could do to lie there and not yell at her to stop. During one moment when

Effie had the blanket pulled down, Annie glimpsed at what was at the foot of her bed. She saw two black, swollen blobs that were unrecognizable as human feet. Her toes were nothing more than hideous lumps. She turned her head away to put the image of them out of her mind, but she couldn't. A wave of nausea swept over her.

* * *

Day four was when the stench filled the room. As her flesh thawed and began to rot, the miasma was palpable. It made her want to puke, but she held it in. Effie was not so fortunate. Annie watched helplessly one time as Effie dashed to the open front door just in time. The sound of her retching made Annie feel sorry for the poor girl.

Effie slowly walked back into the room, a little unsteady, and sat down with a cup of water in her hand. She took a small sip and glanced over at Annie. "I'm okay, don't worry about me."

"It's not you I'm worried about. It's me."

"I understand. I'd open the window to let in some fresh air, but then we would both freeze. It's so cold outside."

They sat in silence, with the only sound being the cracking of the flames in the wood stove.

"I need another drink, Effie! Hand it to me, or else—"

"Or else what?"

"Or else I'll . . . I'll fall out of this bed reaching for it, break my neck, and die right before your eyes!"

Effie handed her the bottle. Annie guzzled the half-full bottle until it was empty and let it drop to the floor. She wished she would pass out, and after what felt like an eternity, she did.

Annie awoke the next morning in a daze. Now her head was throbbing; her legs felt like they were being stabbed with dull knives that pierced her flesh right to the bone. The stench in the air was thick and putrid. She vomited all over the bed. Effie cleaned it up without a word.

"Whiskey! I need a shot!"

"Doctor Newkirk is almost here. Please hold on a while longer, and it will be all over."

Annie passed out and awoke again. A man entered the room. *Who is that? Must be the doctor.* He pulled back the blanket and gasped, then looked Annie right in her eyes. It was obvious from the look on his face that it was bad.

"Listen to me, Mrs. Morrow. Gangrene has set in. I have no choice but to amputate. If I don't, you'll get sepsis, and you'll die. I brought a bottle of chloroform. That will put you under, so you won't feel anything. I promise." Annie could not understand what he was saying. He put a sweet-smelling cloth over Annie's mouth and nose. She had no strength to resist.

Chapter 34

Annie awakened and tried to sit up. The room spun around, so she let herself fall back on the pillow. She couldn't feel her feet, but the stench of rotten human flesh was gone. Her knees hurt, but it was a dull pain, not the burning and throbbing like before.

"Did they do it, Effie?"

"Yes. They did, but I couldn't watch. Nurse training never taught me about amputations. I'll be changing your bandages every day. We got to keep them clean so you don't get infected."

Effie was tireless; she cooked, she cleaned, she wiped the sweat from Annie's face when she vomited in the night. She never lost her temper, never raised her voice. If Annie refused the water, Effie would wait an hour and bring it back. No more whiskey. When Annie swore a blue streak, Effie would calmly quote her favorite verse about patience, "Rejoicing in hope; patient in tribulation; continuing instant in prayer, Romans 12:12, King James Version", and then carry on as if the room wasn't a battlefield between Annie's anger and Effie's patience.

"I can tell you a thing or two about tribulation, Effie girl. You ain't been through as much tribulation in your whole life as I have been through in the last five days. Think about that before you say anything more."

Once, out of pure frustration, Annie threw her tin cup across the room. It bounced off the wall, dented the oil lamp, and splashed water on Effie's dress. Effie didn't shout or scold. She wiped the water off her dress and picked up the cup, humming a hymn all the while. That did more to break Annie's anger than any punishment. *I don't take kindly to displays of righteousness, especially from a simple Christian girl.* Despite Annie's misgivings, she could see that Effie's wisdom was the subtle, creeping kind, the kind that seeped into the soul. She didn't lecture Annie about right and wrong. Instead, she asked questions and let the silence answer for itself when Annie refused to answer.

"Do you ever regret it?" Effie asked one morning while changing the bandages. "The life you've lived?"

Annie gritted her teeth as the strips of bedsheets were peeled away from her legs. "What's the point of regret? I can't grow new legs by wishing for them. I can't undo a damn thing that I ever did."

"True," Effie said, wrapping the stump with practiced hands. "But sometimes regret means you're ready to change. Or at least to stop repeating the old mistakes."

Annie stared at the ceiling. "What would you have me do, Effie? Start singing at church? Wash the feet of the poor? I'm nobody's idea of a saint."

"You're not supposed to be," Effie said, tying off the bandage. "I'm not either. We do the best we can with what we got."

After that, Annie watched Effie closer. *This young woman is not as pious as she pretends to be, must be Methodist. She never once prayed before a meal, but she always set it on the table and waited for me to take the first bite.*

The next day, Annie noticed something. "I see you're not reading the Good Book. Lost your faith, dear?"

Effie rolled her eyes. "Not everything I read has to be scripture."

"Really? I'm surprised to hear that coming from you."

Effie held up a thin publication with a light green cover. "It's a dime novel. Famous Fiction by the World's Greatest Authors. Published by F. M. Lupton in New York. They mail these out once a week. I have a subscription. Three dollars for an entire year. They reprint a complete novel in only twenty-one pages. The print is super tiny, but it's readable."

"So, what are you reading this week?"

"The Wizard of Granada by M. T. Caldor. It's a story about a Spanish knight who travels to the Alhambra in Spain searching for somebody. He encounters all kinds of mysterious characters. Can I read a little to you?"

"If you must."

"I'm on page thirteen, where chapter seven starts."

> Early in the day came the royal summons to the Alhambra. Prince Azim accompanied his guest, and at the gateway they met Basilio coming forth. There was a fierce flash in his eye as he bowed to the knight, which startled the prince.
>
> "What's amiss?" exclaimed the latter. "I know that evil flash of Basilo's eye; it means mischief."
>
> "There has been a heavy weight on my own spirit, foreboding calamity. I would I had brought Alana. We two, with our trusty blades, would meet whatever fate comes manfully."
>
> "Hush, dare not draw your sword in the king's presence, at any provocation. Remember that. We will manage to rescue you, whatever betide; but a rash word or movement might draw upon you instant doom."

"I enjoy reading about knights, kings, and princesses in faraway lands. Don't you?" asked Effie.

"I'm not much for reading. Seems like I always got something to do or something that needs my attention. Keep reading if you like. I need to close my eyes for a while." Annie did not want to admit it, but she enjoyed being read to. Effie's voice was pleasant and soothing, and reminded her of the nights when she read to Anna Eliza and John Henry, cuddled next to her in bed.

It became a game, Annie trying to catch the nurse in hypocrisies. She once asked her, "Tell me, what's the best sin you ever committed?"

"I don't believe there is such a thing as a best sin, but once I pushed my little brother in the creek. Broke his tooth on a rock. Lied to my father about it for weeks." When Annie laughed, Effie didn't smile, but her eyes twinkled.

* * *

Some days they didn't talk at all. Annie would stare out the window, watching the last of the snow melting and the muddy street reappearing, thinking about the places she'd never go to again. *I wonder if I'll ever see Rocky Bar or Beaver Creek, where me and Hazel spent summer afternoons reveling in each other's company. I wonder if anyone will remember me as anything more than a curiosity or a scandal. No matter. I'm not dead yet.*

Effie's Methodist minister came by once to check on her progress. He was a tall, thin man with a mustache that looked glued on, and a voice that never quite matched his face. He brought Annie a book of sermons and told her, "You're lucky, Mrs. Morrow. God must have big plans for you."

"Ha. If He wants to give me a new set of feet, He'd better get a move on." The preacher turned red and changed the subject.

Effie waited until he left, then told Annie, "He means well, but he's never had an actual job in his life. Don't take him too seriously."

That was the first time Annie realized Effie wasn't only tolerating her but liked her a little. *Turns out Effie girl has some compassion for me, even when I get nasty. I've never seen her get upset at my antics. Impressive.*

Late at night, when the pain was at its worst, and Annie couldn't sleep, she'd ask Effie hard questions just to see if she could come up with one that Effie couldn't answer.

"Why is the world so miserable?"

Effie considered. "Because most people want more than they need. Because nobody forgives anyone anymore. Because men think they're owed something from God, and women think they're owed something from men."

"That's a bleak way to see things."

Effie shrugged. "It's not so bad. There's still good in people, even when they don't show it."

"You think I'm good, Effie?"

"I think you're strong. And I think you know how to survive. That's a kind of goodness."

Annie mulled that over, unsure if it was a compliment. She stared at her bandaged stumps. "If God made me, He did a damn sloppy job. Look at me now. I'm half a woman, and not a soul to blame but Him."

"Or maybe He's not to blame at all. Maybe He's waiting for you to stop shaking your fist long enough to hear Him."

"Tell me, Effie, what kind of loving God leaves a woman to crawl through snow like a dog and come out with less than what she started with?"

Effie paused her sewing. "I don't know. I won't pretend to know. But I do believe suffering is not the end of the story. Sometimes, it's the middle."

"You ever suffer, girl?"

"My mama died of consumption. My brothers are buried under a cottonwood tree without a cross to mark them. I've known grief." Effie got up from her chair and came over to the bed to straighten out the crumpled blankets. "You don't scare me, you know. You talk like there's no meaning to life, but here I am—sitting with you, changing your bandages, and singing to you when you sleep. I pray for you every night. If that's not grace, I don't know what is."

"Maybe it's pity. Or boredom."

"No, it's love. That same old stubborn kind that made the earth and sky and sent me to you."

Annie shook her head. "You really believe all that, don't you?"

"With all my heart."

Silence enveloped the room for several minutes. Annie rolled over onto her side in order to get more comfortable. Effie walked over to the wash bin and wrung out a few soaking wet bandages.

Annie turned her head to look directly at Effie. "Let me tell you something about suffering, Effie. You know what I think suffering means?"

"What?"

"It means life's got teeth. And it bites indiscriminately. Children, whores, honest men, crooks, liars—it don't matter. Pain don't come with a reason. It just comes. And now I lie here and have to listen to you all day."

Effie moved her chair over and placed it next to the bed. "When Mama was sick, I used to ask God why He let her suffer. She'd wheeze so hard she'd cry, and I'd pray till my knees were raw. Want to know what she told me?"

"No, but I bet you're gonna tell me, anyway."

"She said suffering's like a plow. It breaks the ground. Hurts like hell, but it makes room for something to grow."

"Your mama ever work in a saloon or a brothel?"

"No."

"Then she don't know what the hell she's talking about. Suffering ain't some holy tilling of the soul. It's a man pressing your face into the floor while he breathes down your neck. It's having your children stolen from you. It's being forgotten on purpose. It's being abused by a man you thought loved you but who turned into a monster. It's waking up in the middle of the night and finding your best friend in the world lying next to you dead."

"I know I don't understand it all. But I believe that none of it is wasted."

"Oh, I wasted plenty. Wasted my youth, my beauty, my chances. All gone up in smoke and whisky and men with gold teeth and filthy minds and dirty hands."

"But here you are. Alive. Still fierce enough to argue with me. That means something."

"It means I'm too stubborn to die, that's all." *She's got no comeback for that one.* Neither spoke for a while.

The fire in the wood stove faded. Effie opened the door and tossed in a few pieces of wood. "It'll warm up in here in a few minutes." Outside, the Idaho sky was streaked pink and gold with the last of the day. Effie sat at Annie's bedside, half in shadow. Annie, now propped upright with pillows behind her, stared out the window.

"You ever wonder why you were born, Annie?"

"What kind of question is that? How is anybody supposed to know why they were born? You just are. Period. Most days, I reckon it was a cosmic accident. Some poor girl on an Iowa farm got knocked up in a barn by the boy next door. That was my father. My mother was fifteen years old when I was born. If that's not an accident of nature, then I don't know what is."

"I think we're here for a reason. Maybe not one we understand right away. Maybe not even one we like. But I believe God breathes life into us on purpose. We're not just . . . accidents."

"That's sweet. Naive, but sweet. You think I got dragged through brothels and snowbanks and back alleys because some big, bearded Sky-man had a plan? What kind of plan ends with a woman cut in half and pissing into a tin basin?"

"The point isn't where you end up—but who you become on the way."

"I became a mother with no children, then a whore, then a cripple. That's the arc of my great divine purpose?"

"You became someone who tells the truth. Who sees through lies. You care about people. You can look suffering in the eye without blinking. You know how to survive. Listen to me, you Angel of Mercy, that matters. There's goodness inside that stubborn soul of yours, Annie. You should let it out more often."

"What about you? You believe your life's got meaning just 'cause you sing and pray and scrub floors?"

"Yes. Even the small things. Especially the small things. There's a kind of holiness in them. I don't need to be important. I just want to live a life of kindness. Serve where I'm needed. Be a light in dark places.

"Sounds lonely."

"It isn't, not when I remember who walks with me. When I pray, I'm not talking to the clouds. I'm talking to someone who knows me, even the parts of me I don't know." Effie leaned in towards Annie. "You'll walk again someday, Annie. I feel it in my bones. Don't give up, Annie."

I've heard that before. Come to think of it, those words popped into my head when Thomas left me for dead on the road to Mountain Home. And the day Hazel walked out of my life, and . . . that night after Em froze to death. "I never give up, Effie."

Annie took a deep breath. "I think the meaning of life is to survive. To keep going no matter what life throws at you. Did I ever tell you about the time Thomas almost killed me? I was lying flat on my back on the ground in the middle of nowhere, and he was standing right over me with a gun pointed at my chest. He stood like that for the longest time, just to terrify me. Never pulled the trigger. He got up, walked away, and told me I would never see my children again. That was worse than dying."

"I can't imagine. I'm sorry to hear about that," Effie said, as tears welled up in her eyes. "I had no idea."

Neither of them spoke after that. Effie wiped the tears from her eyes and moved her chair away from the bed and back to the corner. It scratched the floor as she pushed it. Annie rolled over again, but this time facing away from the window. They were both mesmerized by the orange light from the open stove flickering on the walls.

When Effie wasn't looking, Annie reached under her blanket, pulled out a flask, took two quick swallows, and put it back under the blanket. A few minutes later, she did it again, but this time Effie glanced over just as she tucked it away.

"How did you get that?"

"I got connections."

Effie let out a long sigh. "I can see that."

Silence followed for several minutes.

"Annie, can I tell you something I've never told anyone?"

"You? You got secrets? Well, I'll be—"

"Damned?"

"Watch your mouth, girl. That's my line."

Effie laughed. "You're funny. Anyway, yes, I have secrets."

"Alright, then. Let's hear it. Let the wicked woman bear witness."

"When I heard about your surgery, the first thing I prayed was, 'Please God, don't make me care for this horrible woman'. "

"That so?"

Effie nodded, her chin sinking into her chest, and she gazed at the floor. "I'd heard things. About you. That you were bitter. Filthy in speech. That you'd lived in sin so long you'd forgotten what decency looked like. I thought—I assumed—that you didn't deserve kindness or care. And I felt proud of myself for judging you in silence."

"And now?"

"Now I'm ashamed. Because I've learned more about grace from you than from a dozen sermons. You speak honestly. You don't pretend. And you're braver than most people I know. I . . . I feel like a hypocrite sometimes. Preaching love and mercy, while condemning the very people I'm supposed to serve."

"Welcome to the human race, sweetheart."

"It doesn't feel right. I pray every day, yet still I envy, I judge, I doubt. I want to be pure-hearted, but I fall short."

"Of course you do. That's what makes you a person, not a statue. The only folks who think they're pure are liars or fools, or both."

"Sometimes I even wonder if God's disappointed in me. Like I'm wasting the faith He gave me. But I just . . . I want to be worthy.

"That's the trap, Effie. You think worthiness is something you earn. But life ain't a damn bank ledger. If love—yours or God's—only comes after you've scrubbed every sin clean, then it ain't love at all. It's a transaction."

"I was raised to believe we should be spotless."

"You were raised wrong. Spotless things never survive in the real world. They get torn, stained, lived in, used, broken, and repaired."

Effie walked back over to Annie's bed and sat down. "So, you think . . . it's okay to stumble?"

"Not only okay. It's expected. The trick is what you do after you fall. That's the part that counts. You fall, and then you get back up and keep going."

"I can imagine my husband Gilbert telling me, 'What, you, a Christian girl, learning about life from a prostitute? What's gotten into you, Effie?' as he peers at me over his reading glasses."

That made Annie chuckle. "And how would you respond to that?"

Effie thought for a moment. "I don't know. Maybe I'd say, 'judge not lest ye be judged,' or something like that."

"As much as I don't like your being here, Effie, I have to give you credit for being a smart girl."

Effie blushed at the unexpected compliment. "Thank you, Annie. I believe that's the first time you ever said anything nice to me."

"Don't get used to it."

The fire burned low, and the flickering on the wall faded away, replaced by a soft orange glow in the room. Outside, the mining town was still, with only the wind whistling between crooked buildings and the occasional clip-clop of a distant horse breaking the silence. Even the stamp mills were silent. Annie was motionless except for long breaths. She stared at the ceiling until she fell asleep.

* * *

Over time, their conversations became more respectful. Annie decided it might be worthwhile to listen more closely to what Effie had to say. One afternoon, Effie was seated in the chair beside Annie's bed, having finished replacing a set of bandages. Effie opened her mouth to say something, but stopped. She tried again, but no words came out for several minutes.

"Annie . . . do you mind if I ask you something personal?"

"That means you already decided to."

"I did. But if you'd rather I didn't, I'll hush. I'm so embarrassed." Effie blushed.

"Go on, then. I'm half-dead and got no place to go. I can handle a question."

"Why . . . uh . . . why did you . . . never mind." She stood and turned away.

"Why did I what? Come on now, out with it."

"I shouldn't. It's none of my business."

"Too late for that. You got a question, so ask it already."

Effie turned back, sat down, took a deep breath, and whispered, "why did you become a . . . a prostitute?"

"Not the kind of question they teach you to ask in Sunday school, is it?"

"No. But I think sometimes we judge things we don't understand. And I want to understand you."

"You're married, right?"

"Yes, to Gilbert."

"How long?"

"Our second anniversary is in three months."

"And how's it going for you?"

"Gilbert is a wonderful God-fearing man. I couldn't have asked for anyone better."

"Let me tell you something. My marriage to Thomas was the worst thing that ever happened to me. The man I fell in love with and married ended up beating me more often than not, made my existence miserable, robbed me of every shred of happiness that I could ever have had. He made my life a living hell for thirteen years. That's what marriage means to me. We had five children, but he turned them against me. Now they all hate me. That's why I left my family in Pine Grove. To escape with my life. I haven't seen or heard from him or my children since I moved back to Rocky Bar and then here to Atlanta. The one thing that I knew I could do was run a business. I am a survivor. I don't give up. If my marriage and family were destroyed, well, at least I could have my own businesses. I owned a boarding house, restaurant, and saloon in Rocky Bar, and they all made a nice profit. Then I came here to expand my businesses, and I did. I became known as the Queen of Atlanta, and I'm sure you know why. I never intended to become a madam. Marriage was out of the question for me, and so was love from any man. I learned that lesson the hard way from a man named Jacob. I'll tell you about him some other time. If you can't have love, the next best thing is companionship, the more intimate the better. Even if it's not permanent, a little is better than none. One thing led to another; one encounter led to the next. There are a lot of lonely men in these mining towns, Effie. Men who will never know the comfort of having a girlfriend, much less a wife and children. Is it fair to them to be deprived of one of life's most enjoyable experiences? I don't think so. I'm fulfilling a need, something these boys and men may never otherwise get to experience before they grow old, die, and find themselves six feet under. Think about that. Does that answer your question?"

"Yes." Effie looked down at the floor. "I'm not judging. Believe me, I swear I'm not. I just . . . I wish the world had been kinder to you."

"You and me both, sweetheart."

"You didn't become a prostitute because you were a bad person. You did it because the world failed you. You know what I see when I look at you?"

"A cranky half-woman with a foul mouth?"

"I see a woman who's still standing—without legs. That takes more grit than anyone in town that I can imagine."

"You're too tender for this world, my dear Effie."

* * *

As the weeks wore on, Annie's strength resumed. Somebody, she didn't know who, made a pair of woolen pads for her stumps. She learned to use her arms to hoist herself from the bed to the chair, then from the chair to the window, then finally to the privy out back. When that failed, she crawled on her hands and knees. Effie fashioned a set of wooden crutches from scrap lumber and showed Annie how to balance on the stumps without falling. It was awkward at first, but after a while, she moved without too much of a hobble.

One afternoon, memories of Em dancing at the Silver Moon Dance Hall kept flooding into her head. As clear as day, Annie could see Em spinning around so fast that her dress would fly up and reveal her petticoats. *The men howled every time she did that, and she loved it as much as they did. Em had such a passion for life. She invested everything she had in what she did.* The scratchy melody of Camptown Races on Em's hurdy-gurdy competing with the piano man's version played in her mind over and over. *Em loved music so much. She could sing better than anyone at the dance hall. I told her that once.* Annie couldn't make the memories stop, and she didn't want to.

"Effie dear, can you do me a big favor?"

"I'll try, but no promises."

"I know it would kill you to ever set foot in the Silver Moon, so can you have somebody fetch Em's hurdy-gurdy for me? I can't play the damn thing, but it would remind me so much of Em. Could you do that for me, please?"

"I can do that. I'll send Gilbert over there tonight after he gets home from work."

"Thanks, Effie, you're an angel."

"I'm no angel. I'm just a girl trying to do her best in this world," she said with a smile.

Effie returned that evening with the case that contained Em's hurdy-gurdy. She set it on the table beside Annie's bed. "Should I open it for you?"

"Please."

Effie opened two metal clasps and lifted the cover to reveal the odd-looking instrument. "I've never seen one of these up close before. It looks like a fat violin with a crank at the bottom end. How does it work?"

"It has strings like a violin, but instead of a bow, it has this wheel under the strings. You turn the crank, which turns the wheel, which rubs against the strings. These levers over here make the different notes."

Effie handed the hurdy-gurdy over to Annie as if it were a sleeping child and set it in Annie's lap. The wood gave off a faint scent of rosin and lavender—Em's mother's trick, Em had once said, to keep the wood from drying out in the high-altitude air. Annie stroked its curved body with her fingers.

"Oh, Em," she whispered.

Near the top end of the instrument, where the pegs that tightened the strings were located, Annie felt something rough, like a scratch. She tilted it towards the window to get some light on it. It was an inscription in tiny, engraved letters.

For Emma-
Your music is the place where the world can't hurt you.
-Mama

Annie pressed her thumb over the inscription, feeling the grooves like the ridges of old scars. She swallowed hard, the burn rising into her eyes. Em had spoken several times of her mother's lessons with a kind of shy pride, as though she feared that wanting anything from childhood might seem foolish in a mining camp like Atlanta.

She set the hurdy-gurdy down on her lap. She turned the crank, slow and steadily. A single wavering drone, like the buzz from a bee, filled the small room—a hollow, mournful sound that vibrated through her bones. For a fleeting second, she could almost imagine Em sitting beside her, rolling her eyes and teasing her about her awful tuning. She turned the crank again. The buzz continued, the same unbroken note, for as long as she kept turning the crank.

Annie placed the instrument back in its case, and was about to close the lid when she noticed a small piece of folded paper tucked into a crease in the fabric on the inside of the lid. She plucked it out and opened it with care. The handwriting was Em's, bold and looping as if she'd been in a hurry. As she read it, tears formed in her eyes.

Effie noticed. "What is it?"

"It's a note from Em. It's a note I wish I never had to read."

"Would you like to share it? If not, I'll understand."

"I'll keep it for now, if you don't mind." Annie folded the paper and placed it back in the same crease in the lid and closed it. She whispered, "I promise, Em."

* * *

The next morning Effie arrived on time as usual. She sat in her chair by the wall, but her gaze never left Annie. "Are you ready?"

"Ready for what?"

"You know very well what I'm talking about," she said, tilting her head towards the peg legs across the room.

"As ready as I'll ever be."

The chair scraped against the floor as Effie dragged it closer to Annie's bed. She helped Annie onto the chair. Annie stared at the two wooden pegs leaning against the wall like tools laid out for punishment.

"Bring 'em here," she said.

Effie hesitated. "Annie, perhaps we should wait until—"

"Now." Annie's voice snapped. "Before I lose what little courage I have."

Effie crossed the room and lifted the prosthetics. Up close, they looked even more unforgiving—scarred wood, darkened by oil and sweat, the leather cuffs stiff and curled. She set them gently at Annie's feet.

Annie rolled up her skirt with shaking hands. The ends of her legs were wrapped in linen, already stained where the cloth had rubbed too long against tender skin. She swallowed and reached for the first peg. The big leather cup at the top end was stiff. She pressed it open, trying to guide her leg into the socket. Sharp pain flared instantly. She gasped and jerked back. "It doesn't fit."

Effie moved closer. "Let me loosen the straps."

"Don't." Annie clutched the peg. "If they're loose, they'll slip. I won't have them slipping."

She tried again. The rough seam of the leather scraped scar tissue. She winced.

"Stop," Effie said softly. "You're hurting yourself."

"Fiddlesticks! I have to do this, one way or another."

The peg tilted as she forced it down. One strap gave a dry creak, then snapped free. The prosthetic slipped from her grasp and struck the floor with a hollow crack.

Effie reached for her arm. "Annie—"

"Don't touch me." Annie's voice shook now, angry at herself and frustrated. "I need to do this. If I can't manage this much, I might as well be in a grave with Em. I don't want to have to crawl around on my hands and knees forever."

Silence pressed between them. Effie gathered the fallen peg and re-threaded the strap with careful fingers.

"Lean back," she said. "Just for a moment."

Annie obeyed reluctantly, jaw clenched as Effie spread the leather socket wider.

"On three," Effie said. "One. Two—"

Annie shoved her leg down before the count finished. She gasped. The peg twisted, refusing to seat properly.

"Pull it off," she sobbed. "Pull it off, I can't—"

Effie did, and the relief was immediate but fleeting, replaced by a deep, throbbing ache. Annie sagged against the chair and sighed.

"I can't do it," she whispered. "I can't wear them. I can't stand on sticks like some sorry cripple."

Effie knelt in front of her and looked up into her eyes. "You can," she said, firmly, "because you want to walk again."

Annie laughed weakly. "Walk," she echoed. "Is that what you call it?"

Effie tightened the leather again, slower this time, more deliberate. "Try once more. Just once."

Annie closed her eyes. She nodded. This time, she guided her leg inch by inch, breathing through clenched teeth. The peg resisted, then—at last—settled with a dull, final pressure that spread like fire through her limb. She cried out, but she did not pull away.

"There," Effie said quickly. "It's seated."

They repeated the ordeal with the second leg. Twice it slipped. Once the strap twisted and had to be undone. Each failure drained her further, until her hands shook too badly to hold the leather. Together, they tried again, aligned the peg. The leather creaked. Then it held.

Effie exhaled. "It's on."

Annie sat motionless. Both pegs stood beneath her now, rigid and foreign. "If I fall . . . . "

"I'll catch you."

Annie nodded once. She placed her hands on the chair arms and pushed, trembling as she rose. The pegs struck the floor with a deadened thud. She stood—only for a breath, only with Effie gripping her waist—but she stood. When she sank back into the chair, sobbing, she pressed her face into her hands.

"They hurt," she whispered.

"I know," Effie said, holding her. "But you'll get used to it in time. That's enough for today. Let's try again tomorrow. One step at a time. I'll help you as long as you need me."

* * *

Morning light crept through the thin curtains, pale and unforgiving. Annie stood between the bed and the window, the peg legs strapped tight, her hands braced on the back of a chair. The leather straps felt colder today, heavier, as though they had gained weight overnight.

Effie hovered a step behind her. "We can sit first. There's no shame in resting."

She shifted her weight, testing the pegs. The familiar stab of pain came, but it no longer startled her. She breathed through it, slow and deliberate.

"What do you feel?"

"Besides the pain, nothing below my knees," Annie replied. "I can't tell where the floor ends and I begin."

Effie placed a steady hand on Annie's elbow.

Annie swallowed. She lifted one peg an inch, set it down again.

"That was a step," Effie said quietly.

"No," Annie snapped. Then, after a moment, "It was not walking."

"Walking begins with standing," Effie said. "And you're doing that well enough."

Annie drew a breath and shifted forward again. The peg loosened, and panic flared.

"Effie—"

290

"I've got you," Effie said, tightening her grip. "Lean towards me, not away."

Annie did as she was told, heart hammering. The peg steadied. She exhaled shakily.

"All right," she murmured. "All right."

They stood like that for several seconds.

"When you're ready," Effie said, "move the other leg."

Annie laughed, a brittle sound. "You make it sound as easy as picking up a spoon."

"I make it sound like it can be done."

Annie stared at the floorboards, memorizing the grain, the knots, the narrow gaps between planks. She lifted the second peg and placed it carefully ahead of the first. The jolt traveled up her spine, but she did not cry out.

"There," Effie said. "Two steps."

Annie blinked. "I didn't fall."

"You didn't."

A smile tugged at Annie's mouth, faint and unbelieving. "Again?" she said.

This time she did not rush. She moved one peg, then the other, each placement deliberate, measured by breath rather than distance. The room seemed impossibly big; the window impossibly far away. Halfway there, her arms began to tremble.

"I can't hold myself," she said.

"You're not," Effie replied. She loosened her grip a little.

Annie froze. "Don't let go."

"I haven't."

"But you will."

"Yes," Effie said. "In a moment, when you're ready."

Annie took another step. The pegs struck the floor in uneven rhythm—thud, scrape, thud—but they held. She took one more. Effie stepped back. Annie felt it at once—the terrible, exhilarating absence of support. She swayed, arms lifting instinctively, a gasp tearing from her throat.

"Effie!"

"I'm right here," Effie said, close but not touching. "Stand still. Let them carry you."

Annie did. The pain flared, sharp and hot, but beneath it was something else: a strange, solid certainty.

"I'm standing," she whispered.

"Now," Effie said softly, "one step. Just one."

Annie nodded. She moved the first peg forward, then the second, her balance teetering but intact. Another step followed, then another. She stopped, stunned. "I walked," she said. The words sounded foreign in her mouth.

Effie smiled, eyes bright. "You are walking."

Annie closed her eyes, letting the truth of it settle into her bones.

"I won't be fast," she said. "And I won't be graceful."

"You'll do just fine. You're Annie Morrow, and Annie Morrow never gives up. You told me that yourself one time."

"Except for one thing: I *used* to be a dancer. What fate could be worse for a dancer than losing her legs?"

Chapter 35

After Effie's nursing care had ended, Annie relocated to the Hoffman Hotel, where one maid had the instructions to check on her twice a day and assist her with anything she needed. Annie did not like being waited on, so more often than not, she told the maid she was fine.

Staying at the Hoffman Hotel lasted through September, until she decided it would make more sense to stay in her own place, the James Hotel. Her days of servicing the men of Atlanta were over.

Now that Annie resumed her position as a business owner, she considered that she should look like one, instead of a cripple. *I don't want sympathy, especially from out-of-towners. There's no need to advertise my condition, so I'll wear long men's pants for a while and see how that feels.* She purchased a pair from the mercantile and after struggling to get them on, found it easier to walk around in them compared to wearing her dress. The next day she purchased another pair and, this time, several men's shirts as well. *Got to be coordinated.* It worked, and from that time on, Annie wore men's clothes more often than not.

Less than a month later, Annie received a note from Mr. Campbell, owner of The Claim Jumper saloon. *Please come see me. It's urgent.* Within a few minutes, Annie set out. The autumn rains swelled the creek that wound along the edge of Atlanta, sending the smell of wet pine and wood smoke into the mountain air. The town's muddy main street was filled with miners stomping boots free of slush and pack mules braying against their loads. Being adept with her new peg legs, Annie stepped over a rivulet of runoff and onto the warped front porch of The Claim Jumper.

The batwing doors hung askew, one hinge loose enough to groan with each gust of wind. Inside, deep scratches marred the once-polished bar, and tarnish covered the brass foot rail. The spittoons were tipped over. A few empty whiskey bottles were scattered on the floorboards. Behind the bar, a stocky man in a stained waistcoat straightened when he saw her. He was bald except for short hair around his ears.

"Annie," he said, the tone of voice caught between hope and shame, "I'm so glad you came."

"You sent word that it was urgent," Annie replied, removing her gloves. "What's the trouble, Mr. Campbell?"

He rubbed a hand over his jaw. "Trouble's the only thing I've got left in here. The Claim Jumper's dyin'. She'll be foreclosed before month's end unless I can pay the bank what I owe. You know I've never been much with the books. Too much credit given to fellas who never pay their tabs."

Annie looked around. "I can see that. When a saloon looks this empty on a Saturday afternoon, the town's already voted."

His eyes darted to hers, desperate. "I'm beggin' you, Annie. You've got a head for business—everyone knows it. If you buy the place, you could turn it around. The miners trust you. They'll drink here just because your name's above the door."

Annie crossed to the bar, running her fingers over the sticky bar. "And how much are we talking about to clear your debt?"

Campbell swallowed hard. "One thousand three hundred and fifty dollars."

"That's a mighty sum for a failing saloon. And I'd be buying more than the business—I'd be buying your mistakes."

He nodded and gazed at the floor. "You'd be buyin' the building, the liquor stock, the license, and the goodwill—what's left of it. And you'd be savin' me from bein' run clean outta town."

Silence filled the room except for the faint clink of a loose window shutter outside. Annie stared at the empty shelves behind the bar, imagining them stocked, the lamps polished bright, the piano tuned, the tables full of miners shaking gold dust into drinks and laughing loud enough to drown out the winter wind.

She turned back to him and set her gaze upon him for a minute. "Tell you what, Mr. Campbell. I'll do it. I'll pay the bank and take The Claim Jumper off your hands. I'll throw in a few dollars for your assets. The James Hotel is a profitable business, and a few of my grubstakes have paid handsomely. That's given me some cash to work with."

Relief washed over Mr. Campbell's face. "Bless you, Annie. You won't regret it."

"I hope you're right," she said, pulling on her gloves again. "But from this day on, The Claim Jumper will answer to me, and I don't run tabs for men I don't trust."

As she stepped back into the cold, the sign above the door creaked in the wind. She hesitated mid-step. *The Claim Jumper is a stupid name. Claim jumping is a crime. Nobody likes claim jumpers; they're the most hated men in town. Sometimes they get shot or end up in jail. This place needs a new name, something with gold in it. After all, that's why everyone's here in Atlanta—for the gold. Let's see: Gold Dust Saloon, Gold Pan Saloon, Gold Bucket, Whiskey & Gold, Golden Star Saloon—that's it: Golden Star Saloon. Everyone likes gold, and everyone likes looking at the stars.*

* * *

Less than a week later, Annie stood behind the polished bar. She had scrubbed it clean and applied a fresh coat of varnish. Its pungent odor lingered in the air. The shelves behind her were stacked with bottles that caught the lamplight like stained glass windows. The brass spittoons were burnished and looked like new. She'd hired a local boy to keep the stove stoked and the place clean, and a fiddler named Red Connally to play in the corner, his bow sawing over the strings in a reel fast enough to keep the miners' boots tapping.

Annie let her eyes survey her new acquisition. A pair of trappers leaned on the bar, swapping tall tales about snow as deep as their shoulders. Near the stove, three miners played poker under a hanging oil lamp, the flicker of its flame catching on the chips and coins piled high on the table.

Mr. Campbell slipped in, hat in his hands. He lingered near the wall, watching the room full of men. Annie caught his eye and gave a small nod of acknowledgment.

When the fiddler broke into *My Darling Clementine,* the entire room clapped along, the floorboards trembling with the beat. Annie allowed herself the smallest of smiles. *This is mine now, and it's going to stay mine.*

It was a chilly night in Atlanta, but the stove inside the Golden Star Saloon radiated warmth, and cigar smoke thickened the air. Red's fiddle sang over the muted conversations, creating a jovial atmosphere. The front doors banged open with a sudden crack.

A young miner walked in with an exaggerated swagger, heavy boots scraping the floor. His canvas coat hung open, his shirt half-untucked, and his eyes were glassy. A pouch of gold dust swung from his belt like bait for a thief.

"Annie!" he slurred, slapping a hand on the bar. "I'm thirsty."

Annie recognized the man, Cody Drummond, known for his temper when the whiskey got into his brain. She took a pinch and put the shot glass and bottle on the bar.

"That's all for you tonight, Cody."

He blinked at her, then laughed. "One? Are you kidding me? I ain't paid my way in dust for one drink, Annie Morrow. I'll tell *you* when to stop."

A few of the other miners fell silent, watching. Red's fiddle trailed off into a squeak.

Annie leaned forward, her wooden peg legs planted firmly behind the bar. "No, Cody. You've had enough. I won't have you startin' trouble in my place."

He reached for the bottle on the bar, but Annie's hand came down first. "Leave it."

Cody's face twisted. "You think you can run me off? I was drinkin' here long before you—"

"Would you like to meet my friend Mr. Colt?"

One of the poker players at the corner table stood up. Jim Sloan was a big man, who had settled more than one fight in town. He crossed the room and stood behind Cody.

"You heard the lady," Jim said as he rolled up his sleeves.

Cody swung around and stared at Jim's broad chest and then at Annie's steady eyes. After a long, tense pause, he backed toward the door, muttering curses under his breath. The doors swung shut behind him. Annie wiped down the bar and looked around. "All right, boys—music's back on. And somebody buy Jim here a drink."

The conversations and laughter resumed, the fiddle struck up a reel, and the Golden Star Saloon hummed as if nothing had happened, except that everyone now understood that Annie Morrow owned the place and she meant business.

* * *

By June 1897, she was "Peg Leg Annie" to every man, woman, and child in Atlanta. The miners liked her because she poured a stiff drink, never watered the whiskey, and she could out-cuss a mine foreman without half trying. The wives and church ladies still avoided her, but that was to be expected. She was on good terms with the sheriff, as long as she paid the fines on the James Hotel that came in like clockwork. Everybody in town knew he was putting on a show by slapping her with fines. It was the girls at the James Hotel who appreciated her more than anyone because she took care of them and never let the johns abuse them.

She couldn't dance at the Silver Moon Dance Hall anymore, but business at the James Hotel and now the Golden Star Saloon kept her busy. When the out-of-towners came through, she'd smile extra wide, tell them how she'd lost her legs to a bear for some and to a mine cave-in for others, and pocket the sympathy tip before they even realized she had made it up. *It's entertainment.*

On a sunny spring morning the following year, Effie walked over to Annie's cabin and found her outside, sitting on the porch, her legs wrapped in an old blanket. Annie was watching the street, counting how many men slipped in and out of the saloons before noon. Even though Effie was no longer charged with caring for Annie, she came by occasionally for a visit.

"How are you doing, now that it's been two years since that fateful day? Are you going to keep the James Hotel running?"

Annie shrugged. "What else is there for a woman like me? You know there are few options for a woman in a mining town."

Effie sat beside her, hands folded in her lap. "Teach the girls in town to read. There's a few that don't go to school."

"Ha. You think their mothers would let me anywhere near their children? Not a chance."

"You're smarter than most men around here. Smarter than me too, probably. Don't waste it on men and whiskey."

Annie didn't know what to say to that. She massaged her stumps beneath the blanket. She had removed her peg legs and left them on the floor. "We'll see."

"You're good with bookkeeping, aren't you? Didn't you tell me once that you ran businesses in Boise City and Pine Grove? You have experience. I could ask around at the mills to see if there are any openings."

"I appreciate the offer, Effie, but I can manage on my own. I always have."

For a long moment, neither woman spoke.

"Thanks, Effie. For saving my life. And for not making me feel like trash, even when I deserved it."

Effie nodded. "You're not trash, Annie. You're a woman with a hard story."

As Effie got up and walked out into the street. Annie watched her go, then called out, "Effie?"

She stopped and turned around.

"Did I ever show you the note from Em that I found in her hurdy-gurdy case?"

"No, I don't believe you did."

"Would you like to see it now?"

"Yes, if you don't mind. I was always curious."

"The hurdy-gurdy is inside, under the bed. Go ahead and open it and take out the note."

Effie did as instructed and sat down again, holding the unopened paper.

"Go ahead and read it to me, please."

Effie carefully unfolded the paper and held it with both hands.

> If anything ever happens to me, Annie,
> don't let them throw my hurdy-gurdy away.
> Play it. Or don't. Just keep it.
> You're the only one I ever trusted.

"That's beautiful, Annie. You must have been close. What was she like?"

"I've never met anyone like Em. She was so excited about life. Em would light up the dance hall just by walking in and twirling around in one of her satin dresses. I've only had two best friends in my life: Hazel back in Rocky Bar and Em here. Everyone loved Em." She paused. "Em was the one that got me into the sisterhood. That's part of having a best friend; you gotta take the good with the bad. What's that saying about finding and losing love? I read it somewhere a long time ago."

"Do you mean the poem by Lord Tennyson?

"Not sure."

"The one I'm thinking of goes like this, 'Tis better to have loved and lost, than never to have loved at all.'"

"That's the one. It describes me and Em. I was never one much for poems, but that one strikes me right in my heart."

"I have to tell you, Annie, you're lucky to have had a friend like that. I have Gilbert, but a husband is different. Em was a real friend to you. I've never had a real friend like that."

"Not to worry, Effie. I'm sure there are real friends out there for you. You just haven't met them yet."

Effie looked Annie directly in the eyes. "I hope you're right."

Annie gave her hand a gentle squeeze. Effie squeezed in return.

"I should be going. Gilbert will wonder where I am. I promised to make him venison stew for dinner." She rose and headed back out into the street.

"Effie, if I ever see you at the Golden Star, drinks are on me."

Effie grinned. "Don't bet on it."

"Bye, Effie."

"Bye, Annie."

Chapter 36

Annie stopped by the Silver Moon Dance Hall one night to find the place buzzing with excitement. Laughter spilled out of the open doorway in bright, tinkling waves, carried on the warm glow of lamplight and the familiar twang of a fiddle tuning up. For a moment, Annie stood outside, letting the sounds wrap around her like a remembered embrace. This rickety, smoke-stained dance hall had once been the center of her world.

She liked to drop by now and then, just to see the new girls who drifted into town with nothing but a carpetbag and wide, nervous eyes. Watching them gather in clusters, helping each other lace corsets, fixing a fallen curl, sharing nervous smiles, tugged at her heart. It reminded her of another night, so long ago, when she herself had stepped into that dressing room and an unknown future.

Annie slipped inside, moving past the crowded bar and toward the corridor that led to the dressing area. She paused there, her eyes misting as the memories rose so vividly she could almost reach out and touch them. She remembered the scent of powder and rosewater, the rustle of petticoats, and the nervous flutter in her stomach, before a girl with laughing brown eyes looked over to her and smiled. *That was Em. That smile had changed my life. What an amazing girl you were.*

How many nights did we share in this place? Whispering secrets between dances, stealing bites of supper in the wings, helping each other pin hair and mend stockings, laughing until tears rolled down our cheeks. Em, you had a way of turning the darkest day bright again.

The Silver Moon Dance Hall had been loud, chaotic, sometimes downright brutal—but with Em beside her, it had felt like home, a real home. The kind that wrapped around the heart, not the type built of lumber and nails.

Annie rested a hand on the worn doorframe of the dressing room, balanced on her peg legs, and let the pulse of the dance hall vibrate through her fingers. The ache of missing Em rose so suddenly that she had to swallow against it. *I would give anything to hear Em's laughter ring through the dressing room one more time, to feel the familiar bump of her shoulder as we passed each other in the hallway, to catch her rolling her eyes at some drunk miner showing off his bravado.*

Annie whispered under her breath, blinking hard as tears glimmered. "I was so lucky to have you as a friend." She closed her eyes and let the familiar sounds and scents drift into her awareness.

A voice called out, "Can I help you?"

Annie opened her eyes to see a young girl seated before a mirror, her long blonde hair spilling over her shoulders as she drew a brush through it in careful strokes.

"Sorry, Miss," Annie said. "I was just daydreaming."

The girl studied her reflection for a moment, then turned, her brows knitting as recognition dawned. "You're Annie Morrow, aren't you?"

"Yes," Annie replied. "I am."

The girl's face brightened at once. "I knew it. You're famous, Mrs. Morrow. I heard you used to dance here—before my time, of course." She rose partway from the chair, clearly uncertain whether or not she ought to stand. "My name's Jasmine. It's an honor to meet you."

"An honor?" Annie smiled, the word feeling strange on her tongue. "You flatter me." Em's voice echoed in her mind, firm and knowing, and Annie found herself repeating the old lesson. "I'll tell you something. Don't let anyone hand you a scrap of paper with 'free dance' written on it. There ain't no free dances in this place."

Jasmine's eyes widened, not with fear but with interest. "I've heard stories about you. They used to call you the Queen of the Silver Moon Dance Hall, didn't they?" she said quietly.

"They did, indeed."

"You lasted here a long time, didn't you?"

"Longer than most," Annie said. "Long enough to learn which smiles to trust and which ones to keep at a distance."

Jasmine set her brush down and turned fully toward her. "That's exactly why I'm glad you're here. The older girls talk about you like you were somehow different. Strong. Like you never let anyone take more than you were willing to give."

Annie looked away, uncomfortable with the praise. "I made my share of mistakes."

Jasmine shook her head. "Maybe. But you survived them. That counts for something." She hesitated, then added, "I hope I can be half as good as you were."

Annie met her gaze again, surprised by the sincerity she found there. "You'll do okay here. The girls watch out for each other."

A shy smile crossed Jasmine's face. "Hopefully, I'll see you around here sometime? I'd like to get to know you, Mrs. Morrow. I think you could teach me a few things—about more than dancing."

"That I could," Annie said, warmth creeping into her voice. "It's nice to meet you, Jasmine."

"Nice to meet you too." Jasmine stood and held out her hand, her posture earnest, almost formal.

The gesture caught Annie off guard. She took Jasmine's hand and gave it a gentle squeeze. "Good day, Jasmine."

"Good day, Mrs. Morrow," Jasmine replied, her tone of voice carrying unmistakable respect as she watched Annie go.

Annie turned around and headed back to the main room. The miners were jabbering something about Alaska. She walked over to one of the regulars. "What's the fuss about, Leroy"?

"It's gold, Annie, gold's been discovered in the Klondike. Prospectors are stampeding up there by the thousands. Lots of the men here are planning to go. I'm going." He pulled on his suspenders with his thumbs. "Atlanta's seen enough of me."

"That discovery was years ago. Don't you think all the good claims have been taken? Isn't one gold rush enough for you? Besides, if you think winters in Idaho are tough, you ain't seen nothin'. Winters in the Yukon can kill you if you don't starve to death first or become lunch for some polar bear. The first thing you need to know is that the Klondike isn't in Alaska. It's in Canada, the Yukon Territory."

"I know that. The Canadian government won't let anyone across the border unless they have a year's worth of supplies, and you can buy most of that in Seattle."

"Seattle, huh? I heard it rains there all the time."

"A little rain never hurt nobody. I'd be there only until the next ship sailed." Leroy's face lit up as he revealed his plan. "I read all about it. The steamships go through the Inside Passage to a place called Skagway. It's an eight-hundred-mile voyage, but it only takes three days in a fast ship. From Skagway, you hike up to White Pass, which is where you cross over from Alaska to Canada, and then down to the Yukon River. From there, you float downriver to Dawson City. That's where the goldfields are." He waited with bated breath for Annie's acknowledgement.

"Well, good luck, Leroy. It's been nice knowing you." *If these men go, some of them will not return alive. I hope they realize what they're getting themselves into. The Klondike ain't no picnic.*

* * *

On a warm afternoon in the summer of 1902, a man walked into the Golden Star Saloon that Annie had never seen before. That was not unusual. What caught Annie's attention was not his thick brown moustache contrasting with his receding blonde hairline, or his bowler hat. It was his nose, which was big and stuck out like nothing Annie had ever seen before.

He sat down at a faro table and spoke to the dealer with a heavy Italian accent. She watched him. He won several times and then moved over to join a poker game. He won there, too.

Annie watched him each day for a week, waiting for the catch. There was always a catch. He alternated between spending his evenings at the Golden Star Saloon and Whiskey Gulch. One evening, she found him over at the Whiskey Gulch running the faro table. He wore a blue necktie that matched his three-piece suit, which set off his gold cufflinks. His blond hair was slicked back with some kind of pomade that made the whole place smell like aftershave. The regulars watched him with wary respect. Within two weeks, the whole town was talking about the Little Italian with beady eyes.

One evening, Annie limped over to Whiskey Gulch and found the man dealing at the faro table. *Looks like he got the job as the faro dealer.* "You planning to rob the whole town before payday, or just the idiots who don't know the odds?"

The man smiled. "Only the ones who are convinced they can beat the house," he said. "The rest I leave alone. You could try your luck."

She shook her head. "I don't gamble on anything I can't control."

"Neither do I," he said, eyes glinting. "That's why I deal."

Annie stood up straight. "Doc Holliday was a faro dealer too, you know, in Colorado and Texas, and he kicked the bucket when he was only thirty-six. Wasn't he shot in the back in the middle of a card game, with a hand of two aces and two eights? Don't they call that Dead Man's Hand?"

"No, that was Wild Bill Hickock, not Doc Holliday. They were both gunslingers. I'm not, so I'm expecting to do quite well, thank you. My name's Henry Longhini."

"I'm Annie. I own the Golden Star Saloon up the street and the James Hotel, which is more than just a hotel, if you know what I'm saying. I see you're pretty good with the cards. I've been looking for a faro dealer at my place. Come by sometime if you're interested."

"I'll do that." He returned to the game, and Annie walked back to the Golden Star Saloon.

A week later, he was the new dealer at the faro table at Annie's place and the newest boarder at the James Hotel. Henry appeared to be a gentleman and smart enough to stay out of fights. He wore the same three suits in rotation, pressed and spotless, a bowler hat, and tipped the housemaid a nickel for every chore, even when he knew Annie would scold her for taking it. He ate his meals in the parlor, sitting nearest the fire even in July, and read every page of the newspaper from Boise City before the sun came up. Annie never saw him drink more than a single glass of beer, and he never let his voice rise above a hush, even when the other boarders tried to draw him out to talk politics. He never talked about himself, except to say he'd come from Montana, and that he'd once worked as a "mining consultant" in there, which Annie took to mean gambler or swindler, or both. *There's something about him I don't like, but I can't tell what it is. Should I trust him?*

After a month had passed, he assisted Annie with the bookkeeping for the James Hotel and Golden Star Saloon, offering minor corrections that saved her money. He found two staffers skimming from the till, fired them before Annie even noticed, and had the replacements trained before she asked for an explanation. When a group of prospectors threatened to burn down the Golden Star Saloon over a gambling debt, Henry talked them down with a whispered conversation in the back alley. She saw them back there, but she never found out what he said. The prospectors returned the next night, smiling and sober, and left a ten-dollar tip for Annie.

Henry moved through the town as if he belonged. He made friends with the blacksmith and the postmaster, sent Christmas cards to the mayor's wife, and once saved the sheriff's kid from drowning in the Yuba River. Annie knew a social campaign when she saw one, but she couldn't help admiring his skill. She sought him out in the evenings, just to hear him talk about the world outside. He told stories about the gold rush in Bonanza and Custer, the con men in Idaho City, and the underground war between competing mine owners in Silver City. He never bragged, never lied outright, but Annie spotted the exaggerations and called him out every time.

Some nights, Henry walked Annie from the James Hotel to her cabin on the edge of town when she wanted to savor some peace and quiet. He steadied her when the boards were slick or the pain was worse than usual. He kept her company, as if that was all he wanted. Annie didn't trust it, not at first. Someone had fooled her before, and worse. But Henry never asked for anything: not a loan, not a favor, and not even a free drink. He understood her, and she appreciated that.

One afternoon, she caught him in the hotel office, counting the week's receipts. He was sitting in her chair, feet up on the desk, hat tipped low. She was about to tell at him, but he looked up and said, "I balanced the ledger for you. You were missing three dollars and seventy-five cents."

She narrowed her eyes. "And what do you want for it?"

He shrugged. "Nothing. It was bothering me."

She grunted, took the seat across from him, and eyed the stack of bills. "You sure you're not skimming?"

He looked hurt. "Annie, if I was skimming, you'd never catch me." He twirled the hair at the ends of his moustache.

She laughed out loud. "Fair point."

He leaned forward. "I hear you're buying into the Buffalo Mine."

She studied him with suspicion. "Who told you that?"

"I have ears." He smiled again. "It's a smart play if you can trust the partners. I could look into it if you like. Discreetly. I know some people."

Annie thought it over. For the first time in years, she considered letting someone else in on her business secrets. It made her feel exposed, but also lighter, like she didn't have to carry everything alone.

"I'll think about it," she said.

He nodded, satisfied. "You do that."

* * *

A few weeks later, a letter arrived at the James Hotel, postmarked Boise City. It was from her youngest daughter, Ethyl Frances. She read the letter three times, then locked it away in a drawer. It was brief, written in the clumsy script of a fourteen-year-old girl, and it said Anna Eliza got appendicitis and died last year. *I had no idea. She was my first baby, and now she's gone? Eighteen is too young to die. The last time I saw Anna Eliza, she was twelve, looking at me from the stagecoach as she and the others were stolen from me. That was the worst day of my life. I miss my babies so much! Ethyl must be eight years old now. I wish I could send them birthday gifts, but how could I?* Annie wanted to cry, but no tears came. She sat slumped in her chair, not knowing what to do. She couldn't write back. *Thomas would intercept my letters, so what's the point?* Sometimes, late at night, she'd take it out, read it again by candlelight, and wonder if her children would recognize her now, or if they'd even want to. *What fate could be worse than a mother having her children taken away? It's not fair.*

As if the loss of her children wasn't enough, the guilt over Em's death never left. It haunted her, like the ache in her legs. She knew she'd never see Em again, never hear her sweet voice, or give her a hug after a busy night at the dance hall. She knew she'd never be whole again. People continued coming to her through the back door of the James Hotel with their problems: miners down on their luck, girls who got pregnant by the wrong man, gamblers who lost more than they could afford. Annie helped them when she could.

Chapter 37

The economy in Atlanta was stable until the Panic of 1907. The upgraded 150-ton Monarch Stamp Mill, built the year before, was now running at half capacity. Businesses across the country were going bankrupt and banks were failing. There weren't any banks in Atlanta or Rocky Bar, but she feared the worst for the banks in Boise City. This was enough to confirm her distrust of the entire banking system. It gave her pause to question whether the country's economy was stable. *People think things will always be the way they are now. That's not true.*

Something Effie once said many years ago to her came back. She remembered the concern in Effie's voice. *"You shouldn't profit from the sins of others. I believe you've lost your moral compass, Annie. Deep down inside, you know the difference between right and wrong, and what you've been doing is wrong. You don't have to continue in that line of business. You think you're giving these men a taste of happiness with your girls, but it never lasts. Everyone aspires to be appreciated and loved, but if they have to pay for it, it's not love, it's a purchase. Think about it, Annie. I care about you. It's your decision. I said what's in my heart, but it's up to you to take the next step."*

Annie mulled over her words. *Effie could be right. But people have expectations, and I have expectations of myself. Running a hotel house with upstairs girls is a steady income, and I help any miner when he's down and out. On the other hand, even without my girls, it probably would still be profitable. It would be a challenge, but I thrive on challenges. Maybe it's time for a change. Maybe the title of Proprietress is more fitting than Madam. I could transform the James Hotel into a proper hotel.*

The next morning, Annie woke up earlier than usual. The smell of coal smoke clung to the ceiling of the parlor, mingling with coffee, damp wool, and the wisps of perfume that the girls wore upstairs. It was past breakfast, and the men had long since cleared out. Annie stood at the foot of the stairs, hands on her hips. She had thought about it long enough. And now that the first frost had crept in around the windowsills, it felt like the right time. She yelled, "Parlor! Now."

A few minutes later, the girls gathered as requested.

Molly came in first, her red corset only half-laced. "What's the matter, Annie? Trouble?"

Jewel followed, eyes sharp. "We behind on rent?"

Last was Scarlet, the youngest, the most recent addition, clutching a shawl around her shoulders like it might protect her from whatever was coming. "I didn't do nothin'," she whispered.

Annie motioned for them to sit behind a table while she remained standing before them.

"I've made a decision. I'm closing the upstairs side of the business."

They stared at her, wide-eyed, jaws dropped.

"Closing?" Molly scoffed. "You mean for a week? Like last winter when the preacher came sniffin' around?"

Annie shook her head. "No. I mean it. I'm keepin' the hotel business, meals, and beds for the locals and travelers, but no more upstairs business. No more whiskey deliveries through the back door. And no more of you takin' tricks in here behind my back."

Jewel's face flushed. "What brought this on? You goin' holy all of a sudden?"

"No," Annie said gently. "Just tired. I've run this place for eleven years now, and I'm tired. Tired of watchin' you girls get older and more worn out every year. And I'm tired of men thinking they own the ground we walk on."

Molly stood. "We gave you everything we got."

"I know," Annie said. "And I ain't forgetting what you've done, what you've given up to be here. That's why—"

She reached behind the tea cabinet and pulled out a small metal cash box. She laid it on the table and opened it. Inside, there were three envelopes. She pushed one toward each of them.

"Bonus," she said. "Call it severance. Enough to head to San Francisco and start fresh, or open a dress shop, or anything else that suits your fancy."

Nobody reached for the envelopes.

"You're not throwin' us out?" Scarlet asked.

Annie's face softened. "No, Sugar. But I'm giving you the chance to leave before this life wears you down to the bone."

Silence settled in. Then Jewel sat back, eyes still on the envelopes. "I always figured I'd die upstairs, in that red room. Maybe this is better. Maybe it's time for a change."

Scarlet crossed her arms, looking out the window. "Don't know nothin' else."

"You didn't know this when you started," Annie replied. "But you learned. You're clever, all of you. You'll learn something else."

One by one, the girls took their envelopes, went upstairs, came back down with their bulging satchels, and walked out the front door in silence.

Outside, life in the boomtown of Atlanta continued as before: new lodes discovered and old ones played out, miners moving in and miners moving out, fortunes made and fortunes lost. But inside the James Hotel, now a proper hotel, something shifted. A chapter closed, but not with violence or a scandal or a foreclosure, but with envelopes, quiet words, and the understanding that existed only between women.

Even with the girls gone, there was no shortage of business. When the Monarch Mill started paying out again, the whole town went wild, and every bed in the hotel was booked for weeks. She hired a new grub slinger, Swede, whom she knew from Rocky Bar. Annie didn't eat much, but she liked to sit at the end of the table and watch the men shovel it in, their faces red and sweaty, their voices rising with each shot of Old Overholt.

Annie made good money. Rumors circulated that she was one of the wealthiest women in town. The hotel did better than ever, and by mid-summer, she had grubstaked shares in three more claims that made a handsome profit. Every night, Annie would sit at the open front window of the James Hotel and listen to the sounds of the town. Sometimes she heard music from the Silver Moon Dance Hall down the street, sometimes a fight or a shout from the alley.

Annie bought herself new clothes, tailored to fit her changed body. She cut her hair short but kept it neat. Sometimes, when she wanted to feel fancy, she'd paint her cheeks with a touch of rouge and wear the old blue dress she'd saved from Rocky Bar. She was no longer pretty, not in the way she had once been.

One frosty night in October, as she hobbled her way to the James Hotel after visiting old friends at the Silver Moon Dance Hall, she heard muffled footsteps behind her. She turned around and realized it was a mutt. It stopped in its tracks. This reminded her of the day Jack had shown up behind the hotel, cold, wet, and nothing but fur and bones. This one wasn't much better off. She called out to him, "Come here, boy, I won't hurt you." It approached cautiously, taking a few steps at a time, but did not get too close. Annie turned around and continued her walk, glancing over her shoulder to make sure the mutt was still following her. It did, all the way to the front door of the hotel. She went inside, found a few scraps of meat, and set them back outside the door. The mutt wolfed them down, then sat down with its tongue hanging out, hoping to get more.

"Well, boy, you know I've been through this before. His name was Jack, and I sure miss him. He was a Newfoundland, a handsome one. I have no idea what you are. You're not exactly a handsome one, but I believe I can take a liking to you anyhow. How does that sound?"

The mutt laid down, muzzle resting on his paws, and let out a sigh.

"Hmm. Looks like you're here to stay. Come on inside." He sniffed around the room and plopped down in the exact spot that the first Jack did when he arrived that long time ago. "You know, there's a reason I like your kind. You know what it is? I'll tell you. Dogs can't lie. It's impossible for you. That's it. You wear your feelings on your face and in your voice and with that tail of yours. Dogs are honest. You can't say that about every human. We're gonna get along fine and dandy."

* * *

Around noon on a crisp afternoon on September 13th, 1908, there was a knock on the front door of Annie's cabin. *Who could that be? Nobody visits me anymore.* She hobbled over and flung it wide open.

"Well, I'll be damned! Effie, what are you doing here? It's been a long time."

She smiled with that girlish smile Annie remembered from their days together during her recovery. "I brought you something," she said as she held out a small cardboard box. "May I come in?"

"Of course."

Effie strolled in with a lift in her stride and gently placed the box on the kitchen table. "Open it."

Annie sat in the chair next to the table. "I don't like surprises."

"I think you'll like this one."

Annie lifted the top to reveal a small round cake with white frosting decorated with tiny red roses around the edge.

"Happy birthday, Annie!"

Annie gasped and put her hands to her chest. "Why, thank you, Effie. I do declare! It's gorgeous! How did you know today was my birthday?"

"You know, Annie, you're not the only one in town who has connections. Rumor has it that you're turning fifty today."

"It's true. I ain't gettin' any younger."

They sat together for the rest of the afternoon, savoring each other's company as much as the cake and the fresh coffee.

"There's something else, Annie."

"What?"

"I heard you let your girls go and you're no longer in that line of business."

"Also true."

Effie placed her hands on Annie's and leaned in. "I never thought I'd ever say this to you, but I'm proud of you. For what you just did. I know it wasn't easy, but you did the right thing. Give yourself some credit."

Annie took a deep breath and let out a long sigh. "You're part of the reason I did that. You'd be surprised by how much a decent person like you can influence others. You influenced me. You made me think. Thank you."

"I heard what you did for a Chinese girl in Rocky Bar. You probably saved her life. That shows me that you have a good heart inside that crusty personality of yours. I'm proud of you for that too. I never saved anyone's life."

Effie gazed into her coffee cup. "There's something else too. A confession. When I first heard about you, before your accident with Em, I despised you. I even hated you for what you represented. But I changed. When I had to take care of you for those three months, I learned things about life that I never knew, like there is goodness in even the worst-looking people. You showed me that, Annie. Thank you."

"I believe we were good for each other."

"Yes, I believe so too."

As the daylight faded, Effie said her goodbyes and walked over to the door.

"Can you leave the door open when you leave?"

"Of course."

"Thanks, dear."

Annie positioned herself in the doorway so she could watch Effie as she walked down the street until she disappeared around a corner. *What a good woman she is. The world needs more people like her. I hope she comes again someday.*

One regret Annie allowed herself to entertain these days was that she couldn't dance anymore. *What could be worse than a dance hall girl losing her legs?* She missed the feeling of being light, of spinning across a floor with everyone's eyes on her. Some nights, when the pain kept her awake, she'd close her eyes and imagine the music, the laughter, the way her old legs had carried her as if she weighed nothing at all. Now she was the one and only Peg Leg Annie, the meanest, smartest, toughest woman in Atlanta. The pain was still there, but it was a small thing compared to what she'd survived. She ran her businesses and her life as she wanted.

Annie got a kick out of the Peg Leg Annie stories that floated around town. They had some truth, but none were complete. Her favorite was the one about the bear attack. That one garnered the most sympathy until people realized she made it up. The miners said she could break a man's nose with a glance, and then patch him up before the swelling set in. The wives said she was mean as a rattlesnake, but sometimes she left a loaf of bread on their steps when their baby was sick, or the husband spent the week's wages at the saloon. They still called her an Angel of Mercy.

Annie and Henry shared coffee in the mornings in the hotel kitchen, sometimes in silence, sometimes in simple conversation. At night, Henry would read to her from one of the Boise City newspapers, since the Elmore Bulletin shut down years before. He put the newspaper on the table.

"You used to live in Boise City, didn't you, Annie?"

"Yes. That was a long time ago. Times I would rather forget."

"Well, here's something interesting. It says here the city fathers want to drop the 'City' from Boise City."

"What on earth for? As if I give a hoot."

"That's the interesting part. Seems there is a Boise City in Oklahoma. It was founded last year by three land developers who sold thousands of lots that they did not own. It was a complete fraud, and they all went to prison for it."

"Okay, so they got what they deserved. What's your point?"

"That, my dear, is why the city fathers want to drop the 'City' from Boise City. The name has been ruined. Says here they will make the name change official soon."

One Christmas, he bought her a new set of peg legs. They were lighter, easier to maneuver, with brass fittings and polished leather straps. Rumors spread that they were lovers. They weren't, but Annie didn't care. Henry never said a word about them. He smiled when anyone teased him, as if he liked the idea

* * *

The batwing doors of the Golden Star Saloon flew open on a gust of wind strong enough to make the oil lamps sway. A man stepped in, shoulders hunched against the cold, left foot dragging like it weighed more than the rest of him. He looked to be in his forties, with a thick black beard and a tattered hat. His clothes were old and dirty. One of his suspender straps was missing.

Annie looked up from behind the bar, a towel in her hand. She knew that kind of walk, the kind a man gets from something that didn't heal right. "What can I do ya for?"

He leaned onto the bar and put his injured foot on the bar rail.

"Old Forester, if you got any." His voice was deep and hoarse, as if he was suffering from a sore throat.

She reached for one of the best bottles she kept for miners who came in looking older than their years. She placed the bottle and a shot glass in front of him. He poured one and downed it.

"You're not from hereabouts. You come far?" she asked, keeping her tone light.

"Far enough. Coeur d'Alene."

Her brow lifted. "That's a real limp you got there."

A flicker of pride crossed his face. "April twenty-ninth, 1899. Wardner, Idaho. You hear of it?"

"I heard," she said. "That's the day the Bunker Hill and Sullivan Mill blew up."

"Aye. We loaded three thousand pounds of dynamite into a boxcar in Burke. The whole train crew was on board with us. Some people say we forced the engineer at gunpoint, but that's a lie. He was with us the whole time. We rode her down the canyon, from Burke to Wallace, straight into the yard, cut loose the ore car loaded with dynamite, and let her sit like a Christmas gift on the siding. We'd barely cleared the switch before it went."

His eyes widened as he yelled out, "KABOOM!" and threw his hands up in the air. "The shock wave almost knocked me over. The sky turned black. There was wood splinters and whole timbers and pieces of machinery everywhere. For good measure, we burned down the company office. On the ride back to Burke, folks was lining the tracks, cheerin' and wavin' their hats and kids runnin' alongside the train. Felt like we'd shown the bosses we weren't their dogs, and they couldn't stop us from joining the union. We even had the sheriff on the train with us."

"What happened after that?" she asked, even though she already knew.

"McKinley sent in the damn Army! The soldiers went house to house looking for any man who looked like a miner. Rounded us up, shoved us into bullpens. Guard decided I was too slow one morning, stomped my foot with the butt of his rifle and busted three bones. It's been ten years now and it ain't been right since. They had to let us out after a month, but only after treating us like animals in that place."

"Sounds like you paid more than your share. This is on the house."

"Does Atlanta ever have trouble with unions?" he asked.

"Nope."

"I hate politics. I just want honest work and earn a fair wage."

One of the regulars, who was standing at the other end of the bar, blurted out, "Hey Annie, how come I don't get nothin' on the house?"

"Shut up, Buck. This is my place, and I'll do whatever I damn well please."

Annie leaned over and put her elbows on the bar. "You like pork and beans?"

"Yes, Ma'am."

Annie grabbed a bowl from underneath the bar and walked over to where she kept an enormous pot of pork and beans. She scooped out two cups' worth and poured them into a bowl. "Here, try this. Tell me what you think."

The man's eyes widened and then closed as he inhaled the sweet aroma. He took a spoonful, then another, and another. "I think I just died and went to heaven. I could eat nothing but this every day for a week."

Annie smiled.

"How'd you make this? I tell you me, these are the best damn pork and beans I've ever had."

"If you must know, I use the recipe in Cooking for Profit, by Jessup Whitehead, published in 1886 in San Francisco. First, you let the beans soak overnight. Dump out the water, add fresh water, add baking soda the size of a bean, toss on a slice of rinsed salt pork and boil for an hour. Pour out that water and add fresh water again. Boil them again for a few minutes until they're soft. Season with a pinch of salt and a tablespoon of molasses and bake for half an hour."

"You're an amazing cook, and that takes more than just a great recipe."

"You're welcome. On the house this time. Ten cents next time."

Buck yelled out, "Hey Annie, I like your pork and beans too." He let out a bottom burp.

"Aw, come on, Buck, go outside if you're going to do that. You're gonna stink up the whole place."

"Sorry." Buck turned around and walked out.

The newcomer finished his pork and beans, then looked at Annie, searching her face. "Thought Atlanta might have a place for a man who can swing a pick."

"Atlanta's full of busted folks. You'll fit right in."

"I'm Annie, as you heard."

"Clint. Nice to meet you, Annie."

"I got a nickname."

"Really?"

"Yes, really. It's Peg Leg Annie."

"That's a might unkind. Whatever for?"

Annie had been standing behind the bar since Clint walked in. She strode around the end of the bar and pulled up the legs of her pants.

Clint gasped. "What happened?"

"Well, I was walking in the forest one day near the Yuba River south of town minding my own business when this black bear sneaks up behind me and grunts. I turned around and tried to stare him down, but he kept staring back at me like I was to be his lunch. He jumped on me and started chewing on my legs when somebody fired off some rounds from their shotgun. That scared him, and he ran off, but my legs couldn't be saved." She cleared her throat.

"I'm sorry to hear that, but you survived. It coulda been worse."

"Ain't that the truth." She turned around to hide the grin that crept across her face.

Neither spoke for several minutes, and they let the muffled conversations of the saloon's customers fill the air between them.

"If you need a place to stay, I run the James Hotel up the street."

Annie's gaze fell upon Clint's hands. Years of hard labor had made the hands calloused. "If you're looking for work, one supervisor at the Monarch Mill owes me a favor. Wait a couple of days and go to the Monarch office and ask for Burt. He'll be expecting you."

Clint looked at Annie, astonished. "Why, thank you, Annie. This means a lot to me. You're truly a decent woman."

Annie smiled at him. "Not everyone agrees with that, but I appreciate it just the same."

Two days later, Clint was back, beaming, and wearing a set of clean clothes.

"Welcome back, Clint. How did it go at the Monarch?"

"Got me a job thanks to you. Much obliged."

Clint rested his elbows on the bar. "There's one thing, Annie. I mentioned to Burt how good it was of you to put in a word for me, and how amazing it was that you survived the bear attack. He laughed at me! I said it's not funny, and he laughed even harder. What a strange fellow he is!"

"Well, my memory gets kind of fuzzy sometimes. Maybe it wasn't a bear. It could've been a cougar, wolf, or even a tiger."

"Wait a minute, there ain't no tigers in Idaho, nohow. That's impossible. What are you talkin' about?"

She put down the glass she was wiping. "Tell you what, Clint. Stick around in this town long enough, and I'll tell you what really happened."

He looked confused. "Okay. Fine by me."

* * *

In spring, the town celebrated the discovery of a new lode of high-grade quartz with gold, and the James Hotel filled with strangers. The celebrating did not last long, however. The new lode turned out to be a scam by the mine owners back east. The ore was salted with gold from another mine. Around this time, Annie began to doubt Atlanta's future.

She sat across from Henry, watching as he salted his eggs. Their morning conversations were getting less and less optimistic about their future.

"You ever going to leave?" she asked.

Without looking up, he replied, "not unless you ask me to," as he twirled the hairs at the ends of his moustache.

"I don't mean from me, I mean from Atlanta. Do you want to stay here? It's happening all over Idaho. Same old story. When the ore plays out, the miners leave, the mills shut down, and businesses close. In a few years, I believe Atlanta will be nothing more than a ghost town. You know that a few businesses here burned down. Might be arson. That's one way to go. Burn down your business, collect the insurance, and hightail outta here."

Chapter 38

Annie signed her name with a hand steadier than she felt, the old nickel pen biting its way across the last page. There was a vase on the table, some kind of pink carnation wilting at the edges, which made her think of nothing so much as a cheap funeral. She was about to end seventeen years in Atlanta, and it felt like it was time to move on. It was just a matter of time before the mills shut down for good, the lodes played out, and the miners left. Atlanta was destined to become a ghost town, and she had no desire to be here when that happened.

The lawyer, a gray-bearded man with a knack for talking past her shoulder, shuffled the sheaf of papers and said, "Here you go, Mrs. Morrow. Selling the James Hotel at a loss wasn't easy. I've seen this story a dozen times. I'm afraid more will follow. I remember the days when there were more than a thousand miners working in Atlanta. Now there are barely a hundred, and the stamp mills have shut down. I hope things are better for you in Rocky Bar. I hear there's a new dredge operating on the Feather River. That should be good for business. Since you and Henry are going to Rocky Bar, I took the liberty of buying a small cabin for you from the proceeds of the sale of the Golden Star Saloon. I'll give you a map showing the location."

On her way out the door, she crossed paths with the new owners of the hotel. She overheard one say to the other, "Montezuma Hotel is a wonderful name. Much better than the James Hotel." She kept walking.

"Listen, Henry, there's one last thing I need to do before we leave. Wait for me at Whiskey Gulch."

"Understood."

Her latest set of wooden peg legs was crude but functional. She made her way south on Quartz Creek Street, then turned left on East Alpine Street. Her gait was stiff and uneven. Henry had offered to help her, but she wanted to go by herself. Up ahead, an old wooden sign nailed to two posts read, "Cemetery". She stepped with care, the ground squishy beneath a thick layer of pine needles.

She spotted the grave marker, about two feet tall with a rounded top. The wood had weathered over the years, but the inscription remained legible.

DUTCH EM

DIED ON BALD

MOUNTAIN

MAY 16, 1896

Annie dropped to her knees and winced from the pain. She steadied herself with one hand on the marker and a bottle of whiskey in the other. She stared at it for a long time. The wind rustled through the pines like distant voices. "I'm moving back to Rocky Bar, Em. I've visited your grave every year, and this is the last time. This is 'goodbye' for good. Oh, how I wish things had turned out differently for us."

She forced a bitter laugh and looked down at her legs, or what was left of them. Every step reminded her of that night on that mountain pass.

"You wouldn't have gone alone. You only went because I said I would go with you." Her eyes burned. "You were sick. The weather was turning.

I knew it. I knew. My intuition told me not to go, but I didn't listen. Biggest mistake of my life."

Her hand trembled as she took a sip from the bottle and let the rest splash on the ground at the bottom of the marker.

"I was right next to you when you died," she said, voice cracking. "I tried to keep you warm, but I failed."

She bowed her head. A tear slipped down her cheek. "I'm so damn sorry, Em. You deserved better." She traced the words DUTCH EM with her finger.

"They took my legs after we got down. Did you know that? You were already gone by the time Bill found me. They cut 'em off below the knee. Doc Newkirk said it was the only way to save my life."

A silence fell, heavy and cold. She let the tears come and let them drip onto the pine needles.

"I loved you, Em," she whispered. "More than I ever told you. More than I knew how to say back then."

A gust of wind stirred the branches overhead, and a shower of dry pine needles rained down. Annie let out a long, shaking breath. "Gotta go. Henry's waiting for me. I won't be able to visit you anymore after this."

As she turned back toward the trail, she glanced over her shoulder. "Goodbye, Em."

* * *

The year that Annie and Henry returned to Rocky Bar, the town had lost its wild edges. The mining rush had faded to a slow grind. They arrived in the back of a supply wagon, Annie perched on a barrel with her peg legs swinging, Henry with his city shoes and a battered trunk full of ledgers. Business had declined for Miner's Haven, Sourdough Sally's, and The Lucky Strike. With most of the mining operations shutting down and people moving away, all the businesses in Rocky Bar were suffering.

On the third day in Rocky Bar, Annie set out looking for Hazel. It had been eighteen years since they said their goodbyes that day at Beaver

Creek. She found the house where Hazel had lived, but it was vacant. The front yard was overgrown with weeds, the paint was peeling off the siding, and the front door was missing. It saddened her to see the place where she and Hazel had shared so many happy moments now in ruins. She found the lot where she expected to find her childhood home, but there was nothing there. The entire house was gone. The lot was now a patch of dead weeds and garbage. She couldn't bear to look at it. At the post office, she inquired about Hazel. The postmaster told her the Jacksons had moved to Portland at least five years ago, and no, they had not left a forwarding address.

Next was Meng Yao. She had quit working at Miner's Haven several years prior with no explanation. She asked around town, but nobody remembered anything about the Chinese girl. Gone without a trace.

As each year passed by, Rocky Bar shrank. As work in the mines evaporated, so did paychecks, and one by one, businesses folded for lack of customers. Annie had to shut down Miner's Haven in 1914, followed by Sourdough Sally's and The Lucky Strike in the spring of 1917. She could not find any buyers. As abandoned properties, they became targets for vandals and scavengers. *What a shame. People have no respect for history. These buildings have so many memories for me. But what can I do about it? Nothing. Nobody cares. Even that old stamp mill where Thomas proposed to me is gone. It's nothing but a vacant lot now.* Annie avoided looking at them every time she had to hobble down Rocky Bar Road. It was too painful. None of this meant anything to Henry. He never asked why she would return from her walks around town with such a melancholy look on her face.

They had saved several thousand dollars from their earnings at Sourdough Sally's and The Lucky Strike. Those savings would run dry someday, so they decided to open a laundry business to earn a living. Their main expense was food, and what little they made was more than enough to cover it. They were able to save some money each month.

Chapter 39

A letter arrived for Annie, postmarked August 23rd, 1917, Kuna, Idaho. It was from Ethyl. It was only the second letter she had received from her. None of her other children ever wrote.

> Dearest Mother,
> I hope this letter finds you well. I apologize for not writing for such a long time. There is no excuse. We live in Kuna on a small farm, and our family is doing well. James is not too happy with the idea of writing to you, but I'm writing anyway. I miss you! I'm ashamed to say that I don't even know what you look like, but I believe your face is full of love and kindness. I will see you someday, when the time is right. Please be patient.
> Your Daughter,
> Ethyl

Annie was about to toss the envelope into the fire when she noticed it was stiff. Peeking inside, she found a photograph. It was a family portrait of Ethyl, her husband, and the two children. Ethyl was a beautiful young woman; she reminded her of Hazel by the way she wore a ribbon in her hair. She turned it over, and on the back, in neat writing, was written,

"James, Ethyl, Edna 5, Mable 2." Henry watched her from across the table, saying nothing. He did not ask why she grew tearful.

By 1918, the Gold Nugget Saloon was the only saloon in town still operating. Rocky Bar was on a death spiral. Annie was sitting at her favorite table chatting with Sammy, the barkeep. He was Annie's only real friend, and this was how she spent most of her afternoons.

The Spanish Flue hit Rocky Bar hard, and it claimed a surprising number of lives. She had heard what the people of Challis did, over on the other side of the Sawtooth Mountains. The city officials posted armed guards on every road into town. They refused to let travelers in. That worked until Governor Alexander ordered them to stop. The flu lasted until the spring of 1919. Annie and Henry were among the lucky who never fell ill.

By that winter, the mines had played out, and only a few placer miners on Beaver Creek and the Feather River downstream remained. The town shrank to half its size, and the only businesses left running with any viability were those that provided only the necessities of life: food, whiskey, and clean clothes.

Still, Henry was indispensable. He managed the books, negotiated with suppliers, and ran every laundry delivery with a clockwork precision Annie admired. Sometimes, though, Henry's business sense crossed the line to something questionable. He'd come home late, smelling of cigars and cheap whiskey, and talk about "opportunities" that bothered her. He never shared details, not unless pressed, and even then it was half a story: "I helped a friend settle a debt" or "I took a minor risk for a quick return." Annie told herself it was harmless, just Henry being a wheeler and dealer, but the seed of doubt was planted. One night, Henry returned after midnight, face pale and lips pressed tight. He poured himself a drink and sat at the kitchen table, staring at nothing.

"You in trouble?" Annie asked.

He shook his head. "Not me. Business."

"What kind of business keeps you out all night?"

He gave her a tired smile. "You don't want to know." He fingered his mustache.

You're doing it again—the thing with your moustache. She let it drop, but for the next week, she watched him closely. Something was bothering him. Every so often, she'd catch a look, like fear, cross his face when he thought she wasn't looking. After that, Annie started locking the safe when she was away, even for a minute.

Rocky Bar was shrinking, the way Idaho mining boom towns did once the gold or silver played out. The Alturas Hotel, once the biggest business in town, went bankrupt; the Gold Nugget Saloon changed hands three times, and half the shops on Rocky Bar Road had boarded up their windows. Annie's laundry business declined as fewer and fewer miners remained. She didn't trust banks, not after hearing about the robberies in Boise or the bank failures during the Panic of 1907.

Henry pressed her sometimes. "You should enjoy yourself, Annie. Buy one of those horseless carriages people call automobiles. We got the money. Go on a trip, even if it's just to see your children."

Annie shook her head. "They don't want me, and what on earth would I do with one of those infernal machines?"

He shrugged. "But what about me, then? What if I want something nice for once?"

She eyed him. "What are you getting at?"

Henry grinned. "A new suit, one from Italy. Or a better watch. Or a box of imported cigars."

She relented sometimes. She bought him a silk cravat and a fancy pen for his birthday. But even those small gifts made her feel uncomfortable. Winter was the only time business slowed down. When the snow got too deep for wagons, Annie would close the shop at noon and spend the afternoons in the kitchen, reading old dime novels like Effie used to do while Annie was recovering from her surgery.

* * *

The summer of 1920 came late, with dirty snow still clinging to the mountain tops in June. Rocky Bar Road was empty most of the time except for the three dogs that made their rounds through the town begging for food. Annie usually found a few scraps for them. Her laundry business still ran, but with fewer customers with each passing month. Most days, less than half a dozen people showed up. Henry spent more time in the kitchen, reading or writing letters, and Annie noticed that he often sat by the window, staring outside.

Early one morning, on a gray day like any other day, Annie set a can of ground coffee on the counter next to the stove and went outside to get some water. She came back in and noticed the coffee can was not there.

"Where's the can of coffee I left here?"

"It's in the cupboard exactly where you left it," Henry replied without looking up from his newspaper.

It was on the counter next to the stove a minute ago.

"I've been sitting here all morning. You didn't put the coffee on the counter. You're getting forgetful in your old age."

She took the coffee from the cupboard and made an extra potent brew.

"Annie, we need to talk."

She grunted, but sat across from him, hands wrapped around the coffee mug. "If you're about to ask for money, you can forget it."

He smiled. "Not exactly. But I need a favor."

Henry laid it out, careful as always. He'd gotten a letter from his cousin, something about an inheritance, a chance to buy land back in the old country. He wanted to take a trip to Italy, just for a month or two, to see his family and handle the business. "And while I'm in San Francisco," he said, "I could put your nest egg in a real bank. It's not safe here, Annie. Anybody with a crowbar could walk off with your life savings."

Annie sipped her coffee, stony-faced. "Nobody knows the safe combination except me."

"That's true," Henry said, "but there's still fire, or thieves, or . . . ." he let the sentence hang. "It was last week you couldn't open the safe. I think you forgot the combination. Memory is one of the first things to go when you get old. You don't even remember that, do you?"

What? The safe opened just fine. What's he talking about? Just because a person is sixty-two, that don't mean they're losing their mind. She set the mug down. "Anyway, I don't trust banks. You know that. Never will."

He leaned forward, elbows on the table. "It's the modern way, Annie. Everything is moving in that direction. And if you're ever sick, or need to send money to your children, it's easier if it's in a proper bank account."

"I don't want anyone poking into my business. Especially not some banker in California."

Henry tapped his fingers on the table, then smiled. "You don't trust anyone, do you?"

She shot him a look. "Should I?"

He laughed, but it sounded more tired than amused. "You've trusted me all these years, and I've always come through for you." He moved one hand up to touch his moustache, but quickly placed it back on the table.

Annie went silent, weighing the truth of it. *I never caught Henry stealing, never once in eleven years, but he keeps doing that thing with his moustache. That concerns me because I don't know what it means. He handled the books, paid the bills, and never skimmed more than an occasional cigar or bottle of gin. He's kept my secrets, and more than once, protected me from men who wanted to see me fail. Still, something about him is off. I wish I knew what it is.*

Henry reached across the table and laid his hand on hers. "I promise, Annie. I'll take the money straight to the bank. I'll wire you from San Francisco and send the papers back by post. Write down every detail if you like."

She wanted to say "no" but her self-confidence was slipping away. There was the missing coffee can, forgetting the combination to the safe, and several other times when she was sure she did something, but Henry always said it never happened. *Maybe Henry's right. If I can't trust myself, then trusting Henry would be the right thing to do. Right?*

"Okay, Henry. But you sign a paper before you go. And you count it, every dollar."

"Of course," Henry smiled. "We'll do it together."

That afternoon, Annie took the cash out of the safe, one bundle at a time, and stacked it on the kitchen table. She held up a crisp one-hundred-dollar note. She never took the time to study the artwork on them. This series 1914 bill featured a pudgy profile of Benjamin Franklin. The back was in green ink and was more interesting. Across the top was *Federal Reserve Note*. In the center was an engraving of what looked like a Greek goddess on a throne with lesser goddesses reclining on either side of her. On the left was a man carrying a huge sheaf of wheat, and on the right was Mercury, judging by the wings on his feet and the wings on his helmet.

She pulled out a wrinkled hundred-dollar note. It was a series of 1880 and had a portrait of Abraham Lincoln with a half-smile. This one was more ornate compared to the 1914 series. On the right was an engraving of a lady in a dress, who was measuring a block of stone, as if she were building something. Sitting in front of the stone was a little boy holding a big scroll on his lap. There weren't any illustrations on the back. *One Hundred Dollars* was written in four places, and on the left side was a paragraph of text written in cursive. The rest had intricate patterns of curvy lines.

She thumbed through the thickest stack of bills and found what she was looking for: the one-thousand-dollar bill. This was the only one she had. On the right side was a portrait of Wm. L. Marcy. *Don't know who that is.* On the left side was a picture of a lady wearing a wreath on her head and grasping the hilt of a sword. On the back was a big "1000" surrounded by squiggly lines. *These bills represent eleven years of hard work and frugality. I never squandered money on frivolities.*

She counted every bill, her lips moving, with Henry writing it all down in his neat, slanted script. The total was $12,000. It would have totaled $12,287, but she kept $287 aside. When they finished, she tucked the whole pile into an oilcloth, then wrapped it with string and sealed it in a battered suitcase.

Henry signed the currency tally with his flamboyant signature, then kissed her on the forehead, a rare gesture. "I'll be back before you know it," he said. She watched him go, suitcase in hand, coat flapping in the wind. He walked down the muddy road to the old stagecoach stop, where a hired Ford Model T driver waited to take him to Boise. She stood on the porch, arms folded, watching until the car disappeared out of sight.

For a long time after, Annie stared at the spot where he'd vanished. She checked the safe twice, even though she knew it was empty, just to make sure. That night, Annie sat by the stove and replayed the morning's events in her mind. *I'm sure I've done the right thing. Henry said he would come back in a month, that everything would work out the way he promised.* She kept the currency tally by her bed, tucked into a Bible that Effie had once given her that she had yet to read.

* * *

She received a postcard from Henry with a photo of Fisherman's Wharf in San Francisco, postmarked July 24th. He wrote that he will make the deposit tomorrow at the Wells Fargo on Market Street and send her the details as soon as it was done. Annie went to bed, the postcard on her pillow, wishing it was true.

The next postcard arrived two weeks later. Henry wrote that the bank was solid, the paperwork slow, and that he'd be on the train to New York City and then the ship to Italy in less than a week. He would mail her the deposit receipt as soon as it cleared.

Another postcard arrived a few days afterwards. Henry's handwriting was different. It was sloppy, as if he had written it in a hurry. He said the bank was giving him trouble, something about delays with the transfer, but that she shouldn't worry. He would sort it out, no matter what.

Annie was worried. *What transfer? He's only making a deposit.* She kept busy and put Henry's troubles out of her mind. She did the laundry, cooked her meals, made coffee, and had her daily drink. After two weeks, she started asking around: the grocer, the station agent, the old men on the benches outside the mercantile. Nobody had heard from Henry, and nobody cared enough to wonder. She waited until the end of August before sending a letter to Wells Fargo in San Francisco. The reply took three weeks, and when it arrived, Annie's hands shook so much that it was difficult to break the seal. She hoped it contained the deposit receipt.

"We regret to inform you . . ." was all she could read before she let it fall to the floor. She collapsed onto the kitchen chair and sat there, paralyzed. There was no record of a $12,000 deposit.

In the weeks that followed, Annie wandered through her days as if caught in a dense fog. Sleep came fitfully, leaving her adrift between tangled dreams and the stark reality of her loss. The safe, once a symbol of steadfast security, now mocked her whenever she looked at it, a cruel reminder of both her naivety and misplaced trust.

Annie's thoughts swelled back and forth in her mind every waking hour. Perhaps Henry was cornered by desperate thieves in some dingy alley of San Francisco, or maybe he succumbed to darker forces she couldn't comprehend. She spun each theory, which provided fleeting relief but then unraveled under scrutiny, leaving her with the gnawing certainty that Henry had conned her. She yearned for an alternative truth, one in which he would return with explanations and apologies that would make sense.

Somehow, the miners figured out what happened. She was surprised one morning when a regular paid her double the amount of her usual laundry fee. It happened again a few days later with another regular. The third time it happened, she asked the man for an explanation. He told her that everyone knew about how kind and generous she had been over the years with men down on their luck, both in Rocky Bar and Atlanta, and now it was their turn to give back.

"Thank you, Johnny, and tell the others how much this means to me. I really appreciate it."

No one ever heard from Henry again. Some folks said he had run off to Nevada, or was robbed in San Francisco. Annie didn't care. She'd stopped caring the day she lit his last postcard in the stove and watched it curl into black ashes and fall apart. *Don't give up, Annie,* came the thought that sounded familiar, as she gazed into the flames.

Chapter 40

By October 1922, Rocky Bar was a hollow shell of its former existence. The day started the way every day started: with the crack of her knees against the side of the cot, the embers of a dying fire, and the knowledge that if she didn't light the stove herself, she would freeze before the sun cleared the ridge. She dragged her stumps into the kitchen, bracing on the walls, and set a match to the last of her kindling. Her hands shook less than they used to. Her world had shrunk to the size of her cabin.

Every Monday, Annie started before first light. Her laundry business barely enabled her to survive. She boiled water over an open fire, the air thick with the sharp tang of lye and the heavier stink of men's sweat. She worked the washboard with calloused hands, her stumps wrapped in old towels and wedged inside a shoe with the toe cut off when the peg legs became too uncomfortable. By mid-morning, the yard filled with a chorus of flapping shirts and drawers, dozens of white flags surrendering to the wind.

It became routine. Annie was up to her elbows in suds, her hair tied back with a rag, when the first shift of miners came through. They would sling their soiled flannels onto the rock outside, sometimes with a coin or two tucked in the sleeve. Annie never asked for tips, but she kept every extra two-bit piece. She liked the secret pleasure of watching the coins pile up week after week.

Miners came and went, but the regulars always brought their business back. Some of them remembered her from Atlanta, how she provided free meals to the men down on their luck and the kindness she had shown when no one else cared. One time, she had to confess to a new customer, "Yes, they called me an Angel of Mercy, not that I deserved it." They told stories, sometimes in front of her, sometimes behind her back: how Annie once beat a man at poker with nothing but a pair of twos, how she carried a gun in her petticoat and shot the thumb off a gambler who cheated her, how she'd dragged a dying miner three miles through a blizzard and then nursed him back to life with whiskey and opium. And then there was her favorite, the one about the bear attack.

Annie measured her success by the weight of gold coins, the neat stacks of tattered bills, and the perfect balance of columns in her ledger. The Rocky Bar Laundry was all she had.

Some nights, she sat on the worn-out chair on the porch with her stumps propped on a barrel, watching the sun slide behind the hills. Sometimes she thought about leaving, of picking up her two battered trunks and taking the stagecoach to Mountain Home or Boise.

People were abandoning the town, some with formal goodbyes, others sneaking away in the night, leaving behind only a debt and an abandoned home. The worst were the ones who died here, the old miners who'd worked themselves to death, widows who died of a broken heart, children who didn't survive the last round of consumption. By 1923, it was just Annie and a handful of others: the old-timers who could not bear to leave their claims, and the handful of men who ran the government survey camps up in the hills every other year.

The day the town doctor left, Annie watched him pack his bags into the Model T with a sour, silent respect. He had done little doctoring in recent years. Instead, he served as a notary and read the mail to those who were losing their vision. His absence created a new level of emptiness.

He drove away without a backward glance. Annie watched the dust settle on the road, then went inside and heated a pot of yesterday's baked beans. She thought about how much she disliked beans, and how she was the only person for fifty miles who remembered the taste of sourdough pancakes or hot bread baked in a real oven. After the doctor, it was the postmaster who left a note in the window saying, "Closed until Further Notice," even though everyone knew "further notice" meant "forever". That signaled the demise of her laundry business. There were not enough miners with dirty clothes still working in Rocky Bar to support it.

That night, she dreamed of the old days: of Em, alive and grinning, spinning in circles at the Silver Moon Dance Hall while the piano man played, with the boys stomping their boots in time. She dreamed of her own children, their merry faces, calling to her from the other side of a sunlit grassy field. When she woke, the world was silent, and the bedsheets were tangled around her stumps. Annie stared at the ceiling for a long time, then rolled over and pulled the blanket up tight.

Annie had never liked the taste of moonshine, but she liked the taste of hunger even less. By the end of her third year since Henry left, she'd run through the last of her savings, sold off every stick of furniture that wasn't nailed down, washed her last load of miner's clothes, and pawned Henry's old watch to a traveling peddler for three quarts of bootlegged rye and a basket of dried peaches.

It was a peddler who gave her the idea. He was a scrawny man with a bird's nest of a beard and a backpack that jingled when he walked. He stayed the night in the empty bedroom and left the next morning with two of her oldest blankets and three jars of her pickled beets, in exchange for a gallon of his "good stuff".

"Split this up into small bottles and sell it. Men pay double, even triple for it," he told her with a twinkle in his eyes. "Law's got no teeth up here. Prohibition's not going to end any time soon."

That's an intriguing idea. In the spring of 1924, Annie tried her hand at bootlegging. She started small. First, she swapped favors with the Chinese gardeners out on Steel Creek, two bags of dried beans for a flask of nasty stuff they called "dragon's blood." Next, she traded eggs with an old trapper for bottles of what he swore was bourbon, but tasted more like watered-down turpentine. Her favorite deal was the one where a one-eyed prospector traded his shotgun for a bottle of Annie's best. *He had no business pointing that thing at anybody, anyway.*

For a while, she bought whiskey from a distillery that was still operating somewhere. She didn't ask questions, so she didn't know where it came from, but it worked. She would then mix it with whatever she had on hand and resell it. This was a common practice in some saloons.

Annie ran her operation with the same rules she'd run the boarding house: no credit, no questions, and no patience for double-talk. She traded on the front porch, shotgun across her lap, her new guard dog a mongrel with teeth like railroad spikes and a mean streak to match. Word got out quickly; anyone with a thirst and a dollar to burn could get a bottle of rotgut from Peg Leg Annie, but only if they minded their manners.

One of her customers was an old prospector that she had seen wandering around town. He limped up to her porch on a Monday morning, hat in hand, face red as the dawn. "You got any of the real stuff left, Annie?" he asked, his eyes not quite meeting hers.

She let him stew for a minute, then jerked her head at the woodpile. "Pay first, one dollar." The man pulled a paper dollar from his pocket and handed it to her. "There's a bottle in the hollow log, next to the axe. Go get it."

He shuffled over, pulled out the brown glass, and cradled it like a lost child. Annie watched, unimpressed. She'd hidden it in plain sight, just to see if the old man had any brains left. He did.

Some customers were less friendly. One man showed up after sundown, his Model T coughing up dust at the edge of her yard. Annie listened to the engine rattle, then pop, then die with a sad little wheeze. The driver stayed in the car for a long time before getting out. He was a city man, wearing a suit and tie, and polished shoes.

"You lost?" she called out.

He stepped onto her porch, eyes darting around the dark. "No, ma'am. I was told you might have a supply of Canadian whiskey."

Annie didn't like the look of him. He was too clean, too polite, and he kept glancing over his shoulder as if someone was watching him.

"Don't know anything about booze from Canada," she said, slowly. "And I don't sell to strangers."

He pulled a crisp ten-dollar bill from his coat, unfolding it with a flick of his wrist. "Well then, consider me your newest friend." He held out the bill. "One bottle. My employer, he's a man who appreciates quality, discreetly."

Annie took the bill and rubbed it between her fingers. *This is brand new. I haven't seen a ten-dollar bill in years. Ten dollars for one bottle. That works for me.* She had memorized the hidden locations of a dozen bottles on her property, and directed customers to the one that they had paid for. Annie nodded toward the shed. "Left side of the shed, under the flat rock. It ain't from Canada. It's better."

She kept her shotgun trained on him, making no attempt to hide it. He cradled the bottle, nodded thanks, and walked over to his automobile. He opened the door and turned towards her. "You ever get lonely out here, Mrs.—"

"I don't. Goodbye." She didn't like the looks of him.

After that, word spread to Mountain Home, Nampa, Boise, and every mining camp in between. Peg Leg Annie earned the reputation of being the most reliable bootlegger in the South Boise diggings. You could buy from her, so long as you paid cash and didn't ask questions. She kept the operation simple: the front porch was her office, the root cellar her bank. Annie never asked names and never kept a ledger.

Annie was enjoying the tranquility on her front porch when a pair of disheveled-looking miners showed up. They stood at the bottom of her porch steps, demanding she sell to them at half price, "on account of the economy."

"Get lost."

They snickered. The taller one called her a name she hadn't heard in years, something about her legs. She let it pass, and without a second thought, she aimed the shotgun between their heads and fired. BANG! The men hit the dirt and froze. "Now see here. You boys done gone and put me in a bad mood. You catch what I'm sayin'? Get the blazes out of here!"

Annie reloaded and pointed the gun at them. They ran. *What a couple of numbskulls!*

The seasons turned, the snow came and went, but Annie's business never dwindled. She became the subject of more than legends: the unstoppable Peg Leg Annie, former madam, Angel of Mercy, and bootlegger extraordinaire. Reporters wrote about her in their newspapers and referred to her as "notorious" or "scandalous". She granted one an interview because he offered her an unopened bottle of Old Overholt.

* * *

It was January before Bill dropped by again, still working as a mail carrier, though this time he brought a bottle of whiskey and a sack of flour. He stood in her doorway, face red from the wind. "Town's dead, Annie. You're practically the last one left except for a few diehards at the other end of town. You ever think of leaving?"

She shook her head. "This is my place. Besides, I'm not much good anywhere else."

Bill frowned. "It's not safe. If you fall, or get sick—"

Annie waved him off. "I'll manage. Always have."

"If you don't mind my asking, whatever happened to Henry Longhini? Did you ever figure out why he took your money?"

"I only think about that when I get bored. It's a waste of mental energy." She leaned back in her chair and took a sip of her whiskey. "But something did occur to me. Henry was a gambler, through and through. It was in his blood. He couldn't stop even if he wanted to. It was a thrill for him to risk losing yet end up winning. Do you ever play poker, Bill?"

"Not often. I guess I'm not the gambling type."

"Well, professional gamblers know that people have a 'tell.' A tell is an unconscious gesture or expression that reveals what you are thinking or feeling, and in the case of poker, whether you have a good hand or not. If you're playing poker and you can read the tells of the other players, chances are you're going to win big. Henry knew this. Yet, Henry had a

338

tell. I remember several times during our conversations where he would touch his moustache, especially when we were talking about our money. A professional gambler is aware of their own tells, and they can control them. Looking back at it now, I think Henry was deceiving me about his plans to put our money in a San Francisco bank. The question is: why didn't he suppress his own tell?"

"And you know why?"

"Yes, I believe I do. Like I said, Henry was a gambler through and through. He lived to gamble. He deliberately allowed me to see his tell. This was an enormous risk for him, if I spotted it and then refused to go along with his plan. It was also a tremendous thrill for him. He was gambling on my not seeing his tell. This would be the biggest and most daring gamble of his life, with the biggest payoff. With him showing his tell and me not spotting it, his win would make him feel like he was a real shrewd gambler. Plus, if I didn't spot his tell, he could claim that it was my fault for not stopping him."

Bill thought for a moment. "You're probably right, Annie. I'm amazed that you could figure it out."

"It's only my opinion, but I'm pretty sure it's correct."

Neither spoke for a while. They let the words settle in their minds. Bill left the goods on her table and went on his way, but before he left, he turned and said, "If you ever need help, you know where to find me." Annie nodded and closed the door. She watched through the curtain as Bill trudged away through the snow, his silhouette shrinking until it disappeared. She poured a drink from the bottle he had left, savoring the warmth as it slipped down. The taste was sharp, almost electric. She finished her cup, then another, and by the time she crawled into bed, the cold and the loneliness had faded to a dull, familiar ache.

Winter passed. Annie's movements were slower, her hands stiffer, her hair gone to silver. She buried two more stray dogs in the yard. She liked the silence. It gave her space to think, and to remember, and to forget when she wanted.

In the spring, the first tourists arrived. They were city folks in shiny cars, poking through the ruins of Rocky Bar's buildings for souvenirs. Annie was well known to the people of Boise. They took her picture, asked for her autograph, and bought her stories for the price of a meal. Annie told them what they wanted to hear, then sent them on their way. Sometimes she would deliberately be more ornery than usual to put on a show. It entertained her to watch their expressions when they couldn't tell if she was joking or serious. She didn't care as long as they didn't stay too long.

One night, as she watched the moon rise over the empty town, Annie thought of Em, and the way she used to dance sometimes barefoot in the saloon, skirt flying, cheeks pink with mischief. She missed her, missed the music, the noise, and the feeling that anything could happen if you survived another night. But she didn't dwell on it. The past was gone, and she was still here. As the last bottle clinked empty on the table, Annie felt a sense of peace. She'd outlived everyone who'd ever tried to run her out, beat her down, or make her small. She was Peg Leg Annie, and she never gave up.

Chapter 41

The spring snow that year was wetter than usual. Annie watched the gray sky sag over Rocky Bar and wondered if the sun had given up for good. She went days without seeing another soul, living on salt pork and boiled potatoes, sometimes on coffee, sometimes nothing at all when her stomach turned sour, and she couldn't stand the thought of food.

It started the way everything started in Rocky Bar: with a knock on the door so soft it could have been the wind. Annie was in the back room, fussing over the stove, when she heard it—a single tap, then silence, then another, more tentative. She scowled, wiped her hands on her skirt, and hobbled to the door, bracing for whoever would bother her this early in the morning.

Three old men stood on her stoop. They wore the same battered felt hats and the same set of expressions: a mixture of regret, stubborn pride, and the deep, unspoken solidarity of men who'd spent too many years staring down the same stretch of mountain.

"And what are you varmints looking for?"

The leader, his beard white as cotton, hands knotted like tree roots, looked her in the eyes and said, "Miz Annie, we come by to see if you's needin' any wood, or anythin' else, really."

"What's it to you?"

"Not a thing," the old man said, glancing at his boots. "We figure it's a cold March. Some folks could use a little help."

"I don't need charity," she snapped. "I get by fine on my own."

The second man, shorter and more direct, cut in: "We ain't here to charity you. We's here 'cause you kept us from starvin' during those terrible years, and y'all never asked for a dime. Now it's our turn."

The third man looked at her. "Be mean all you want, Miz Annie, but you know the rules here. Nobody dies in this town unless the rest of us say so."

Annie tried to muster her usual defense, but the words caught on her tongue. It reminded her of the days when her laundry customers would pay double. She stepped aside, letting the three men file in with their arms full of wood, burlap sacks of potatoes, and a cured ham. The cabin filled with the earthy scent of split pine, and for a moment, she remembered what it was like to come in from the cold and feel the snow melt out of your hair.

She watched as they stacked the wood by the stove, hands working in silence, not looking up. The second man started setting the groceries on her battered table, fussing with the order of the cans.

"You want coffee?" Annie asked more out of habit than hospitality.

"Be obliged," said the leader.

She made the coffee strong and poured it into the mismatched mugs that lined the shelf above the sink. Annie took the chance to glare at each of them, trying to figure out their angle. *I know these men. I've seen them at their worst, in the saloons and backrooms of the old days. They had a tough life, but they were honest.*

"What's really going on here?" Annie said, folding her arms.

The short man shrugged. "Heard you been skippin' meals. Heard you ain't been in town for a week. Figured maybe you was sick, or maybe just sick of us, but we gotta check."

"I'm fine," Annie lied. "Tired of people."

"That makes two of us," the white beard said, with a ghost of a smile. "But you're stuck with us for now. We voted, and you lost."

She rolled her eyes. "What'd you bring the ham for?"

The third man, still muted, still blinking too much, shook his head. "It's the only decent food left in town. Nobody else has to eat like you do."

"Ha. I don't eat at all, sometimes."

They took that in, then the three looked at their hands, embarrassed by the confession. After a minute, the leader cleared his throat. "If y'all need anythin', y'all let us know. We's around most days."

The three men shuffled to the door. The shortest looked Annie straight in the face. "You think you're the only person to lose everythin'? You ain't. Some of us never had nothin' worth losing. But that don't mean we's done for." And with that, they walked away.

The next morning, she found another surprise: a box of kindling, neatly stacked and wrapped in brown paper, sitting outside the front door. There was a note, scratched onto a piece of an old newspaper, "For Annie. Don't freeze. From the old varmints."

It grew into a routine. Every few weeks, another sack of potatoes, another bag of dried beans, sometimes even a bottle of whiskey if the men were feeling sentimental. Sometimes there'd be a loaf of bread, sometimes a jar of sour pickles, once a small wedge of cheddar cheese. The gifts were unsigned, but Annie knew who sent them. She pretended to ignore it, but she let the pile grow, and she started eating proper meals again.

The next morning, around noon, it was the squeal of the brakes that woke her from her morning snooze. It was a shrill, metallic shriek, followed by the unmistakable rumble of an internal combustion engine, spitting and sputtering up the muddy slope from town. Annie pressed her face to the kitchen window and waited for the apparition to come into view. Few cars made it to Rocky Bar, even in the best of summers. The rough road was a test of man and machine.

She watched as the motor car, a black coupe, new enough to still have its shine, as it rambled up the road, with the driver swerving recklessly around the huge mud puddles. It stopped right in front of her cabin, and the engine cut out. The door of the motorcar swung open, and a woman stepped out. *Women never come here to buy my booze. Why is she here? Is she one of those enforcers from the Woman's Christian Temperance*

Union? I don't mind them writing letters to the editor and making speeches, but they have no right to parade around in front of saloons and boarding houses. These are legitimate business. I hear they spy on bootleggers and try to run them out of town. Don't they have anything better to do?

Annie pulled the curtain aside in the front window and peered outside. *I didn't know they hired women to do their dirty work. Either that or she's going to give me one of those pamphlets. They already raided the distillery. What more do they want? I'll give her a piece of my mind!*

She drew back when the woman looked in her direction and stepped away from the window. *Dammit. She saw me. I can handle her.*

She scanned the room and noticed three bottles of her own special mix and tossed them under her bed. *Too bad I can't use my shot gun to scare her away.*

Chapter 42

She rushed to clear the table and comb her hair. She wanted to look respectable even though she didn't care what the woman thought of her. The woman knocked on the door three times. Annie considered ignoring her and stood motionless for a few moments with a load of firewood in her arms. There were three more knocks, louder this time.

"Mrs. Morrow, I know you're in there. Open the door, please." Her voice was stern.

I guess I have to see who the hell it is. I'm in no mood for trouble. She braced herself for whatever confrontation was about to unfold. She unlocked the door and swung it wide open.

"Hello, Mother."

Annie froze. The firewood slipped from her arms and crashed to the floor. She stared at the woman standing before, thunderstruck.

"Ethyl?" Her voice cracked. "Ethyl?" She couldn't breathe. "I . . . I can't believe it's you."

The woman standing in the doorway nodded once, eyes glistening, lips pressed together to keep them from trembling. She did not smile. Tears stood in her eyes, unspilled, as though she were afraid to move. "It's me," she said quietly. "I came to see you, Mother. I heard you were living up here all by yourself. I wanted to come and see you. It's been thirty-eight years."

Annie swayed and almost lost her balance. She lifted her hands, then let them fall again, unsure where to put them, afraid to reach. "The last time I saw you . . . ." Her voice faded. She swallowed hard. "You were a baby. You had a yellow ribbon tied in your hair. I can still feel it between my fingers." Her eyes searched Ethyl's face, desperate, incredulous. "And now—now you're—"

"I'm a mother too," Ethyl said, with a soft voice and a gentle smile. A tear finally slipped free and traced down her cheek.

Annie's knees weakened, and she reached for the table to steady herself. Her mouth opened, but she couldn't say a word. Her hands fluttered in the space between them. She took a step forward and placed a trembling hand on Ethyl's cheek.

"Ethyl, I can't believe you're here."

"I'm here, I'm really here, Mother."

"Come in. Have a seat. I could make some coffee. It's not much, but—"

"Thank you." Ethyl wiped her eyes.

Annie turned abruptly, as if afraid she might look too long and lose her again. "Sit down. I'll—I'll make coffee." Her hands fumbled at the kettle, metal clanging against iron. She could not stop shaking. *What do I say? The thought slammed through her. How do you speak to the child you lost for a lifetime?*

Behind her, Ethyl wiped her eyes and stepped fully into the room, closing the door with care, as though afraid even the sound of it might shatter the tension in the air.

A moment later, she set two white mugs on the table. Ethyl was sitting stiffly on the edge of the wooden chair, her back straight, with white-gloved hands clutched in her lap. Her pale blue cotton dress looked brand new.

Now that they were sitting across from each other, Annie took a moment to have a good look at her daughter. She had a delicate heart-shaped face, gentle almond-shaped eyes, and a sweet bow-shaped mouth. Her hair was thick and glossy chestnut brown.

Ethyl noticed. "Do you like my hair? I had it done the other day. They're Marcel waves."

"You look lovely."

"Some people say that I look like Pauline Garon, you know, the Canadian actress. She played Mathilda Ramsay in the moving picture, Adam's Rib. DeMille directed it. Have you seen it?"

"I've never seen one of those moving pictures. Sounds spooky to me."

"They're actually quite fun. Every so often they put words on the screen so you know what the characters are saying."

"Really? I wonder what they'll think of next."

Ethyl's eyes roamed the cabin, over the patched curtains, the iron stove, the single bed with its faded quilt, and out the window, where the sun was casting a golden glow over the roofs of Rocky Bar.

"It's beautiful up here," Ethyl said, her voice softer now as she accepted the coffee. Their fingers brushed for a moment. "Peaceful."

"I thought I'd never see you again. This does my heart good." Annie wrapped her fingers around her coffee cup. "But to be honest, it gets lonely up here sometimes," she admitted for the first time, the words heavier than they sounded. "But I suppose I earned that."

They sat in silence and listened to the crackling of the fire. Ethyl lifted her eyes and looked straight into Annie's. She cleared her throat and leaned back in her chair. "I have to say this, Mother. I waited. For years, I waited. For anything. Anything from you! You never sent me anything. Not a word! I don't understand it. Why didn't you? Why?" Annie could see the tears forming in Ethyl's eyes.

Annie sighed. "I'm sorry," was all Annie could say, her voice barely above a whisper. Her eyes met her daughter's. They sat facing each other, years of silence straining to be undone in the stillness between them. They sipped their coffee in silence.

Ethyl set her cup down on the table. "Why did you leave us? Father never would say much about it. Just that you got confused."

Annie sturdied herself for what she knew was going to be an unpleasant conversation. She stared at the coffee and turned the coffee mug around with her fingers. "I left because your father was becoming a dangerous man. When he got drunk, he terrified me. I feared for my safety, yours too. One time he broke John Henry's arm. It was an accident, but if he wasn't drunk, it never would have happened. It was getting worse every year. I lived with that man for thirteen years until you came along. That's when I decided we had to leave if we were going to survive."

"We? He told us you deserted us. Took off in the middle of the night."

"I took off in the middle of the night all right, *with* all of you. My plan was to take us to your Uncle George's place in Mountain Home, where we'd be safe. I paid extra to get a stagecoach just for us."

Annie sat in silence for a moment. "He caught up with us, threatened the driver at gunpoint and made him turn the stagecoach around and head back to Pine Grove. He left me for dead on the side of the road in the middle of nowhere. George showed up the next morning and rescued me."

"What? I had no idea. I believed the terrible things that father said about you. I never questioned what he said. Can you forgive me?"

"Listen to me, Ethyl, I'm the one that needs to be forgiven. Maybe I should have stayed with your father. I should have had more courage to stand up against him. I just don't know."

"I don't blame you. You did what you had to do."

They let the stove's fire do the talking for a few minutes, with both of them taking long sips of coffee.

Ethyl broke the silence. "I married James Farmer in 1910. We had two daughters, Edna and Mable. I sent you a letter a few years ago with a photograph. Did you get it?"

"I did. Thank you so much for it. I cherish that picture. That was very kind of you."

Ethyl smiled. It vanished as quickly as it appeared. "Our marriage didn't last more than a few years, so we ended up getting divorced. He wasn't cruel to me; we just drifted apart. I got married again in '23 to Roy Davenport. He's a decent man. No more children yet."

"Do they . . . do Edna and Mable know about me?"

"They know they have a grandmother they've never met. Roy told me I ought to come and see you, especially after Edna started asking questions. Edna is fifteen now, and Mable is twelve."

Annie wiped her eyes with the back of her hand. "I wrote to you. Several times over the years. But I never sent the letters. I kept thinking . . . what right did I have? What could I say that would make up for what I did?"

"I don't know if anything could have made up for it, but I need to understand. I need to see if you are the monster I'd imagined all these years."

"And am I?"

"Lord, no!" Ethyl stared at her mother. She saw the deep lines around her eyes, the tremor in her hands, the loneliness that seemed to emanate from her. "No!" she said again. "You're a woman who's had a tough life."

Annie let that sink in. *Yes, I've had a tough life. I don't know why. I lost my first love, my children, my best friend twice, my legs, my businesses, my life savings, and now my health. But I never gave up. I survived long enough to see you again, my darling Ethyl.* She took a deep breath. "Tell me about the others. I got your letter about Anna Eliza dying of appendicitis when she was eighteen. You're the only one who wrote to me. How are the others?"

"Well, Grandma Marcella separated from James after a few years and married William Floyd some years after that, but that didn't last long either. John William went to heaven in 1901. Father died in 1906. Drank himself to death, I heard. George passed away about a year after that. That leaves me, Susan Margaret, and John Henry."

"I'm glad you're here, Ethyl. More than glad. I thought this day would never come."

They sat in comfortable silence as the sun sank behind the mountains, painting the clouds in shades of orange and pink.

"I best be going," Ethyl said. "I've got to get back before dark. The road is treacherous enough even in daylight."

Annie nodded, though her heart was breaking at the thought of being alone again. "Of course. Thank you for . . . thank you so much for coming."

They both stood up, and for a moment, neither knew what to do. Then Ethyl stepped forward and held her arms wide open. Annie melted into them and squeezed her with all the force her old arms could manage. Annie sobbed, her tears bursting forth, unstoppable.

"I'm sorry, baby," Annie whispered. "I'm so sorry. I'm sorry I wasn't brave enough to be your mother when you needed me."

"I know," Ethyl said, her own tears falling. "It's okay now, Mother."

They held each other as the mountain wind whispered through the pines, two women finding their way back to each other across the years of silence and pain. When they pulled apart, Ethyl reached into her purse and pulled out a small photo photograph. "One more thing, Mother. This is them. Edna and Mable."

Annie took the photograph with shaking hands, studying the faces of her grandchildren. "They're beautiful!"

"Maybe . . . maybe someday you could meet them. If you wanted to."

"Could I?" She walked over to a shelf on the wall and picked up a small wooden box. "I have something for you." She set the box on the table and fumbled through the jumble of papers and knick-knacks until she found what she was searching for. "This is for you. It's a picture a travelling photographer took of me when I was running the Miners Haven. I was in my early thirties."

Ethyl took the picture and gazed at it. "You're so pretty, Mother, but you look kind of sad. Was something bothering you that day?"

"I wasn't in the mood to sit in front of a camera. While the photographer was setting up his camera, I realized that I never had a family portrait taken. When we lived in Boise, Thomas always said it would be a waste of money, no matter how many times I asked him." Annie shifted her gaze towards the window. "I don't have a single picture of my children. Not one."

"But you have me now, in the flesh."

"That I do, and for that I'm grateful."

Annie took a long sip of her coffee. "Anyway, Hazel talked me into getting the picture taken. We had a larger print made and hung it up on the wall of the parlor in a fancy oval frame."

"Who was Hazel? Was she a good friend?"

Annie slumped into a chair and let out a long sigh. "Hazel was an angel. We were best friends during our teenage years in Rocky Bar, and then we got re-acquainted when I returned after being gone for fifteen years. Hazel was the best thing that ever happened to me until it ended."

"It ended? Why?"

"Because her husband didn't approve of me. Simple as that."

"That seems so unfair. I'm sorry you had to go through that. It must have been painful."

"Painful? It tore my heart apart. I hope you never have to experience anything like that." She ran her fingers through her hair. "I suppose you heard about Dutch Em."

"Yes. It was in the papers for days. I wish I could have been there for you."

"How could you? You were only six years old when that happened. You could read when you were six?"

"No, John William would read the newspapers to me. He was eleven and pretty good with his reading and writing, but he didn't like arithmetic."

Ethyl gazed into her coffee cup. "I'm sorry it took me so long to come and see you. I should have come years ago, but I was afraid of you because of the terrible things Father said about you. I know now those were lies. Can you forgive me?"

"It's not your fault. There's nothing to forgive. I'm happy you're here now, with me." They let the conversation lapse until the only sound in the room was the fire crackling in the stove.

"I'll write to you," Ethyl promised. "And I'll come back."

"That would be grand."

They walked out to the Model T together, and Ethyl climbed behind the wheel. As she started the engine, she called out over the racket, "Take care of yourself, Mother."

The words felt like a long-awaited gift. She watched as the Model T disappeared down the road through town. *Am I dreaming? Did this really happen? Ethyl is the most beautiful woman I've ever seen, and she is my very own daughter. After an entire lifetime, I have something I can be truly proud of.*

* * *

Ethyl came back in the spring, and then again in the fall, when she arrived holding a small cardboard box wrapped with a red ribbon and a bow.

"I brought something special for you, Mother," she said with a smile as she walked in.

"Why, thank you, Ethyl. I wonder what it could be."

"I'll give you a hint." She paused, set the box on the table, and flung her arms around Annie. "Happy Birthday!"

"Thank you, my dear. It moves my heart that you remembered and drove all the way here."

"I wouldn't rather be anywhere else today. September thirteenth, right? It's a cake me and the girls made for you. Edna decided you must like chocolate."

"I'd love anything your little ones made for me."

"Near as I can tell, Mother, you're seventy today."

"Yes, I guess I am. Hard to believe, isn't it?"

Each visit peeled away another layer of the thirty-eight-year silence between them. What began with stiff conversations and hesitant glances gave way to warmth, laughter, and an intimacy that felt miraculous.

On her fourth visit, Ethyl returned with the children, two shy girls with freckles and ribbons in their hair like Ethyl had once worn. Annie wept right there on the porch the moment their eyes met.

"Are you okay, Grandma?" asked Edna as she looked up into Annie's eyes.

"Yes, my dear. These are tears of happiness. I'm thrilled to see you two."

She held out her arms, and the children came to her with curious eyes and eager chatter.

She made them blackberry cobbler that night, the kind she used to bake before everything had fallen apart, and the children devoured it with sticky fingers and giggles that filled every dusty corner of the cabin.

On the following visit, Ethyl helped Annie patch the roof. They worked side by side, sleeves rolled up, faces flushed from the mountain sun, pausing now and then to sip cool water and trade memories. Ethyl told stories of her life, the hard years, the good years, the joy of motherhood, and the grief of losing her first husband. Annie listened with her whole heart, not needing to interject, grateful to be allowed into the chapters she had missed, while savoring the lyrical cadence of Ethyl's voice.

They picked wildflowers in the summer and placed them in old jars on the windowsill. Ethyl brought books, and they read aloud by lamplight, laughing at the silly ones and wiping away tears at the sad parts. In the evenings, Annie taught her daughter how to play poker, and they sat cross-legged on the floor with cards fanned in their hands, playfully accusing each other of cheating while the fire crackled behind them.

Sometimes they sat without speaking, both lost in thought. Annie would knit while Ethyl mended a dress or wrote a letter. It wasn't what was said that mattered, but the ease of their silence, the comfort of presence. The heavy ache that had haunted Annie's heart for decades softened with each visit and was replaced with contentment. Nothing they said or did could erase the lost time. They discussed what might have been, even when the words were difficult. Over time, the wounds in their hearts healed.

Chapter 43

The last winter Annie spent in Rocky Bar nearly finished her. The snow arrived in October and accumulated like wet plaster. It was increasingly difficult to have hope. She blamed the stove, blamed the town, blamed her own stubbornness, but by February, even Annie admitted she was beat. She heard about a miner named Shorty McClain over in Gilmore who blew himself up with a stick of dynamite because he was so depressed. *There had been a few suicides in Rocky Bar, usually with a gun. Suicide is not the answer.*

The first day of June, Ethyl showed up in her Model T and proclaimed that Annie was moving to Mountain Home, come hell or high water. Annie did not have the energy to fight back. Rocky Bar was on its way to becoming a ghost town. Ethyl refused to leave without her. Feeling resigned to the inevitable, Annie packed everything she owned into two small trunks, except for Em's hurdy-gurdy in its own case.

Her new abode in Mountain Home was a battered bungalow on the edge of town, rented by the month from a widow who spent most days gossiping with the neighnors over her fence.

There was no work to be had, not for a woman her age or reputation, so Annie spent her days watching people through the warped pane of her living room window. Mountain Home was nothing like Rocky Bar. The nearby train station made it noisy and crowded. Hordes of automobiles rattled up and down the street all day long. Every day, she witnessed men in suits hurrying to the station and women in hats and gloves rushing off in random directions. Sometimes children played in the street, shrieking and chasing a ball or a dog. She had yet to receive any word from Susan Margaret or Jack Henry.

Once a month, Ethyl dropped by with groceries and a fresh pack of cigars for Annie. Ethyl would unload the bags, wipe down the kitchen table, and put away the food with the silent, practiced efficiency of a woman used to doing everything herself. She would pour two cups of freshly brewed Arbuckles and sit across from Annie at the kitchen table.

"Anything new?" Ethyl would ask with each visit, her tone hopeful, as though she expected the world to have shifted in the few days since she was last there.

"Same as ever," Annie replied, smiling despite herself.

Ethyl lingered by the window, glancing toward the road. "Well," she said at last, unable to keep the note of anticipation out of her voice, "I have something new for you. It should arrive any minute now."

Annie frowned. "Arrive?" she echoed. But Ethyl only shook her head, lips pressed together in a way that suggested she was determined not to spoil the surprise.

A sharp knock sounded at the door before Annie could press her further. Ethyl was already on her feet. "That must be Roy. I'll open the door."

The door had barely swung open when a bundle of black fur came hurtling inside, all paws and enthusiasm. The Newfoundland puppy skidded across the floor, nearly losing its footing, then righted itself and charged straight for Annie. With a joyful bark it leapt up, planting paws against her skirt and showering her with eager licks.

"Oh—my goodness!" Annie laughed, startled, her hands instinctively coming up as the puppy wriggled and squirmed, its tail wagging so hard its whole body seemed to sway. It sniffed her face, her hair, her sleeves, as though it had known her all its young life and was delighted to have found her at last.

Ethyl laughed from the doorway. "He's taken to you already."

Annie sank back into her chair, still laughing as she caught the puppy around the chest to steady it. "Why, aren't you a force of nature," she said, her voice softening.

"Roy heard you were partial to Newfoundlands," Ethyl said, her eyes shining. "So he got one for you."

"Glory be!" Annie repeated, scarcely believing it. She ran her hand over the thick, downy fur, marveling at its warmth. "He's beautiful."

The puppy responded by flopping awkwardly into her lap, and wagging his tail as if in agreement. Annie's laughter faded into something quieter, deeper. She rested her cheek against the puppy's head, a broad smile lighting her face.

* * *

After the first summer in Mountain Home, Annie stopped keeping track of the days. Once, in the fall, Ethyl showed up with a pumpkin pie, home-baked and warm, and they ate it together, savoring each other's company.

It was during one of those quiet nights that Annie thought about the nights in Atlanta and Rocky Bar, the wild swirl of music and bodies and laughter. She remembered Em's hurdy-gurdy, the sweet sour of whiskey on her tongue. She also remembered being needed by the upstairs girls in her boarding house and the miners down on their luck.

As the year wore on, so did Annie. Her cough got worse, her appetite faded away, and even Doc Percy's chalky pills stopped working. She took to her bed for days at a time, drifting in and out of sleep, dreaming of snow and fire and the endless black night. Once, she thought she heard a piano playing off in the distance, and in a dream she was dancing barefoot, her body whole and light as a child's.

When she woke, Ethyl was there, sitting in the chair by the window. "You're not leaving me, Mother. Not yet."

Annie smiled, but didn't answer. Instead, she reached for her daughter's hand, held it tight, and closed her eyes again.

By 1932, Annie was frail, but she still managed to get around the kitchen. She survived on money from Ethyl's husband, Roy. He sent a postal order every month, accompanied by a note in pencil: "Write if you need more. - Roy"

On bad days, Annie struggled to drag herself to the window. She'd stare through the dirty glass, watching the parade of beggars and peddlers and lost children. She kept a notebook by the bed, jotting down names and odd fragments of dreams. Much of the time, she couldn't remember why she bothered.

Her dreams worsened. She dreamed of Em, but not the young, pretty Em with the hurdy-gurdy and the laugh that filled a room. No, this Em was old and tired, hair streaked with gray, hands rough from work. In the dream, Em sat in a rocking chair on Annie's porch, playing cards with the devil himself, who always cheated but lost anyway. Sometimes Em sang, but the words were jumbled, a song about chickens or whiskey or nothing at all. Annie woke from these dreams with the taste of loss on her tongue and the feeling that she had forgotten something important.

Other nights, she dreamed of young women in long white dresses. They danced around her bed, chanting in a language she couldn't understand, their faces flickering between young and old, alive and dead, happy and sad.

Every so often, Annie's mind wandered to the lives of her children. Despite her attempts, their faces and voices remained unknowable. She knew she ought to have regrets, and sometimes she did, and other times she wanted to scream or break something out of frustration. Most of the time, she sat in her chair and let the memories settle around her like light snow falling to the ground.

Every time Ethyl came by, she reminded Annie that she would be much better off at the St. Alphonsus Hospital in Boise. Time and again, Annie shrugged off her daughter's words until one day she gave in and agreed to be admitted. *I hate the idea. Old folks go to the hospital to die.*

Chapter 44

"Welcome to St. Alphonsus, Mrs. Morrow. I'm Sister Benedict, and I will make your stay here as comfortable as possible."

The smell of antiseptic hung heavy in the white-walled ward, muffled by the ever-present scent of carbolic soap. As soon as Sister Benedict left, Annie murmured under her breath, "Can't you people do anything about that smell? It's enough to drive a person crazy."

Outside Annie's window, the February sunlight struggled through a veil of high clouds, casting the bed in a pale gray light.

A nurse poured water into a small glass and set it on the table beside Annie's bed. Annie glanced up at her. "Is . . . is nurse Effie here?" she asked, her voice more breath than words.

The nurse, a tall woman in a crisp white cap, leaned closer. "Nurse Effie? I'm sorry, Mrs. Morrow, but we don't have any nurses here by that name."

Annie's eyes blinked with disappointment, and her lips trembled. "She . . . she took care of me . . . when I lost my legs. Thirty-seven years ago. She was the only one who . . . who kept me from losing my mind. I just—" she broke off in a fit of coughing, her shoulders shaking under the thin blanket.

The nurse hesitated, then nodded. "Sorry, Mrs. Morrow, but I don't recognize the name."

"Fine. Go away. Find something useful to do, if you can."

Two weeks passed, and each day all Annie could see outside the hospital windows were grey, overcast skies. The boredom was never-ending.

Towards the evening, the ward door opened, and an unfamiliar woman stepped inside. She was not Ethyl or a nurse. *Must be a visitor for one of the other sorry souls in this place.* Annie paid no attention to her until she walked over and stood at the foot of her bed.

Annie's gaze locked on hers, and for a moment, both women stared in disbelief, their faces working through shock and then recognition. Her frail hands reached out, trembling. The woman was wearing wire-rimmed spectacles. Her hair was grey, tied up in a tight bun with hairpins, but there was a smile in her eyes that looked familiar.

"Effie Prey? Lord in heaven, I didn't think I'd ever see you again!"

Effie pulled a chair close to the bed and sat. She took both of Annie's hands in hers. "Annie Morrow . . . you haven't changed a bit. Still bossing nurses around, I see, like you bossed me around."

Annie let out a long sigh. "You were there when they . . . when they took my legs. When I thought I was done for, you told me I'd walk again. I've carried those words every day since. I did walk again."

Effie's eyes glistened, and she nodded. "Yes. You walked again on those peg legs of yours." She gave a soft chuckle, but the sound caught, and her thumb brushed over Annie's knuckles. "You were the bravest patient I ever had."

Annie's lips pressed together, fighting emotion. "I was only brave because you wouldn't let me be anything else, and I never thanked you. I'm sorry, Effie, I was so mean to you."

"No apologies needed, Annie."

For a long moment, neither spoke. Effie leaned in close. "You're not alone. You weren't then, and you're not now."

Annie closed her eyes, a faint smile softening her features. "I know . . . now that you're here. How did you find me?"

"During a lunch break over at St. Luke's, which is where I work, one nurse mentioned something about a woman with no legs over at St. Alphonsus. I wondered if that could be you, since it's not every day that you hear about a woman with no legs. So, I have come over here to see for myself."

"Effie, can you take care of me here, like you did in Atlanta all those years ago?"

A frown worked its way across Effie's face. "I'm sorry, Annie, since I work at St. Luke's, I can't work here. Hospital rules don't allow that." Her frown gave way to a smile. "But I can visit you . . . as a friend."

"That would be grand."

Effie stayed until the light in the window turned the color of pewter, the two women talking in hushed voices, of the years between, of the hard winters and the faces they both remembered, and of the strange, fierce connection that had survived almost four decades apart.

"I have something for you, Effie. I insisted Ethyl bring it over from my place in Mountain Home. It's under that blanket over there in the corner. Go ahead and get it."

Effie walked over and lifted the blanket. She gasped. "I remember this—it's Em's hurdy-gurdy! What is it doing here?"

"Do you remember the note Em wrote to me? You read it out loud during one of your visits to my cabin in Rocky Bar."

"Yes, I remember the note, but I don't remember what it said."

"I made a promise to Em to keep that thing safe. Seein' as how I may not be around too much longer, I'm giving it to you. It's yours, Effie. I'm trusting you with it to keep my promise to Em. Can you do that?"

Effie was visibly moved. "Yes, Annie, I can do that, and when the day comes when I leave this world, I will pass it on to one of my children, and I will tell them what a wonderful friend Em was for you."

"Thank you, Effie. You're an angel."

"I'm no angel. I'm just a woman trying to do her best in this world," she said with a smile.

When she rose to leave, Effie pressed Annie's hand once more, her eyes saying what words could not: *I care about you.*

* * *

The days wore on, one bout of monotony after another. When her lungs grew so tight that every breath sounded like a windstorm behind her ribs, Annie started making a list. Not on paper; her hands shook too much to write anything. It was in the deep recesses of her mind.

Hazel. My best friend. Hazel, with her braids and the quick, gap-toothed grin, who said I will outlive them all. We had raced through Rocky Bar playing hide and seek, playing tag by Beaver Creek, and gossiping about the boys with the hush of sworn conspirators. And that poem she wrote. I just about died when she read that to me. I remember our last moments together by the creek, when she told me her husband killed our friendship. We never spoke after that, but sometimes at night, I hear the echo of her laugh in my dreams. She gladdens my heart, even now.

Meng Yao. The little Chinese girl with the big, haunted eyes, who worked for Zhi Peng. I like to think that I saved Meng Yao's life, saved her from a life that was sure to become a living hell. I wonder where Meng Yao is now. Hopefully, she is safe and happy somewhere.

Em. Dutch Em, my German hurdy-gurdy girl, the little soiled dove that got me into the sisterhood. The nights in Atlanta, the wild dancing, the way Em could turn a room of sullen miners into a carnival just by singing "Camp Town Races." Em was sunshine bottled up in a short, fierce body. Even after the snow took her, I feel her presence: in the crack of a stick of kindling, in the way the morning light crept through dirty windows, in the scent of oncoming snow. The world never made another woman like Em, and I was glad to have had her, even for a little while. The guilt and the ever-present ache—those were the price of admission. Em was worth it. I'd do it all over again.

Jacob. The man I could have loved, the man I should have loved, who could have saved me. If I had left Atlanta with him, I would have never gotten drunk that night with Em, when we got that harebrained idea to walk to Rocky Bar in the snow. It was her idea to go, but the only reason we went was because I agreed to go with her. Em could still be alive today if it wasn't for that night, if it wasn't for me. I would still have my legs. But what's the use of such thoughts? What's done is done.

Bill Tate, the mail carrier. Honest Bill, who saved me from certain death on Bald Mountain and talked me through the worst night of my life. He never once judged me for the worst decision of my life. After I moved to Mountain Home, Bill sent me a postcard every Christmas, even after his hands went too shaky to write more than "Best, Bill."

Effie Prey, my little Christian nurse. Yes, I gave her a hard time in the beginning, but in the end, I think we were good for each other. She gets credit for putting up with me, and I get credit for listening to her. I can't believe she came to see me the other day. I wonder if she still reads those dime novels. I'll have to ask her the next time she comes by.

Ethyl Frances. My dear Ethyl. The last of my blood, the only child who still came to see me in Rocky Bar, who cared enough to cut my hair and talk about the meaning of life over pie and bring her ugly blankets. She didn't judge, didn't pry, just sat with me when the coughing got bad, holding my hand in the afternoons, humming soft lullabies as if I were a child again.

Me. I'm the main character of my story, right? People called me "Angel of Mercy" and "Peg Leg Annie" among other less-than-flattering names. What's that word authors like to use? I heard it just the other day. "Protagonist", I think. How about "Protagonist Extraordinaire". That's me. I'm not sure which name I like best. I never turned away a soul who needed help. Not once. Those were good deeds. That must count for something. I took risks. I made mistakes. But the people I knew and loved in my life made it worth it. Would I change anything? Of course! Who would ever choose to lose their legs?

She repeated the list every night, the names rolling over and over until they blurred together, a comfort against the rattle in her chest and the hush of the hospital ward. *These are the things that matter in life.*

On September 13, 1934, the room at St. Alphonsus Hospital smelled like bleach, but this time the odor did not bother Annie. She couldn't tell if the shape at her bedside was Ethyl, Effie, or a nurse. Her eyesight was a mess of blurry shadows, but she figured it didn't much matter. Her entire world had shrunk to the rough sheets, the slow drip from a glass bottle overhead, and the thud-thud, thud-thud of her own tired heart.

"You awake, Mother?" asked Ethyl, leaning in close.

"I think so," Annie said. She meant it as a joke, but the words came out slurred, thick with sleep.

Ethyl took her hand, small and cold, and squeezed it once. "Doctor says it won't be long."

"That so?" She tried to laugh, but it came out as a cough.

For a while, they listened to the clock ticking on the wall. The light in the window faded from yellow to gray, then back again. Annie let her eyes close, drifting between memory and nothingness, her mind lurching back to Atlanta, to Rocky Bar, to the sharp rush of wind and snow on the mountain.

The room around Annie grew dim, the edges softening like a photograph fading at the corners. Each breath felt lighter than the last, as though something inside her were loosening its hold.

She found herself standing at the foot of a sun-drenched hill. The entire slope was alive with yellow flowers, countless and trembling in a gentle breeze, their petals catching the sunlight like tiny flames. The air smelled of summer long past: wild honey, warm grass, and that sweet hint of pine she remembered from her happiest days.

And there, at the top of the hill, Em was dancing.

Em twirled among the flowers as if she had been waiting there forever, her bright blue dress flaring around her like a splash of sky. Her long brown hair streamed loose down her back, shining as though each strand had stolen a thread of sunlight. Her cheeks were flushed with the same rosy vitality that Annie remembered so well.

When Em saw her, she stopped mid-turn. Her face lit with a joy so pure it made Annie's heart ache with longing. Em lifted one hand and beckoned, a slight gesture, but filled with more affection than any words. Annie felt it like a pull deep inside her chest, gentle but irresistible.

Em called out to her, but Annie couldn't hear what she said. Em laughed—a sound of pure delight—and opened her arms wide.

Annie heard Ethyl's voice off in the distance, choked with tears. "I love you, Mother."

As the darkness enveloped her, Peg Leg Annie drew her last breath.

"I'm coming, Em."

Epilogue

Anna Morrow and Emma von Losh, known as Peg Leg Annie and Dutch Em, were real people. In 2003, the Atlanta Arts Society Ltd. erected a bronze memorial near the location where Dutch Em froze to death. It reads as follows:

> Dedicated to the gritty resolve and courage of
> ANNIE MORROW aka PEG LEG ANNIE
> and her friend "DUTCH EM." In May 1896
> they were caught in a late blizzard while
> walking from Atlanta to Rocky Bar. Losing
> their direction to the Summit House at this
> site, Em froze to death and Annie's feet were
> later amputated. She died in 1934, but their
> colorful spirit lives on in our hearts and
> minds through the stories, myths, and truth,
> still told about these pioneer women.
>
> Atlanta Arts Society Ltd.
> July 2003

About the Author

Howard Frisk began his creative journey not with words, but with images—capturing the world through the lens of a Kodak Instamatic 104 camera given to him by his mother in his hometown of Seattle. What began as a childhood fascination soon grew into a lifelong passion for photography. His work evolved into freelance assignments, and he started selling his fine art photographs on various online platforms.

In pursuit of dramatic landscapes, Howard purchased a Jeep Wrangler and set out to explore the remote back roads of Washington and Idaho. Along the way, he discovered more than sweeping vistas—he encountered the haunting remnants of history: weathered farmhouses, collapsed barns, and, eventually, entire ghost towns. These forgotten places became both his inspiration and his subjects.

His explorations culminated in a series of five books documenting the ghost towns and abandoned places of Idaho. While researching the mining communities of Rocky Bar and Atlanta, he stumbled upon the story—or more aptly, the legend—of Peg Leg Annie. In his book *Ghost Towns of Western Idaho*, she earned a brief mention, little more than a page and a half. When a friend suggested her tale deserved a book of its own, the idea took root.

Although Howard's previous works were non-fiction, he realized that Peg Leg Annie's life story existed somewhere between truth and legend—territory best explored through storytelling. The result is his first work of historical fiction: a novel that brings new life to one of Idaho's most enduring frontier legends: Anna Morrow.

Other Books by Howard Frisk

All books are available on Amazon:

Ghost Towns of Eastern Idaho

Ghost Towns of Western Idaho

Abandoned Mines of Eastern Idaho

Abandoned Mines of Western Idaho

Abandoned Idaho

Abandoned Washington State

Historical photographs of Rocky Bar and Atlanta can be seen on the publisher's website, at:

www.WesternEchoPublishing.com/PegLegAnnie